Vengeance and Vipers

A WOMAN WITH SECRETS DARKER THAN THE NIGHT.
SIX SEDUCTIVE DEMONS TORN BETWEEN HATRED AND DESIRE.

VENGEANCE AFORETHOUGHT
BOOK TWO

KYRA ALESSY

DARK REALMS

Copyright 2023 by Dark Realms Press

All rights reserved.

No part of this book may be reproduced in any form or by any electronic or mechanical means, including information storage and retrieval systems, without written permission from the author, except for the use of brief quotations in book reviews.

This work of fiction is licensed for your enjoyment only. The story is the property of the author, in all media, both physical and digital, and no one may copy or publish either all or part of this novel without the express permission of the author.

Cover by Deranged Doctor Designs

Vengeance and Vipers

She survived their betrayal, but now she's their captive. When the lines between love and hate begin to blur, will the life she's always wished for be hers, or will her past lead to the destruction of all their futures?

In prison, they told me I was their downfall. But they were mine. The demons betrayed me and left me to die. Guess I should have seen that coming, but I'll bet they didn't expect me to follow them home!

The thing is, I never thought I'd end up back here either.

Sure, I've tricked my way out of sticky situations before, but this is different. I've traded cobwebs and shadows for a Swiss estate and a clan of incubi who think I'm a viper in their midst. My new prison is more lethal, laced with temptation and taboo.

I escaped these guys once before. Now, three of them want to claim me, while the others want to...well, let's just say it won't be easy to go back to my old life without my head attached.

Still, I can't ignore that with every day I spend here, I feel their grip on my heart tighten. The allure of this place is undeniable, and these men are under my skin. Have I changed, or have they? All I know is the demons who were my adversaries are looking less like captors and more like lovers.

But I have powerful enemies. Sooner or later, I'll be found again and the fragile life I've begun to build will come crashing down.

Can I keep the demons I care about safe from them? Will I have the future I always secretly wished for, or will my dark past swallow it whole?

If You're Related To Me...Danger Ahead...

If you are a part of my family, put the book down.
Don't read this!

If you do not heed this warning, never EVER speak of it to me. I don't want to know.

I don't want to hear that you're surprised that I'd write about monster fucking in sex clubs and primal chases in the woods. I don't care if you think noncon is wrong, or this is too dark.

Because I swear to you here and now, if you rile me up about this, we CAN have the conversation and I WILL tell you all the things that turn me on, and you will never view me with the same eyes again.

It's not a threat, it's a promise.

Not you, Granny. I know you'd never ask! I love you!

Triggers

I hope you enjoy this next world in the universe of Jane and the Iron I's. If you haven't read the previous trilogy, you don't really need to, but it might help as the demons in this story appear in the Desire Aforethought series.

Triggers* in this book include (but may not be limited to):
Noncon
Dubcon
Torture
Sexual Assault
Death outside the harem
Emotional abuse
Violence outside the harem
*Author's brain too twisted to realize some things are triggering to 'normal' people and forgets

TRIGGERS

to include them in warning lists. Sorry. If you think something needs to be added, please contact Kyra.

If you find any typos in this book (it happens) please contact Kyra with a screenshot or the sentence where the issue is.

It is important to note that, *probably* because of my neurodivergent brain, I 'HATE' double quotes ("") with an eye-twitching, burning passion that rivals the heat of a thousand suns.

(I also hate commas, but I try to include them for clarity's sake because I hate ambiguity even more.)

Because I live in the UK, where single quotes are almost always used for dialogue nowadays, I made the executive decision to never include doubles in any of my books no matter where they are sold.

EVER.

Sorry, my American friends, but I just can't do it!

Chapter One

MADDOX

'Krase?' I ask harshly into the dark, wondering how he can possibly still be here. *Alive*.

There's a low laugh as he comes to the fore of the second cell, his dark red hair long and matted, his face half hidden by an unkept auburn beard.

'I don't understand,' I mutter. 'Why aren't you dead? How did you get out of the fold I put you in?'

The sad fact is that I left him with a loaded pistol at his own request inside a fae-built cell in his room upstairs. He'd promised me that he'd use it when things got bad rather than trying to escape. I thought he would.

I hoped he would.

After all, he knew what was happening to him, how hopeless it all was ... *is*.

He laughs again, but when he looks at me, his eyes are tortured. I know what I should do and what my duty is as the leader of this clan. He didn't do what he said he would, so now it's down to me. I need to put him down. He's a rogue—a danger. Even I won't be able to control him.

He rattles the door of the cell suddenly, making me step back in case he can get out of there, but the magickly reinforced iron holds.

'You locked yourself in.'

'Aye.' His expression turns lucid. 'Where have you been?'

'You'd never believe me.'

But he's already forgotten I'm there. I can see that as he turns his back on me and goes to the other side of his cell, staring at Jules, still asleep and wrapped up in the blanket.

'You brought an entree,' he murmurs, and I second-guess putting Jules down here even though they're separated.

I should stow her in the tiny, padded fold I had created for Krase to be safe in. But it's fae-made. There's no guarantee that it's secure now that we're hiding from the law. For all I know, it could alert the authorities to our whereabouts if I start playing around with it. No, she needs to stay here. For now, at least. The cell is holding, and if Krase locked himself inside, it was because he knew that he couldn't get out.

Krase sniffs the air and looks confused because he can't smell the figure in the other cell. That's definitely for the best, I muse. He'll be angry if he's not too far gone to understand who's in there.

I watch my clan-mate lumber around the cell, kicking at the debris, mumbling to himself. I could delegate his execution to one of the others, but I was always taught that a leader doesn't ask anything of his people that he isn't willing to do himself. That, and the others said their goodbyes weeks ago. They're all well into the grieving process. Knowing he's still alive now will do more harm than good. I have to be the one.

But not tonight.

I turn away while his attention isn't on me, listening to him rant quietly to himself as I leave the dungeon, turning the key in the lock of the outer door and walking briskly through my wine cellars. On the way out, I grab a *'62 Chateau Latour* and trudge up the stone stairs.

After swinging by the kitchen to uncork the bottle and grab a glass because I'm not a heathen, I head straight for my own room. I shut myself inside, sitting calmly on the bed and pouring myself a large dose. I knock it back quickly, hardly tasting the expensive vintage. This bottle is for getting drunk, not for savoring.

I stare at the floor, my happiness at being home being tempered by the mass of problems I have downstairs as well as in the rooms adjacent to mine.

When Axel and Jayce are up, they're going to be more than furious, and it's going to take time for them to understand that what I did was for the best. I errantly wonder if I should bring in a supe MD. It's clear that Julia Brand did *something* to them in the Mountain. I could call Alex and get him to send Theo, his resident doctor, but discount it almost immediately. Better no one knows we're here until I've started the process of getting us pardoned, not even 'allies'.

I just have to hope that whatever hold Jules has on half my clan will dissipate in time. Although, with her *here*, that could well not be the case. Putting down the glass on my nightstand, I rub my face, running my hands through my hair.

We'll need food. The on-call girls we had before are gone now. I let them out of their contracts when shit started to hit the fan last month, assuming we'd be able to do what we normally do when we're *between* humans, just go to the clubs to feed from supes. Now, if we want to do any of that, it'll have to be in disguise, which means conjures, which means fae trinkets. I wish I knew more about them, but Krase was our resident expert on magickal fae objects, and I don't know what's safe. I don't want to lead the fae right to our door because I used a charm to conjure up a crooked nose.

Tomorrow, I need to start calling in favors and contacting the right people to make sure we don't get sent back to the Mountain once it inevitably comes out that we've returned. Then there's finding help for the daily running of the estate, which is also a must.

I drink the rest of the bottle in record time and flop into my bed, the reality of being back making our stay in the Mountain seem like a holiday.

Given the lengthy list of what I need to do tomorrow, I hope that my unhappy clan doesn't thwart me at every turn.

One thing's for certain. All of them will be a hundred times more unmanageable if they find out I have a pair of secret prisoners downstairs.

But that's a tomorrow problem.

JULES

I wake to a noise I can't really discern, and it takes me a good few seconds for my brain to play catch up. The last I recall, I was lying outside on wet grass and looking up at the stars.

A pang hits me hard as I recall that Siggy is dead. What follows is confusion when I think about the aftermath. There's no way I'm remembering what happened during those minutes after Dante killed my friend correctly. It has to be some kind of trick.

I look down at my hands. They look normal. But I turned into something else.

I KILLED DANTE!

And not only did I kill him. I snapped his neck like a carrot. *Easily.*

That's not possible. He was like a demon Terminator. No one survived him. Not ever.

This can't be real. I must have been hallucinating from all the torture.

I shift uncomfortably. I'm lying on something hard, and I'm wrapped in blankets that smell old. I sit up slowly and look around, my heart waking up and beginning to hammer when I see ancient-looking iron bars and a rough floor. I'm on a stone outcropping in cells that look like they've been hewn out of the rock.

For a second, I'm sure that I'm still in the Mountain, but there's a door in front of me that's wooden with a small, glass window high in the center of it. Beyond it, I can see wine bottles on new-looking shelves, and I know there's nowhere like this in the Mountain.

I'm somewhere else.

But where?

'You're awake,' a voice close to me rasps, and I jump with a squeal, realizing I'm not alone.

There's another cell next to the one I'm in, and inside it, there is another prisoner. He's gripping the shared bars between our cells, grinning maniacally. But as he stares at me, his grin melts off his face.

'Victoria,' he growls.

'How do you know my ...' My mouth falls open. '*Krase?*'

I immediately know with a sinking feeling where I am. The place I fell in love with two years ago. Maddox's Swiss chateau. Guess I'm not a guest this time.

The demon's fingers flex on the iron bars, morphing into claws. He gets taller and broader, his skin turning a dark grey and wings sprouting from his back. A long tail thrashes around, inserting itself through the bars and whipping the air as if to strike me, but it's not long enough by about two inches. I still scramble back, though.

His sudden roar has me huddling in close to the cold stone wall, hiding under the blankets as if he might calm down if he can't actually see me.

I peer out when there's no more noise to see him standing at the bars, holding onto them, his gaze on me unwavering. It's like a weight pressing down on my shoulders, and I shiver, exorbitantly glad that he seems to be as stuck in his cell as I am in mine.

Unless ...

I get down from the slab of stone and shuffle across the cage to the door. I pull, and it clanks in the hinge, but that's it. I'm definitely locked in this place.

Looking down at my arm, I frown at the unblemished skin and *normal* shape. The conjure on me is still working, but it only covers scars, not new wounds. I can't be remembering my final hours in the Mountain right because I'm sure my arm was visibly destroyed by the time Dante had finished his torture games. The pain of his play is seared into my mind.

Isn't it?

I open the shirt I'm wearing and look down at the rest of me. There are thin, scabbed scratches where I remember him cutting me deeply and yellowing bruises from his strikes while I was paralyzed. None of the marks look anywhere near as bad as they felt when he was hurting me.

Maybe it was a trick? Maybe Dante didn't really do all those things, and he just made me think he did. But he was one total asshole of a demon. Why wouldn't he hurt me for real? That theory doesn't really hold water. Or, perhaps the arania venom made me hallucinate or something?

I peer at Krase, who's back in his human form, and try not to think about it anymore for now because I don't have the answers, and it doesn't matter anyway. I'm out of the Mountain, and the portal is closed for another three months. There's nothing to worry about besides my current situation, though I hope the Demon King really is dead.

The demon in front of me looks a lot different from the man I knew from two years ago. He kept his curls longish but always clean and tidy. Now, it hangs around his face, greasy and dirty. His beard is long and needs some maintenance as well. His clothes look like he's cosplaying 'Russian Political Dissident'. They're ragged and soiled and smell like they could walk around on their own. But he clearly put some prep in before he came down here because he's got thermal, warm layers, whereas my own garment is the thin shirt of a dead demon whose body clearly ran hot because I'm freezing my ass off.

I keep my eye on Krase as I move around my cell, but the incubus seems calmer now.

He's back to murmuring to himself. But when I look closer, is see he has something in his hand.

It's a rat or a mouse. He's talking quietly to it, feeding it something from his pocket. I wonder how long he's been down here, how he survived when the others were imprisoned for half a month. Maybe Robertson, their butler, brought him food.

My own stomach rumbles. I have no idea when I last ate, but it was days ago. Food is probably not going to be coming anytime soon, either. Considering how things went in the Mountain, it's pretty safe to say that Maddox and the others are not going to be taking care of *me*.

Though as I look around the dungeon and see a grate built into the stone floor at one end, I guess I should be grateful they didn't put me in the ancient oubliette and just forget about me.

I sniffle a little. I really thought that Axel and Jayce would have fought for me. But they couldn't have because I'm down here. Everything they said and did really was bull, just like I thought it was.

I was right about them, and I should be glad. Vindicated.

But all I feel is loss, like my boyfriends just broke up with me.

I mean, I *imagine* this is what a breakup feels like. I still feel the connections that sparked to life between us like faint, muted, floating tendrils of light that go nowhere. I can't feel them now like I could in the Mountain. In fact, I haven't felt them since Maddox drugged them with the arania venom, I realize.

Did that even really happen, or was all of this Iron's doing? Could he have made me see and feel everything he wanted from the moment he started torturing me in that room? He was certainly strong enough.

I shiver at the thought and then screw up my face in anger. It wasn't just Iron who hurt me. I don't want anything to do with any of them! I push the tendrils of Jayce and Axel away so I can pretend they don't exist at all, and I try not to cry because I'm all alone now.

My hand rubs at my chest, and I gasp as I feel the ridges of the brand over my left breast. I look down, but I can't see it. Whatever Dante did to it while he was cutting on me has disrupted the conjure but not completely dissolved it.

I need to get it fixed. I need to get out of here, get somewhere safe.

I snort at myself.

There's no such place. Without the additional conjure to keep me hidden, they'll find me. It's only a matter of time. The thought terrifies me, so I push that away, too. There's nothing I can do but wait for now.

I side-eye Krase, who's lying on his stone bed, staring up at the ceiling.

And hope my prison buddy doesn't get anywhere near me.

'They told me you were dead,' I say softly, and, at first, I think he hasn't heard me.

But he slowly turns his head towards me, pinning me with a dark look that makes me a lot more frightened than I'd like to admit. The others are big and mean and frightening in their own ways, but Krase is on another level now. His eyes are wild. Unhinged. Crazy. His scariness rivals Dante's.

'They were right,' he says, eyes still on me.

I go back to my own bed and lay down on it. My body may not look bruised and broken from The Demon King, but it hurts a lot. I turn away and open the blanket to look down at myself again. I run my fingers over one of the scratches. They hurt so fucking much when Dante did them; I figured they were way deeper than little flicks of a knife. I really thought he'd gouged me to the bone in some places.

I close the blanket and roll back over, curling into it for warmth.

Light comes into the dungeon through a grate high up in the ceiling. I might be able to reach it. But there are bars on it as well.

The draft coming from the outside is cold, and I'm guessing the season is turning. It must be almost October, and we're high in the Alps. The temperature is going to be dropping fast over the coming days.

I curl up, shivering and closing my eyes as tiredness overtakes me.

I'm in a tunnel. It's dark. It feels like the Mountain, but it's different somehow. Someone's chasing me, and I'm running as fast as I can, but I'm not getting anywhere. It's like I'm stuck in a mire.

A dark laugh rings out from behind me, and I'm grabbed in a punishing grip. I scream, but a clawed hand claps over my mouth, silencing me. A knife teases its way down my body.

'Time to bleed,' Dante whispers.

My heart is beating erratically as I struggle in his grip. He keeps laughing, and it chills me to my core. Goosebumps track their way down my spine.

But when he turns me around, it's Krase, not Dante, who has me.

He looks immaculate. His beard is gone, and his auburn hair is messy, but in that sexy, just-got-out-of-bed-intentionally-ruffled way. He's also wearing a three-piece suit that somehow enhances the broadness of his shoulders and how tall he is compared to me.

He looks down at me and tears away my shirt, a slow smile making his lips turn upwards. But then he frowns, and I feel him messing with my damaged conjure. It'll stop working completely!

'Don't,' I beg. 'I don't want anyone to know what they did.'

But when he's done, whatever was wrong with it has been mended.

He picks me up, and even though I'm scared, his arms are warm on my freezing skin, and it feels nice.

'You're mine, Victoria,' he growls.

Chapter Two

JAYCE

I wake up slowly to birds chirping and the sun streaming through my window. I'm in my own familiar bed, in my room.

Jules.

My eyes snap open, and I bounce off the bed, tearing open my door and stalking down the hallway.

'Maddox!' I yell. 'MADDOX!'

I run down the stairs and to the library because that's where the bastard always is, and sure enough, he's sitting in one of his old-fashioned, high-backed chairs by the cold hearth.

The fucker is working on his laptop. He has a crystal glass of port in his hand.

'Where's Jules?'

Maddox types something and looks up frustratingly slowly from the screen.

'In the Mountain, I'd assume,' he says.

'You left her there.'

He lets out a sigh. 'I did what I had to. In time, you'll see that I—'

I snatch the crystal glass from his hand and hurl it across the room with an angry roar. It thuds into the wall and shatters, spraying shards of glass and sticky port all over.

But Maddox just quirks a brow.

'Do you feel better?' He snorts. 'Good thing my father sold off all the actual family crystal to pay his debts,' he remarks and goes back to his screen. 'You're cleaning that up, by the way. We all have to do our part until we can find some domestic help, with Robertson being a turncoat and all.'

I can't help my snarl when I think of our betraying butler, but his time will come. Right now, my eyes train on Maddox.

I stand over him, my hands clenched into fists, but he ignores me now. I run my hands through my hair, pulling it hard as I try to think. I'm helpless, and Jules is in Dante's power.

What the hell is he doing to her right now? Letting out a tortured sound, I run back upstairs to Axel's room. I burst through the door and find him on his back in his bed. His eyes open as I approach, and he gasps, sitting up abruptly.

'How long?'

'Since the Mountain? I don't know. Eight hours, maybe?'

He looks at me. 'We left her there.'

'I've tried Maddox. He doesn't care.'

Axel gets up, sways, and grabs one of the black beams of his four-poster bed for support.

'We need to get back there. Protect her from Dante. We can get ourselves arrested, we can't let her—'

'Do you hear yourselves?' Daemon growls from the door. 'Get your shit together. The human is gone, left to suffer her well-deserved fate. Be thankful some of us had the gumption not to get ensnared by her tricks, or stolen magick, or whatever it is that has you by your dicks.'

'Get out,' Axel sneers. 'You're not welcome here no matter what Maddox says.'

Daemon chuckles coldly and backs out of the room slowly. 'Have it your way, but if you think any of us are going to let you leave the estate so you can run to the cops and get us all taken again, you're mistaken. Maddox is three steps ahead of you. The border spells are already trapping you on the grounds, and the link keys are set not to recognize either of you. There's no way off the property until the both of you come to your senses.'

He leaves with a laugh that echoes down the corridor.

'Do you think he's telling the truth?' I ask.

'One way to find out.'

We go downstairs and out one of the side doors. The walk is half an hour to the edge of the property, and we make our way in silence, stalking angrily down the gravel drive until we get to the farm track that leads to the nearest main road.

Axel, who's in front of me, glances back at me with a dark look. He puts out his hand and brushes his fingertips against the invisible barrier that protects our home.

He yells as there's a flash, and he's thrown through the air. He lands hard on the ground about ten feet away with an oomph and a low groan.

'Are you okay?' I ask, my anger and frustration rising.

Daemon wasn't lying as I had hoped.

Axel sits up and shakes his head. 'Fuck Maddox,' he growls. 'He's made the conjure draw in power to make itself stronger.'

'He doesn't know enough about fae magick to re-form a spe—' I break off with a loud curse. '*Iron!*'

'Yeah, Iron,' Axel snarls as he gets to his feet. 'Looks like the Mountain's gifts haven't left him. At least not yet. Smart. We keep trying to get out, and it drains us dry. Without a food source, they know we won't even chance trying to break out more than once.'

'We need to get to her,' I snarl, turning to him. 'Can you feel her?'

'No.' Axel looks away. 'Not since the moment Maddox took us out with the venom. But we can't do anything until we can leave the grounds. We have to bide our time.'

'Meanwhile, Jules suffers in that hellhole,' I say quietly, my heart aching and anger coursing through me at my clan as well as at myself for not seeing Maddox coming. 'What if he kills her before we can get to her? What if she's already ...'

'No! He'll keep her alive to suffer for as long as possible,' Axel says very quietly. 'We just have to hope she can hold on until we can get her out of there.'

'How did we let this happen?'

'We were fools,' Axel says.

'Aye, we were.' I look him in the eye. 'How far are you willing to go for her?'

'For our mate? All the fucking way,' he grinds out.

'Good. We might well have to if we want to save her. But we need a plan.'

Axel nods as we begin walking back to the house slowly. After a few minutes of us mulling over our options, he speaks first.

'The problem is that they believe we've been bewitched.'

I nod. 'They'll not take anything we say or do seriously where she's concerned.'

'But Maddox thinks it'll wear off.'

'Aye.'

'So, we let it.'

I give him a look. 'What do you mean?'

'Double bluff. We pretend her hold is leaving us. Quickly. Over the next few hours, we start acting less and less like we give a shit about her. If we play our cards right, they'll let us go free.'

'And what then?'

Axel stops in the road and turns to me. 'Then we break ties

with the clan. We find a way into the Mountain, and we get Jules out of there.'

I nod my head. 'Agreed.'

We walk back to the house and go our separate ways, enacting our plan of pretending Jules isn't our top priority.

For my part, I go back to the library with a dustpan and brush, and I start cleaning up the mess I made in here earlier when I threw the glass.

'I didn't think you'd be back so soon,' Maddox says from his spot in the chair, still on his laptop.

I don't lay it on thick; just grunt my response. 'You said yourself there's no one else to damn well do it.'

He doesn't answer.

'There's someone I could call,' I say as I keep sweeping up the shards of glass.

'Call?' he enquires, not looking up.

I grit my teeth at the smug cunt. 'Aye, to keep the house for us. He and his wife are pixies. Older. Quiet sort. Lived in my village. He's had run-ins with the fae himself over the years, so he's none too sympathetic to their cause.'

Now, Maddox looks up, and I can see he's half surprised, half suspicious. I roll my eyes. 'We need someone. They'll do the job, no problems. No tattling to the fae on us.'

He regards me for a moment.

'Call them,' he says finally, going back to reading, and I resist the urge to snatch it away and throw it out onto the wet lawn.

'Aye, I'll do it now.'

I leave the cleaning supplies in the library and open one of the French doors, walking out onto the terrace and taking my phone from my pocket. It feels alien in my hand, though it's only been three weeks since we were taken in by the authorities.

I dial the number, and Fergus picks up almost immediately. 'Have a job for you and the missus.'

'Aye?'

'Aye.'

I tell Fergus what we need, frowning as I look over the lawn and see a depression in the grass as if a large creature was lying there in the night.

Odd shape for a deer.

I turn away, thinking no more of it while he talks to the Missus, and they agree to come the next day, and I go back inside, ending the call and telling Maddox it's sorted.

The prick just nods, going back to his work, and I walk from the room, forcing myself to pretend I'm not furious about this entire situation, that I don't want to go out to the border and hurl myself at it until it breaks or kills me.

But that won't help Jules.

I go back up to my room and pace. Jules is a smart woman, and I know she's spent a lot of time with supes. I'd guarantee that her position right now isn't the first life-or-death situation she's been in, and she's very good at keeping herself alive. I have to trust that she will do everything she can to survive because I don't know how long we're going to be stuck here. If I had any chance of taking Maddox, I would, but his power as the leader makes sure he can keep us in line even with the extra I got from Jules in the Mountain.

I throw myself in a chair, trying to think of a way to speed things up but coming up with nothing. The clan used to mean everything to me, but after the Mountain, and now that Krase is gone, Axel is the only one I can trust.

I put thoughts of my brother from my mind. I miss him, but there's no point in dwelling on his loss. Jules is what's important now. Nothing else matters.

The clan be damned.

JULES

So close!

The piece of rock my foot is on crumbles under my toes, and I hear it bounce loudly to the ground. I adjust my grip and hold on tight, my fingers screaming from the strain. Siggy's sticky silk was easier to climb than these thousand-year-old walls, that's for sure.

With one last effort to pull myself up the last few inches, I push through the pain with a strained grunt and grab for the iron rungs of the grate above me.

Success!

I hang from it for a second before I can get my other hand up to join it, and I use my feet as leverage against the wall, pulling with one hand and then with the other. But the rungs are solid, and, now that I'm up here, I can see that they're modern, and they've been cemented into place quite recently.

With a growl of frustration, I begin the climb down.

I hear Krase chuckling from his cage.

'I can see your cunt,' he calls out crassly.

I ignore him. Yes, he definitely can, but that's because all I have to wear is Dante's shirt and some smelly horse blankets.

When I get to the ground, I wrap the shirt around me again and sit back on my hard rock bed.

I brush my fingers over my chest for the tenth time. I can't feel the brand. The conjure really is up and working again, but how? In my dream, Krase fixed it, but surely that isn't possible.

I watch him in my periphery. I know that he and his brother play around with fae stuff, so he'd probably have the knowledge to repair it, but how did he from all the way over there?

'How did you do it?' I come right out and ask.

'Do what?' he asks, playing with the rodent in his hand.

'Fix the broken conjure on me.'

He taps the side of his nose and doesn't say anything. I scowl.

'Will they bring us food?' I ask.

'Hungry are you, lass?'

'Aye!' I mock.

I rub my eyes and take a shaky breath.

'I haven't eaten in a while,' I admit.

'How long?' he asks.

'Don't know.'

I actually think my last meal was the one that Jayce procured for me from one of the orc vendors. Thoughts of him make my chest hurt.

He and Axel have just left me down here after everything that we ...

Sadness has me putting my back to my dungeon mate, trying to keep my pathetic tears a secret even from Crazy Krase.

'I can take the pain away if you like,' he says.

'What pain?' I try for a laugh, but it falls flat. I rub my eyes again. 'Even if you could, why would you? Don't you hate me too?'

'Aye, most assuredly, you deceitful little bitch!' he spits.

His sudden animosity has me curling in on myself even though this isn't the first time he's 'remembered' who I am over the past few hours and spewed hate at me.

'Then why?'

He snorts. 'Perhaps 'take the pain away' is the wrong way of putting it. I meant that I could take your mind off it for a while.'

I wipe my damp eyes before I look at him.

'How?'

He dangles something on a chain from his hand. It looks like a piece of jewelry.

'Look, I know you probably think I'm like a magpie, and any sparkly thing draws me into its orbit like it's a giant sun, but I actually have more important things to worry about than a pretty bauble at the moment.'

'It's a tacturn.'

'A tacturn?' I ask, not recognizing the name.

'Aye. Fae. Makes you see things you want to see.'

'Like a dream?'

He nods. 'But more real.'

'How?' I turn to watch him, and he shrugs.

'How does anything fae work? Magick and trickery.'

I'm about to tell him to stick it, but out of the corner of my eye, I notice a small spider spinning a web in the corner.

My lip wobbles as I'm reminded of my lost friend. Maybe I could see her again.

'Okay,' I say. 'How does it work?'

'We both hold it, and you close your eyes and think about what you want to see,' he says.

That seems too easy for a fae device, and when I remark as much, he laughs and holds it out.

'Why do we both have to hold it,' I ask.

'Because I know how to use it, lass.'

'Will you be able to see what I can see?'

He shakes his head. 'I'll be a voice in your head, that's all.'

I get off the bed and walk to where our cells share the bars.

I don't get too close, and he grins at me as he holds out the chain. It dangles down, and I let it snake into my hand a little, gripping it between two of my fingers.

'Close your eyes,' he orders, and, with a final, wry glance at him, I do as he says.

I gasp as I feel a shift in my body, and I open my eyes, but everything's black.

I draw a harsh breath.

'Think of where you want to go.' Krase's voice echoes through my head, and I do it.

The Mountain materializes in front of me. Siggy's lair.

I look around it and, even though I know that logically I'm not really here, the sights and smells and sounds ...

I touch a piece of silk hanging down from next to me. I can feel it brush across my fingers. I'd assume I really was there right now if I didn't know any better.

I start as I see the great arania above me, repairing a piece of her web. Unbidden tears come to my eyes as I watch Siggy, knowing that her web lies empty and her corpse has probably been stripped down to nothing along with the Demon King's.

I wipe a tear away, but another joins it, and pretty soon, I can't see through crying.

'I'm so sorry,' I say brokenly. 'It was my fault. I should have never taken the venom. Then you wouldn't have had to come down to the ground for me. He wouldn't have had a chance to kill you.'

I wipe my tears off with my sleeve. 'I'm so sorry,' I whisper. 'I'm so sorry, Siggy.'

I stand and watch my friend for a long time. She doesn't come closer, and I wonder if it's because this is an illusion. Maybe she can't interact with me.

'How do I get out?' I ask Krase.

There's a chuckle. 'You saw what you most desired to see. Now, you see the memory you least desire. That's how the fae work, silly girl.'

Siggy's cavern disappears into the darkness, and a moment later, there's a door in front of me.

'What is this?' I ask, my heart picking up because I know that door, and the last thing I want to do is go through it.

'Balance,' Krase answers readily.

'How do I get out of here?' I ask.

'Go through the door,' he answers impatiently.

I frown. 'I thought you couldn't see what I was seeing.'

His laugh echoes around me. 'I lied.'

Chapter Three

KRASE

I'm right behind her even though she can't see me, and I'm giddy with excitement. What horrors are through the door, I wonder. I mean, she's just a human, so I doubt it'll be all that bad, but watching her trepidation as she walks to her doom is the best entertainment I've had in weeks. It's almost as good as watching her climb up that wall and trying to pretend I wasn't watching her every movement and craning my neck to see beneath that long shirt. Almost as good as imagining how I'm going to kill her as soon as she stops amusing me.

The door opens with an ominous creak, and she walks inside. I follow and huff in disappointment as I find myself in an old-fashioned scullery.

A kitchen? This is her big, bad nightmare? Maybe the tacturn isn't working correctly.

I look around. It's large. Bigger than the one we have here. Humans are darting around. Servants.

My eyes narrow as I try to figure out where we are, the need for information making my brain feel normal for the first time in

I don't know how long. This is why I kept the tacturn when I locked myself down here. It beats back the madness for a little while.

I move around Victoria and take in her expression. Her eyes are wide and scared. What's so terrifying about a kitchen?

'You clumsy, dirty little—'

A slap and a cry reverberate through the room. A couple of the younger lads laugh, and Victoria cringes, putting her hands over her ears.

But she walks towards the sound, through another door, and into a washroom where a human child is clutching her cheek, tears in her eyes.

The girl is weeping quietly.

'Keep making that noise, and you'll get another one!' an older human woman tells her, raising her hand to punctuate her point.

The child cowers away.

'Why his lordship bought such a useless creature, I'll never know,' a new, commanding voice enters the room.

'Sir,' the human woman mutters, lowering her eyes, 'Apologies, I didn't know you were here already.'

But the lower fae male has already forgotten the human woman in favor of staring at the small girl.

'She looks like she could do with a firmer hand,' he remarks, and the human woman cringes.

He grabs the child and hauls her in front of him. 'Did you just look me in the eye, child?' he booms.

'No, sir,' the girl cries. 'I'd never!'

'I can see a spark of defiance in you,' he murmurs, 'and that won't do at all, not when his lordship let you into his home and feeds you the food from his table.'

I snort at that because it's clear that the girl is half-starved.

He pushes her into the waiting arms of a guard. 'Take her to the cellars.'

Then he rolls his eyes. 'And I shouldn't have to say this, but as it's you, don't despoil her. Mustn't touch what isn't yours.'

The fae guard murmurs his assent and takes the girl's arm, pulling her out of the kitchen and down some gloomy stairs while she whimpers and pleads.

Victoria follows the memories slowly, her face blank.

And I realize why we're here.

The girl child is her.

I tail her. If she looks behind, she'll see me, but she doesn't. She's too focused on this dark road before her.

I descend the stairs, but when I get to the bottom, there's no cellar. Instead, it's the kitchens again, but the girl is now older, maybe fifteen.

She's dressed in a shapeless shift, washing dishes and cowering whenever anyone, human or otherwise, comes near her. She's covered in bruises, old and new. I watch as a fae approaches her. He's dressed well, not some lower fae overseer of staff. This one is a High Lord. When he sees her, his mouth twists into a sneer, and his movements turn stealthy as he creeps up on her.

When he gets to her, he doesn't do anything. He just stands there. The servants in the room are pointedly ignoring him, but I see a few watching inconspicuously from behind their workbenches, relishing what's happening to their fellow human.

I look back, and he's still in the same spot. At first, I thought she hadn't realized he was there, but when I edge around to see her face, I can tell she knows exactly where he is. When his arm comes out and takes the back of her neck in a sure grip, she jumps, but the move is practiced, and it's clear to me it's an act.

But why?

He whispers something in her ear, and she blanches as he walks her out of the kitchens. Some of the humans snigger.

We follow again, but this time, it's up into the main house.

It's opulent and huge, with magickal lights and ceilings of moving skies and sunlight.

Soooo fae.

The fae lord brings her to a room, and, for the first time, I see true fear as he opens the door and pushes her through.

The door slams closed, and Victoria stands frozen at it, making no attempt to enter. I hear noises from within. Low voices and the clanking of chains. A sudden scream has me starting forward before I remember that this isn't real. At least not presently.

I begin to hear the sound of a beating, thudding blows, and the sounds of a whip whistling through the air, punctuated with cries of pain.

Victoria still doesn't move. She's like a statue; her eyes cast to the floor as she listens to what I assume is herself being brutalized.

My own heart is thudding hard in my chest, my suddenly clear mind berating me for doing this to her even though she is an enemy.

It's a few minutes before the door opens, and another High Fae lord exits the room. He's looking annoyed as if something isn't going his way.

The one who brought her follows him, but the figures now standing in the hall are muted, like shadows or ghosts, and their voices are muffled.

Because she was in the room, not out here, I suppose. She could hear their exchange but not see them.

'This isn't progressing quickly enough. Increase the duration by twenty percent and the frequency to every day.'

'But, my lord, she's already—' The fae falls silent at the other's warning look. 'Of course, my lord.'

The realization that this hasn't been as entertaining as I thought it would be has me twisting the tacturn in my hand to end the illusion.

The cells appear before us.

She's standing right where she was, still staring at the floor. There's nothing in her expression to show she's upset, but her body is quivering. I reach through the bars and gently pull the tacturn's chain out of her hand.

'Victoria?' I ask gently, knowing I don't have long before the fog takes me again.

It's the only reason I kept this infernal device. When I'm enveloped in its magick, I can think clearly for a little while. It has a price like everything fae, taking slivers of power I don't miss *until I do*, but I'm going to need it when Maddox returns. If I can't prove I'm still *in here*, he's going to kill me. I know that would be best, safest at this point, but there's something inside me that's telling me to fight just a little while longer, that maybe there will be salvation for me.

Victoria doesn't answer and, in fact, gives no indication that she's heard me.

I glance at the cell door. I probably have just enough time if I make it quick.

I pull it open, releasing the lock with a phrase I've buried deep in my sane mind so that the growing dark part of me doesn't know it when he takes over.

I use the same one at her cage and walk inside.

She doesn't move.

'Victoria?' I ask again.

This time, she looks up at me, but I know she's not really seeing me. She's still in that place. The only difference is that it's no longer the tacturn keeping her there but her own mind.

I pick her up and pull her against me gently.

I wish I could say that I hadn't dreamed of holding her, but I have. Many times. Those weeks she spent with us were some of the happiest that I can recall of my life.

I lay her down on the blankets, wrapping her shaking body and stroking her forehead.

'It's all over,' I murmur, shaking my head at the useless platitude.

She's as much a prisoner here as she was there, and while I doubt Maddox and the others would stoop to such methods of punishment as those fae, I'm not sure about myself anymore.

I can already feel the dark impulses worming their way into me. The more I fight them, the more I want to give in. Intense, insatiable hunger eats at me. I step away from her, swallowing hard at the urge to rip the blankets away and make her scream for me in a completely different way to the fae before I rip out her throat.

Jaw clenching, I turn and rush to the door, flinging it open and closed again, thankful when it relocks automatically. I open my own cell door, and my body freezes.

No!

I force my foot forward into the cell while my head screams. I pull the cell to, hearing the lock and lurching across the space before I give in.

The melody I hear is one of pain, and I revel in it, eyes locking on the female in the next cell who's sobbing quietly on her bed. I hate her, but I can't quite remember why. Not that it matters.

I reach out as I demon-up, trying to grab her so I can feed from her through the bars, but she's too far away. I grin. If I can lure her close to me in my human form and let my glamor down quickly enough, I'll be able to get my claws on her.

I've tried lulling her to do my bidding several times, but it's not working.

My jaws snap in frustration. I'm hungry, and I will not be denied!

JULES

I'm quietly weeping as I realize I'm back in the cell at Maddox's, and I turn around to glare at Krase for his tricks. The fucker just grins at me, cooing at the rat sitting in his hand.

'Fuck you, Krase,' I mutter.

He laughs darkly. 'Soon, Victoria.'

I roll my eyes and force a chuckle of my own. 'No way in hell, pal.'

Luckily, I'm saved from having to speak to the psycho anymore as I hear the lock turning outside the dungeon.

I sit up, pulling the blankets around me as Maddox enters. He's carrying a tray of food, and I practically leap up to see what he's brought, my stomach rumbling loudly.

He puts the tray down on the floor, and I see he also has a small pile of clothes. He throws them into the cell at me without preamble.

'Put these on.'

I grab them off the floor. It's a pair of jeans and a green, long-sleeved top. They look familiar.

'Are these mine?' I ask.

'You left them. They were in the laundry when you fled the estate,' he murmurs as he locks the outer door that leads to his wine cellars and turns back around to face the cells.

He takes a covered plate off the tray and slides it under the door of Krase's side, along with a cup.

He does the same under mine, and I don't wait for him to leave. I uncover the plate and fall on the meal like I've never seen food before, shoveling it into my mouth and hardly even taking the time to chew it. I don't even stop to look at what it is. I don't care. It tastes good. It smells good. But even if it was old, maggoty bread, I'd still be stuffing my face with it to ease the ache in my stomach.

When there's nothing left, I finally sit back to find Maddox squatting outside my cell, regarding me with an odd look on his face. When he sees I've noticed, he stands quickly and peers in at Krase.

The imprisoned incubus hasn't touched his plate.

'Not hungry, my friend?' Maddox asks.

Krase scoffs from the shadows. 'For my last meal? No, thanks, mate.'

Maddox lets out a slow breath, and I feel my eyebrows rise.

'You're going to kill him?' I ask.

Maddox doesn't look at me.

'You can't!' I cry, despite his tricks. 'He survived all this time. He's your frien—'

Maddox is suddenly throwing open the door to my cell and stalking inside towards me with purpose. I scramble back, losing my blanket in the process. He grabs me and pins me against the wall by my throat, leaning in very close.

'Do you think I want this?' he says in my ear. 'Do you think I want to kill a member of my own clan? My brother?'

'But why—'

'He's rogue. Mad. Can't be trusted. It's the most humane thing to do for an incubus like him.'

He squeezes my neck for a split second before he pushes away from me with a curse.

'You've changed,' I mutter. 'Two years ago, you would never have done this. You'd have found a way to save him!'

'You don't know me, Julia. You don't know any of us. If it were up to me, you'd still be in the Mountain playing house with Dante. How did you escape anyway? Did you make a deal with him? Did you tell him where the portal was?'

He snorts. 'Of course, you did. Tell me, how long before he comes through our door looking for revenge?'

I push off the wall and glance at the open door behind him. 'That's not how it happened.'

'Then enlighten me, darling. How did it happen?'

'I ... he left me alone and ... the arania came. She got me out.' I try not to let my emotions get the better of me as I talk about Siggy, recount the story the way I wish it had happened.

'She's lying,' the asshole in the cell next to me rasps.

'Oh, so now you're *sound as a pound*, Krase?' I snarl at him, borrowing one of Maddox's sayings. 'You don't know anything!'

Krase jumps at the bars between us violently, making the cells shake, and I flinch.

'Siggy's dead,' he taunts with a smile.

Maddox's lip curls. 'How do you know about the arania?' he asks Krase.

The crazy incubus lets his fae trinket drop down from his closed fist. The tacturn spins slowly on the chain.

'You tricked her into a fae illusion to get information out of her?' Maddox gives him a long look. 'Shrewd as ever, Krase, even in this state,' he mutters.

I frown, certain he's giving Krase too much credit. I'm pretty sure he just wanted to fuck with me to ease his own boredom.

'I knew you were lying,' Maddox tells me, and I roll my eyes because, no, he didn't. 'Just tell me the truth, Jules.'

I don't say anything. I don't want to tell anyone how I think I changed when I fought Dante and that I killed him because I don't really believe it happened that way ... but I also don't have an alternative story to give.

'Or do I get Iron down here to put you through the wringer again?'

NO!

My eyes flick up to his before I can hide the fear, and I see surprise. He didn't expect to see anything real in my expression. I must be tired, showing something like that to him. He'll use it against me.

Keep it together.

'Siggy *is* dead,' I relent, clenching my jaw as unbidden tears come to my eyes. 'She came to rescue me, but I ... I was tied up. She came down to the floor and freed me, but Dante appeared, and they fought. He ...' I clench my eyes shut to stop the tears. 'He killed her.'

Maddox is quiet, and, in the end, I'm forced to blink back my tears to look at him so I can gauge whether or not he believes my mostly true story.

He has a look on his face I've never seen on him before. Commiserating. Like he gives a shit about some arania. I look away quickly because it's bull, and he's just trying to create common ground between us for his own gain.

He's not going to succeed. He gave me to Dante, and he left me in the Mountain to die. Yeah, the others were involved, but it was down to Maddox, the clan leader. He's the one I blame the most, and my punishment didn't fit my crime. They've been blaming me for a death that hasn't even happened. Krase is standing right next to me. Yeah, he's nuts, but *that's* not my fault!

'I'm sorry,' Maddox shocks me by saying, and I look up into his eyes again, a part of me reaching out to him, wanting kindness from him.

'I know she was the only real friend you'll likely ever have,' he cuts me by saying.

A hiccuping sob almost forces its way out, but I drive it back down relentlessly.

'Thankfully,' I say, shoving away everything that's real and scolding myself for showing weakness to them. 'Anyway, after Siggy was dead, I sat back where I'd been and pretended I was still tied up. When Dante left the room, I used Siggy's silk to climb up into the shafts. I ran for the portal, and I got through just in time. I ended up here. Guess I went through around the same time as the last one of you did, so it brought me to the same place.'

Maddox doesn't say anything; just watches me. Inside, I smirk. He talks a good game, but the truth is he'd never know if I was lying or not. I don't have any tells at all. And I know that for certain because, if I did, I'd have been dead long before he met me the first time.

He backs out of my cell. 'Put on the clothes,' he says again, his eyes flicking down my open shirt to look at the goods before they leave me completely like he's trying to make sure I know he's not interested.

Works for me, asshole.

I don't move. I don't cover myself.

'Before you freeze, human,' Krase murmurs, and I turn to look at him.

He's staring openly at my body even more than Maddox, and, to be honest, I don't want to antagonize him even if he *is* locked up. I stoop to pick up the clothes I dropped and throw on the underwear and jeans with my back to them both.

I turn around for the bra and the shirt, backing into the corner by the slab. They aren't paying attention to me anymore, though. Maddox is outside Krase's cell. He's touching the tacturn. Both their eyes are open and looking around. Their mouths are moving, but no sound comes out.

I throw on the bra and shirt, not taking my eyes off the disturbing scene in front of me. Was that how I looked while that fucking thing took me into my nightmares? I thought I was screaming the whole time. That's what it felt like, but was I just standing there like a puppet?

That's fae shit for you, I guess. It's either sublimely ethereal or creepy as fuck.

While Maddox is indisposed, I go back to the dish and lick

the remaining residue of food off my plate. Hunger still gnaws at me, though, and I wonder if I can reach Krase's meal, too.

Keeping an eye on them, I shuffle to the shared bars of our cages and stick my arm through. My middle finger just brushes the plate, but I can't reach it well enough to pull it closer. With a small noise of frustrated displeasure, I stop trying, stalking back over to my bed and sitting on it cross-legged.

Chapter Four

IRON

I watch Jayce and Axel from my position in the hallway, looking through the crack in the door like a voyeur. They're talking about cars, and it seems like they're coming out of whatever love spell Jules had them under. They're acting *normal*.

Too normal.

My eyes narrow, zeroing in on their faces. I can't see any outward signs that this is a trick, but we'd better be damned sure they're back to themselves before we ease up on the security, or they'll cause a heap of trouble for us.

I was right to change the estate's conjures to stop them from leaving, though it was Maddox's idea for the spell to steal energy from them every time they tried. I have to admit that was pretty inspired. As it is, we've got maybe a couple of weeks before we'll all need to feed properly. They won't risk their energies trying to escape more than once or twice.

I turn away and head back upstairs. There's something niggling at me, and I can't work out what it is. Or maybe I just don't want to examine it closely. I told Maddox I didn't care that we'd left Jules in the Mountain, but every time I think about it, I feel sick.

So, I try *not* to think about it.

But everything just keeps circling back to the fact that we left a defenseless human girl in a prison of supe monsters. In the hands of Dante, one of the worst of them all. It was on Maddox's orders, yeah, but I can't blame him for this. I should have gone back for her, found a way to get her out of there.

Maybe the arania saved her.

I sigh, giving myself a nervous shake. I need to do something other than wander around this house.

And I need to forget Jules. She deserved what she got.

I go up to one of the round turret chambers in the west tower. The Sunroom. The walls are painted in fae symbols. Maddox had this room created for me to practice my fae magick in when I first joined his clan. It had only been a few months since I'd been kicked out of the military when they found out I was a supe. Now, of course, there are special supe detachments in all branches of the forces, but back when they first learned of us, it was a 'get the fuck out, you freak' type of deal.

I make a turn of the room, taking it in. I haven't been up here in a long time. I'd forgotten how calming and centering it is. My magick was so weak before that there wasn't much point in trying to perfect it because it wasn't any more useful than Krase and Jayce's fae toys that they were always playing around with, but I did enjoy coming up here to meditate.

Now, I'm wondering how powerful I actually am because the Mountain did something to me. I felt it then, and I can feel it even more clearly now that we're back, in this room especially. I never could have changed the estate's magickal defenses before. We used to have to pay some mid-level fae kid to come here and tweak it for us when we needed something altered. It would take him all day. This morning, I fixed it in five minutes.

I close my eyes, my countless childhood lessons with GiGi coming to the front of my mind. I sense rather than see the symbols on the walls when they start to glow as I push out with the tendrils of my personal magick, or at least the magick from my mother's side.

I'm shocked when I feel them, ropes of magick so thick and infused with power, tinged with my demon side as well. When I was a child, these same ropes were like tiny, limp threads of nothing that embarrassed my mother's fae kin.

Something in my mind relaxes, and it's like dust being blown off a table, clearing it. I can see the conjure around the estate, the little clouds of blues, greens, and purples that come from the many old spells added over the years to the house and surrounding land. The maze, especially, is like a watercolor painting, being one of the older and historically more favored parts of the garden.

My brow furrows as I see the house itself. Most of those little conjures I know, like the one that Robertson used to use to call objects to him from around the grounds or the golden glow of the portal keys locked up in the safe in the library. I can even see the lone ones secreted around the house for emergencies. But there are a few other spells that I'm not sure of, and one in particular, down in the wine cellar, draws my attention. I get closer to it, but it's muffled. Isn't that my own—

Someone bangs on the door, breaking my focus and my connection to my magick.

'Maddox wants you,' Daemon says from the other side of the door. 'The pixies Jayce called are here, and he wants you to check them out for spells and stuff.'

I roll my eyes; the conjures I was looking at forgotten.

'What the hell did he used to do before?' I mutter.

'Used Jayce and Krase's collection of fae crap,' Daemon snorts. 'But that sure as shit isn't going to work with one of them being dead and the other one outside the trust circle.'

I wince as Daemon mentions Krase's death so casually. I know he was gone for a couple of years, and I know that time wasn't kind to him, not just because of what I heard but also because he seems harder now than he was before. Despite his past, there used to be a playful boyishness in his eyes that's gone. Now, all I see reflected when I look at him is a world-weariness and jaded melancholy that he hides behind anger.

I open the door.

'Krase was my friend,' I say, not able to let it pass without comment.

He at least looks abashed. 'I know. Sorry. I didn't mean anything by it.'

I sigh, 'Yeah, I know. Look, I'm not saying we pretend that the last two years didn't happen, but we're clan. We need to *be* clan.'

He nods. 'That's something we can agree on. Divided, we're weak.'

I frown because, although that's true, that's not what I meant, and that that's where his mind went first is further evidence that he's still in survival mode.

'We're clan,' I say again, putting my hand on his shoulder. '*You're* clan. Julian should never have kicked you out like that. It wasn't right.'

He looks uncomfortable and moves back a step. My hand falls away.

'I deserved it for letting her in.'

'We were all to blame for that. Not just you.'

He shrugs. 'Doesn't matter now.'

'No, I guess not,' I mutter, frowning as Daemon turns around and descends the spiral staircase, moving out of sight.

He *is* right. Divided, we're weak, and we need to be as strong as we can be right now.

I follow him slowly, deciding the library is probably the best place to locate the visitors.

I enter and find I'm right. Two pixies in human form, both looking like they're in their sixties, stand in the middle of the room, each with a small suitcase.

'Ah, Iron.' Maddox ushers them forward. 'This is Fergus and Tabitha. Our new members of staff.'

I give them both pleasant smiles and shake hands, using my contact to inspect any magick they're carrying.

Tabitha, who's about a foot and a half shorter than me, looks up into my face, her eyes crinkling.

'We didn't bring anything fae,' she mock whispers, and my eyes widen a little.

How did she know what I was doing?

She grins and gives me a wink. 'We're older than we look, incubus. Not our first time aiding and abetting.'

'You're not just a pixie,' I mutter.

She laughs. '*Just* a pixie?' she feigns umbrage. 'No, I'm a tiny part orc on my father's side. Gives my magick a little kick.' She raises a brow. 'Not like yours, though. Odd pairing, fae and demon. They like to keep the bloodlines *separate*, don't they?'

I give a small smile to hide my surprise that she can see my magick's sources. I'll need to figure out a way to keep that under wraps.

'My mother and father weren't fans of the rules,' I say.

'Rebels, eh?'

'Something like that.'

I hear Maddox chuckle.

'Well, I think you'll get on well here. Welcome to our home. Let me show you the cottage that comes with the position and whatnot.'

He ushers the couple out of the library, and I stare after them, Tabitha especially, with a bemused expression. There's certainly more to her than meets the eye, but I'd wager she's not dangerous. At least not to us.

I leave the library and wander around, the crack of a hard ball against another drawing me to the Billiard room.

There, I find Axel and Jayce playing a game together. They look relaxed like they don't have a care in the world. Like we didn't leave Jules in that place. That feeling creeps up again, even more magnified, and I tense up.

Guilt. That's what it is. And if I'm feeling it, then there's no way these two are over it, either. Not after all the time they *spent* with her in the Mountain. I pin them both with a glare.

'You're not fooling anyone,' I say.

They both turn to look at me, pausing their game.

'What are you talking about?' Axel asks.

I scoff.

'Please! If I took down the shield right now, the first thing you two dumbasses would do is get yourselves arrested and thrown back into the Mountain to go save Jules.'

They just look at me, false incredulity all over their faces. I roll my eyes. 'You aren't going to get the chance,' I tell them. 'None of us can leave the grounds until we've paid the right people to forget we were ever arrested in the first place. Not for any reason.'

They both just stare.

'Look, maybe you aren't the only ones who think we did something wrong by leaving her there,' I blurt, not sure why I'm admitting it to them.

Jayce and Axel look at each other and shrug.

'Perhaps she got to you as well, Iron?' Jayce says with a sneer. 'Wouldn't tell Maddox if I were you, you'll find yourself out here in the Badlands with us.'

I look from one to the other and sigh. They don't believe me. They think it's a test.

They both go back to their game without another word, ignoring me.

I leave them, feeling frustrated and oddly alone, thoughts of

Jules making me freeze in the hallway for a moment. Did she get to me with whatever it was that turned Jayce and Axel to her cause? If she did, it was no magick I've ever felt before because I know that I'd feel its residue if that's truly how she did it.

But if it wasn't magick, then what was it? How did she do it?

I walk the corridors aimlessly, deep in thought, and I find myself outside the room that Jules had while she was with us.

I go inside, closing the door quietly behind me, taking in a deep breath through my nose, and pretending I can still pick up her lingering scent, even though it's been over twenty-five months now since she was here.

But who's counting?

I go to the top drawer of the bureau and open it, expecting, as always, to see the clothes she left here. But they're gone.

It's been a long time since I last came in here. Someone must have got rid of them. Inordinately bothered by this, I turn away with a small growl. I go to the bed and pick up one of the pillows. I push it into my face, smelling it, and I swear I get the barest whiff of her perfume.

What the hell am I doing?

With a snarl, I throw the pillow back down on the bed and stalk from the room, unable to push away the feelings warring within me.

It doesn't matter what she did to me to make me feel this way. It's not going away. In fact, the shame and guilt and the fear are getting stronger, and it's like I'm coming out of a fog, seeing everything with sudden clarity.

Maybe it was a latent magick in the Mountain itself messing with my mind, or suddenly having power at my fingertips after so many years of being told I *should* have it, yet not being able to manage more than a weak conjure. Either way, I turned into something I hate in there, I realize. A cruel, power-drunk fae. And Jules bore the brunt of me at my worst.

But now everything is shifting on its axis. My mind is

clearing when I didn't even see that it was murky. The Sunroom, I realize. If some lingering magick from the Mountain was affecting me, that would have burned it off.

Now, when I think of what I did and said, how I tormented her and made her break down and sob ... it doesn't feel like it was me.

But it was, and I helped to give her to a psychopath and left her there when we could easily have brought her with us. How could we have done that to her?

I pull myself together and practically sprint down the hallway to the Billiard room, cursing when I find it empty. I need to find them; I need to tell them.

I reach out with my magick, searching for them. They're in the gardens, walking together. Plotting more like. It's one of the only places where they can be sure they won't be overheard.

I leave the house via the side door, and I wait until they're closer to the house, away from the library where, no doubt, Maddox is watching. I don't want him knowing about this. I don't need him suspicious of me, too, because, even though my fae power is stronger than it's ever been, Maddox is still the clan leader, and the magick of that position will always be stronger than mine, I suspect.

When they get close, I walk out into the path in front of them.

'We have to go back,' I blurt. 'We can't just leave a human girl in that place.'

JULES

'How long have I been here?' I ask Krase.

He doesn't respond; just lays on his slab of stone and stares at the ceiling. He was lucid for a little while after Maddox was here the last time, when he and Maddox used that fae thing.

When he lets his head fall to the side to look at me now, though, his expression makes me want to hide because whatever is staring at me from behind those eyes, it's not him.

He knows I'm scared. He likes it. Is this what they really are without their sanity or their human sides?

'I'm going to come in there and rip out your insides,' he whispers.

I roll my eyes. 'Yeah. You told me,' I mutter.

Actual threats in words I understand, and, weirdly, it makes me happier to know what Krase's plans are for me if he does catch me than if he said nothing at all, and I had to wonder.

He sniffs at me again and frowns.

'Why do you keep doing that?' I ask, not really expecting an answer, so I'm surprised when he actually gives me one.

'You don't have a scent.'

'I don't?'

'No,' he growls like he's annoyed by that.

'I guess Iron didn't take his conjure off me after the Mountain,' I mutter, half to myself.

'Iron,' he scoffs. 'That fool has less power in his whole body than this tiny little fae toy.'

'Maybe that was true before,' I say, 'but things are a little different now.'

He doesn't say anything back, just spins his tacturn, staring at it. 'I know why you brought this,' he says, and I look up, but he's not talking to me, I don't think.

'But you're just delaying the inevitable. Soon, you won't be coming back out, and it'll just be me.' His eyes find me. 'Me and the pretty human.'

His fingers clench, and, for a second, it's like he's at war with his own body, jerking and shuddering until there's a low laugh and the tacturn is flung away.

It hits the bars of his cell and falls to the floor just outside mine.

'No more fae toy to bring you back,' the demon taunts, closing his eyes.

I stare at the tacturn on the ground. He won't be able to reach it, but I bet I can.

I slip off the stone slab I'm sitting on and ease myself silently across my cell to the front where I sink to the floor and poke my arm through the bars. My fingers easily grab it, and I rise, holding the tiny magickal item in my hand for a moment before I wrap the chain around it and put it in the back pocket of my jeans.

Maybe I am a little magpie-ish, but a fae bauble is always worth something, and if I can get out of here, I can sell it.

I shiver a little as I feel its magick, and it makes the other conjures on me tingle, the one Iron put on me that I can't do anything about and the one I had from before that Krase somehow fixed after Dante broke it when he touched the brand.

I wrap my arms around myself as I remember being on that bed, unable to do anything but lie there while he touched me, hurt me. Even though it can't have been real because my body is completely healed from everything he did. I still can't work out what really happened, but it keeps rolling around in my head without me wanting it to.

'Stop torturing yourself,' I whisper.

I go back and sit on the blankets I've piled up on top of the stone to try to stop the cold from seeping through. The worst part of this is having nothing to do down here. Maddox appears once a day to bring food and, other than that, it's inane conversation with Crazy Krase,

Sometimes, he sits at the bars between our cells and just stares at me for hours. Other times, he talks to himself about something he needs to find, but he doesn't look around for whatever he's lost. Most of what he says makes no sense, but he gets himself all riled up and throws himself at the bars. He does it when I least expect it, making me scream involuntarily at the sounds of him losing it. He likes to *hear* my fear, I think, because he can't smell it on me.

The sun has moved down low by the time I hear Maddox today. He's later than he was yesterday, and my stomach is clenching in anticipation of food.

I rush to the front of my cell to get my meal, already salivating at the clank of the keys like a Pavlovian dog, excited to have some kind of interaction to break up the monotonous hours down here.

Maddox enters with the trays stacked on top of each other. He sees me by the front, but he takes his time, making me wait as he gives Krase his food first. I try to stay patient because I know he's doing it on purpose to mess with me.

I fail.

'You're very good at playing the bad-guy, sadistic jailor,' I find my errant mouth saying.

'Thank you,' he answers without missing a beat as he stands outside my cell with the tray, making no move to give it to me.

He quirks a brow, and I move back to the slab, jumping up onto it and sitting down because if he thinks I'm going to beg him for food, he can go fuck himself.

I'd rather die.

But he surprises me by putting it down and sliding it under the bars without much more delay.

I get up and go over to it a little warily, taking up the cover and finding a hearty stew with some bread.

'This is my favorite,' I say with some shock.

'Yes.'

I look up and regard him even more warily. 'Last meal?' I quip and side-eye Krase because Maddox hasn't killed him yet like he said he was going to.

'No, but Axel made it, and there was some left over. I remember how much you enjoyed it before.'

He stands in front of my cell, and although I'd rather wait and eat without being stared at, I can't. I dive into it with a sound of appreciation, the taste of buttery meat and carrots, of the gravy and peas making me remember when I last had this. It was the night before I left. We all sat in the dining room and ate together, drank fine wine. We'd all talked and laughed, and, at the end, I'd fallen asleep between Maddox and Axel on the couch.

I'd been happy and content.

And that's why, the next day, I'd destroyed it all and left.

The memory makes me sad, and when I glance up at Maddox, he has a look in his eye that makes me think he's remembering the same thing. His gaze hardens as I watch.

Yep, he's remembering all right.

'What did you do with all that money you took?' he asks suddenly.

The question takes me by surprise. I swallow what's in my mouth before I answer, buying myself a little time because it all went on an expensive charm to keep me hidden from magick for eighteen months.

'Oh, you know me,' I say airily with a little shrug. 'I like nice things.'

'Yeah, you do,' he sneers. 'How does it feel to be in there, dirty and cold and hungry?'

'It's not so bad,' I lie. 'Step up from the Mountain.'

I gesture to the blankets and my plate of food. 'Could be worse.'

I should shut up. What if he decides he wants me to be more miserable and takes the blankets away? Makes the food less palatable, or stops bringing it altogether? He could just stop coming down here and kill both Krase and me that way. I wouldn't put it past him. He's a supe no matter how human he looks, how civilized he pretended to be when I was here before. He could do it easily and probably wouldn't feel a thing if it was just me, but Krase is a different story. He's family, after all.

'What are you going to do about Krase?' I ask him point-blank.

His eyes flick to his clan mate, who's in the corner staring at the wall and hasn't even made a move towards his food, though he must be as hungry as I am.

'Have you reconsidered?' I ask, hoping that he has, even though Demon Krase is a dick.

'For now,' he answers.

'Why?'

He stares at Krase. 'Because he asked me for more time, and he's my friend.'

He looks back at me, clearly surprised that he just answered me like that, like we're not prisoner and jailor.

'How do you do that?' he asks me quietly, coming closer to the bars.

'Do what?' I say, looking up at him from my knees.

His eyes move over me, and I can tell he likes me in this position. He never said anything, but I always had a feeling that he and Daemon especially had certain proclivities.

Guess I was right.

I should probably use them to my advantage.

I lean forward a little so he can see down my top just a smidge. His eyes flick down, and I pretend not to notice.

'You always know how to make me relax, tell you things.'

I don't break our eye contact.

'It's not on purpose,' I say.

He huffs, and the spell is broken.

I look down at my plate and finish eating, but despite the food, the hollowness in my belly hasn't been assuaged. Reluctantly, I push the tray back under the bars, wishing I'd have eaten slower because now I have nothing to do.

'Would you do me a favor?' I murmur, grasping the bars in front of him.

After all, if you don't ask, you don't get.

'What is it?' he asks, his eyes darting over me in suspicion but still lingering on the breasts that are squished against the bars.

He steps so close we're almost touching, and I gasp a tiny bit. He smells *so good*. For a second, I forget my question as I breathe in the scent of leather and neroli. My eyes have drifted closed, and I feel something coming from him.

He wants me, I realize.

My eyes snap open at the same time his do, and he leaps back with a snarl. 'Don't you fucking dare, Julia!'

I try to hide my surprise at his visceral reaction, taking a couple of steps back into the cell while I watch him. I jump as an arm darts through the bars beside me, and I dance away from Krase's claws that are trying to grab me. He's staring at me with such a hungry look in his eye that I shudder because, despite his threats of physical violence, it looks like that isn't what he really wants to do to me. He's been lying, maybe to us both.

I hear the door open, and I let out a cry.

'No, wait! Please, Julian! I didn't mean it. I'm sorry.'

I say everything I can think of to delay him even though I have no idea why he was so upset, nor any inkling of what I'm actually apologizing for.

'Stop doing it then!' he thunders.

'I will, I promise. Please don't go yet.'

He pauses at the door and looks at me expectantly, looking almost fearful of getting too close again.

'Books,' I blurt. 'Please bring me something to do. I'm going nuts like Krase down here.'

He looks at me like he's going to say no, but he doesn't.

'I'll think about it,' he says gruffly before closing the door and locking it behind him.

I sink to my knees by the bars, not knowing what just happened between us but needing more.

'Come to me, and I'll give you what you need,' Krase growls from his cage.

I jump because he sounds close enough to grab me, but when I look, I'm just out of his reach.

I laugh. 'No fucking way.'

'It's only a matter of time,' he says.

'Until you kill me? I'm not going to let you do that, Krase,' I say with more confidence than I feel because he was very close to snatching me a few moments ago, and I don't actually know if Maddox would have intervened on my behalf.

I stay like that for a few minutes, and my thoughts slowly turn back to Siggy as they always seem to. Maybe it's normal after a bereavement, but I can't really remember feeling this when my parents died. Maybe there was just too much going on, so there wasn't time to feel like that. I had other problems around that time.

I mean I have other problems now, but nothing else is going on. There's just time stretching out in front of me. I go to the only spot in my cell where Krase can't see me, behind the slab of rock that serves as my bed. It's a little nasty because the waste bucket is back here, too, but at least it has a cover on it. And, besides, I literally lived with a giant spider over rotting corpses for three months. A little poop in a bucket is nothing.

Thoughts of Siggy have me crouching down to cry as quietly as I can.

I can hear Krase moving around his cell. He sounds agitated.

'I can hear you,' he finally rasps. 'I know what you're doing.'

'So?'

'So why hide?'

I think about that for a second. 'Because I don't like to cry in front of people.'

He chuckles. 'I'm not people. I'm a monster.'

I peek over the stone at him. He's standing right at the bars, gripping them hard.

'What do you care?' I ask, rolling my eyes.

'I don't, thief.'

'Seems like you do,' I retort.

'Are you hungry?' he asks, changing the subject.

'Yes,' I admit, clutching my aching abdomen.

He lets out a snort. 'I could help you.'

I return the sound. 'How? You have another dinner in your cell?'

'I do, actually.'

I peek over my bed again and find him holding the bowl of stew Maddox brought.

'A deal,' he says, and I have to admit, my interest is peaked as I stare at the bowl that's still steaming a little.

'What kind of deal?' I ask, wondering how lucid he is. He sounds all there, but sometimes I think it's just the darkness in him pretending, so I let my guard down.

'You feed me, and I feed you.'

I stare at him for a minute, turning his words around in my head. 'What do you mean?'

'Come out, and I'll tell you.'

I suppose this exchange is at least taking up some time, I think as I leave the confines of the back of the slab, emerging into the cell once more.

'Okay. I'm out,' I say, eyeing the food in his hand. 'What is it that you want from me?'

'Come to me,' he murmurs low, his voice seductive, and I roll my eyes.

'You demon voodoo doesn't work on me, Krase.'

'Just making sure. It doesn't matter. If you want this,' he waves the bowl around, 'you'll do what I want anyway.'

I decide to play along. 'Sex through the bars?'

His eyes light up, and I know I shouldn't mock, but I can't help my laugh. 'No fucking way.'

'I'm starving,' he whines, 'and I don't need to touch you. It needn't be any more than you sticking your own fingers in your cunt and making yourself come.'

I wince a little at his crass words, but the image of me doing just that while he watches is, surprisingly, not as abhorrent as I'd have thought it would be.

In fact, my lady parts clench pleasantly at the idea.

'So, you want me to drop my pants and get myself off?' I ask, just making sure I have it straight.

I have no intention of doing it, of course, but ... I mean, it wouldn't be the *end of the world* if I did, would it? I've arguably done worse things; they just didn't involve sex, but is there really any difference?

My stomach twists, and I look at the bowl and then at Krase.

It would be easy to do, and then I get food.

'Do you need to see what I do?' I ask quietly.

A light appears in his eyes. He knows he's got me.

'No,' he growls.

I nod, glancing behind me at the stone bed. I don't really want to crouch behind it next to the waste bucket. I have some standards. But I could do it under the blankets on top of the slab itself.

'And you'll give me the bowl?'

'Cross my heart,' he grates out, putting it down on the floor just inside my cell.

I nod. 'Okay.'

Holy shit. Am I really going to do this?

I undo the top button and unzip my jeans, not looking at

him, my cheeks getting hot. I sit up on the slab and lay down on it, pulling my jeans down a little for easier access. Closing my eyes, I try to think of something hot, my mind settling on Jayce and Axel double-teaming me in the Mountain, but I find the memory tainted now that I know it was a trick.

I don't really have anything else ...

I glance at Krase, who's still by the bars, staring so intently that it's almost as if he can *see* under the blanket.

'Take off your shirt,' I mutter, and his eyes cut to me.

'Why?'

'Because my highlight reel sucks,' I say, 'and even though you're nuts, you're still a hot as hell incubus.'

He grins at me, practically preening under my gaze. He rips off the rags that cover him, baring his chiseled body, his eyes not leaving mine.

'Like what you see?' he drawls.

My eyes move over him, following the contours of his biceps and pecks, down to the muscles of his abs and the V that leads lower.

'Yes,' I breathe.

'Watch me then.'

My eyes widen as he unbuttons his pants and pulls out his already hard shaft. He fists it, leaning against the bars and touching himself as he stares at me.

It should repulse me. But it doesn't. Not at all.

I watch his movements, and my fingers slip down beneath the band of my underwear and find my slit, pulling it open a little and settling two fingers on my clit. I start moving them in circles, zings already making my hips want to move, too.

I widen my legs, dropping them off the side of the stone slab to hold myself wide.

He groans, his hand moving a little faster, his unblinking eyes taking in not just my movements but my face, too.

'Fuck yourself with your fingers and pretend they're mine,' he instructs, and my eyes fall close as I imagine just that.

But my jeans are in the way.

I kick them off with a sound of frustration, settling back down, making sure the blankets are in place, and spreading my legs wide. My fingers work my clit faster, and I shove a finger inside my pussy. It's already not enough, so I immediately add a second, thrusting them into myself and pretending it's Krase.

I imagine him over me, holding me down, forcing himself into me even if I'm not ready, making me do what he wants, telling me to take it like a good girl.

Fuck!

My eyes open to see him pulling at his thick, hard cock, his hand squeezing it, his eyes closed as he pants. My gaze focuses on his dick, and I imagine it fucking me instead of my fingers, adding a third. The delicious pain of the stretch makes me moan, and I come suddenly, my hips bucking as I work myself hard and cry out loudly, the sound echoing through the chamber.

He follows not a second later, grunting and growling that I might be a thieving little bitch, but at least I'm hot, and I grin in spite of myself, collapsing under the blanket and pulling my fingers out of myself.

My head rolls to the side, and I look at him. He's still watching me. I'm still the center of his attention, and I like it. I show him the three fingers I used to fuck myself, and, very slowly, I put each one in my mouth, licking them clean.

His shocked face is priceless, but the expression that settles over him afterward is sated and predatory ... and *admiring*?

'Was that good?' I ask breathily, still in the throes of my submissive imaginings, I guess.

'Very good,' he purrs. The sharp intake of breath that I try to muffle has his eyes boring into mine.

'*Very good girl*,' he murmurs, cocking his head to the side as if trying to gauge my reaction. I try not to give him one, coming out of the sex stupor now and not wanting to give him any more of me.

He watches me as I put my jeans back on under the blanket and refasten them. I go to jump off the stone, though, and my knees give out. I grasp onto the stone with one hand, trying to make them work.

When I turn around, the bowl is still where he left it on the floor. I approach warily because he still hasn't moved, although I notice he's put his dick away.

'Gonna stick to the deal?' I ask, looking into his eyes and finding them surprisingly clear.

He looks at the bowl. 'Yes,' he whispers. 'That was exactly what I needed.'

He takes a step back so that I can grab it, but at the last second, he darts forward, grabbing my arms and pulling me to him. I struggle with a cry.

'Let me go!'

But all he does is stand there with an arm wrapped around my middle and the other grasping my hair as he looks into my face.

'Now, more than ever, don't trust me,' he says. 'You stay away from the bars no matter what. Promise me, Victoria. *Julia.*'

'I promise,' I whisper with wide eyes that bulge further as he pulls me in and kisses me hard on the lips through the bars.

'Good girl,' he breathes and lets me go abruptly, pushing me away.

I stagger back, reeling, but still have the presence of mind to grab my prize and slink to the back of my cell.

I eat the still-warm stew, though the hunger that was gnawing at me has disappeared.

Maybe it was just boredom making me want to eat.

I still finish the bowl off, though, and scrape it clean before I put it outside my cell, pushing it over to his side a little.

'You were very good, little thief,' Krase drawls from the shadows, making me crab crawl back quickly out of his reach when he leaps towards the shared bars, his tail coming through to grab me. 'Too good.'

AXEL

'Did it work?' I ask in frustration, watching Iron for signs that he's fucking with us.

'I can't tell,' he mutters, sounding far away.

I guess he sort of is since he's focusing on the magick.

I snort. 'Thought you were all-powerful now.'

'The estate's defenses are old and complex. Bringing them down isn't a two-second job.' He opens his eyes and gives me a look of disdain. 'The lessons I had in all this shit were a long fucking time ago, okay? Give me a damn minute!'

I put my hands up in placation, stepping away and turning to Jayce with a roll of my eyes.

'This is bullshit,' he mutters. 'Iron is trying to delay us, keep us distracted.'

'I don't think so,' I say, taking a look behind me where Iron is sitting in a chair at the table with his eyes closed again. 'I can't see him bothering. He's not like you. Doesn't get off on playing those kinds of games.'

'When why is this taking so long?' Jayce heaves a sigh. 'What if she's ...?'

I look away. 'She's strong. She just has to hold on,' I say quietly, my fists clenching.

'And here we sit, useless as chocolate teacups,' Jayce seethes, walking briskly to the window that overlooks the gardens. 'What if she's dead?'

I rub over my heart. I can feel her there still if I concentrate hard. I'm sure I can. It's not just wishful thinking.

'I think we'd know,' I whisper so Iron doesn't hear because I don't trust him despite my defense of him.

Jayce puts a hand on his own chest and closes his eyes. 'You're right,' he says finally. 'She is still there, but faintly.' But when he looks at me, his eyes are tortured, much like mine probably are. 'But we wouldn't feel if he was hurting her, letting others hurt her.'

I shake my head. 'Have to be closer for that, I guess.'

'When we ... when we get her back, she's going to be broken,' he whispers.

'She's strong,' I say to him again, 'stronger than the Demon King. She won't be broken, only bruised.' I put my hand on his shoulder. 'We'll help her to heal from whatever he's done to her. She won't be alone. Not ever again.'

He grips my hand hard and nods. 'Never again,' he echoes.

'Well?' he turns with a snarl to Iron. 'Did it work?'

'I still can't tell,' Iron mutters from his seated position. 'He's done something to it.'

'Who?'

'Maddox, I think. Suspicious fucker has locked me out somehow, and I can't figure out what he's ...'

He trails off, going silent, and my eyes narrow at him. Maybe he is playing us, making us think he's trying to help us to keep us distracted from going to save Jules.

He jumps up. 'I need to go to the Sunroom. It's easier to focus my magick. Maybe I can figure out what he's done from there.'

Jayce and I glance at each other. 'Why didn't he do that from the start?' Jayce mutters. 'I'm telling you, he's fucking with us.'

'We can't actually do anything until the border conjure

comes down or lets us out. He's our best bet even if he fucks it up accidentally because he has no clue what he's doing.'

That draws a reluctant chuckle from Jayce. 'Aye, maybe you're right.'

We follow a very distracted Iron upstairs into the round sunroom, painted in blues and golds with magickal fae symbols meant to increase and focus power. He sits cross-legged in the middle of a circle, already closing his eyes and breathing deeply.

He used to do this all the time when he first joined the clan, when Maddox first had the Sunroom made for him in the hopes that it would bring out his latent power, but it never did. It took the Mountain to bring it out, or so he believes. But something about that niggles at me. He can't be the only part-fae ever sent there, so why weren't any others leveling up inside that prison? The inmates gossiped like neighborhood moms. If it was a thing, we would have heard about it while we were there.

It makes me think that maybe Iron has it wrong. Maybe it wasn't the Mountain at all. But what? Maybe a defense mechanism from being in such a dangerous place for more than a few hours, I muse.

'This is weird,' he mutters almost to himself.

Cue another shared look with Jayce, who closes his eyes and shakes his head.

'I thought I sensed it before, but it's not … How is this possible?'

'What?'

'What is it?'

We both ask at the same time as we move to the edge of the circle.

'What the fuck?' Iron suddenly exclaims. 'That sonofabitch!'

There's a whoosh, and he's thrown backward, hitting the invisible side of the circle that keeps any conjures inside of it and falling to the carpeted stone floor with a low thud.

He doesn't move.

'Iron!'

'Get him out of there!'

Jayce hits the emergency button on the wall that opens the sprinklers in the ceiling, spraying salt all over the room. The circle dissipates immediately, and we rush to where Iron is lying on his front, his eyes closed.

'He's breathing,' I say, checking his pulse. 'He's just knocked out cold.'

'What was that?' Jayce asks with a frown. 'Never seen anything like it before, not inside a circle.'

I tut. 'Maddox,' I mutter. 'He probably put in a booby trap or something in case we started messing with the estate's defenses.'

Jayce looks doubtful. 'Maddox knows even less than Iron does about the border conjures. They're old magick; legacy spells from his forebears. He has to get that fae kid in every time he needs something messed with.'

'He did until Iron found his way to power,' I correct. 'Maybe the half-fae dick did something dumb. You know fae shit. It never goes the way you expect.'

We turn Iron over carefully and give him a once-over, making sure he's not seriously hurt. When we're satisfied, we leave the prick on the floor.

'Think we can leave the estate yet?' I ask.

'One way to find out.'

Chapter Five

KRASE

She's a danger.

I should have realized as soon as she appeared in that cell. I knew who she was, but I figured she was just a human. How much trouble could she be to me? But trouble she is.

I stand before our shared bars and stare at her, asleep now under her blankets, thinking she's safe from me, as if metal bars and a couple of blankets are a sure defense against me.

Somewhere in my mind, my other half struggles to get free. He's stronger. Somehow, her little show under the blanket, her breathless moans, and her climax fed him enough to come at me in a way he hasn't had the strength to for some time. She's piqued his interest the way she probably intended, the way human women do when they want that high we give them. I've always been on the fringes before, deep inside and removed from it, but I remember their faces when we were done with them. Happiness and bliss. That's what they always want.

But she didn't count on my interest as well. Unfortunately

for her, mine is a little more fatal. An incubus I may be, but this human does not equate to my survival out in the open. It's time for me to get out of here.

My mind is working against his even now. He doesn't realize it yet, but I'm close. So fucking close. He thinks I'm a simple beast, but I'm as intelligent as he is. I should be. I'm just the other side of the coin.

He's pulling hard at his chains, trying to take over, but I push him back. I'm still stronger, and he doesn't have the tacturn to help him now.

Almost have it.

He realizes what I'm doing and what my plan is.

'Yes,' I whisper. 'The human is as good as dead, and then I'm leaving this prison.'

The physical one he put us in and the mental one at the same time. Soon, there will be nothing left of him. Only me.

He doubles down, trying to break free and save the human in the next cell.

I smile and demon up, doubling in size. I have what I need.

I say the words he's been keeping from me, and I hear the door to my cell unlock.

I can't help my laugh as I open it.

Almost free in more ways than one.

My body freezes, and I grimace as I fight him. She's made him stronger than I thought, and it takes all of my effort to beat him back.

I leave my cell, and I go to hers, forcing out the words he uses the last of his waning strength to try to stop me from saying.

Her cell opens, and I walk inside.

I stalk the room a little, playing even though she has no idea that she's in terrible danger.

I approach the bed, unable to wait any longer, my claws opening to choke the life out of the unsuspecting human in front of me.

Her eyes flutter open, dazed from sleep, but she realizes quickly that I'm in the cell with her. Her eyes widen, and she opens her mouth to scream.

I don't bother stopping her from making noise because no one's going to hear it anyway, but I do grab her throat so she can't flee. It might be diverting to chase her a little, but all of my effort is going into staying in control of my body, so I don't really want to exert it now. Once I'm out of here, I'll find prey to stalk and play with. This isn't the time.

I squeeze, and her eyes bulge, her mouth moving, no doubt pleading with me to let her go if I'd let her actually get the words out.

'Hush, little human,' I coo. 'Your pathetic existence will be over soon.'

She wriggles around, and I can't help but bask in it, enjoying her pitiful struggles as she bucks on the stone slab in the final death throes.

I frown as I see a glint of something in her hand, realizing a split second too late as she gets a triumphant look on her face that it's the fucking tacturn I threw away!

She wasn't dying, she was rooting around in her fucking pocket for it!

She slaps it down on the claw at her throat, keeping hold of it.

'No!' I snarl, but it's too late.

'How did you get in my cell?' she asks a little breathlessly.

I look around us. We're sitting on the edge of a cliff in the dark, the Milky Way looming over us in the night sky. It's a beautiful sight.

'It wasn't me,' I say distractedly. 'How did you work the tacturn?'

'Fae shit is pretty simple, really. Why are you trying to kill me?'

'I'm not. The demon is.'

She heaves a sigh and touches her neck. 'Are you still choking me? Am I dying right now while we're in here?'

'No. I took over as soon as the tacturn was placed on him.'

'So, what? You've got like multiple personality disorder?'

I snort. 'That's a very human way of looking at it, but I suppose it's a bit like that. That's what going rogue as a demon means. The darker side gets stronger; the *human* part gets weaker. I can't control it now.

'Are you ... is he going to *feed* from me ... like without my consent, I mean?'

I try to hide my grim look, but I know she sees it. 'No,' I say. 'He wants you dead, Jules.'

'Why?'

'Because when he got you to feed us, he was playing with you. He didn't think your energy would make me stronger.'

I look at her to watch her reaction, see if she knows anything.

'It shouldn't have; once we're that far gone, nothing can bring us back. There's no cure for this. How did you do it?'

Nothing shows on her face. 'I didn't do anything except let you feed from me for a bowl of stew.' Her cheeks turn pink. 'And I didn't even want it after that anyway,' she mutters.

My brow furrows. She's self-conscious about what she did. I don't think I've met a human who was embarrassed about sex before, but then the usual ones are on-call girls, used to life around us ... although there was that one from before whom I can vaguely recall Maddox bringing to me. She was similar, but the energy she let me have to give me a little more time to get my affairs in order was nothing compared to the power-up Jules provided. It looks like she has no clue about any of it, though.

'Listen,' I tell her. 'I'm in control in here, and I will be for a few moments after we get out. I'll give you as much time as I can.'

'For what?'

'To run. He will kill you, Jules. I underestimated him, and

now he knows the words to open the cells. You need to get out of here.'

'But the door to the wine cellar is locked,' she says. 'There's nowhere to go. How long can we stay in here?'

'Not long enough. The tacturn has a safety, so you can't get trapped in the mirage.'

'Perfect,' she mutters. Then she side-eyes me and cringes a little. 'What if I did what I did before, but in here?'

I tilt my head. 'What you did before?'

She looks down. 'Feed you. Make you stronger. Then you can fight him, right?'

I look down at her, at war with myself and not the demon for once. I should tell her no, that it won't work, but I don't know that for certain. The truth is that she's practically irresistible to me at the moment. I thought I was past caring, past feeding. But I guess not. Maybe this is the glimmer of hope I've been waiting for because her energy did make me stronger, a lot stronger than she should have been able to, considering we didn't even touch before. What would sex do for me?

'It might work,' I hear myself saying.

I'm trying not to lie to her. There have been times when I would have said or done anything to feed just a little, but as I take her in, I just can't bring myself to do it.

This is new. Why I care what this slip of a charlatan thinks of me, I have no idea. I don't know how long we've been down here together. My perception of time hasn't been great lately. But I know I hated the sight of her as soon as I figure out who she was. Because of her actions, the demon was able to swallow me whole, though I concede much of this wasn't her fault directly. Wrong place, wrong time.

I let out a dry laugh. *Wrong place, wrong time.* What a fucking understatement.

I step closer to her and kneel down. She's still staring at the ground. I cup her chin and angle her face up to mine.

'Look at me.'

Her eyes flick to mine. 'Ready?' she whispers.

'I'm not going to hurt you.'

She lets out a laugh of her own. 'This is not how I thought it would be if I ever got out of the Mountain.'

That's news to me, and I don't like it one bit. 'Why were you in that place?'

'It doesn't matter,' she deflects, and I let it slide because now isn't the time, and she owes me no explanation of how she spends her moments.

I'm the incubus who's about to kill her if we don't pull this off.

I swallow hard as I pull her up to stand, feeling the kind of trepidation I haven't experienced since I was, for all intents and purposes, a human youth. She comes with me easily, no hesitation, but I don't for a moment believe it's because she wants me. This girl is nothing if not pragmatic. She'll do what she has to do to survive.

And that I understand.

I make her look at me. 'I'm not going to hurt you,' I say again.

She nods, 'I know you're not,' she says, 'but you can't really speak for the other guy, can you?'

'Not yet.'

I draw her closer, wondering if the energy she gives off here will actually feed me and hoping with everything in me that it does. For once, I don't give a shit about feeding for me, I just don't want *him* to kill her.

I liked her before. She was a bright light when things had started to go grey for me two years ago when we'd first begun to realize what was happening to me. I tried not to get too close to her while she was staying with us just in case I did something I couldn't take back, but her energy and the way she lived in the moment were contagious. I secretly crept into her room on more than one occasion while she slept to watch her. Even though I knew it was dangerous and wrong, I couldn't help myself.

Just like I can't now.

I pull her closer, putting my lips to hers, my tongue invading her mouth, and her wide-eyed squeak, followed by almost instant arousal, is enough to make me growl with need. I pull her shirt over her head and use it to capture her arms and cover her eyes. A claw slices through her bra, letting her ample tits bounce free.

I weigh them in my hands, scrape the calloused pads of my fingers across her nipples until they stand to attention.

I bend down to lick, pulling one into my mouth to suck gently and reveling in her mewl, groaning as I feel energy trickling into me already.

I don't say anything as I rip her jeans down her legs and lift her to yank them from her body. The effect is immediate. She likes sex the way she likes life. Unpredictable and dangerous.

My fingers flex on her arms, digging in just a little, and I grin when her fear morphs quickly into quivering need.

I put her legs around me and tear off her shirt the rest of the way so I can see her face as I enter her.

Her eyes are wide and unfocused. She's panting and impatient. Her mouth opens as if she wants to say something, but all that comes out is a breathy, 'Now.'

I don't make her wait, plunging into her wet channel. Her hands on my shoulders curl, her nails biting into my flesh, and I fucking revel in it. I've rarely taken a human outside the lull, and it makes them docile. Jules is all fire and passion, and if we survive this, I promise myself I'll have her in the real world, too.

My pace is fast and desperate, and her cries fuel me to go faster, her energy taking me to heights I've not felt in a very long time.

He's distracted by the beauty in his fae-induced vision. My fingers shake as I will them to move. I just need my hand to tip, and the tacturn will be on the floor ...

I put everything into it. I can feel him getting stronger, and I commend him. I wouldn't have thought that what amounts to a sex dream would give him what he needed, but his coffers are filling quickly, and I only have seconds.

My hand jerks with my effort to control it, and the chain of the golden, fae bauble falls, sinking to the stone bed and, mercifully, taking the fucking tacturn with it.

Free!

I feel him realize what I've done, but I keep him back, taking complete control; I demon-up, and my claws close around her throat again.

Her eyes flutter open, still in the throes of whatever they were just doing. She's not even focused on me. Instead, she moans, liking my firm grip around her neck.

The foolish female doesn't seem to realize that I'm not going to fuck her; I'm going to crush her pretty little neck.

I know I shouldn't, but I can't help but play, my thick fingers closing incrementally around her until she can't breathe and claws at my arm ineffectually. Her eyes finally clear and find mine, full of terror, and I grin as the life begins to leave her.

Without her here, there will be no energy for him to keep me in the dark. I'll have won our war within the day.

My nostrils flare as I straighten, and I frown. There's something in the air that wasn't there before. I sniff. It's her.

It's odd. I've never scented anything like it before. I take in a deep breath, and I shudder at how divine she smells. With a very human gasp, I drop her lifeless body immediately and back away.

What have I done? How could I not have *realized*?

My back hits the bars with a clang as I shake my head in disbelief. I didn't know. How could I have known? She didn't smell like that before. She didn't smell of anything except dried blood before.

I've killed her.

Just as I think it, though, her eyes snap open, and she springs up, darting across the cell, through the open door, and slamming it closed behind her.

I watch her dart this way and that, my horror and self-loathing rapidly transforming into excitement and ... joy?

My grin is large as my prey works herself into a frenzy, trying to open the locked door that leads into Maddox's wine cellars. She pulls and pulls, looking back at me in terror every so often.

She doesn't know I no longer wish to kill her.

Quite the opposite.

She's mine!

JULES

I look behind at Krase. He's still in his demon form, and I try not to look at it because it's making me weirdly *excited*.

He wants you dead, you idiot!

I pull again at the handle, but it doesn't budge, and I glance behind me. He's at the cell door. He says some words in a language I know all too well, and it makes my skin crawl. *Fae.*

The damn thing swings open, and I stifle a cry of fear because I know he'll take joy in the sound. I pull with everything in me, and there's a great crunch. It finally comes loose!

I tear the door practically off its hinges as I fling it open, and I run through the wine cellar, but I can't see the stairs. This place is fucking massive!

He's behind me. I can feel him but don't look back as I race down one of the many aisles of wine. This really is a helluva collection.

Fucking rich supes. All I took was a few hundred grand, but there must be millions of dollars worth of aged grape juice down here.

I get to the end and slide into one of the shelves, making the bottles clink as the whole thing shudders a little, and a tiny part of me worries that I'm going to break something, which is the dumbest thing ever. What do I care if Maddox's pretty bottles break? The thing is, I know my evil captor must care a lot about this cellar, and it makes me not want to destroy it.

Yeah, I don't get it either.

I use the shelf to propel myself around the corner and up the next aisle, but when I get to the end, I hear nothing.

I'm breathing hard and loud and try to quiet everything down, but I can't hear him. I look this way and that, up and down and all around, but he's not there. He wouldn't have just quit. He wanted to kill me a minute ago. He would have if I wasn't great at playing possum.

I tiptoe to the end of the next aisle and peer around the corner. There's an echoing laugh that I can't pinpoint.

The demon is stalking me. I know he is. He's making me play his game now.

I cross my arms over my chest, scowling and getting my head on straight. I don't play other supes' games. They play mine! If I'm going to die anyway, it's not going to be out of breath and sweaty and running for my life like I'm the token first victim in a 90s slasher movie.

'Come out!' I demand. 'Face me properly, coward.'

'Is that what my female wants?' comes a whisper that's much closer than I anticipated.

His female?

I frown as I turn in a circle, trying to locate him. 'I'm not yours, demon,' I say with more strength than I feel, trying not to let him see my fear.

'Aren't you?'

I finally realize where he is much too late to still be getting out of this alive, and I roll my eyes upward to the tower shelves, cursing my stupid ass. Sure enough, he's gripping onto the wooden frame like fucking Spiderman. I curse softly as I turn to run, even though it's hopeless. He barrels into me.

I go down with a thud, the wind knocked out of me, wheezing on the floor as my own boobs stop my lungs from expanding.

Death by double D asphyxiation. What a dumb way to go.

Is it really going to end like this? Tears come to my eyes. Was everything I did to survive for the past few years actually for nothing?

I'm turned over, and I suck in a hard breath like I've had my head stuck underwater. My hands grip his forearms as he leans over me like that's going to delay him even a little.

My pleading eyes lock onto his face, and I see something in his eyes that I don't understand. It looks like remorse, but he's got to be fucking with me, so I let my face fall to the side so I can't see it anymore.

But a hand, not a claw, cups my cheek and urges my limp head back towards him. My eyes flutter to him again, wondering what he's doing, why he hasn't just killed me.

Probably wants to play with his food.

Demon fucker.

But then he speaks, and I'm more confused than ever.

'Sorry,' he half-growls. 'I didn't mean to ...'

'Well, you did!' he seems to say to himself. 'I can help her. You'll just hurt her more.'

I stare at him. *Them*? This is so weird.

'It's called an internal monologue for a reason,' I wheeze, turning my head to cough and wincing when my ribs twinge.

At least one is cracked, I'm pretty sure.

'Maybe you could keep it down,' I whisper. 'I don't want your argument with yourself to be the last thing I ever hear, you know? Give a dead girl a break, huh?'

He lets out a low, long-suffering grunt.

'Fine. You deal with the female, but this isn't over.'

Krase's fingers, which I realize have been digging into my waist, gentle.

'I'm in control,' he promises, and I snort softly.

'For how long?'

'Long enough to get you somewhere safe.'

He starts to pick me up, but I wave him away. I get to my feet on my own and give myself a nod of approval. I don't need help from a dude who was just going to—

I stagger to the side, smacking into one of the shelves, and I wince. The floor pitches.

'Ok, fine,' I mutter, glancing at him and waving him over to me.

I let him pick me up and cradle me against him. I know

when to accept help. I'll be my usual bad-ass bitch self as soon as I feel better.

Krase carries me across the cellar floor to what looks like a wide closet, but when he opens it, I see it's an elevator with a spiral staircase next to it. I huff and roll my eyes. No wonder I couldn't find the exit.

'Where are we going?' I ask.

He doesn't answer. Instead, he walks into the elevator with me, the door closing silently behind him.

He presses a button, and I feel us going up.

'It's really quiet,' I mutter when the door opens again a few seconds later with no dings or anything.

No answer.

He peers out and darts into a hallway I recognize as the upstairs landing. We're in his room before I can blink, and he seems to relax as soon as the door is shut and he's closed us in together.

'The lift used to ping when the doors opened,' he says as he lays me on the bed. 'I cut all the wires so I could travel straight up and down without any of *them* hearing me.'

'Why?'

'Because ...' he stops and frowns. 'I actually can't remember why now. It seemed important at the time, though.'

He turns away and goes into the adjoining bathroom. I hear water running, and I immediately sit up in anticipation, grunting as my ribs smart. I prod at them with my fingers and find that they're thankfully not broken.

Krase comes back into the room and regards me. 'I'm guessing you'd like to bathe.'

I nod. 'It's been a minute.'

He raises a brow and sniffs the air. I scowl.

'Okay, three months. But, in my defense, there was only a river, and it was frigid.'

He walks over to me, and I get up from the bed.

Force of habit.

His eyes are piercing as he hands me a glass of water. 'I'm not going to hurt you.'

I shake my head at him and give him an incredulous look. 'You literally almost broke my ribs ten minutes ago and then strangled me, demon. You've told me how you're going to kill me in great detail multiple times.'

'I know, but it wasn't *me* me.' He frowns. 'Do you need me to look—'

I roll away from him to the other side of the bed, ignoring my ribs when they protest.

'Nope. I'm a big girl, Krase. I don't need you to play the chivalrous doctor.'

He steps back with his hands up. 'I deserve that. I'm sorry about before, but I promise you that things are different now. I won't hurt you, Jules. *Neither of us* will hurt you.'

He turns and goes back into the bathroom. 'The water's hot,' he calls.

If I could prance across the room in excitement, I would, but I get up and walk calmly, my hands shaking a little.

How nuts is it to be this excited over a shower?

When I get inside, the room is already steamy. Krase has his hand in the water, checking the temperature for me. What is his deal?

He turns around and finds me watching him.

'It's ready.'

He doesn't move, and I jerk my head towards the door.

He smirks. 'I've already seen you.'

I give him a look. 'Dreamland doesn't count, incubus.'

With a grin, he leaves, closing the door behind him, and I don't wait. I tear off my clothes and enter the large cubicle, moaning at the heat of the water that warms my body. My body has been constantly on the cusp of cold for months, so this is heaven. I bask in it, feel it pummeling the dirt from my skin. I wash my hair until the run-off is clean, and it takes three shampoos. The rest of my body is soaped and exfoliated with a convenient sea sponge on a rope until my skin is pink, and I grab a razor from by the sink to get rid of the body hair that's been plaguing me. When that's all done, I lean into the spray and cry tears of relief. Not because my pits don't resemble a sasquatch anymore, but because I'm alive, and I really didn't think I was going to make it quite a few times over the past weeks, months, *years*.

Sure, things aren't perfect, but they rarely are, and sadly, being in this shower might actually be the closest I've felt to safe in two years. I've lived this way for such a long time. I hadn't realized that I'd been trying so hard to stay a step ahead of my past that I'd stopped living for the future. I've been in a limbo of the present, moment to moment. And I know it's not really the shower.

For some inexplicable reason, I feel the kind of safe with Krase that I did when I was Axel and Jayce in prison, the kind of safe I felt on this estate when I was last here, and I don't understand. My nature hasn't been trusting in a long time, so why do I keep finding it so easy to let this clan of incubi in, to relax in their house? Krase tried to kill me, and now I'm bruised and naked in his shower, hanging out in his room like he's not a psycho demon killer who either wants me dead ... or for dinner.

Can this place, these men, really be as safe as they feel? I mean, no one has come looking for me as far as I know. Unless they've stopped trying to find me, which is highly doubtful, something here must be acting like the wards of the Mountain, keeping me invisible to magick.

I try to count how many days I've been out of the Mountain without a conjure. It's got to be coming up to a week at least. There has to be some magick here that's keeping me safe, I decide. There's no other explanation that I'd accept. He'd never have stopped looking. I was an important possession, even if I never knew why.

The irony isn't lost on me. If I'd been able to stay here two years ago, I might actually have been safe. I might never have needed to buy another conjure to stay hidden. I wouldn't have had to to steal from the clan in the first place.

I heave a sigh and turn off the water. I wrap myself up in a towel, take a breath, and leave the steamy sanctuary of bliss, hoping I'm going out there to face a Jekyll, not a Hyde.

I regret leaving the heat of the bathroom almost immediately anyway, the cold of the outside room making me shiver as I locate Krase lounging on his bed.

He's watching me.

'I'm not going to pretend that I don't love seeing my marks on your neck,' he growls, eying the bruises that have begun to appear around my throat.

I try not to flinch, wondering if he's lost control again already.

'You about to Mr. Hyde-up?' I inquire with a lot more calm than I feel.

He shakes his head. 'No. I don't think that's going to happen again. I feel better. Stronger.'

He looks at me like I should know what's going on.

'What's different?' I ask.

'Pardon?'

'You said before that things are different. What's different? You wanted me dead less than an hour ago. Has that much really changed?'

I touch the bruises around my neck, and his expression darkens.

'Yes. Things are very different than they were earlier. I don't understand it myself, but I give you my word that you're safe here in this room from me. From the others, too. There's a conjure on it. They could come straight through the door and not even know we're here unless we leave.'

'So, I'm basically still in prison?'

He snorts. 'At least this one comes with a bathroom and not a bucket.'

Can't argue with that.

He rises and goes into said bathroom. I hear the water start up again, and I wonder how long we have until one of the other members of the clan barges in to find us, regardless of what Krase says. Maddox will know we're missing soon.

While Krase isn't in the room, I dry off and get the excess water out of my hair.

I lay on the bed for a bit, closing my eyes. It's soft, and I like it at first, but then I think about how it feels a little like the fluffy floor of the web bunker that Siggy made for me.

I sit up with a shuddering breath, not wanting to think about her and break down right now.

The water goes off, and Krase comes out of the bathroom a minute later.

I swallow hard. He looks how he did before he went nuts. His red curls are wet and shorter now. The matted beard is gone. He has a small towel wrapped around his waist that opens a little as he walks, and I make myself look higher only to see a drop of water fall from the end of one curly lock and make its way down his chest to one very chiseled peck. My eyes dip again without them meaning to. There's a shit ton of abs down there leading to a pleasure trail I'd love to …

'Are you staying in here too?' I blurt.

'For now,' he says carefully. 'Maddox won't be happy that he's not in control anymore.'

I snort. *That's an understatement.*

He walks closer, the towel flapping a little and giving me glimpses of …

I clear my throat hard, trying to get a handle on this desire I have to lick him all over.

'And you aren't having murderous thoughts about me anymore?' I ask.

I hope he is so I can give myself a proverbial slap in the face for my thoughts and then start planning my escape.

'No, not *murderous* ones.'

My heart skips a beat.

Get a hold of yourself. He tried to kill you today!

'But how can it change that fast?' I ask. 'What happens when you go all demon-crazy and choke me out again, and I don't have the tacturn to save me?'

Instead of answering me, he gives me an indulgent smile that makes my eyes narrow. He beckons me to him.

'Sit on the bed,' he says, but it's more of a question, not a demand.

I do as he asks because it *wasn't* an order and because I want to be closer to him. But I don't want him to know that. I sit next to him gingerly, trying not to touch him even though I want to.

He laughs.

'No, with your back to me.'

'Why?'

He shows me what's in his hand. A hairbrush. I tilt my head at him, but, for some reason, I indulge him further, shifting so I'm sitting cross-legged in front of him and wondering what this is, where it's going to go.

Where do I want it to go? Why am I feeling like this? Another trick? I wouldn't put it past him. Even in non-nuts form, he must still hate me as much as the others do. I have to remember that.

But then he begins to tease the tangles out. He starts at the bottom of my matted hair, working out the knots gently, taking care not to pull it. Minutes go by. He works slowly upwards, patiently until it's done, and when he is, I feel like …

I glance back at him, not sure what I feel, actually.

'You like this,' he murmurs, and I can't help my tiny nod, blinking back insidious tears.

I do like it.

'Where were you with only a cold river to bathe in for so long then?' he asks with a chuckle. 'Camping wasn't really your scene from what I remember.'

I frown. We talked about this in the tacturn sex dream.

'The Mountain,' I say.

I feel him stiffen behind me. Maybe he doesn't remember that we already spoke about this. He was sort of *demonic*.

'Ah, yes. You mentioned. Who put you in a prison for male supes?' he asks. His tone is calm, but his body is coiled.

'Me. I found a back-way in.'

'If anyone could, it would be you,' he chuckles, and I relax a little, 'but why would you go to that place voluntarily, deamhan àlainn?'

'What does that mean?' I ask.

'Don't avoid the question.'

'Hiding from the last supe I stole from,' I say lightly, but as soon as I say the words, I have a feeling he doesn't buy it.

A rumble comes from his chest, and I'm suddenly pulled backward and turned, so I'm sitting in his lap.

His smoldering eyes make an unwelcome thrum of heat go straight to where I don't want it, and it has me trying to shift away from where his pelvis and mine are so close.

'Let me go,' I breathe.

He clutches me tighter and groans. 'I don't think you really want me to, but fine.'

He turns me over quickly but carefully, putting me face-down over his lap with my bare ass in the air.

'What are you—'

A stinging slap of his massive hand on both cheeks has me gasping and struggling to get away, but he holds me easily.

'No more lies, my pretty little conwoman,' he murmurs. 'I think you've given us enough of those, don't you?'

I go lax under his hands immediately, my angry ego buttoning my lip. I silently refuse to say another word, not even making a sound as he keeps up his punishment. I wriggle around a little, but the pain is nothing, even though it goes on for long enough that I know my ass is going to hurt for a couple of days.

In truth, there's something happening that's more embarrassing than being half-naked and spanked by a man ... *a demon* I hardly know.

He finds out a minute later when his hand delves between my legs, and he tuts when it comes out wet.

'So, you like this too, you naughty girl,' he murmurs. 'I'll have to remember that.'

I refuse to say anything, but he pulls me back up into his arms, and he immediately notes my pink cheeks.

He makes a contemplative noise like he's learning things about me, and I clench my jaw.

'I'm not going to get answers out of you that way, am I?' he says quietly.

My defiant eyes meet his.

It'll take a lot more than you're willing to do right now.

'You're an interesting woman, Jules,' he says lightly, but there's an undercurrent of gravity in his words, and I wonder what else he just found out about me because I suddenly get the impression that this was all just a learning exercise.

I push away from him, but he doesn't let me go.

Instead, he holds me close, stroking my hair and down my back in soft caresses like he's calming an angry feline.

Annoyingly, it starts to work, and I feel myself leaning into him even though I don't want to.

'Are you going to tell me why you were in the Mountain?' he whispers.

'I can't,' I say after a moment, and he sighs.

VENGEANCE AND VIPERS

'At least it isn't a lie.'

I think he's disappointed and prepare myself for more wrath, but then he shifts, putting my legs around his waist and opening me to him.

'Good girls who tell the truth are rewarded,' he growls.

My eyes widen as I look up into his, but he just pulls me closer and against his very hard length.

'Rub yourself against it.' He murmurs the order, and I shake my head a little.

So, he does it for me, picking me up and grinding my clit against his shaft.

My mouth parts on a gasp, and he seizes it, his tongue mingling with mine as he moves me against him.

This isn't exactly what I've been craving, but it's close enough, and without even really realizing it, I begin rubbing myself against him.

It feels so good!

My climax isn't an explosion or a thunderclap but a subtle pleasure that rolls through me, making me whimper as I bury my face in Krase's neck.

'Good girl,' he grunts, and I practically feel the energy of my orgasm go through him, feeding him.

My movements still, and I pull away to look at him. His eyes are closed, and his head is thrown back. Between us is sticky, and I look down to see that he came as well.

What am I doing?

I scramble up, but his arm shoots out, and he grabs me, hauling me back to him.

He gives me a rueful look. 'Sorry, it's been a while.'

He ignores my attempts to extract myself from him and instead lays me on my back on the bed.

'Stay,' he mutters as he goes into the bathroom.

I sit up with a huff, but he comes straight back with a washcloth. He pushes me back down and cleans me up while I frown at him.

'I can do that,' I say.

Another grin like he's humoring the human.

'I know you can,' is all he says.

He leaves me again, throwing the cloth into the bathroom and opening the top drawer of his bureau. A second later, a slinky, fire-engine-red dress drops onto the bed. Designer. Expensive.

I eye it and quirk my brow at him.

'It's all I have in here that might fit you,' he says, glancing at the door.

I grab it and throw it over my head. The chest is a little tight, but a cowl neck hides any bulging. It's long with a slit up the side, but it mostly fits.

I run my hands down the satin.

'Who's was this?' I ask, not liking the jealousy I feel.

'No one's,' he says with his back turned.

I recoil a little at his hesitation, his lie, and then I roll my eyes at my dumb self. He's an incubus, I remind myself *again* ... but I'll probably stop bothering soon. Every rule I ever had I've broken with these guys. What's a few more? I'm not listening to myself anyway. Maybe I'll learn when everything goes to shit, and I'm left running for my life like always, but this time I'm heartbroken as well.

The door to the bedroom flies open, and I gasp, springing off the bed and stumbling back towards the wall as a furious Maddox stalks in. But as his eyes move around the room, they pass right over me.

Krase winks at me. 'Told you. He can't see us.'

Chapter Six

IRON

'What happened?' I ask, sitting up and wincing at the light in my eyes when I open them.

I rub the back of my head. There's a lump the size of a golf ball back there.

'You tell us,' Jayce says from close by over to the right.

I glance around, trying to ignore the shooting pains through my left eye and down the side of my neck. I'm on the floor of the Sunroom. Light streams through the tall, western-facing windows.

'How long was I out?'

'About three hours, give or take,' Axel says.

He sounds worried.

'What the hell happened?' he asks. 'You were doing your thing, and you said something, that someone was a son of a bitch, and then you went all Superman and smacked into the wall. It was nuts. We had to salt the entire room.

So that's the gritty stuff I can feel under me.

I get to my feet and feel Axel take my shoulder to steady me.

'Weird,' I say, continuing to massage my head. 'The last I remember was being in the circle and looking for a way to break the shield. Then, nothing.'

I frown. There's something niggling at me, bothering me. But the more I try to remember whatever it is, the further away it slips.

Jayce opens the door. 'Well, I'm guessing we still can't leave, but I'll go see anyway.'

'We already checked,' Axel mutters.

'Aye, but maybe there was a delay. We should try again.'

'Only once,' Axel warns with a roll of his eyes when Jayce isn't looking. 'Remember, it'll sap your energy.'

Jayce leaves with a derisive 'Och!' and I regard Axel.

'Did I say anything else?'

Axel shakes his head. 'No, but you were pissed. You sounded like you get with Maddox. You don't remember?'

I shake my head. 'No, but I think—'

We hear a loud crash from inside the house somewhere. Axel is already halfway to the door before I register that he's even moved, and I follow as quickly as I can. We race down the spiral stairs and along the corridor, listening for more sounds.

Another thud echoes through the hall a few seconds later. It's coming from Krase's old room.

I'm just behind Axel as he bursts in to find Maddox standing in the middle of the room in all his golden demon glory.

'I know you're in here!' he bellows. 'Come out, you craven cunt!'

We glance at each other, wondering if our clan's leader has finally cracked up. He never loses his shit. Who the hell is he talking to?

I sniff the air. It smells like Krase, but it would in here. This was where he spent a lot of his time tying up his affairs towards the end.

'I'm glad Jayce isn't here to see this,' I murmur, and Axel nods.

He sniffs the air as well, and his brow creases.

'What the fuck is going on?' Daemon growls as he enters the room behind us. 'What the hell is he doing?'

'Maddox,' Axel calls.

Our leader turns at the sound of his name. 'What?'

'Why are you tearing Krase's room apart?'

He hesitates before he answers. Whatever he's going to say next will be a lie. I try not to let my suspicion show. I know Julian well, and I can tell when he's spin-doctoring, though he is very good at it.

'I just ... I miss him,' he growls. 'Fuck him for not being here!'

I watch Axel and Daemon swallow the bullshit, and I pretend to as well.

But Julian Maddox, our leader, is hiding something. The others somehow don't see the worried look he gives the room, but I do.

'We all feel the same,' Daemon says quietly, and I glance at him.

He's looking away. Are those tears in his eyes? I grit my teeth. I've been hard on him since he came back. I didn't think he'd feel Krase's loss as keenly as us, but maybe that was unfair of me. He was clan ... he *is* clan.

I give him a commiserating look, which he returns. Then, I go to Julian, putting my hand on his shoulder.

'Jayce will be in here in a minute,' I say. 'He can't find you doing this.'

Maddox gives me the barest of nods, donning his glamor and leaving the room. The others go with him, probably to the library to share a strong drink, but I hang back.

I pick up the chair that Maddox threw and set it back by the wall where it was. It looks like he got to a vase before we arrived.

I grab the largest shards, surveying the room as I do. It looks exactly like it did when Krase was alive, which doesn't seem right when he's no longer here living in it.

I step into the bathroom to throw the pieces of pot away, and I freeze. Someone's showered in here recently. The air is still damp. Who would do that? We all have our own bathrooms ...

I go back out into the bedroom and look again. The bed. The covers are rucked up a little. The bureau. The drawer isn't closed. The rug. It's askew. Maddox may be responsible for one or two of these things, but not all. Someone's been messing around in here. Fergus and Tabitha, the new help, maybe?

But why would they? They've only just arrived. What would they be poking around in a dead demon's room for? And they have their newly renovated cottage. They don't need to use the main house's amenities.

I try to focus to see if there's some conjure working in here, but there's so much magick lingering from Krase's fae *toys* that there's no way of pinpointing anything specific.

Julian has had plenty of time to lose it over Krase. Why now? The longer I think about it, the more I'm sure there's something else going on, and Maddox is hiding it. This wouldn't be the first time he made decisions for the clan without talking to us. He's the leader. Technically, it's his right, but we usually tend to be a little more democratic. If Julian is deciding things unilaterally, he's doing it for a reason he thinks is valid.

But I don't like it.

I leave the room, closing the door behind me and taking a deep breath in through my nose. I halt and sniff again, wondering what I can smell. It's faint, like the remnants of a rose that's no longer in bloom. It's gone as soon as I smell it, and I put it from my mind as I go down the grand staircase slowly, deciding to see how the land lies with the clan before I do anything else.

When I go into the library, all of them are in there. Maddox,

Jayce, and Axel each have a snifter of port. Daemon has a whiskey. The mood is somber because, of course, it is. I grab one of the decanters. I don't even bother to look at which one as I pour myself a decent amount of whatever expensive liquor is sloshing around inside the crystal vessel. I knock it back, letting it burn its way down, not even tasting it.

I need to figure out what Julian is hiding, I think as I watch him. He's staring out the window. His face is blank, but he's worked up. The others might not notice, but I'm his lieutenant. It's my job to see him when the others don't.

'How's the new help?' I ask.

He glances at me. 'They seem to be settling in well. As a matter of fact, Tabitha has cooked a dinner for tonight. It'll be served in the dining room in a few minutes. It would be good if you could all be there. We have some things to discuss.'

I see Axel and Jayce share a look. I know they wanted me to try again to bring down the conjure that's keeping us in, and I will as soon as I can. But they have to be realistic. What are the odds that Jules is still alive? Suffering by Dante's hand for this long, would they even *want* her to be at this point?

I feel hollow and sick when I think about it. I'm just as culpable as Maddox is. I could have tried to change his mind. Instead, I was a good little soldier and did as I was told. My fists clench when I think again about all the things I compelled her to do with my shiny new power, all the vicious words I said to break her.

I promised myself all my life that I'd never act like my mom's fae family, but all my high and mighty ideals fell like rotten apples from a dying tree as soon as I was given an ounce of power. It doesn't matter if my mind was affected by the Mountain's magick somehow. I should have noticed the change in my thoughts.

I find myself sitting at the table in the formal dining room with a plate in front of me and only a vague recollection of following the others in here. Everyone's quiet. What is there to say?

Maddox regards us all, pretending to be the attentive host at the head of the table, but I can see that even he's distracted, troubled by whatever secrets he's harboring.

'I've made some headway in getting us off the naughty list,' he says finally, and everyone's eyes move him.

He nods. 'It'll cost us, but it can be done. It *will be done* over the next few days and cemented in a masque.

'A party is going to ensure we stay free?' Jayce mutters. 'Fucking fae.'

'It's not just the Council we're contending with,' Maddox answers him, 'but, yes, a masked ball. Here. At All-Hallows. Everyone who matters will be in attendance, and it will be proclaimed that we were framed or some such tale,' he says with a wave of his hand as if he hasn't bothered to find out the specifics.

But he has.

Maddox enjoys playing the feckless fop when he wants to be underestimated, but *he's underestimated me.* Now I'm certain he's hiding something. And whatever it is, it's big.

But what?

The remainder of the meal has me playing a role of my own, the loyal friend and right-hand man who definitely isn't doubting his best friend's integrity.

But as soon as the meal is over, I slink down to the back of the main halls. I see Tabitha bustling around in the kitchen. I think I've eluded her, but she's suddenly in front of me.

'Can I get you something?' she asks with a smile.

'No, thank you,' I say, trying to think of something plausible as to why I'm sneaking around. 'I just came by to tell you how delicious dinner was.'

She gives me a small but genuine smile. 'I'm glad you enjoyed it. I hope there was enough.'

'Enough?'

'Yes,' she says, wiping her wet hands on her apron. 'I set the table for five, but I realized halfway through dinner that there are seven of you in the house.'

She taps her nose and gives me a wink. 'More than just a pixie, remember?'

Seven.

Time stops for me as I try to figure it out, pieces not fitting together properly with this new information.

Seven people. Not five.

She shuffles her feet. 'Well, I'm glad there was enough,' she says brightly, giving me a funny look as she goes back to the Range and stirs something in a pot.

My eyes zero in on the new door to the cellar. My original destination. If there are two extra people in his house, I know where they'd be.

I open it and, ignoring the elevator, I go down the spiral stone steps to the bottom. The lights are on sensors, so they go on as I move downward. At the bottom, I walk with purpose to the very end, where another new door was put in not too long ago when the cellars were modernized and became temperature-controlled.

I pull it, wondering if it'll be locked, but it comes easily. The entire door does, in fact. It's been ripped off its hinges and propped back up.

I go inside and immediately smell him. *Krase*. He's been here. I look into the two cells. One smells more of him than the other does. The one on the left has no scent at all that I can discern, but perhaps Jayce, with his better nose, would be able to pick something up.

Krase must have been down here for weeks, not feeding, slowly dying. We'd all said our goodbyes weeks before we were even arrested and had begun to grieve in our own ways. I thought Maddox had done what had to be done before we were taken by the authorities. He never said, but with how far gone Krase was, he had to have ... He wasn't our clan brother anymore. Krase was dead. We all tried to accept it.

But he never did it. Whatever is left of Krase isn't dead, after all.

The thought doesn't fill me with joy. He's rogue. His mind has to be gone by now.

And he's free in the chateau.

Except I know where he is. I snort.

Even in insanity, he's a creature of habit.

I turn and go back the way I came.

I'm going to need my gun.

JULES

I'm trying not to feel rattled, but when Maddox burst in, my stomach leaped up into my throat, and I pretty much threw myself across the room away from him as he demoned up, equal parts scared and intrigued by his golden form, the dark, swirling tattoos I glimpsed. I tried to ignore that second feeling, though ...

It was pretty obvious that he couldn't see us because of whatever conjure is on the room, but he knew we were in here, and it didn't stop him from throwing stuff around.

The way Krase immediately grabbed me and turned me away from the vase Maddox hurled in my general direction made it obvious that it wouldn't pass right through me.

It was also weirdly protective of him... *and confusing.*

I glance around the room, my eyes falling on the door for the hundredth time. I'm alone. I'm not sure where Krase went, but after Maddox's little temper tantrum, he mumbled something and disappeared into a hidden passage behind the wall next to the bed.

A hidden passage.

Yeah, fine. Sounds about right.

I'm trying not to worry, but my eyes just keep going back to the door that leads to the hall. What if they come in again, and they *can* see me this time?

What would I even say to Jayce and Axel if I saw them again? My heart aches, and I try not to think about what happened in the Mountain between us. It wasn't real. They were playing me. It's so obvious now. I was so stupid and pathetic. An easy mark. I can't blame them for it, I guess. They wanted to get out. I knew how. It makes sense that they'd get close to me, make me think things that weren't true.

I mean, yeah, Maddox *seemed* to poison them, but was that really what happened, or was it just another ruse for my benefit? With Iron's shiny new skills and his ability to put stuff in my head, I don't really know what's true from pretty much the moment they made that deal with Dante.

But, at the end of the day, what I do know for certain is that Maddox's clan left me to be tortured, raped, and killed. That's what's real, and that's all I actually need to know. I didn't escape because of them. I escaped because of *me ... and my spider buddy*.

But the only one I can rely on is *me* now. That's it, and I need to stop forgetting that.

There's a click beside me, and the secret door swings open. I let out a small, involuntary sigh of relief. Krase is back. I move to greet him, trying to stifle a ridiculous, happy grin that is somehow plastered to my face. But I freeze as the barrel of a gun is the first thing that emerges from the darkness. The hand is tattooed, as is the corded forearm it's attached to.

By the time I see his face, I already know who it is, and I'm ashamed that my body freezes, the details of what he did and said to me in our last meetings flashing before my eyes. I stumble back as Iron comes over the threshold into the room, and his eyes find me.

He can see me! I'm stuck in place like somehow he's not going to see me if I stay completely still. As if that's going to help.

He halts, looking as shocked as I feel.

Of course, he is. He thought I was dead.

'Jules? But you ... you're in the ...'

I find my voice. 'In the Mountain?' I finish for him with a sneer. 'Please! Like some supe prison can contain me.'

He scowls and takes a step forward. I shuffle back two. I can't help it. Even my bravado has its limits. His eyes move over me, taking in the red dress. He hasn't lowered his gun, although I have no idea why he's brought one.

My eyes widen as it comes to me. I do know why. For Krase. He probably thinks he's gone incubus psycho killer.

'How did you escape Dante?' he asks, his eyes flicking over me as if he's trying to see what Dante might have done through my clothes.

'What do you care?' I mutter. 'You all left me there to die.'

He gives me a narrow-eyed look that chills me, reminds me that even without the gun in his hand, he's a very dangerous half-fae. He can torture me into telling him anything he wants. I don't think I can take that again so soon after all the stuff he did in the Mountain.

I try to keep from showing him my fear, wrap a little bravado around me. I give him the same bullshit story I told Maddox.

'Siggy rescued me before the portal closed.'

'You bring her back too?'

I don't say it, but he must see it in my face.

'I'm sorry,' he says. 'I know she was your friend.'

I clench my jaw, but my lip still quivers at his words that actually sound genuine.

But the gun doesn't get lowered.

'How did you find me?' I choke out.

'I know Krase's little tricks,' is all he says. 'Where is he? He's dangerous, Jules. You shouldn't be anywhere near him. He'll kill you.'

I can't help my incredulous look. 'He hasn't hurt me.'

Not like you did ... well, except for the choking out and the bruised ribs, but I've decided to let that go because he let me shower and made me come.

He gestures to my throat, and my hand goes up to the bruises still visible around my neck.

'I can see that isn't true, Jules. You don't have to protect him. He's rogue, he's—'

I see movement in the passage, and I stop listening to Iron's hypocritical diatribe on how evil his clan brother is as Krase moves into the room, silently coming up behind Iron. I don't let my eyes move to him, not wanting to give him away, but, at the last moment, Iron turns, hitting Krase on the side of the head with the butt of the gun.

Krase staggers to the side with a grunt and a curse but rights himself immediately and barrels into Iron with a snarl.

They fall onto the bed.

'You'd pull a gun on her?' he yells at Iron as they grapple in the sheets.

'Better than what you were going to do!' Iron retorts.

The gun isn't in his hand anymore, but it's not on the floor either. I glimpse it on the bed close to them and move around the bed to grab it, not sure what else to do.

I take it in my hand. It's big and kind of heavy. It's not my first time, but this is a little different than the .38 I carried for a while.

'Freeze!' *I always wanted to say that.*

They don't listen, and I raise the gun above my head, yanking back the hammer and pulling the trigger. The blast has them doing what I told them immediately and me exclaiming in pain at the kickback that I wasn't expecting.

I switch it to my left and shake out my other hand, the top of my thumb and wrist, smarting.

The two demons are still, their hands wrapped around each other's throats. They're watching me.

'Get up,' I say to them both, and they extract themselves from each other, standing side by side at the end of the bed, looking a little sheepish.

I look at the gun and then at Iron. He looks defiant.

'Do it,' he snarls. 'I know you're aching for payback for what I did to you in the Mountain.'

Krase growls next to him. 'You were there too? Payback for what?' He glances at me. 'What did you do to her?'

'We were all there,' Iron mutters, 'and I did,' he looks away, emotions flitting across his face, 'what I was ordered to do.'

He looks a little ashamed, but I don't buy it.

'Krase isn't a danger,' I say, changing the subject. 'Look at him. Does he seem mindlessly deranged?'

Iron does what I say. I mean, I *am* still holding the gun.

I lower my arm as I let out a long breath. 'I don't want payback,' I say. 'What I want is for you to be nowhere near me.'

I see remorse in his countenance, but I'm not having it. I don't want to see it. I turn away and put the gun on the bureau.

'I just want to leave,' I say quietly, glancing back at the two incubi.

Krase's expression is barely readable, but he looks ... disappointed.

Iron's face is hard and unyielding, as usual. 'That's not going to be possible, Jules.'

'Why?'

There's a loud banging on the door next to me, and I jump, leaping away from it.

'Because your little gunshot has brought the cavalry,' Iron says as it bursts open, and four pairs of eyes lock onto me. 'And they can all see you now.'

Chapter Seven

MADDOX

Iron and Krase are in front of me, but I hardly notice them, my eyes glued to Jules.

She's alive. He didn't kill her. I look for signs of distress, of pain, but there are just a few bruises. She looks remarkably well, her curves accentuated by the red dress she got from who only knows where. I try not to notice, but it's more than a little difficult. Where the hell did that come from? Trust Jules to somehow trade her dirty clothes for a well-fitting and frankly dazzling ensemble fit for an evening soiree in a house no woman currently even resides in.

I swallow hard, finally able to rip my eyes away from her to look at Krase.

'What were you thinking?' I explode, my fearful anger rising to the fore. 'What if you'd—'

My words die in my throat as I belatedly take in my friend's appearance. I've spent the past few hours fearing the worst, but Krase looks ... better. In fact, he looks normal. He's cleaned himself up, rid himself of the tatty beard and dirty clothes.

I hide my relief and bury my confusion at this impossible outcome for now. Coming back from the brink like this is unheard of, and I can't explain it. I glance at Jules again. Could she have something to do with it? I discount that ludicrous idea almost immediately. She's human. I'm sure of it. What power could *she* possibly have to save him from the darkness?

I feel Iron's eyes boring into me, and I can't help my slight grimace. I should have known he'd suspect something wasn't quite right.

'What the hell is this?' Daemon growls from behind me, his wide eyes going back and forth between Krase and Jules.

I grit my teeth and decide to start with Krase's presence first.

'I found him when we got back. I didn't kill him, as you can plainly see. I know I should have, but he requested time to settle his affairs, and then we were taken to the Mountain before the time I'd allotted him was up.'

'And you just let us believe he was dead?'

Axel's words cut me.

'Of course not! I left him in the fold with a pistol. I thought ...' I stalk to the bureau and take the gun in my hand, stowing it in the waistband of my jeans before I turn to face them all.

Krase tenses, but I roll my eyes. 'If I were going to do it now, I already would have.'

From the corner of my eye, I see that Jayce has arrived now as well. He doesn't see Jules at first because she's not in his line of sight. He shakes his head at Krase and springs forward. At first, I'm afraid he's going to wring his brother's neck, but he pulls him into a tight bear hug, laughing.

'You're alive, you fucking cunt!' He pulls back and laughs again. 'Alive!'

Then he punches his brother right in the gut. Krase doubles over with a grunt.

'Aye, I deserve that,' he wheezes.

Jayce notices Jules and does a double-take. The smile on his face is quickly replaced by shock. 'Bana-Phrionnsa?'

I almost roll my eyes again. *Here we go.*

He crosses the room quickly. She steps back when he tries to touch her.

'We thought ... we feared the worst,' he says, frowning at her faint scoff. 'Leaving you wasn't our doing. The arania venom ... we didn't wake until we were back here, and it was too late. We *were* coming to get ye. You know that, lass.'

She snorts. 'You're really going to tell me you didn't know I was here?'

Jayce and Axel both stare at me.

'You hid her from us!' Axel exclaims. 'You sonofabitch!'

Nothing shows on Jules' face, but I see her throat working. She takes another step back.

'Well, you needn't have worried. I made it out on my own, as you can see.' Her tone is devoid of emotion.

Jayce reaches out for her again, but she shies away, keeping her distance from all of us. His face falls further.

'Bana-Phrionnsa ...'

She flinches at the term, and he looks back at Axel, a helpless expression on his face.

I get between Jules and my clan and turn my back on her. If they want answers here and now, fine, but I'm not explaining myself to *her*.

'I didn't know Krase was alive until we returned,' I say. 'I found him in the cells downstairs. He'd locked himself down there.'

'And Jules?' Axel snarls. 'Are you going to tell us you didn't know she was here either?'

'Of course, I knew,' I grind out before she can start complaining to them about how I kept her in the dungeon and whatever other tales she can use to try to drive us all apart.

'How long has she been here, Maddox? How many days have you kept her from us?'

I glance back at her. She isn't saying anything, but I refuse to lie. I did my duty to ensure my clan's safety. Nothing more or less.

'Since the night we returned. She must have come through just after we did,' I tell them. 'I found her unconscious in the garden.'

'You made us leave her! You gave her to Dante! You made us think that she was still in the Mountain! We thought she was being tortured to death!' Jayce roars.

'Yes.' I meet my clan brothers' eyes head-on as I say it. 'And I would do it again. I'm only sorry she isn't still where I stowed her so this obsession you have with her would cease!'

I glance back to find Jules gone, and my eyes narrow.

Daemon swears under his breath. 'I don't remember all of you being so fucking dramatic before I left,' he mutters. 'Don't worry, I'll find her and bring her back before she causes trouble.'

With that, he pushes himself off his perch by the door, ignoring the anger-filled looks of the rest of the clan and disappearing through the secret door to follow Jules.

I ensure that none of the others can follow Daemon, keeping them where they are, though I hear Jayce grunt as he tries to fight me.

'When were you going to tell us?' Axel asks quietly. 'Or were you not going to bother?'

His features twist with disgust. 'Were you going to take her out into the wood with Krase and put them both in the ground without any of us being the wiser?'

'No,' I say, drawing myself up to my full height because fuck him for questioning my integrity, 'I wasn't.'

Krase glances at me and shakes his head at Jayce. 'I asked him not to tell anyone about me. I wasn't myself, ye ken. I needed a few more days. Had a feeling in my gut that this wasn't the end for me.'

'And you're yourself now?' Jayce asks.

'Aye. Almost.'

'How did you survive?'

Krase shrugs, and I scrutinize him carefully. He knows more than what he's saying. He must.

'And Jules?' Iron asks. 'What *did* you plan to do with her?'

I fix him with a cold look. 'I wasn't going to murder a helpless human in cold blood if that's what you mean. I was ... keeping her in the cells until we'd dealt with the Council, had our records expunged. You know she can't be free to leave while all this is going on.'

At their accusatory expressions, I throw up my arms, aiming my words at Iron, potentially my last ally in this room. 'What else could I have done? If she's allowed to go to the law, we'll be back in the Mountain before we know it. And what if she tells them about the portal? They'll seal it, and we really will be stuck there.'

Iron sighs, and I can see he agrees with my thinking. He might not like that I kept him in the dark, but he knows we can't trust her just as I do.

'Maddox is right. She might be here now and pretending she's not holding a grudge, but we tortured her. We left her for dead in the Mountain. She won't forget that, and she has no reason not to go straight to the authorities.'

'You agree she should be put back in the dungeon?' Jayce spits, his eyes flashing in anger at Iron.

'No,' Iron says, his gaze moving to the window where the signs of autumn are becoming more apparent outside. 'The weather's turning. A human will freeze down there soon.'

'We'll put her in a room up here then,' I say, glad that Iron is still thinking with his head and not his cock like the others seem to be.

Not that I'm surprised. Her hold on them is as strong as it was in the Mountain.

Iron raises a brow. 'Even a magickal supermax couldn't keep that woman confined. Do you really think we can keep her in a room? As I see it, we have two options. We give her an incentive to stay—'

'What kind of an incentive?' Jayce asks.

Iron chuckles patronizingly. 'Well, it's Jules. Payment, of course. As I was saying, we give her the promise of money if she doesn't try to leave, and she keeps that pretty mouth shut. In return, she gets the run of the property. Of course, we still ensure she can't get through the defenses the same way we stopped Jayce and Axel ...' he looks at them apologetically, 'and we beef up security to keep all our bases covered where she's concerned.'

'And option two?' I ask even though I already know.

He gives me a hard look. 'We put a bullet in her head.'

JULES

I know I'm pretty lost as I walk slowly through the maze of secret passages, but it's not bothering me, really. I'm strangely at home in this dark, rocky labyrinth after so many weeks in such a similar environment. I also feel ... I don't know ... a lot of things I can't explain and wouldn't want to.

The truth is, between Axel and Jayce's 'concern' over me, Krase's Jekyll-and-Hyde personas despite the pleasure he's given me in his bed, and the other three's ire, it was just too much to deal with all at once.

The darkness and the quiet are soothing in a way it never was for me before the Mountain. Who knew that I'd be left with a love of cave-like spaces after that ninety-day horror show?

I let my steps falter to get my head on straight and plan my next move, and my progression through the narrow space halts at a sort of passing point where it's a little wider. I lean against the wall in the designer dress Krase pulled out of nowhere, not caring if it gets soiled and ripped. It's not mine. It belonged to someone Krase cared about. That much is clear, or else why would he have bothered to keep it?

Why am I jealous?

I hear the tell-tale scuff of a shoe on stone behind me and cover my mouth to cover my gasp. How did they find me so fast? I've taken a ton of turns.

There's nowhere to hide, so I start sprinting, running my fingers along the stone walls to guide me. But the wall ends abruptly, and I find myself in an actual cave. Faint light comes through from the ceiling, where there's an opening with ivy creeping down from somewhere on the grounds.

Frantically, I search for another tunnel, but I've lost precious seconds, and a body barrels into me, throwing me down hard. I stifle a cry as I hit the floor, but I'm up within a second and running again.

'Did you think we'd just let you go?' comes a taunting whisper from behind me.

A thick arm wraps around my waist and picks me up off my feet. I kick and claw, but all he does is laugh darkly.

The laugh.

It's just like Dante's in all of my nightmares.

I freeze, transported by the sound into Dante's throne room to his stage at the moment he let the two supes rip off my clothes for the amusement of the others. He laughs darkly behind me while I struggle in their grasps ...

I'm turned and held with my back against the cavern wall. I

look up, lip quivering, breathing hard through my nose, but the demon holding me isn't Dante. It's Daemon.

My eyes are swimming, and my mouth opens. I'm trying to catch my breath, but I can't. The hands that are gripping my upper arms tightly gentle a fraction.

'Jules? Hey, it's okay.'

I shake my head. It's not okay. Nothing's okay.

But in the next second, his concern turns to anger.

'I can't believe I almost fell for that,' he growls. 'Stop fucking with me. Stop playing the fucking damsel in distress. It might work with Jayce and Axel, shit even Krase, but it sure as hell isn't going to work on me!'

He gives me a shake, which I know is meant to scare me but actually snaps me out of the nasty memory. I'm not in the Mountain. Dante can't hurt me.

'I don't care if Krase is alive,' Daemon continues. 'The rest of them might forgive and forget, but I lost my clan for two years because of you. They were still sitting pretty after you fucked us and left while I was out on my ass and barely surviving! You don't know what it was like, the things I had to ...'

He breaks off and levels me with a venomous look.

'We aren't square, baby,' he says quietly, gipping me hard again. 'Not even close.'

He pushes me in front of him, but when I stumble, he doesn't let me fall. He catches me, rights me, and makes me walk before him into another tunnel across the cavern that I couldn't see from where we were.

He doesn't say anything more as he marches me to wherever he's bringing me, to the others, I assume ... unless he's planning to start making us 'square' now.

'Where are we going?' I ask as I wonder what his personal revenge is going to entail.

'Back to the house,' he grunts.

We reach some stairs, and I trip on the hem of the dress I'm wearing as I climb.

Daemon curses, stopping me from hitting the ground again.

'Thanks,' I mutter.

'Pick up your fucking feet,' he growls. 'Where the hell did you get this thing, anyway?'

He plucks at the thin strap, and I feel his warm fingers brush against my shoulder blade. My skin wakens under his touch, making me shiver and my core pulse.

What is wrong with me?

'Krase,' I say breathlessly, and I hope he thinks it's because of the exertion.

'Krase just *had this dress* lying around?' he sneers.

He doesn't touch me again, and I'm glad. I shrug, knowing he can probably see me with his demon eyes. 'I guess.'

His chuckle has me turning on him with a scowl. 'What?'

But he doesn't say anything, just spins me back around and, putting a hot hand on my shoulder that feels like a brand, half-pushes me up the steps. Heat pulses through me like a battering ram, and I resist the insane urge I have to turn and kiss him, not understanding why I'm feeling this way and definitely not liking it.

I can just imagine his humiliating reaction if I did, his condescending sneer, the spiteful words he'd say to make sure I knew I wasn't worth anything to him ... to *them*.

Those thoughts combat my unwelcome sexual thoughts like a mental bucket of ice water, and my body cools.

He makes a strangled, choking noise above me, and I'm afraid he somehow knows the nature of the things that are going through my head, but he's completely silent after that.

At the top of the stairs is a dead-end, and he presses a stone beside my head that looks just like all the others as far as I can see. I hear a click, and a door opens in front of me. The library is on the other side. The smell of the books assails me, and I breathe it in. I always liked this room the best.

I push the door wider and go inside before Daemon can touch me again, and I halt in my tracks when I find Maddox sitting behind his desk, facing me.

He surveys me, clearly not surprised to see me emerging from his secret passages with his clan brother.

'Are you putting me back in the dungeon?' I blurt, still unnerved by Daemon, whom I can feel standing behind me.

Maddox continues to look unmoved, taking a small sip from a small, stemmed glass in his hand. He leans back. 'That depends entirely on you, Jules. Why don't you sit down?'

I shake my head, but Daemon's hand on the small of my back urges me over to one of the upholstered wooden armchairs in front of Maddox's desk. His hand on my shoulder forces me down into it, and the full-on contact of his skin pressing against mine has my hands squeezing the arms of the chair hard as my abdomen clenches and I choke back a moan.

He looks at me sharply, but I ignore him, trying to shy away from his hands before I embarrass myself. Thankfully, his fingers leave me, and I try to pull myself together, focus on Maddox.

'Was it difficult to find her?' the clan leader asks.

Daemon, who I know is still staring at me, finally steps away. He scoffs at the question. 'Of course not. She's so predictable. Even not being able to smell her, it was stupidly easy.'

I roll my eyes but wonder what he means by not being able to smell me. I would have thought Iron's conjure from the Mountain would have worn off by now. But if I still don't have a scent, that gives me an advantage I didn't know I had.

Maddox chuckles and gives Daemon a nod that must be an invitation for him to leave because he turns, his eyes finding me again. As he walks past the back of my chair, a lone finger brushes across my bare back, and it takes everything in me not to give an outward reaction, though my thighs involuntarily press together hard.

'Be seeing you, Jules,' he mutters.

As the door closes behind Daemon, Maddox steeples his fingers and regards me.

'Jules, I have a proposition,' he starts, not wasting any time. 'If you agree, you have my word that you won't be returned to the dungeon.'

I blink at his statement and clear my throat, trying to buy myself a few seconds because we've just entered into the negotiations for my freedom and potentially even my life. I try to get over my confusing reaction to Daemon as I surreptitiously sit up straight in the chair. I also lean back a little like I'm getting comfortable because I want Maddox to think I'm not fazed by any of this. I'm not going into this discussion on the back foot.

'And if I don't agree?' I ask, just to show him that I'm not afraid.

I feel that side of me who knows how to navigate these supe-infested waters slide into place like a warm, fitted glove on a freezing day, and I'm instantly more at ease.

I've done this a hundred times at a hundred desks with a hundred supes, and I've always come out on top. Granted, none of those others knew me the way Maddox does, but so long as I'm not put back in the cold dungeon, I feel like that's a win.

He smiles coldly. 'Well, I'm sure you'll be happy to know that you still won't see the dungeon again, darling, but you will get a brief yet exhilarating tour of the ancient woodlands on the estate before you're dispatched.'

'Dispatched?' I grin. 'What a charming way of saying you're going to slit my throat and throw me in a shallow grave on your property, Julian.'

'Indeed.' He takes another sip from his glass.

My eyes flick to it. 'Any chance of refreshment while we discuss my fate?'

'But of course.'

Maddox gets up and pours me a finger of cognac. I reach for it, but he ignores me, instead putting the glass over the flame of a candle that I hadn't really noticed on the sideboard. He swirls it around, warming it to his satisfaction before he finally hands it to me.

I take it gingerly, taking care not to let his fingers touch mine just in case my reaction to Daemon wasn't an isolated incident. I cup it in both hands, appreciating the warmth of the glass on my cold fingers as I take a sip.

He quirks a brow.

'Lovely,' I say. 'Louis 13?'

His lip twitches. 'Very good.'

I sit back in the chair, allowing the silence to stretch on, letting him be the one to speak first. I sip my drink slowly, taking the fact that he poured me a glass of *very* expensive brandy as a good sign. Even Maddox wouldn't have wasted the good stuff on a dead woman. I take in the room as I wait. It's exactly as I remember it: ornate plaster moldings with gilt accents and periwinkle panels. Floor-to-ceiling books on every subject take up most of three walls, while the fourth is dominated by tall windows and multiple French doors that look out over the gardens.

'I assume you'll be choosing to agree to my terms then?' Maddox finally breaks the silence by saying.

My eyes move over him. 'I think I'd like to hear them first before I commit.' I give him a small, insincere smile. 'Death might be preferable.'

His grin is genuine. He's enjoying this exchange, and I realize I am too. I'll agree to whatever he wants. He knows that already. But getting to the conclusion of our talks isn't really the goal. This is a game, a diversion that we're both enjoying in spite of ourselves.

That realization is another bucket of cold water on my brain.

Whatever was happening with Daemon is happening with Maddox now, too. It's different, though, more subtle, and that makes it far more insidious.

With a frown, I put down my glass. 'I can't leave then.'

Maddox notes the sudden change in my demeanor because the humor that was dancing in his eyes disappears, but he doesn't say anything about it.

'No. Until we've sorted our *misunderstanding* with the Council, you'll be staying here. Whether that be as a guest, a prisoner, or a corpse, you decide. But if you're our guest, Julia, there will be some rules to follow.'

I nod.

'You may have run of the house and the garden, but no further than the maze. You'll be treated as any honored guest here.'

He stands up and towers over me, suddenly intimidating, but I don't let myself cower. 'But you don't try to escape, and you don't attempt to steal from us.' He levels me with a stare. 'And whatever hold you have on Axel and Jayce, you relinquish it.'

I open my mouth to ask him what he means about Axel and Jayce, but he doesn't let me speak.

'When all of this is finished, you can leave, and if you haven't caused any mischief, you'll be two hundred grand richer.'

The money surprises me, but I don't let it show. A few months ago, I would have said yes without a second thought. But tonight, the offer and the condescending tone it's delivered in give me a nasty taste in my mouth. Does Maddox think he can buy anyone with money, or is it just me?

His expression says he thinks I'll jump at the chance to get more out of him. I want to prove him wrong, show him that I'm not what he thinks. I wish I didn't give a shit about his opinions, but the truth is that I've always cared what he and the rest of the clan thought of me, and I'm sick of him looking at me the way he does.

What does any of that matter? Swallow your pride and survive.

I have a couple of hundred thousand saved, but I'm going to need at least double that for a decent conjure as soon as I get out of here. Assuming it's the estate that's hiding me, I can't go outside of the grounds unprotected. If I am still being hunted, they'll find me in a matter of days, and I can't let that happen.

As I watch the demon in front of me, I wish I could tell the smug prick where to stick his money, but I don't have that luxury.

'Two hundred and fifty,' I counter because I have nothing to lose.

'Two twenty-five.'

'Two thirty-five.'

'Done.'

I feel a little sick as I rise to shake his proffered hand, seeing that look in his eye like he knows exactly who I am because I did exactly what he expected.

I want to tell him he's wrong, that not all of us were born into wealth and power, that honor and decency don't fill your belly or keep you safe and warm at night when you're running.

Our hands touch, and I grit my teeth as I feel that same unwelcome lust that I can't explain. He doesn't seem to notice whatever it is, though.

I don't ask what he meant about Axel and Jayce or what 'hold' I'm meant to be relinquishing. For that kind of cash, I'll just keep away from them completely. The house is huge. It can be done. I'll make sure of it.

'I'll have Tabitha show you to your room.'

'Tabitha?' I ask. 'What happened to Robertson?'

'Gone.' Maddox's jaw tightens. 'He betrayed us. *Me.*'

I give him a look of surprised commiseration. It isn't forced.

He and Robertson were as close to friends as an employer and employee could get, and I remember the butler telling me once that Maddox had given him a job when no one else would. I'd thought he was as loyal as they came.

'I'm sorry,' I say. 'He'd been with you a long time, hadn't he?'

He doesn't answer, but his eyes flash, and I wonder if this was how he looked when he realized I'd stolen his money two years ago, too. Did he take my actions to heart the way he did Robertson's?

As I watch his face, I know he did.

'It wasn't personal,' I whisper before I can stop myself.

His eyes snap to mine. 'Neither was giving you to Dante,' he sneers.

I wonder if he really believes that, but I turn away so he doesn't see my wince, and I give a small chuckle instead. 'Touché.'

I don't trust myself to look at him again as I go to the nearest bookshelf and read some of the titles. I hear him sit back down behind his desk, and a moment later, the library door opens.

'Ah, Tabitha, please take Julia to her room. I trust it's ready.'

'Aye. All aired and sorted. Come along, dearie.'

She bustles along in front of me, leading me away. I do glance back at Maddox, but I've already been forgotten. His attention is back on the papers on his desk.

Guess I'm dismissed.

Feeling hollow and unsettled, I let Tabitha take me up the stairs in silence, and I'm glad she's not asking me questions I might find difficult to answer, though I know she must be curious about me. We turn left at the landing, and she leads me to the room I had while I was here before. It's in the opposite wing to where the clan's rooms are.

Last time, it was for my protection. This time, I can't help but think that, in Maddox's mind, it's for theirs.

We go inside, and I look around. It's been redecorated since I was last here. It was lavender before with flowered wallpaper. A quaint yet sophisticated space that reminded me of Regency England. Now, everything is white and utilitarian. Even the sheets are devoid of color.

'Apologies,' Tabitha mutters, looking slightly abashed. 'I hope you don't mind me asking, but I have a very good nose, and you don't smell ... are you human?'

'Yes,' I say with a small smile, 'but I don't think I have a scent at the moment.'

'Ah,' she says faintly, 'I see.'

But she doesn't look convinced.

'Iron put a conjure on me a few days ago,' I explain. 'I guess it hasn't worn off yet.'

I don't know what she suspected, but at my words, Tabitha nods and looks suddenly much more at ease.

"Ah! Of course. That explains it.'

She turns down the bed and shuts the curtains before she returns to the door. 'Are you hungry? Can I bring you anything?'

I shake my head. 'No, thanks. I ate earlier.' *In the dungeon.*

She smiles and leaves me to it after asking me to ring for her if I need anything. I promise her I will, but I already know I won't. The thought of ringing a bell to summon her like some rich, supe asshole doesn't sit right with me.

When I'm alone, I brush the curtain aside and peer out into the darkness. I glance at the clock. It's after ten now. I look around to make sure there aren't any *surprises*, even spending a few minutes seeing if I can locate any secret passages out of the room, but I don't find anything.

Afterward, I get on the bed and lay in the middle, staring at the ceiling. I'm as much a prisoner as I have been for the past three months, I think. Sure, it's more comfortable, and at least I'll be able to move around the house, but I'm going to have to be careful. I need to stay away from Axel and Jayce to keep to Maddox's rules, and after what happened with Daemon and Maddox, I should probably avoid them, too. That leaves Iron, who I'm pretty wary of after the Mountain, and Krase, who may or may not still be on the brink of insanity.

I heave a sigh. Looks like I'll be even more lonely here than I was in the Mountain. At least there I had Siggy.

I blink back a few tears, but in the end, I let them fall, hoping that it'll make me feel better. I cry until my pillow is too wet to sleep on, but it doesn't help, so I close my eyes and try to sleep. Maybe tomorrow will seem brighter.

Chapter Eight

JAYCE

I enter her room silently, and I find her asleep on the bed on top of the covers, still in the dress Krase gave her to wear, though it looks a little worse for wear after her schlep through the catacombs.

I watch her for a little while, taking in the way she's curled up on her side, one hand under her pillow, and her gentle breathing. I think I could stand here forever and never get bored of looking at her.

I gently tuck her hair away from her face, tracing a lone finger down her jaw. My body springs to life, wanting more than this tiny, illicit touch, and I take a step back at the force of my desire. It isn't the time, and it may not be for quite a while, I think, letting out a small sigh.

The way she looked at me in Krase's room speared my heart. She thinks that everything that happened in the Mountain between her and Axel and me was contrived for our escape. I could see the betrayal in her eyes, and I don't blame her after everything that happened to her in there because of us. But, in that moment, it took everything in me not to go to her and explain everything, declare my undying love. The only reason I didn't was because we had an audience ... and because I knew it wouldn't do any good. Whatever small amount of trust we earned in the Mountain is gone.

I've been cracking these past few days while I thought she was still in Dante's power. I went to the barrier more than once and hurled myself at it despite it sapping my energy. I thought I couldn't feel worse, but now I realize her indifference towards me is far more terrible.

I try to feel for her and can almost see the connection between us, but it's so faint that I don't get anything from her. Its dormancy is perhaps why neither Axel nor I felt her, though she was so close.

I'm glad she was here all that time, even though Maddox did put her in the cells, but only because the alternative would have had her dead by now. I was trying to rally my spirits, but I was lying to myself.

I should be furious with Julian. I *am* furious. But I'm so relieved that she's okay, that he protected her when he could have just killed her when he found her that night, and we would never have known. Despite his actions in the Mountain, I could forgive him if he stops being such a prick where she's concerned.

Whether Jules can is another matter.

How can he not see that she's ours? We've been searching for so long, but his obsession with finding the clan a supe mate has clouded his judgment. Who cares that Jules is human? The fact that Krase's mind has been healed is proof that she's meant for us, but Maddox refuses to acknowledge it. He can't see past what she did, her dishonesty and greed.

He lives by his own code, and, to him, there's no excuse for those sorts of character failings. But he's never had to sacrifice his own ethics for his hide. Jules has. I might not know the specifics, but I can see she's had a tough life when her mask comes down.

I pull myself away from her and go into her closet, quietly hanging up the clothes I've brought, just things I've seen over the past couple of years that I thought she'd look good in or that she'd like. It was a guilty pleasure I kept under wraps from the others. A weird, frustrating, outlandish hope that she'd somehow come back into our lives even though I hated her.

In hindsight, it's laughable that I ever thought I actually despised her. Guess that's why it's 20/20, though. I look back at her in the bed, taking in the red Haute Couture dress she has on and grinning. I shake my head. If Krase had that just lying around, I'm a High Fae prince. He's my twin, after all, and we've been on the same wavelength more than once. I'd bet good money he's got a few things in his closet that would miraculously fit our human girl perfectly.

With that thought, I leave her room through the main door, closing it softly behind me. I head for Krase's room. I knock twice and then once more after a pause, our code so he knows it's me.

'Come in,' I hear from inside.

I open the door. Krase is sitting at his desk. As I go in, he shuts his laptop, and I smirk at the glimpse of ladies' jewelry I see before it closes.

He gets up and comes to me. We regard each other for a moment before we both grin, chuckling a little as we hug each other tightly.

'Thought you were a goner, brother,' I say.

'Aye, so did I.'

I tap the side of my head. 'You're well?'

He nods. 'Better than I have been in months. And you?'

'I never said I was feeling it.' I give him a look, and he rolls his eyes.

'I'm your brother. I knew it was taking you as well. But it isn't anymore?'

'No,' I say. 'It isn't anymore. I'm myself.'

'I'm better, but ...' He frowns. 'But I can still feel it. *Him*, I suppose. It's odd like he's separate from me, an entity deep inside. I can speak to him, and he answers me. Though he's a mardy cunt.'

'What does he want?'

'For months, he was only motivated by escape from the dark recesses of my mind, power over me, death, mayhem, sex. The usual old-fashioned demon desires.'

I nod at words that echo my own experiences, though I never got so bad as Krase. I could never actually speak to the darkness that lives within me and receive a response even at my worst, and now it's like it was never there at all.

'And what does he want now?' I ask.

'Jules.'

I tense, wondering if I am going to have to kill my beloved brother after all because I'm not going to let his dark side hurt her.

'What does he want with her?' I grind out.

He looks up sharply at my tone and then snorts in amusement. 'What do you think?'

'If not death, then sex,' I murmur.

Krase surveys me, looking for what I don't know. 'Not quite.'

'Stop being so cryptic,' I growl. 'Am I going to need to kill you after all, or not?'

He doesn't say anything for a moment, and I wonder what the hell my brother's deep, dark demon could want with her if not the usual.

'I'm not sure,' Krase says, turning away. 'He wants to mate. Properly.'

'With Jules? But she's human.' I shake my head at him. 'That doesn't make sense. Why would your fully demon side be interested in a human as more than food?'

'Why are you?' he counters.

'It's not the same,' I argue. 'I'm not rogue.'

Krase is watching me closely again. 'She's human, you say? Are you sure about that, brother?'

I frown. 'Of course. What else could she be?' My eyes narrow at him. 'What do you know that you aren't telling me?'

He sits back in his chair and purses his lips. 'How much did you get to know her again in the Mountain?'

'Intimately,' I say without hesitation. 'I spent time with her, fed from her, fucked her. But I was thwarted by the others at every turn, bar Axel who also fed from and fucked her.'

'He became close to her as well?'

'Aye.'

'But not the others?'

'No. Daemon, Maddox, and Iron ... they thought there was something wrong with us both, that she had us under some spell. They ...'

I hesitate, wondering how much I should tell him. He'll rage, but perhaps it's better to tell him everything now while we're alone rather than wait for it to come out later when there might be others around.

'She was hiding in the Mountain. I still don't know why or from whom. The Demon King knew she was there. He'd been trying to find her for weeks. We thought you were dead, and we all blamed her for it because of what she did two years ago.'

I sit down on the bed. 'We made a deal with the King in the Mountain that we'd find her and deliver her to him. She captured Axel, and then we caught her, but she wouldn't tell us where she'd stowed him. She was ill for a few days with a fever. When she finally woke, I took her with me to find Axel, and when we did, he was starving ...'

'She had a fever?' Krase's voice is sharp.

I look up to find Krase staring at me.

I frown, not seeing the importance. 'Aye.'

'Tell me the rest then.'

'She made friends with an actual arania. Can you believe it?' I smile at the thought, but Krase's face falls a little.

Mine does, as well. 'Siggy's dead.'

Krase nods. 'She grieves deeply for the arania. What else should I know?'

'Iron's fae magick is a lot stronger. The Mountain, maybe ... it did something to him. He was able to compel us to leave the safety of Siggy's nest. He made us walk right out to where he and the others were waiting. We tried to reason with Maddox, but he wouldn't believe that our feelings for Jules were real. He wanted to know the location of the portal she used to get into the Mountain before Dante. He kept us subdued while Iron ...'

'Tortured her,' Krase finishes, standing up abruptly and saying a soft 'fuck'.

'Aye. It gets worse.'

Krase makes an effort to sit back down in the chair. 'Go on.'

'Iron tricked her into telling him what he wanted to know when he couldn't make her crack. Then, Maddox poisoned Axel and me with arania venom to keep us from getting in the way of his deal with Dante. While we were incapacitated, he gave her to Dante.'

Krase doesn't say anything at all.

'She didn't tell you any of this?'

He shakes his head. 'She'd never volunteer so much about herself. You know that. She doesn't like to feel vulnerable.'

'Aye.' I stand.

Krase's anger melts away, but instead of being relieved, I'm the opposite. He's saving it for later, and that doesn't bode well for any member of the clan who hurt Jules.

'Iron tried to help us get off the estate to help Jules when we thought Dante had her,' I say.

Krase snorts but doesn't say anything more.

I regard him for a minute, watching as he considers all I've told him. 'If she's not human, what is she, Krase?'

He grins and gives me a wink. 'I'll let you figure that out for yourself, Jayce.'

I scowl at him. 'No games with her. She's been through enough.'

'No games,' he agrees. 'At least, no games with dire consequences.'

I huff out a breath. 'Still the same, aren't you?'

'Aye.'

JULES

I hear Maddox speaking to someone, and the library door clicks open, pulling me out of the book I was reading. Shuffling further back into the reading nook so I can't be seen, I put a couple of the larger cushions in front of me in case he comes in, but the voice fades, and I breathe a small sigh of relief.

I've successfully avoided the incubi clan for four days except for passing Daemon in the hall once, which was more than a little uncomfortable. I could feel his eyes boring into me. He muttered something about my clothes that I didn't hear, and I hurried away without making eye contact. That's not like me, but after my weird reaction to him and Maddox the other day, I'm wary of being around them.

There's no more noise, so I settle back into the cubby that's been built into the library since I was last here. There are cushions and a blanket, even a small lamp. Not for the first time, I wonder how it was created. I'm no architect, but the wall isn't that thick, and the corridor is right on the other side. But I checked yesterday, and the hallway is exactly the same as it was.

It must be a conjure of some kind, but I've never seen

anything quite like it. It's quickly become my favorite place in the house, more so because no one's found me here. I mean, it's not as if anyone's looking for me, but it feels nice that no one can sneak up on me, and I can secret myself away.

I hear Tabitha come in with a tray. I guess it's Elevenses. I'm certain she knows my hiding spot because she keeps bringing food and drink to the library, but she hasn't spoken to me nor told anyone else where to find me, I'm pretty sure. I give it a minute to make sure the coast is clear before I slip out and pour myself a cup of tea. I take it back into my refuge with me, placing it gently on the convenient little shelf on the side.

I get back into my book, whiling away the time in yet another limbo. I mean, as prisons go, this one is by far the best I've been in, and it's definitely miles better than the Mountain. Although pretty much anywhere would be after getting used to that place. The bar is still very, *very* low. Nothing like running water and hot drinks to make you realize how lucky you are.

But however luxurious this *in-between* place is, it isn't real life, and it won't last long. I know I should take advantage of the respite, relax and get my strength up. I'm relatively safe here. I mean, no one's going to kill me ... *probably*. But the truth is, I don't want to get too comfortable because I remember how easy it was for me to love this place, to care about the clan, and that terrifies me. Two years ago, I couldn't see that, but I can now, and I can't allow myself to fall into the same trap.

I need to stay away from them, keep my head down, and not engage. I need to follow Maddox's rules, and when I get out of here, I need to find a solution that doesn't involve running for the rest of my solitary life.

I haven't made any plans for when Maddox lets me leave the estate because I have no idea when that'll be. But I have calculated that with the money Maddox gives me for following his rules and the cash I already have saved, I'll be able to purchase at least a mid-level conjure. It'll only last about six months, but hopefully, I can come up with a more sustainable plan by then.

I just have to make sure I get that money. That's all that matters.

Unwelcome thoughts try to push their way to the fore of my mind: what the clan will think of me, how much they'll despise me for caring about the money, how smug some of them will be when they see that I do, how some of them will feel.

They'll judge me no matter what, but I can't let them get to me. They don't really know me. They can't.

'I thought I'd find you here.'

I shriek at the voice, throwing the book I'm holding at the speaker as I scramble back. I didn't hear the door.

Axel catches the book and takes a step back. I try to get myself under control while I level him with an accusatory look.

'Sorry, I thought you'd have heard me come in.'

'Well, I didn't,' I reply breathlessly as I crawl out of the reading nook, a feat made that much harder by yet another of the long, expensive dresses that have appeared in my closet.

I stand up and take my book back from him, careful not to touch his skin.

'Sorry,' I mumble.

'No, Jules, I'm sorry. I'm so sorry for what happened in the Mountain. I wanted to tell you that. I tried to wait, to give you some space after everything and let you come to me. But you've been avoiding us.'

I don't let the cringe out when he mentions *everything* so casually.

'It's fine,' I say. 'I understand. You needed to get out of there, and I knew how. I would have done the same.'

I give him a polite smile and side-step him in an attempt to escape the room.

He frowns. 'I don't think you understand.'

He steps closer, boxing me in, and I move back, feeling the ledge of the reading nook at the back of my knees.

'I'm not sorry for what happened between us ...' He rubs his temples. 'Well, I am sorry for how it happened. You deserved better than what I ... What I'm trying to say is that I'm sorry for not seeing what Maddox was up to, for letting myself get drugged and not being able to help you, save you. We tried to get back, but Maddox wouldn't let us leave.'

I look up at him, trying to take in his rambling apology, getting angry with myself because his pretty words have already begun to make me think he really cares. What is wrong with me? I know better than this.

'I'm not a princess, Axel, and you're not a white knight. I got myself out of the Mountain fine. You don't have anything to beat yourself up about. I didn't need you.'

The last part makes him wince, but I press on.

'And let's just call apples, apples. The time we spent together in the Mountain was just a way of passing the time for me and a way of getting out for you.' I shrug. 'I don't hold a grudge. It meant nothing. I'll be telling Jayce the same thing if I see him before I leave.'

'You're leaving?' he asks.

'As soon as I'm able.'

He frowns like that's the last thing he expected. 'You can't mean that.'

His hand cups my cheek, and my eyes widen in panic before I realize that there's not that sharp spike of lust that I felt with Daemon and Maddox. Instead, all I feel is his misery as our physical connection makes the faint tendrils between us that I buried in the dungeon flare to life.

I push them away again, the act making me want to burst into tears.

'I do mean it. Stay away from me.'

His sadness intensifies and merges with what might well be

my own deep despair. My lower lip wobbles, and I bite it, but that doesn't help. I feel as if I could start sobbing at any moment and never stop. I don't want to know how he's feeling, how I'm making him feel. I'm hurting him, but it's not real. It can't be. This is a trick because they want something from me.

They're stuck at the chateau, and they're going to need to feed. That's what he wants, and he'll do and say anything to get it since the lull won't work.

I need to get away from him before I cave and give him what he wants, before I do exactly what I did in the Mountain and let myself pretend that they give a fuck about me when it's so obvious they don't.

I don't look at him as I sidle past and leave the room quickly, glad when he doesn't follow me.

Why are there tears in my eyes?

I blink them away, wanting to go back and tell him that none of that was true, but I can't. I need to follow the rules. I need to get out of here with the prospect of ...

I'm pushed hard as I turn the corner, and I fall into the wall with a small cry.

Daemon turns me around roughly, and his hand grips my throat. I claw at his fingers, only just able to breathe. They feel weird. He's wearing a glove on the hand he's holding me with.

Relief mixes with my fear of being throttled, and I glance up at him, wondering why he's wearing it, but lowering my gaze again just as quickly because he looks more than a little pissed.

'What were you doing alone in the library with Axel?' he snarls.

'Who are you, my keeper?' I snap, pushing ineffectually at him.

'Yes! So, answer my question.'

His covered fingers grip me tighter.

'Nothing!' I gasp.

'Liar!'

I try to swallow. 'I was reading. He came in. We talked. I told him to leave me alone. That's all!'

'What's with the waterworks?' he grates out.

His other *ungloved* hand comes close to my face, and I recoil as he catches a tear on my cheek with his finger, which he puts to his lips and licks, never touching my skin.

For a moment, all I can do is stare with my mouth open. But I come to my senses quickly. I shake my head.

'Involuntary,' I wheeze. 'I was attacked in the hallway by a one-gloved assailant.'

One side of Daemon's lip curves upwards for a second before his frown returns. He stares at me for a moment before he seems satisfied, and his hand loosens but doesn't leave me entirely.

'Another dress?' He smirks.

'I don't have anything else.'

His eyes flick down to my chest. 'No underwear?'

I take a deep breath, crossing my arms over my chest so he can't see my nips.

'Let me go, Daemon.'

He doesn't move for a long, tense moment. Then, he pushes himself away from the wall, and his hand falls away.

I eye it. 'What's with the glove?' I whisper.

'My hand was cold.'

'I'm glad,' I say pointedly as I look into his face.

I see confusion followed by ... *hurt*? He *did* feel whatever it was the other day. That's why he's wearing it. He assumes it's me, and he's taking precautions so I don't lure him in like he thinks I did with Axel and Jayce.

An incubus afraid of being lulled *by little old me. Ironic.*

I think he's just going to leave, but instead, he pushes me hard against the wall again, pinning me to it.

'Stay away from Axel and Jayce, or you'll see who I became without the clan to temper me,' he hisses.

He turns on his heel and disappears down the corridor. I stay where I am, staring at the spot in front of me where he just was, my hands rubbing my neck.

That afternoon, I run into Jayce twice and Axel three more times, both in the garden and the house, and by the end, I decide that if they don't stop, I'm going to have to live in my room until Maddox releases me. I know they're doing it on purpose, but Daemon made it clear that I'm to blame if I'm caught alone with either one of them.

It's not fair, I think to myself as I pause at the closed library door. But what is fair? I know by now that *fair* is for supes like Maddox, not humans like me. Happiness and a decent life aren't things that will just drop into my lap. If I want them, I have to take them. Imbued with determination, I knock on the door softly, knowing by its position that Maddox is in there using the library as his study at the moment.

'Come in.'

I take a breath and enter.

He's not at his desk. He's in one of the plush, high-backed chairs by the empty fireplace, working on a tablet.

I disregard his sneer when he sees who's come. 'I need to speak to you about our deal.'

'Reneging on it already, Julia?'

'No, of course not. But your clan is making it almost impossible to keep to it,' I tell him. 'Jayce and Axel have tracked me down several times today. I'm doing everything I can to follow your rules, but I can't be held accountable if your clan—'

'You really do need that money, don't you, darling,' he interrupts, looking up from the screen. 'What for?'

His eyes move over the black dress I'm currently wearing. 'Clothes, perhaps? Jewelry? To be honest, I can't see where it all goes.'

I shift uncomfortably under his gaze.

'What else would you do for it, I wonder?' he continues, rising. 'How important is it?'

I step out of his way as he returns his tablet to the desk, ignoring questions that I hope are rhetorical because I shudder to think what tricks he might want me to perform to get paid if he continues in this vein.

'We made a deal,' I say, 'and regardless of Axel and Jayce's actions, I'm ready to stick to it. But it's been made clear to me that the fault will be laid at my door if we're found alone together, no matter the circumstances.'

'Has it?' Maddox asks, his piercing eyes holding mine captive as he sits behind his desk.

'Yes,' I breathe, my hand touching my neck subconsciously.

He doesn't miss it, his gaze sharpening on my throat. He frowns.

'I'll speak to them.'

I nod and turn to leave.

'Jules?' he calls, and I swing back. 'You'll come to me if you're in any difficulty with the others. Daemon and Iron can be—'

I can't help my scoff. 'Daemon and Iron are exactly what you want them to be. They were in the Mountain, and they are now. And I wouldn't come to you for help with them even if they pierced me with a poison arrow, and you were the only one who had the antidote, Julian.'

I retreat from the library, pettily leaving the door wide open so he has to get up and close it.

I head for the grand staircase, intending on spending the rest of the day alone in my room, but instead find myself walking past the stairs, stopping outside the Billiard Room. The door opens just as I get there, and I enter, not realizing what's happening until the door shuts behind me, and I'm met with four sets of eyes.

My mind clears, and I forget my fear of Iron. I walk right up to him and slap him across his cheek so hard his head turns. The crack of my hand against his skin is one of the most satisfying things I've ever heard.

'How dare you? How dare you use your fae compulsion on me here!'

Chapter Nine

IRON

I grab her wrist when she attempts to hit me again and squeeze it a little, angry that she'd just assume I forced her to come here even though I know it's warranted, and I can see how upset she is by the tears in her eyes. I know her head is back in the Mountain in that room where I hurt her.

'It wasn't me,' I hiss, inclining my head towards Krase, who's holding one of the little fae objects he and Jayce like to play with, his eyes sightless and clouded over with magick.

'You?'

Her broken tone has me loosening my grip on her arm to a soft caress without thinking and then letting her go completely in pseudo-alarm.

When Krase's eyes clear a few seconds later, he looks bemused by Jules' countenance.

'What's wrong?' he asks.

'You made me come here!' she replies angrily. 'You controlled me.'

'Aye, as I would with any of the others,' he says. 'What's the problem?'

She throws her hands up in the air and seems to notice that it's not just Krase and me here but Jayce and Axel as well.

She tenses immediately. 'I can't be here,' she says. 'I can't be around you.'

I note her choice of words. She 'can't' be around them. This has Maddox written all over it. I'll bet he followed my advice.

'Why not, lass?' Jayce asks.

'You already know,' I say, unable to keep the conceit from my tone. 'Because she made a deal with Maddox for money, didn't you, sweetheart? She's not allowed near you two, or she doesn't get paid.'

Axel and Jayce look upset, and she balks a little.

'It's always about the money, right, Jules?'

She meets my eyes. Hers are still glassy, but her voice comes out strong.

'Yes, it's always about the money. You should try to remember that so there aren't any more misunderstandings.'

She gives a tiny wince as she turns to leave.

'Let me go,' she says to Krase as he bars the door, 'and don't use fae magick on me again.'

'Come,' he tries to cajole. 'Talk to us. Play a game with us.'

'I told you, I can't.'

'You can't be alone with them, aye, but we're all here. Surely, this isn't breaking the rules.'

She shakes her head, and he sighs.

'Leave,' Krase says to Axel and Jayce, and surprisingly, they do, each casting longing looks at her.

Pathetic.

She didn't deserve to be left in the Mountain, granted, but she doesn't deserve their loyalty either. I lean forward.

'I understand why you need to stay here for now,' I tell her through clenched teeth. 'But I want you to know that it was my idea to offer you money. I knew you'd go for it. I knew we'd be able to use it to control you. What does that say about you?'

Jules snorts at me. 'That you think about me far too much, demon.'

She flicks her hair at me, and my traitorous nostrils flare in anticipation of her scent, but there's none. There hasn't been the entire time. Why has it taken me this long to realize?

'Why can't I smell you?' I ask her. 'I broke the conjure the night you got out of the dungeon. I should be able to.'

I didn't actually remember what had happened until the next day, but I found her that night, a split second before I got blasted by magick in the Sunroom and knocked out cold. I picked up on the brightly colored conjures in the cells. She has at least one good one on her that isn't mine, but I'm not sure what it does. I'm going to find out, though. It'll just take me some time to figure out how to access it.

In the meantime, maybe I should keep her close, form a friendship with her. Then I'll know if she's planning anything. I could spend some time with her. Riding, maybe. She liked it when I taught her to before.

She shakes her head at me. 'I don't know.'

My eyes swing knowingly to Krase, who shrugs. 'I wanted to keep her secret when we got out of the dungeon, so I hid her scent with one of my charms. It'll take it off when I get the chance.'

Jules frowns. 'Stop using fae magick on me without my consent.'

He raises his hands in placation. 'I vow I'll cease immediately.'

She looks at me, obviously hoping for the same pledge.

'We'll see,' I growl.

She just looks away with a small sigh, like she knew what I was going to say.

'Why did you want me here?' she asks Krase.

'For your company,' he answers readily.

'Bullshit. You're hungry.'

'That as well.'

She chuckles. 'At least you don't lie about it, I guess.'

'Are you crazy?' I snarl at him. 'You can't feed from her!'

'Aye,' he says with a grin. 'I am crazy, and I already have. *Twice.*'

He licks his lips, and her cheeks redden.

I look from her to him. Jayce and Axel and now Krase, too.

'Maddox should know—' I begin.

Krase laughs. 'You aren't going to tell him.'

'The hell I'm not!'

'You breathe a word of this, and I'll make sure he finds out about your nocturnal activities with Jayce and Axel,' he snarls, and I see darkness leaching into his eyes. 'How do you think he'll react if he finds out you were working with them against him to get Jules out of the Mountain?'

'They were? *You* were?' Jules asks.

I ignore her. 'How do you know that?'

He laughs. 'Doesn't matter how I know, but Maddox won't forget. You know how he feels about turncoats.'

'I'm no traitor! I'll go tell him now,' I bluff, but he just rolls his eyes.

'Don't play with me, Iron. *I'm* the Master of Games, not you.' He turns to Jules, who jumps a little when she sees his eyes. 'And that reminds me of something I'd *love* to do with you.'

'Mr. Hyde?' she asks in a small voice.

'Not yet,' he answers, 'but he wants out. He wants *you*, deamhan àlainn.'

'You can't hurt her—' I start, but Krase just laughs again.

'I don't want to hurt you, little rabbit,' he growls at her, his voice low and gravelly. 'I want to chase you and fuck you where I catch you. Tha an t-acras ort, nach eil, Jules?'

'I don't know what you're saying,' she breathes.

And we're on the same page because I don't know either, I think as I look between them. She seems scared, though her pupils are expanding with lust, and I step towards her to intervene. Maddox will have promised her safety here so long as she abides by the rules. She seems to be, but Krase's idea is nowhere near safe.

'You can't do that, Krase, for a thousand reasons. Not least of which, what if you *do* hurt her?'

He makes a sound of derision. 'We'd never! You know that, don't you, coineanach beag?' He asks her.

We'd? He talks about his crazy like it's another version of him.

But the stupid girl nods at him, having no idea of the danger she's putting herself in by agreeing.

'When?' she asks.

'Now.'

'No!' I snarl. 'She's human. You can't play with her like this. You'll kill her.'

'Ach! She's strong and capable. You underestimate her. Besides, she already said yes. Rules of the game, you don't break your word.' He turns to her. 'You understand what you've agreed to? When I catch you, I will have you, Jules. Doesn't matter where; I'll spear you on my cock. There's no going back once we begin.'

She nods hesitantly again, and he caresses her face. 'You're everything,' he whispers, and her eyes widen while mine roll.

He'll say whatever he thinks she wants to hear, and she's eating it up like an idiot.

He glances at me. 'You keep an eye out for Maddox. If he finds out about this, he finds out about *you*.'

Fuck!

I look from him to her helplessly, trapped between a rock and a hard place, knowing that I need to keep Jules safe from Krase's recklessness no matter what.

'I'll give you a thirty-second head start,' Krase says to her.

VENGEANCE AND VIPERS

'You can go anywhere in the house or the grounds, but don't try to pass through the border spells, or you'll get a nasty zap.'

She doesn't move.

'Run, little rabbit, run!' he snarls, and she gasps, springing into action and fleeing from the room.

Krase laughs as he demons up, his thick tail swishing, his wings elongating. He smiles at me.

'Shall we make it a little more interesting? If you find her first, she safe from me,' he taunts, and I give him a long-suffering look.

'You're a cunt, Krase.'

Will she forgive me if I compel her to come to me?

Ah!

What do I care if she hates me or not? Still, if I want to get closer to her, I'll need to curry her favor, not her distrust.

So, instead of reaching out with my mind to find hers, I watch the clock, and as soon as the second hand gets to thirty, I'm out of that room before him and sprinting down the hallway, wondering how I can find a human with no scent, if I'll be able to use my fae senses to locate her by the magick on her as I run.

I must. I have to get to her first. It doesn't matter what she thought she was agreeing to. As soon as she sees Krase in his demon form, she'll change her mind. But it won't matter to him. This is his game.

And to the winner go the spoils.

JULES

My own hand is clapped hard over my mouth so I don't give myself away. Why did I agree to this? I have no clue. But I didn't feel like I was being controlled when I did. It was all me when I nodded my head. He just ... I could see the darkness leaching into him, hear the change in his voice, and I thought that if he fed, maybe he could push it back.

It definitely didn't have anything to do with his rippling muscles, the chiseled jaw, his powerful body ...

I roll my eyes at myself. There was something else too, something I don't understand. The prospect of being chased by him, taken by him if he catches me, lit a fire in my veins that I've never felt before. I'll do everything I can not to get caught, but I also want him to find me and do what he threatened. *Promised*.

I'm pretty stoked that I've made it as far as the forest. From the Billiard room, I ran straight up to Krase's room, thinking he wouldn't expect that. From there, I took the secret passages to the well I found when Daemon caught me and took me to Maddox.

I saw the gnarled, ancient trees from below in the daylight and realized how far from the main house I'd come through the tunnels. There was a collapsed staircase leading upwards that I was just able to make it through, and I thought that was it, that he wouldn't find me.

But now, as I look around the forest, I realize two things. Firstly, he hasn't put a time limit on the game, so we're playing until he wins. Rookie mistake on my part. And secondly, what I at first thought was a large bird flying high in the sky ... is actually him.

He dives down while I stare up in complete shock. I saw his wings in the dungeon a few times, but it hadn't occurred to me that they actually worked. He's fast, like a bullet headed straight towards me.

I finally make myself move and run into the thickest part of the trees nearby, my dress getting caught on brambles and slowing my progress. I hear him land in the clearing by the well behind me, just a low thud that's totally at odds with the speed at which I saw him descending.

I peek around a tree, my heart in my throat. I'm shaking, terrified, but exhilarated too. It's like tag, but instead of a light tap if I'm caught, I'll be drilled with a giant demon cock instead. In fairness, I hadn't understood that he was allowed to demon-up before I agreed.

I strain to listen. I can't hear him, but that doesn't mean anything. For such a hulking form, he's surprisingly quiet now that he's hunting me on foot through the forest.

I'm hiding in a dense thicket, holding my breath and trying to figure out where he is. I hear something, a noise I can't quite make out, a thudding. It's low and constant, thump-thump, thump-thump, thump-thump. That can't be ... a *heart beating*, can it? Impossible!

It gets louder. If it's Krase, if it is his actual heartbeat that I can somehow hear, he's very close.

I keep still, adrenaline pumping through me as I hide behind a tree. A twig snaps no more than a few steps away. He's coming!

I push off the trunk and sprint, jumping over a log, following a vague animal trail while I try to stay away from the thorns and gnarls that keep slowing me down. I notice my hand is bleeding, and I errantly wonder if it has a scent he'll be able to track.

A figure is suddenly right in front of me, and I smack into his hard chest, looking up with fearful eyes. Krase's grin is languid, and his arm snakes around me, pulling me flush against him. He caresses my face and down my throat, pulls the neck of my dress out so he can see my heaving breasts. He groans and kisses me hard on the lips.

'Try again, little rabbit,' he breathes, letting me go. 'Last chance.'

I turn and stumble away, my lips tingling. I try to stay off the paths, dodging branches and splashing across a brook that's deeper than it looks.

I don't know how long this has been going on, but I'm tired, and my lungs are screaming. Cardio has never been my thing.

There's no sound behind me, but I don't dare look back. There's a structure ahead of me, a stone building. Maybe I can get back into the catacombs from there, and he won't be able to find me. I head for it. I'm almost there, but as I break through the tree line, I trip, going down hard on the remnants of a stone path. I stifle my cry and get up, my knees definitely skinned. I limp the rest of the way to the building, but it's just a shell, the roof open to the elements. There's no door or windows, just holes in the crumbling stone walls.

I make my way around the periphery first to see if there's any opening leading down, battling through tall weeds and wild rose bushes that scratch at me. A nature girl I am not, I decide.

I get to the doorway, hoping that there'll be somewhere to hide inside, but I realize quickly that there's nothing but more weeds and a stone slab that I suppose once served as a table. I turn to go, but a shadow looms over me, and I gasp as I'm grabbed around the waist and lifted off my feet.

'Got you.' He grins. 'No more chances. You lose, little fuck toy.'

I struggle in the incubus' grasp, kicking at him and throwing punches. He laughs and tosses me high into the air. I scream loudly, my body scrambling. He catches me, and I grip onto his massive forearms with all of my strength so he can't do it again.

But he doesn't. Instead, he puts me down, taking both my wrists in one hand and pulling them above my head, rendering me helpless.

'Krase—' I begin, but he doesn't give me the chance to say anything.

He takes hold of the neck of my dress and rips it down to my waist, displaying my bra-less tits to his eyes.

I let out a cry of outrage and fear ... *and anticipation*. A mortifying heat coils in my belly, a dirty little secret that I'm afraid he'll somehow sense.

Do I *like* this?

He casually fondles my breasts, plucking at my nipples and making a sound of appreciation deep in his chest when I try to twist away.

'I've been waiting for this ever since I smelled your sweet scent in the cell,' he rumbles. 'To think I would have killed you and never known ... Tell me, gràidh, have you been fucked by a demon before?'

I blink at him, still panting heavily from all the running and the shock of being caught. I shake my head a little, staring into his black eyes.

'Good,' he coos.

'Let her go, Krase.'

I look past Krase to see Iron step into the building.

'You can't do this,' he says, drawing his gun.

Krase laughs, turning me towards Iron so he can see my half-naked state.

'You could try to stop me, Iron. You won't be able to, though. Even with your firepower and newfound fae magick, you'll find you're no match for me at the moment. Or,' Krase picks me up, dangling me in front of Iron like a snack, 'you could join me, and we can make her sing with pleasure together.'

Iron doesn't speak. I watch his eyes move over me, pausing for a few moments at my bare breasts. He licks his lips slowly, not meeting my eyes. He's tempted. My gaze moves from him to Krase and finds him watching Iron, watching me.

'Thinking of how well she'll take your prick, brother?'

That snaps Iron out of it. 'No. Let her go.'

'Pity, but don't say I didn't warn you.'

Krase chuckles and snaps his fingers. Iron immediately turns transparent in front of my eyes, and I gasp, struggling anew.

'What have you done to him?' I cry.

I don't know why I care, but it's the same protective urge as I feel with the others. I need them to be safe as if they're something more to me than ... whatever it is they are.

Krase pulls me to his hard body with an impatient growl. 'He's safe, deamhan àlainn, just in a fold.'

His amused eyes return to Iron, who's pacing and glaring furiously back at him from wherever he is as he puts away his now useless weapon. The demon chuckles but then frowns when he sees that he hasn't alleviated my concern.

'Give her a wave,' he says to Iron, 'so she stops worrying I've hurt you.'

Iron shakes his head, still looking livid, but gives me a half-hearted wave, turning away and going to lean on the wall on the other side of the building.

Krase sets me down again but doesn't let me go.

'Could we ... do this another time?' I ask in a small voice.

'I told you I'd fuck you if I caught you, and you agreed,' he growls, caressing my cheek with the back of one massive knuckle. 'I won, and you're mine, Julia. Here and now, you're going to take my thick cock. You're going to scream for me while Iron watches and wishes it was him.'

He lets out a low growl and rips off what's left of my dress. I cringe before him, trying to hide, but he doesn't let me, kicking my legs apart and pushing one thick finger into me immediately. I squeal as I'm impaled, going up onto my toes as he enters me.

The sound of contentment he makes is like a purr, and it turns me boneless for some reason. I've been wanting this, craving it since he pounced on me in the wine cellar. I just didn't know what I wanted.

He holds me against his bare chest and lets go of my wrists as he picks me up and sits me on the cold, stone table.

'Stay.' He snarls the command as he steps back.

I want to do as he says, but then he unzips his pants, and my eyes widen as I take in the size of his cock. It's grey and hard, veiny and ridged, and thick as a soda can.

Before I know what I'm doing, I'm jumping off the table and making a run for it.

I hear him roar behind me, and I scream as he grabs me midstride. He picks me up, turns me to face him, and impales me on his cock without any more delay. I squeal, struggling as he pushes into me, not giving me any time to get used to his invasion as he fills me. I'm clawing at his shoulders and chest, whimpering and writhing.

'Please,' I cry, 'it hurts, Krase!'

He seems to come to his senses, his tight grip on me easing and his movements slowing.

'You're taking me so well,' he praises, and I calm down, letting myself relax. 'You were made for me. For this. Let me show you.'

He pulls me up and lets me fall onto him, using gravity against me. He drives in further, and I whimper.

'You feel just as good as I imagined,' he growls, his claws circling my waist as he moves me up and down on him. Every motion makes me whine and squirm, but the discomfort quickly morphs into pleasure.

My pained whimpers turn to moans, and, driven by a desperate need, I try to make him quicken his pace. A strange longing overtakes me, a primal urge, a deep desire to bite the demon in front of me and draw his blood into my mouth.

I resist, turning my face away so I don't do it.

'You see, Iron?' I hear him mutter. 'You thought I'd have to force her, but she knows what I am to her, don't you, lass.'

I mutter something incoherent, wanting more of him, that need to bite him intensifying, but I stop myself.

With a chuckle, he calls me insatiable, pulling me off his now glistening member. Hardly knowing what I'm doing, I mewl for him, afraid he's not going to continue.

But he hauls me over to the table and pushes me down forwards onto it. The stone surface digs into my sensitive nipples, and I feel him thrust into me from behind. He takes hold of my hair and pulls me upwards to arch my back, setting a harsh pace that makes my core clench as he drives my hips into the table.

'Harder,' I plead. 'Please, Krase.'

I still want to sink my teeth into him, but I can't now that he has me like this. In my periphery, I see Iron standing close to Krase, watching him fucking me, a look on his face that I can't discern in my present state.

Krase sees him as well, and he laughs, kicking my legs further apart. 'Look how her tight pussy stretches around me.'

He smacks me hard on the ass. 'Show him,' he commands.

When I don't immediately do as he says, he slows his thrusts. 'Do it, or I stop,' he threatens, and my hands practically fly to my cheeks, pulling myself apart so that Iron can see everything.

'Good,' he praises, and I close my eyes in ecstasy as I feel him pistoning into me, driving me higher, hitting all the sweet spots that make me shudder and moan.

'Please,' I beg brokenly, 'I can't take anymore.'

His pace quickens and my body tenses as I feel the beginnings of pleasure wrapping me up tightly. It takes me to a precipice so high I don't know what's going to happen when I fall. I teeter on it for a second before I come with a long scream that Krase doesn't try to muffle. In fact, I can suddenly feel his male pride at what he's done, where he's done it, how, and with whom. But my thoughts are jumbled. All I can do is ride the waves of sensation that he's drawing from my body, and I hear him roar loudly, heated bursts pulsing into me as he finds his own release, his rhythm becoming erratic.

As I lay boneless on the table, wetness sliding down my thighs, I begin to come back to myself. Pain radiates from my knees when I fell, my legs where they're digging into the table, my pussy where Krase is still fucking me at his leisure.

Tears leak from my eyes, not sure what just happened, why I wanted Krase so much, why I needed him like that, why my body still seems to want more. I don't want them to see me like this, but something else inside me revels in it. Who is this person? I'd never been with anyone before the Mountain. Survival was the most important thing. Isn't it still? Why do I want these demons to touch me? Hold me? Why do I crave them? Why do I care about them? They're supes. I know better. What the hell is wrong with me?

The feel of Krase's body leaving mine and the cold breeze dancing over my skin chills me. I shiver, confused and suddenly so alone. A hiccupping sob bubbles out of me. I clamp my mouth shut immediately.

But the damage is done.

'What's wrong with her?' I hear Krase ask.

He sounds more himself now. Guess he fed.

Conflicting emotions getting the better of me, I stay where I am, pushing away the connection I now have with Krase, wishing they'd forget about me so I can make my way back to the house through the catacombs and clean myself up before anyone else sees me.

'I told you not to do it,' Iron mutters angrily.

Krase has let him out of the fold.

I'm picked up and placed back on the table in a seated position.

I don't look at them, my eyes trained on the ground. I don't want to see me anymore, and I feel more tears tracking their way down my cheeks.

I try to stand, but my legs feel like Jello, and they collapse under me.

Iron takes my arm and tries to pick me up, but I slap his hands away.

'Let me help you,' he murmurs.

I ignore him, grabbing onto the table and pulling myself up. I make the mistake of glancing up. I see a hardness in Iron's eyes and, in Krase's, there's anger. I cower, looking at the ground again immediately, wrapping my arms around myself, trying to hide from their eyes and their judgments.

'Please, can you leave?' I whisper.

Iron turns away with a sigh, and I hear him hit Krase hard.

'Look what your selfishness has wrought,' he snarls.

'Enough!' Krase hisses. 'We can discuss this later. Go on ahead to the house. We'll meet you there.'

Iron does what Krase says, swearing loudly as he leaves.

When we're alone, Krase steps closer to me and tilts my chin up to look at my face.

'Mo chridhe, I can feel you here now, I think.' He presses his heart. 'And I ken your sadness, but I don't know the reason for it. Did I do something you didn't want?'

I shake my head because he didn't, but that's the problem. More tears well in my eyes.

Who am I? I thought I knew.

I'm gathered into his arms, and before I can react, we're airborne. I grip him tightly, shutting my eyes and pressing my face into his chest.

I don't want to go back to the house right now. The thought of the rest of them seeing me like this makes me feel sick. I can just imagine Maddox and Daemon's angry, supercilious faces, and who knows what Axel and Jayce are going to think when they find out I fucked Mr. Hyde when I just told them I couldn't be around them.

Why do I care what they think anyway? In a few weeks, I'll be gone from here.

But the thought doesn't make me feel better. It makes me feel worse.

We land on a balcony upstairs, and I count my blessings that he didn't decide to carry me over the threshold of the front door after ringing the bell to summon literally everyone.

He opens the door and carries me inside. He's brought me to my room. I shift in his arms, but he holds me fast, not letting me down.

'Are you still in here?' he calls.

Iron appears at my bathroom door and nods. 'All ready for her. I'll see you later,' he says to Krase in a tone that promises violence.

'Stay,' Krase mutters. 'I might need your help.'

I'm taken into the bathroom, and there's a steaming bath waiting for me. Krase checks the temperature with his hand, and then, with a kiss on my forehead that makes me frown, he lowers me into the tub gently. I hiss as the hot water makes everything sting for a moment.

'Is it too hot?' he asks.

I shake my head, drawing up and hugging my knees.

'Talk to me,' he murmurs as he gets the shampoo and begins to wash my hair.

'Why are you doing this?' I ask. 'You don't have to.'

'I want to,' he replies.

'And Mr. Hyde? What does he want?'

Krase snorts. 'He wants to fuck you again as soon as possible, but even he doesn't want to force you, Jules.' He sighs. 'He thought you'd enjoy the game. We both did.'

'I did enjoy it,' I whisper.

'Then what is it? Were we too rough?'

I shake my head and look up at him.

'I loved it,' I say so quietly that I don't think he's heard me.

But he answers.

'Then I don't understand. Why are you upset?' he asks in confusion.

'Because I loved it.'

His brow furrows, but he doesn't ask me anything else. He rinses my hair and conditions it. Then he washes my body, carefully getting the grit out of the scrapes on my knees. He helps me stand and wraps me in a warm, fluffy towel. Before we leave the bathroom, he insists on putting healing crème on my knees and all the other various scratches and scrapes.

Out in the main bedroom, Iron is sitting in a chair by the window.

His piercing gaze lands on me, and I freeze, wanting to go straight back into the bathroom, but Krase just picks me up and cradles me against him. He sits with me on the bed.

'Is she okay?' Iron murmurs.

I feel him nod. 'Just a little overwhelmed.'

I hide my face in Krase's chest as they continue the conversation like I'm not even there. Krase strokes my hair as he holds me.

'You shouldn't have done that,' Iron says. 'If Maddox learns—'

'So long as you keep your mouth shut, by the time he does, it'll be too late.' He snorts. 'You're just jealous because you weren't allowed to participate.'

'Too late? What does that mean?'

Krase's hands continue to absently caress me. 'Not here. You'll understand soon enough.'

'Jayce and Axel lost perspective once they'd had a taste of her. Has the same thing happened to you?' Iron asks warily.

A rumble of laughter goes through the demon holding me. 'I haven't had *perspective* in months.'

I peek up at them and find Krase looking at me with a reverence that I don't understand, but it makes me feel safe and cared for.

'She saved me,' he says, and my eyes widen. 'And so long as we have her, the dark part of me has agreed to let me hold the reins ... most of the time.'

Iron stands up. 'What does that mean, Krase? Are there two demons inside you, and the rogue one is kept in check by a lone human girl? Can you hear yourself? You sound insane!'

Now, Krase laughs loudly. 'I am!'

Iron swears and walks to the door. 'I won't tell Maddox about any of this, but you need to stay away from her for her sake, if not yours. She's a human girl. You're going to hurt her, Krase.'

'I'm not the demon in this room who hurt her.' Krase's tone is arctic, and I shiver in his arms. 'I heard from my brother what happened in the mountain, the things you did to her when you let that power go to your head.'

I tense at the reminder, and Krase's arms hold me a little tighter.

Iron doesn't say anything but leaves quietly, and Krase lets out a long sigh.

'They don't understand, but they will.'

I peer up at him. '*I* don't understand.'

He smiles at me. 'You will, too.'

Chapter Ten

DAEMON

'Will you stay with me?' she asks Krase.

'Would that please you?' he murmurs.

She nods her deceptive little head, and my eyes narrow from where I'm watching from the hole in the hidden door. That's three. Half of us are under her spell, and if Iron's constant doe eyes at her are anything to go by, it'll soon be four.

Are Maddox and I the only ones here who remember what she is, what she did to us, that we can't trust her?

'Then I'll stay for a little while, deamhan àlainn, so long as you lay in the bed and try to sleep.'

She nods again, looking so innocent.

'Give me the towel then. It's damp.'

Her practiced hesitation has me rolling my eyes but still staring at her to see if I can catch a glimpse of her creamy flesh.

I'm as pathetic as they are.

I make myself watch Krase take the towel into the bathroom

instead of ogling Jules, and when I look back at the bed, she's under the covers. He lies next to her, stroking her hair, and I just about vomit.

But I stand there and wait, and when the clock hits nine, he kisses her gently on the cheek and leaves the room. As soon as the main door closes, I open mine and slip into the room, silent as a ninja.

Jules is still in the bed, her breathing even. I creep to where she sleeps and look down at her serene face.

'What am I going to do about you, viper?' I whisper.

I could kill her the way Maddox should have the night he found her on the lawn, but a quick death seems too good for the likes of her. The bare bones of a plan begins to materialize in my head like a muse just whispered it in my ear.

Tamadrielle.

I don't know who that is, but I heard Jayce and Axel talking. She's scared of him, and I'd bet that's who she was hiding from in the Mountain, too. What would happen if he learned where she was at an opportune moment? He might well come and take her off our hands. I might even get a finder's fee, which will definitely come in handy as soon as my return from the Mountain is noted by some of my business associates.

I grin. I knew that listening in on that conversation would be worth my while. Now I just have to find this Tamadrielle and keep him as an ace up my sleeve until it's time to show my hand.

I finger the edge of her covers, remembering when Dante had me make her come all over my demon fingers at the dinner table. I've tried to forget her pleas, her cries, the way she moved, the way she felt when she climaxed around my flesh. The way she *tasted*. But I can't. It's seared into my mind, and I fucking hate it.

I lift the covers and peer at her naked body. It's nice, well-formed, passably pretty with good-sized tits, but that's all. There's nothing overtly special about her. And yet she has half of us scrambling after her like puppies. What is it about her? I stare until she shifts and draws herself into a ball, her brow furrowing in sleep. Then, I let the covers down and do what I came here to do.

I open her closet and close the door behind me, turning on the light. What I see has me rolling my eyes hard. So many designer dresses, but I know there haven't been any deliveries. These fools bought them for her before and had them saved for if she ever returned. I open a drawer and dump in the stuff I brought.

'It's not the same,' I mutter to myself.

I'm just sick of seeing her nipples poking out through the thin fabrics of all these gowns every other minute and knowing she doesn't have any panties on either. Why did none of those assholes even think to buy her any fucking underwear?

I turn off the light and leave the closet, going back to the passage and escaping through the tunnels. I decide to take a look at what the others are doing and creep through to the library. Maddox is the only one in there, though, sitting with a drink by the cold hearth and staring listlessly into it.

I move through to the Billiard Room and find that the others are all there. Axel and Krase are playing. The other two are spectating.

'But she's okay?' Axel asks.

Krase nods. 'Just ashamed by her reaction.'

Jayce shakes his head. 'You shouldn't play those games when you aren't sure how she's going to react, how *you're* going to react. The darkness in you ... we all see it, brother.'

'*This* darkness?'

Krase's eyes go black, his face twisting in amusement when everyone tenses. 'Don't worry,' he rasps. 'We've come to an understanding, Krase and I.'

'Which is?' Axel asks.

VENGEANCE AND VIPERS

'That Jules is mine, ours. The clan's. We aren't letting her go.'

'Maddox won't allow us to keep her,' Jayce says. 'He'll never trust her, not even enough to contract her as an on-call girl. She's gone as soon as we're in the clear. He won't change his mind. Even you can't stand against him.'

Axel nods. 'None of us can match a clan leader's strength. If he wants her gone, she's gone.'

Krase shrugs. 'We'll see.'

'What if she wants to go?' Iron asks.

Krase's eyes turn back to their normal blue. 'She doesn't,' he says, taking his shot. 'She only thinks she does. We need her to realize that she wants to be here with us.'

'How do you propose we do that?' Axel asks. 'She's stubborn ... and afraid of letting her guard down.'

'The Iron I's will be here by tomorrow. Maddox wants to meet with Alex and have Paris set up the security cameras to keep an eye on Jules at the same time. They'll be here for a few days.'

'So?' Jayce says.

Krase lands another ball in the corner pocket. 'So, they're bringing their female with them. Jane. Remember Jane?'

'Aye, I remember Jane.' Jayce gives him a knowing grin. 'You want us to use her to make Jules jealous?'

Krase laughs a little. 'No, I doubt we'll have to do anything at all. I just think it will be obvious to Jules that Maddox wanted Jane, and it will make her view the clan *differently*.'

'You think she'll care?' Jayce tuts. 'She'd never give Maddox the satisfaction of envying a female he was interested in, even if she did notice. Besides, Alex and the others won't let Jane out of their sights after what happened.'

'Do you mean when I tried to fuck her, and she beat the shit out of me, or when Maddox made her feed me for his help?'

Jayce puts his head in his hands and groans. 'You pick, but I was actually talking about when Maddox was this close,' he demonstrates with his thumb and forefinger, 'to slitting Korban's throat when we thought the rest of the Iron I's were dead so we could steal Jane out from under them.' He sits back in his chair. 'That's not something even Vicious will easily forget.'

I grit my teeth at the mention of my brother. Alex and I haven't been on the best of terms in a long time. Even less so now since I made him get me back into the clan before I'd help him get his girl back from our psycho father and his equally messed up clan, who were trying to brainwash her into being theirs.

I'd heard she wasn't in great shape by the time they killed those pieces of shit and got her out of there. Alex blames me for the extra time she was with them, and he's right to. I refused to help until I'd got what I wanted. But I needed to be back in Maddox's clan. I don't feel bad about it. If I hadn't made Alex help me, I'd be in a shallow grave somewhere, or worse by now.

I keep listening, wondering what I'm going to do, if anything, about this idea they have that Jules, a woman devoid of real feelings, could actually fall for them the way they all seem to have for her. It's sad.

Is Iron really on board with this? I stare at him, watching his expressions, the way he's standing slightly away from the others. He doesn't look like he's on board from where I'm standing. He *looks* like he's making sure he's in the loop, and that's it.

I can work with that.

I make my way back down the passage and let myself out via the main hallway panel right in front of a very surprised Tabitha.

Her gasp as I appear out of the passage is quickly replaced by a stern look.

I frown. 'What?'

'You don't remember me, do you, boy?'

'Should I?'

I smirk at her, wondering if we slept together. I mean, she's

VENGEANCE AND VIPERS

in her sixties and definitely not my type, but there were times over the past couple of years when I'd been hungry and desperate enough for feed from just about anyone.

Inwardly, I groan. I hope she doesn't know me from then. It's a time I'd rather forget.

She tilts her head. 'Maybe not. You were only a boy, maybe five.'

I take a step back. 'You knew me when I was a kid?'

She nods. 'Your mother and I were friends. You used to love sitting on my lap.'

I regard her, sifting through old memories, wondering if she's lying. 'Did I call you Tabby?' I ask finally, and she smiles.

'Yes, you did! I'd forgotten that. Your brothers were older, weren't they?'

I nod. 'Alex was fourteen. Andy was ten.'

She puts a hand on my arm. 'I'm sorry about your mom. It was terrible what happened. Your father was never the same.'

I scoff. 'Understatement of the year, *Tabby*. By the time I was seven, Mom was gone, and Dad and the others had had their memories wiped of their mate. After that, they didn't give a shit my mom was dead. They couldn't remember anything about her except what her name had been.'

I pull away, not wanting to talk about this anymore.

'I have to go,' I mutter, and she looks at me with the pitying expression I saw on so many faces when my mom was found murdered and my dad and his clan went nuts.

Filled with anger, I make my way down to the gym to beat the shit out of some pads alone, but the talk with Tabitha has long-forgotten memories surfacing, the times Alex and Andy would play with me even though they were older. But Andrew is dead now. Our father killed him on a fucking whim and then had him erased from his brain like he never existed, either. After that, Alex left and got his own clan together. He forgot about me. I went from having a real family to nothing until Maddox found me and gave me a new one where I felt like I actually belonged.

I can't lose my clan, not again.

JULES

I wake up the next morning feeling rested and pretty silly for yesterday's drama. I put my head under my pillow and groan. I'm so ridiculous.

I get out of bed and shower, surprised that all my cuts and scrapes from yesterday are healed over. That cream Krase used must be magick, I decide. But my down below feels fine too, and I figured after Krase's demon dicking down, I'd hardly be able to walk today.

I go into the closet and choose a dress from one of the hangers. This one is a plain purple chiffon, long with flowy little sleeves. I notice something sticking out of one of the drawers and slide it open to investigate. It's now full of expensive, lacy bras and matching underwear. Clothes have been appearing for days, so I'm not fazed. I choose a set that fits, of course, and get dressed, wondering what I should do today. My options are pretty limited, and I'm starting to get a little bored, which sounds nuts after Krase's little game yesterday, but I don't think I'm up for anything like that again so soon.

The first few days out of the dungeon weren't too bad. It was nice to have a little R&R after months of evading the other inmates, but it's been days of sitting around being waited on and reading in the library. I mean, I'm not complaining, but my brain is starting to get antsy. I need something to do to occupy it besides thoughts of primal sex and hot demons.

Truthfully, I've been thinking about what happened with Krase yesterday for hours, and I still don't know how I feel about it, only how I *should* feel as an uncontracted human being played with by demons, which is petrified. I am scared, but it has less to do with Krase and more to do with *falling for Krase* the way I did for Jayce and Axel.

That has me terrified and thinking I need to keep away from them all.

I leave my room and take the grand staircase down slowly, the little ballet flats I'm wearing making no sound as I make my way to the library. The door is closed, so I knock, but there's no answer. I go in, but he's not there. I let out a small huff. It's ten-thirty, so earlier than he's usually at his desk. I wonder what he does in the mornings.

Not feeling like sitting around with a book in the reading nook for once, I decide to go looking for him. It's earlyish, but Maddox has never struck me as the type who lolled around in bed until noon.

I try the Billiard Room, Gym, Reception Rooms, Ballroom, Drawing Room, and Parlor, but other than finding a ton of spaces that I'd enjoy passing some time in, there's no Maddox. None of the others are around, either.

I go by the kitchens and find Tabitha at the stove.

'Do you know where Maddox is?' I ask.

She turns with a smile. 'Morning, dear. He's usually out in the forest around this time.' She closes her eyes for a moment. 'Yes, where the spring feeds into the pond.'

'Do you know where the others are too?' I ask out of interest.

She smiles. 'Or course. Daemon and Axel are in their rooms, Iron is in the Sunroom, and Jayce and Krase are sparring out on the lawn.'

'Useful gift,' I mutter.

She laughs. 'It has its moments. Here.' She hands me two mugs of steaming coffee. 'Could you take the other to Maddox?'

'Sure,' I nod, happy to be useful to someone, even if it's only for a few minutes.

I look down at my in-doors outfit. I need some other clothes. I can't keep walking around like this now that the temperature is dropping.

I go to the side door from the kitchen that leads outside, putting on one of the long coats on the hook next to it. It dwarfs me, but at least I won't be cold.

Outside, I take the white gravel paths towards the wood past where Jayce and Krase are sparring on the lawn, and causing Jayce to get punched in the jaw when he turns to stare at me going past. I grimace, mouthing a sorry that no one can see and not breaking my stride.

It's hard to stay away from them even though I'm angry and I don't trust them. I don't even think I am angry anymore if I'm honest with myself. I'm just using it as an excuse to try to make it easier to keep my distance. But that is getting more difficult as the days pass. I thought I was imagining it, but this morning, it takes everything in me not to turn around and go back to Jayce just to be in his presence. Is this an incubus thing because we slept together? I feel the same way about Krase and Axel.

I stop in my tracks. Am I addicted the way on-call girls get?

I start walking again quickly. No, it doesn't feel like I'm craving a sexual fix; I feel like I need a cuddle. I just want a hug. Is that all it is?

Melancholy hits me so suddenly that it takes my breath away, and my pace falters. I scoff at myself. I'm being ridiculous. I went years without affection. I do fine without it. I clearly have too much time on my hands, and it's turning me into a drama queen.

I walk faster, wanting to speak to Maddox even more now. I enter the woods and head for the stream, remembering when I

VENGEANCE AND VIPERS

crossed it yesterday during the game. My stomach flips when I recall the chase, and I try to put that out of my mind, too.

I find the brook and follow it, reaching the pond a few minutes later, but there's no one there. I sigh and take a long sip of my coffee. As I do, I see a ripple in the surface of the water.

I take a step back into the trees, almost without realizing it. None of them have told me to be careful of anything dangerous on the grounds, but that's just the sort of thing supes forget to mention around humans, and I've been in enough magickal places to know that there are some very nasty creatures in their sanctums.

But what breaks the surface isn't a monster; it's Maddox! My mouth drops open as he wades to the shore naked, trying and failing not to take in the contours of his body. I mean, I knew he was built under all those suits he wears, but holy shit! Knowing something and seeing it with your own two eyes is very different when it comes to Julian Maddox.

I swallow because I feel like I'm drooling all over myself. I watch as he dries himself off and throws on some low-slung jeans that somehow accentuate his abs, the tattoos all over his arms and chest.

I step back onto a stick that snaps under my shoe, and I recoil.

'Who's there?' he calls, his eyes trained on where I am.

I come out of the trees, pretending I've been walking towards him the whole time and not standing there watching like some kind of inanimate pervert.

'Tabitha asked me to bring you this,' I say a little breathlessly, handing him the cup.

He takes it, and I forget to be careful. His fingers brush against mine, and desire slams through me with the force of a meteor striking the earth. I don't know how my knees don't buckle or how I keep myself from jumping on him and begging him to fuck any way he wants. The dirtier, the better.

I mean, I don't even know what *dirty* sex even entails, but I want it from him. Now! Something flares in his eyes, a fire of lust, and one of his hands reaches out toward me. It's so close.

No!

I turn away, tears in my eyes because it feels like my entire being is crying out for him, and denying myself this is actually making my body hurt. My cup shakes in my hand, and I grip it with both to steady it.

'Are you all right?' he asks, but his tone is imperious and flat.

He's clearly not feeling the same earth-shattering impulses that I am.

Did I imagine that look in his eyes? Did I just want it to be there?

The thought of my need for him being one-sided is enough to dampen my intense feelings enough that I can turn with a polite smile and a suitable response.

'Of course,' I say.

He glances at the trees where I emerged only seconds ago.

'Were you watching me?'

'No, I—'

I break off, my focus on his tattoo. It's large, taking up his entire torso. In the middle of his chest is a woman with long hair. No, not a woman, a demon with sharp, little horns protruding from the top of her head. I stare at it. Is that face meant to be mine?

My eyes flick to his and back to the artwork on his skin. It looks like me ... if I was a demon. I'm not imagining it. He has a tattoo of my face on his body. What does that mean?

'Like what you see, Julia?' He sounds bored but amused.

I feel my cheeks heat even more than they already are.

'I'm sorry,' I say. 'I just – nice tattoo,' I finish lamely.

He looks down at it.

'Thank you,' he says. 'I got it a few months ago.' He turns away, giving me no explanation.

Surely he knows ...

'Who is she?' I ask.

'Who?' he asks, taking a sip of his coffee.

'The demon in your tattoo.'

He shrugs. 'No one in particular.'

I frown at him. I don't think he's lying. Doesn't he know? Can he not see it?'

'Did you design it yourself?'

He arches a brow. 'Did you really traipse all the way out here to give me a lukewarm cup of coffee and interrogate me about my body art?'

I blink. Why is he changing the subject?

'No,' I say, deciding to let this go for now because he doesn't seem to realize it. 'I was trying to find you to ask you something.'

'All right.' He looks at his watch. 'I have a call in five minutes. Make it quick.'

He picks up a black tee shirt and throws it on, covering the markings I can't stop staring at.

'Come on, Julia,' he says with a roll of his eyes. 'I have better things to do than let you ogle me all day.'

I scowl. 'As if,' I say sweetly.

'Four minutes,' he says with a smirk and starts walking off through the woods.

I hurry after him. 'Maddox, wait.'

'No, no time.'

He keeps going, and I literally have to jog to keep pace.

'I need to talk to you. You're going too fast.'

He stops so abruptly that I run into him. He turns with an exasperated look on his face.

'What is it, Julia? We can't all just swan around. Some of us have work to do.'

'I'm bored!' I practically yell.

He stops as if that wasn't what he was expecting me to say at all.

'Bored?'

I nod. 'Is there something I could do? Like to earn my keep or something?'

'Like what,' he asks suspiciously.

I shrug. 'Anything. Filing or helping you with admin?'

'As if I'd let you anywhere near our businesses, woman!' he laughs, and I try not to let his opinions regarding my character get to me.

'Helping Tabitha then. I don't care what it is, Julian, but I need something to do. I'm not used to just sitting around.'

'You're serious.'

'Yes, I'm serious.' I give him a look. 'I wouldn't have come to you otherwise.'

His phone rings. He digs it out of the back pocket of his jeans and regards me for a moment. Then, he silences it.

'They'll call back,' he mutters.

He starts walking again, slower now, so I can keep up.

'I might have something,' he says. 'Ever planned an event before?'

I shake my head. 'No, but I can do it. Just let me know what you need.'

'All right,' he acquiesces. 'We're having a masked ball on All-Hallows Eve. I don't have time to sort the details past the guest list. I was going to ask Iron since he's my second, but, really, he's no good with that sort of thing. We'd probably end up with no Champagne or a Yank country music band for music.'

He actually shudders at his own words as if that would be the worst thing to happen at this party.

But I nod. 'I can do it, Julian.'

'It's important,' he says. 'High-level supes. Council types. It marks our success at putting our 'lawlessness' behind us. The formal announcements of our pardons will be made that night.'

My stomach lurches. 'So, after the ball—'

'After the ball,' he interrupts, 'there won't be any reason to keep you here. You'll be free to go as promised.'

'Four weeks then.'

'Four weeks,' he agrees.

I nod and plaster a fake smile on my face, though, for some reason, I don't feel even remotely happy. Don't I want to go? Of course, I do; I just don't have a plan yet, that's all. Now that I know when I'm leaving, I can come up with one, and I won't feel so adrift.

We walk out of the woods and back onto the main path.

'I won't let you down,' I say.

'Good. I'll give you all the details in the library later, and you can get started. And, Julia?' His phone rings again, and he looks at it. 'The rules still stand if you want your money.'

I nod, looking away so he can't see what I'm really feeling.

What am I really feeling?

He answers the phone.

'Maddox,' he says, walking away from me.

I stare after him for a minute, sighing heavily as I try to make sense of why I feel sad when I got what I wanted ... and why Julian Maddox has a tattoo of a face on his chest that he doesn't seem to realize looks exactly like me.

Maybe I was imagi— No, it was there, and the similarity to me was uncanny. I need to stop second-guessing myself all the time. That is *not* the way I've survived.

I start walking back to the house at a brisk pace. I notice the lawn is deserted. Guess the twins have gone inside.

I go back in the house the same way, via the kitchen, to leave my now empty mug in the sink.

I go past the gym and hear the thudding of someone working out. The doors open, and I glimpse a shirtless Daemon glistening with sweat. He's hitting the pads with a fervor that makes me think he's imagining beating the crap out of someone he hates.

'Probably me,' I mutter to myself to lighten my somber mood, but it doesn't feel funny anymore.

I hear him pause and hurry away in case he saw me, going to the library. I push the half-open door, finding it empty. Guess Maddox is taking his call elsewhere.

I go to the shelves and choose a book at random, deciding to sit out in the open in one of the chairs in front of Maddox's desk for once.

I've only just started reading when there's a flash, and a dull roar sounds from my right.

I glance up to find the library door is now a glowing portal.

I scramble up in surprise, not knowing what to do.

A figure comes out of the light. He's huge and broad, and his face is scarred.

They've found me! They've come for me!

I back up, looking this way and that for an escape route. Belatedly, I remember the windows behind me. Half of them are doors! I curse my dumbass self and run to one of them. I pull at it, but it's locked, and the key's gone. I look down the row at the others. None have keys.

I turn around, pressing myself into the window. There are three men now. Demons. Incubi.

They work for him. They have to! Who else would just be able to portal in here?

My mind flashes back to his cruel face, the way he always looked bored when he told his men to hurt me and maim me ...

I clench my eyes shut and feel myself sliding to the floor, curling into a ball.

I'm suddenly in someone's arms, and I immediately know it's Axel. I can feel his concern, his protectiveness when he touches me, and I grip him hard. I'm making noises, I realize, whimpering like a tiny, scared animal. I bite my lip to stop.

I'm picked up and cradled against Axel's chest.

'What the hell?' he growls. 'Maddox said you were coming,

but some fucking warning might have been nice. Pick up the fucking phone next time.'

'I spoke to Maddox earlier,' says an authoritative voice that sounds familiar. 'He knew what time we'd be here.'

'Well, why'd you send Sie through first? You just about scared our human to death!'

Axel knows these guys. I tap his shoulder for him to let me down, feeling like an idiot, but he doesn't release me.

'I'm sorry,' I mutter. 'I'm fine.'

He holds me closer. 'It's okay, but I'm not letting you go.'

'I'll let Maddox know you're here,' Axel says, still sounding pissed.

I'm carried out of the library through the main door, tensing as we pass through it because it was a portal thirty seconds ago. But we go through into the hallway without incident.

'Don't worry, the bridge is closed,' Axel mutters. 'They used a link key. They don't stay open long.'

I nod. 'You can put me down now.'

He releases me.

I cringe as I look up at him, more than a little mortified.

'I-I'm sorry. I don't know what came over me. I just saw them come through, and I ... I didn't know who they—'

'Hey, hey. It's okay,' he says, cupping my face. 'Sweetheart, you have nothing to apologize for. Nothing.'

I stare up into his eyes and him down into mine, and, for a second, we're connected in this fundamental way. I let out a small sigh, feeling properly at peace for the first time since I got here, and I know he feels it, too.

'The connection we have is different than it was before,' he murmurs. 'I know you feel it too, and I know you think you have to stay away from us, but I don't think that's going to work, not now that we're ... whatever we are.'

I want to give in. I want to so badly.
But I can't.

'You left me in the Mountain,' I say to make him go.

I watch him flinch, but I press on.

'Siggy *died* trying to save me, and then I got here, and I was put in the dungeon. And you never came!'

My voice breaks. I realize that while I may not be angry anymore, I'm still very hurt.

'I'm sorry about the Mountain. We had no idea Maddox would go so far. We thought we'd convinced him to bring you with us.' He clutches me, pulling me to him and holding me tight.

'I'm sorry about Siggy,' he murmurs. 'So sorry, Jules.'

He gives it a moment, and I hug him back tightly, trying not to cry about her again.

When I pull away a little, he speaks again. 'And I'm sorry you were here, and we didn't know it.'

He grimaces. 'After Maddox drugged us, we couldn't feel you at all, not until we saw you in Krase's room and,' he rubs his chest, 'it's muted even now. Frail. We really did think you were still in the Mountain. We were desperately trying to get back there to get you out. Please believe me.'

I stare into his eyes. Is this a trick? I feel his emotions a little, and I don't think he could fake them. But I pull out of his arms and turn away anyway. What if Maddox is right and what they do feel about me isn't real?

'Maddox thinks I've caught you in some love spell or something,' I say, not looking at him, 'and I don't ...'

I think back to some of the times I've touched these demons, and they've got this *look* in their eye like I am doing something to them.

'Not wanting to be around you ... it's not about the money ... I mean, it is because I need it, Axel, but I'm also starting to think I *am* doing something,' I finish in a whisper. 'I'm sorry. If I am, I don't mean to be. But I can't be around you.'

My chin quivers. Even saying the words is hard. I turn away, but he pulls me back like we're in an old movie.

'I don't give a shit what anyone thinks. I love you! It's real, not some trick.' He sighs heavily. 'What if Maddox didn't find out?'

'You can't love me,' I argue with a shake of my head. 'I'm leaving.'

He freezes. 'When?'

'After the ball at All-Hallows,' I say miserably.

'That's a month away, Jules.'

'What about after that?' I ask in a harsh whisper. 'This is already so hard. What happens when Maddox kicks me out, and we can't ever see each other again? I can't be yours.'

'You're wrong,' Axel says, forcing my face up to his. 'You're already ours.'

Chapter Eleven

AXEL

I kiss her hard, the way I've been wanting to for days. She fights me at first, scared Maddox will somehow know, but I feel it when she gives up, when her curves melt into me. I press the wall blindly. There's a reason I stopped here. I feel the tiny button under the wooden panel, and the wall slides back almost silently. I pick her up, my lips not leaving hers, not giving her a moment to re-think this.

I know most of these passages like the back of my hand, so most of my attention is on the woman in my arms. It feels so right. It makes me realize how *wrong* everything's felt since we got back from the Mountain without her with us.

Jules is a part of this clan, and I don't think it's just me, Jayce, and Krase who think so, either. Whether the others want to admit it or not, this female is ours. Maddox can try sending her away, but it won't take. I know it won't. But Maddox's arrogance will cause her pain, and we can't allow that. Jules has already had more than her fair share where we're concerned.

She's clearly still suffering the effects of her experiences in the Mountain, and we need to start helping her.

I climb the steps in the dark, skipping the one that I know creaks, and take the left fork. It's only a minute or so later that we come out in Jayce's room. There are canvases everywhere, most half-finished because my clan mate has been in a manic frenzy that I'm pretty sure only one person can assuage.

'Get out,' I hear him mutter from the small, secret anteroom where he does his painting.

I tear my lips from a much more relaxed Jules. Her eyes are closed, and her breathing is even. It's almost like she's under a spell or hypnotized. I put her on Jayce's bed, but when I attempt to leave her, she pulls me back.

Fuck, she's strong.

'I said, 'Fuck off!' Jayce calls angrily but comes out a few minutes later when I don't leave, dressed in nothing but some low-slung jeans and no shirt.

He freezes in his tracks, and Jules' half-shut eyes widen a little as she takes him in. Her tiny gasp has him across the room and on the bed next to her in less than half a second.

'You shouldn't be here,' he says a little bitterly.

Her choosing the money Maddox offered over us has rankled, though I've tried to explain that there are things she hasn't told us. Maybe she's in debt with the human mob or needs to help a sick relative. I just don't believe it's that she's obsessed with buying shoes or something. Maybe I did think that once, but not now. I know her, and it doesn't make any sense.

She looks at me. 'How did you do that?' she breathes.

'I didn't do anything, baby girl,' I murmur low.

'I shouldn't be here. I can't be here!'

She tries to slide off the bed, but I take her arm to stop her.

'Will Maddox know she's here?'

Jayce, who hasn't taken his eyes off her, shakes his head. 'Not unless he saw you walk in the door. There are conjures all over this room. No sound, no scents, nothing gets out. He'll be none the wiser so long as we shower the scents off after.'

'After what?' she whispers.

He lets out a feral snarl as he rolls on top of her, pinning her to the mattress. 'Fucking guess.'

'We can't,' she whispers, but she's nowhere near as adamant as she was before.

'We need to feed,' I murmur in her ear. 'You wouldn't let us go hungry, would you, princess?'

'What do you need me for?' she asks a little petulantly. 'We aren't in the Mountain anymore. Maddox already mentioned he was planning a club visit soon for some snack time.'

Jealousy is thick in her tone, and I love it, but I also want to banish it forever. She's not as confident as she pretends. I need to remember that.

'They aren't you,' I growl in her ear. 'I never want to feed from any female except you ever again.'

'Aye,' Jayce mutters, his hands running up her sides and behind her neck to unzip her dress.

I wait with bated breath, a little frustrated because I'd just rip the damn thing off her. Then I grin. This one is one of the outfits *he* bought for her. He wouldn't be so careful otherwise.

He peels it away, and I watch as her body comes into view, inch by tantalizing inch. The lingerie she's wearing is black and laced and sinful, speaking of a much more experienced woman than I know her to be.

I swallow hard as I take her in, and she makes an impatient noise that makes Jayce grin.

'What is it that you want?' he asks, playing with her.

'You,' she breathes. 'Both of you.'

'What do you want us to do?' Jayce breathes.

'Say the words,' I murmur from her other side.

'I want you both to … fuck me.'

Her cheeks pinken at her admission.

'One here.' Jayce pushes at her pussy entrance.

'And one here,' I finish, delving under her panties and pushing at that other orifice that I know no one's touched when she bucks away from my exploratory probe.

'You've had other firsts with her,' Jayce growls. 'This one's mine.'

He ignores the small shake of her head as he leans over to rifle through a drawer, straightening a moment later with a black velvet bag. He opens it, showing Jules a small, golden plug with a red jewel in the end.

He winks at her. 'Never been used, don't worry.'

Jules' eyes widen, and, again, she shakes her head, but she can't hide from us. I feel her muted spike of lust.

'She doesn't seem to want it,' I say to Jayce with a playful smile.

'She'll take it anyway,' he snarls. 'But I'll be a gentleman, lass, not put it in *unprepared*.'

He wraps his lips around it, wetting it, warming it.

She squirms, pulling away and sitting up. She tries to move around me to get off the bed and flee, but I grab her before she can.

I tut at her. 'We can have a chase next time,' I promise, 'as you seemed to enjoy your games with Krase yesterday. But today, you lay in this bed and take what we give you like a good girl who knows her place.'

I punctuate my words with a sharp slap against her inner thigh.

Her sharp intake of breath precedes her suddenly heightened arousal at my words, and I close my eyes as her energy sates me.

But I'm by no means full. I can take much more, and I will.

I grin at Jayce.

'Naughty girls get spankings,' I say.

Jayce's door opens, and I tense. Jules does, too, but Jayce doesn't even look up from the bed.

'Just Krase,' he says.

His brother enters the room and closes the door quietly.

'I thought our female was in need, but I see you both have her in hand,' he says, eyes moving over an increasingly excited Jules.

'Look, naughty girl, Krase has come to spank that pretty ass before Jayce fucks it. Do you want to be put over his knee?'

She shakes her head adamantly, not looking away from Krase.

'Then be good.'

I haul her back towards us by her legs, widening them as I bring her closer. Jayce tears the flimsy panties away, and I look my fill of her pretty pink holes as he opens her outer lips for us.

'No lasting effects from yesterday,' he remarks, easing two fingers into her cunt.

I see Krase crane his neck and then settle against the wall to spectate.

'You're welcome to participate,' Jayce tells him as he takes the plug out of his mouth and lines it up with her ass, probing gently.

'You know I like to watch,' Krase answers easily, not moving from his vantage point.

'No, don't tense up. Breathe out and relax,' Jayce admonishes Jules, and I see her try to do as he says.

'Such a good girl,' I murmur as he pushes, and the plug begins to disappear.

'You're taking it so well, lass,' Jayce murmurs, thrusting his fingers in and out of her pussy.

She wriggles a little, and I slap her mound just as Jayce pops the rest of the plug into her. She whimpers, her body tensing around it, testing it.

Jayce continues his lazy movements with his fingers, and I let go of her legs, moving up her body.

'What do you think?' I ask her.

'I don't know,' she whispers back.

'If you don't like it, we'll stop, okay?'

She nods, and I smile, kissing her. Her tongue intertwines with mine, insistent and excited. I groan into her mouth, kneading her tits through her lacy bra.

'This needs to come off,' I grumble, demoning up to cut the cups apart with one sharp claw.

Her eyes open wide, and she takes in my dark mauve skin, the silver tattoos along my chest and arms.

'You're beautiful,' she breathes, and I preen at her words.

'Do you want to be ravaged by a beast?' I ask.

She doesn't reply, but another crest of energy from her is more than enough of a response.

I groan. 'Your wish is my command.'

I sink down next to her on my back and pull her over me, her knees wide on either side of my body. I yank her down as I raise my hips, forcing my hard, purple cock into her and making sure she takes every hot inch of me.

I haul her down to me and take her nipple in my mouth, biting it and pulling it. A cry followed by another wave of lust has me rutting my female hard. I lick her smarting nipple before I let it go, so I can watch her tits bounce as I fuck her.

I notice that Krase has moved closer so he can better see what's going on, and I can feel Jayce moving the plug around, stretching her ass.

I know when he pulls it out because I see her jolt and sit up. She turns her head to look over her shoulder at him, concern in her eyes, but he hushes her.

'Human form for the first time, mo chridhe, and I'll be gentle.'

He pushes her forward and eases in carefully. I cease my

movements, holding her over my cock. Jayce pulls her down a little so that both of us are just inside her.

'Breathe,' he says in her ear, and we lower her slowly, letting gravity do most of the work. It's slow and arduous, and I ache to seat myself fully in her hot, wet heat. But, despite her enjoying it rough, we'd like her to want this again, and that means taking it at a leisurely pace for our inexperienced mate's pleasure. Although I want to go faster, I find watching her face as we take our time more than makes up for the wait.

This is how it should have been that first time in the Mountain, I realize. Instead, I was brutal and uncaring with her in my anger. I will carry that regret to my grave, but here and now, with this other first, we can do it properly.

JULES

I feel so full that I can't imagine there can be much more, but as I look down, my arms braced on Axel's, his hands around my waist, I see that they're not even halfway.

'It's too much,' I whimper.

'It's not,' Krase says. 'You can take them, gràidh. You were made to take them.'

I ignore his cryptic words as I'm lowered another inch, and the air is driven from my lungs. Krase drifts closer, his eyes not moving from the illicit scene in front of him as he sits on the edge of the bed.

'You won't tell Maddo—' I begin.

'If you're still able to overthink this much, Axel and Jayce aren't attending to their task very well, are they?' he chuckles.

'Their task?'

'Aye, turning our female into a boneless, thoroughly pleasured heap.'

'We're attending to her just fine,' Axel snarls without malice just as Jayce pulls out and thrusts back in with a growl.

Axel does the same, and they settle into an alternating rhythm, each going in a little further every time and making me whimper with pleasure.

'Shall I help?' Krase murmurs, sliding closer.

I glance down at Axel, wondering if he'll mind, but he just smiles indulgently at me. I can't help my nod at Krase's offer, and he eases closer.

He shows me two of his fingers, and he licks them slowly, putting them in his mouth before trailing them down my stomach to where his brother and friend are stretching my holes.

He puts them directly on my clit, and I let out a breath, assuming he's going to start moving them in circles or something. But he doesn't. Instead, his fingers start to vibrate!

I jump, gasping as the two cocks in me slide a little deeper.

'How?' I manage to cry practically incoherently.

'Incubi,' he hisses, and the tempo of his fingers increases. 'Don't you dare come until I tell you!'

I close my eyes, moaning loudly, throwing back my head, my hips undulating without my say-so, forcing Axel and Jayce even further into me, but I don't care. Any discomfort is gone, and in its place is pure, unadulterated pleasure.

I pull Axel's hands from my waist with a snarl and sink down hard the rest of the way onto them, taking them both completely. I vaguely hear their sounds of pleasure, but I'm already rising, only to let gravity impale me again.

One of them growls, maybe both of them do, but I'm taken in their hard grips as they both come to their senses and begin to move the way I want them to. There's no more alternating. Both of their thick lengths are driven into me and out. The torture is exquisite.

'I need to come,' I gasp. 'Please!'

Krase says nothing, and I open my eyes to look at him, silently begging him as I begin to crest and vaguely wonder what his punishment will be if I can't stop it.

He says nothing.

'Please!' I cry as I go higher and try to wriggle away from his fingers. He doesn't let me, the glint in his eye telling me that he wants me to come without his permission so he can do whatever dark deed he's imagining.

So I do.

I let the pressure that's been building up bubble over, screaming as my whole body explodes into sensation like thousands of tiny dildos are fucking each and every nerve. My muscles lock up, and my rigid form is held tight. I hear Axel and Jayce come at the same time, my name on their lips, and I'm filled with contentment so deep it's in the very fiber of my being.

Jayce kisses my neck as he slides out of me, and I feel him climb off the bed to go into the bathroom. I hear him turn on the shower.

'Jules?' Axel asks, sounding concerned.

I open my eyes but can't see. I realize I'm crying.

'What's wrong?' he asks, cupping my cheek. 'Was it too much?'

'No,' I hiccup, 'and yes. I'm sorry. It's just—' I put my hand over my heart. 'It's just—'

The connections between me and Jayce and Axel have exploded into life again. I can feel them strongly again, just as I could in the Mountain, and it's suddenly overwhelming. I feel Krase lift me off Axel and cuddle to me to him.

'I know, mo chridhe,' he says. 'I know.'

I cry into his chest. He holds me until I quiet and my tears dry. I know the others are hovering, and I can feel their concern, but Krase is reassuringly calm.

'You were alone for a long time,' he murmurs. 'But you aren't any longer, Jules.'

He stands, taking me across the room. My eyes are still closed, but I feel the humid warmth and know he's brought me into the bathroom. He takes me into a huge walk-in shower and puts me under the water.

'Almost time for your reckoning,' he grates out, and I tense, peeking up at him through the spray. 'Will you take your punishment well, or do I need to subdue you?'

He gestures to something behind me, and I blanch as I see restraints coming out of the stone tiles.

'I'll be good,' I squeak.

He snorts. 'We'll see.'

He pours some soap into his hand and begins to wash me. I stand docilely, feeling his calloused hands moving over me, making my nipples pebble under them. He kneels before me and unhurriedly washes my toes, feet, and legs. When he gets to the apex of my thighs, he rises and, without further ado, turns me and bends me over a bench.

I expect him to do something similar to what Axel and Jayce just did in the bedroom, but instead, I'm told to stay still.

I jump as cold water sprays my pussy.

'Spread your legs,' he orders.

I do as Krase says, letting him do what he wants just as I told him I would. After a few moments, the temperature changes. It gets hotter, and I moan as he concentrates it on my clit, warming it up. I come without warning, rising on my toes as a relaxing climax takes me. I moan, collapsing onto the bench. Krase's fingers squelch in and out of *both* channels that were just so thoroughly ravaged by Jayce and Axel, but it doesn't hurt.

He's making sure he cleans me completely, I realize, so Maddox won't find out.

I feel a pang of guilt at deceiving him, but I couldn't go any longer not being near them. It was literally physically painful for me, and I think it was for them, too.

I try not to wonder again what's going on, how I'm going to leave here after All Hallows, how long this addiction or whatever it is will take to wear off, and how bad I'm going to feel while I'm kicking the incubus habit.

I also hope that Axel didn't mean what he said earlier, or at least will realize once I'm gone that he doesn't really love me.

'Good girl,' Krase murmurs, pulling me out of my thoughts.

He hauls me up to standing, only to push me down to my knees in front of him.

He looks down his nose at me.

'Have you ever sucked a cock before?' he asks.

I shake my head.

'Then it's time to learn, deamhan àlainn,' he murmurs. 'I'm going to enjoy teaching you how to please me.'

I eye his dick. 'In this form?' I ask just to make sure we aren't starting with the high board.

He laughs. 'For now. We'll work up to my demon cock, eh? Take it in your hand.'

I do as he says, feeling how silky soft his dick is and lowkey wondering if he moisturizes it. I move my hand up and down the length of it, squeezing a little, and his rumble of pleasure has me doing it a little harder, my confidence growing.

'You're a minx,' he says, caressing my wet hair. 'You'll be the death of me. Put it between your lips. I want to feel that pretty mouth on me, lass.'

I bring it closer and hesitate before I draw my tongue over the tip. His groan has my eyes flying to his as I do it again, watching his reaction, and I can't help my small smile. There's power in this, I realize. And I like it.

I open my mouth and take in as much of him as I can, gagging a little as he reaches the back of my tongue. I suck a little, my cheeks hollowing, and I move my head in and out to see what he thinks of that.

His hands curl into fists as I work him with my mouth. I think he likes it, but he doesn't move to touch me.

'Faster,' he breathes, and I do as he asks, sucking harder and trying to take him deeper.

His hips buck a little as I watch him and his hands plaster themselves onto the tiles behind me. I hear him muttering in Scots Gaelic, and though I don't know what he's saying, I can feel the sentiments behind the words. This isn't just sex or the need to feed. He cares for me deeply.

The realization has me going faster and deeper, sucking him harder. I want to give him the pleasure he gave me. I need to.

He tells me he's coming and pulls out of my mouth at the last second, groaning a curse with his eyes closed. He comes on my face and chest as I kneel before him, and I cringe a bit, not sure how I feel about it because isn't that meant to be humiliating?

My eyes don't leave him, and I watch as his eyes open, and his relaxed expression morphs into one of intense satisfaction as he takes in my painted body.

'Don't move,' he mutters. 'I want to sear the sight of you on your knees before me, covered in my come, into my mind forever.'

His eyes move over me, seeming to do just that before he takes my hand and pulls me up, where he proceeds to wash me all over again.

When he brings me out of the bathroom, Axel and Jayce are still lounging on the bed. Jayce immediately comes over, but Krase whisks me away.

'Don't taint her scent,' he warns. 'I've already washed her twice.'

'Aye, I'll be careful,' Jayce says and gives me a chaste kiss on the lips as he hands me the dress he took off me.

Axel kisses me as well, then cups my cheek in his hand.

'You're amazing,' he says, and I look away, my cheeks heating, not sure what to say back.

I thought that they'd betrayed me, that everything that happened in the Mountain between us was a lie. It was easier to believe that than the alternative, that they really did ... *do* care about me. It makes something deep inside me settle even as I worry what this means for them and for me.

Krase puts me down long enough to slip my dress back on sans my expensive underwear that didn't survive the incubi sausage fest. He picks me up again immediately to take me back through the passages, but it doesn't really bother me. I'm sort of starting to like them holding me as much as possible. When we emerge back into the corridor near the kitchen, he doesn't put me down right away as if he wants to keep me close for as long as he can.

'Axel was right, you know. You are amazing.'

I chuckle this time. 'You're only saying that because I sucked your dick in the shower.'

He grins back. 'Well, not *only* because of that.'

I hear a noise from down the hall, and I step away from him like a teen caught kissing their boyfriend at a school dance.

He sighs. 'You don't have to do that.'

I look down. 'I do have to do that,' I say. 'Maddox already thinks I'm like the worst person ever. What would he say if he found out what I've been doing with half his clan when he told me the rules? I made a deal with him, Krase.'

'If he knew, he would never have forced something so cruel upon you,' he mutters vehemently and seemingly to himself.

'Knew what?' I ask.

He turns away. 'Nothing. We'll sort it, Jules, I promise.'

My lips press into a line because that's bull. I know it, and he knows it. We just know it for different reasons. I hope he never finds out mine.

I force a smile. 'Yeah, we'll sort it.'

He takes my hand and squeezes it. 'The Iron I's are here. They will be for a couple of days while Paris, their tech guy, ramps up our non-magick security.'

'The ones who showed up in the library?'

He grunts. 'Aye. Don't be alone with the big one, the blonde one, or the shaggy-haired one with the beard if you can help it.'

'Why not?' I ask.

He doesn't really answer; he just mutters something about revenge as he walks off, leaving me in the hall feeling confused. I heave a sigh, even though I'd be in mega trouble in more ways than one if Maddox found out about this, and I'm feeling guilty as hell. I'm also a lot calmer than I was earlier and more energized.

With a pep in my step, I go to the library, pausing when I hear voices within. I don't mean to listen, but something makes me pause. They're talking about the fae.

I strain to hear.

'What are you doing?' asks a feminine voice, and I jump, muffling a yelp by clapping my hand hard over my mouth.

'Holy shit, you scared the hell out of me,' I whisper, putting my hand over my heart.

She grimaces. 'Sorry. It's not like I care if you're listening outside the door, but Alex's brother is just behind me, making sure I don't take a wrong turn to the bathroom or something.' She sighs, her eyes moving around, not staying on me for long. 'It was bad enough getting my guys to let me go alone, and then *he* started keeping tabs on me. I mean, I know I broke a Ming vase last time, but that was really not my fault. I should be allowed to pee alone.'

'Daemon, you mean?' I ask after a moment of sifting through her diatribe.

'Daemon The Dick,' she nods. 'I'm Jane.'

'Jules,' I say, stifling a laugh at the apt nickname she's given him.

'Are you an on-call girl?' she asks, and I tilt my head at her, sort of liking her directness.

'Not exactly. More like a loathed houseguest,' I answer.

'What the hell are you doing out here?' snarls a voice I know all too well.

I shy away from his tone, but Jane just wrinkles her nose at him.

'I was going to the bathroom,' Jane says like he's the dumbest guy in the world. 'You legit just followed me there.'

He rolls his eyes. 'I was talking to Jules.'

'Well, *she* was talking to *me*,' Jane says, giving him a what-the-fuck look that I swear makes his eye twitch, and I have to force myself not to laugh.

'Want to take a walk?' she asks.

'Sure,' I say. 'The maze?'

'Nope. Me and the maze don't get along.'

She doesn't elaborate; she just turns and starts walking down the hall without me. I stare at Daemon for a millisecond while he looks like he's about to try to stop her, but he clearly thinks the better of it, and I turn on my heel to catch up.

'I can't go all that far,' she says, pointing to her stomach. 'Theo will give me so much crap later if he thinks I've overexerted myself.'

I stare at her stomach; it taking me far longer than it should to figure it out because she's not really showing.

'Oh!' I exclaim. 'Congratulations!'

'Thanks.'

I scramble for something else to say about it. 'When are you due?' I blurt.

'Early next year.'

'Great,' I say.

'Not really,' she mutters. 'I mean I'm excited, and I already love the baby, but, ugh, being pregnant sucks. My feet hurt, my back hurts, my moods are all over. A thousand tiny things no one tells you that are misery-inducing. Blah!'

'If your feet hurt, would you rather sit in the Parlor than walk around?'

'Yeah, that would be nicer, actually,' she nods, and I guide her to the right room, where she immediately sits down heavily on one of the sofas.

'Do you want anything to eat or drink?' I ask, ready to pull the bell for Tabitha, but she shakes her head.

'No, thanks. Maddox had some tea served, so I'm good.'

I sit down across from her.

'So, are *you* an on-call girl?' I ask.

'Not exactly,' she says.

I wonder if she's a surrogate for the other clan to have a kid, and I frown. Will they take her beloved baby from her once it's born like Iron told me they'd do to me if I got pregnant when we were in the Mountain?

'So, the fae, huh?' I ask, changing the subject abruptly.

It doesn't faze Jane, though.

'Yeah, they're such assholes.'

I nod. 'That's for sure.'

She looks at me for the first time, really looks at me. 'You know a lot of them?'

I shrug noncommittally. 'Not that many, but I've been in Supeland for a while, and they turn up from time to time.'

Jane nods. 'Yeah, they do do that.'

'I've actually been out of the loop for a while,' I say. 'What's the latest news with the supe, human fighting that was going on?'

'Well,' she ponders for a moment, 'after the skirmishes in the cities, most people figured out that the Ten were kind of behind everything.'

I tense at the mention of the Ten but force a normal nod to

encourage her to talk. Even though I was in the Mountain during those weeks, we still heard about the 'Troubles'. It was a pretty big deal, but I didn't know they'd made the Ten for it. Forcing the 'inferior creatures' to fight each other for their personal gain has their fingerprints all over it, though.

'But they're the Ten, so,' she continues with a shrug, 'they're still in charge and doing whatever they want and probably will be forever.'

'Yeah,' I say faintly, my hands clammy.

'Are you okay?' she asks.

'Sure,' I say, plastering a smile on my face. 'So, you guys are here for a few days?'

She nods. 'Yeah, Maddox and Alex had some stuff they needed to talk about, *not* on the phone, and since you guys are on the run from Johnny Law *and* Paris needs to set up some security stuff, we're all in your hair for a little while.'

I grin at her, and this time, it's genuine. 'Well, let me know if you need anyth—'

The door swings open, and two of the other clan, the shaggy-haired one and another one, stalk over the threshold.

'Here you are!'

Jane rolls her eyes. 'I told you I wouldn't leave the house, and I didn't. I'm not *hiding* from you.'

They start arguing a little, but I'm not listening because my eyes are locked on the second one.

He's familiar, and I can tell he's thinking the same as he stares at me with a small frown, like he's trying to place me too. I stand up as it comes to me.

'You!' we say at the same time.

'You got out!'

I nod, smiling. 'So did you.'

'You two know each other, Theo?' Jane asks, and he nods.

'Remember, I told you about the human woman in the Mountain who was in the ceiling?'

He gestures to me. 'This is her!'

'You were in the Mountain?' Jane asks, and the question is loaded. She's asking all the things.

'Yeah, I was hiding out,' I say, leaving it at that.

She makes a gun with her hand and clicks with her mouth as she points at me. 'Right on.'

I grin in spite of myself, deciding I like her.

'Man, when we first got in there, I didn't think we'd be getting out alive.' Theo chuckles.

'Most people don't get out alive, isn't that right, Jules?' Daemon enters the room, a look on his face that makes me tense. 'I'm mean, just think about Siggy. But then maybe *people* isn't the right word.'

I swallow hard. His sudden mention of Siggy so out of the blue is like a punch to the gut.

'Yeah, I guess so,' I say quietly, not able to think of a retort and feeling sick as I sink back down to the couch. No one seems to notice anything's amiss, though. They say 'later' and lead Jane out of the room like she's made of glass. She waves her fingers at me, rolling her eyes again as they go and leaving me alone with Daemon.

'What the hell is your problem?' I hiss.

He stalks towards me and leans down, caging me in.

'You're my problem,' he snarls.

He grabs for my throat, and I dive away, trying to scramble off the couch, but he gets hold of me, pinning me down. I thrash, catching him in the face and scratching his cheek, but he ignores my struggles, grabbing both my wrists in his other hand and hoisting them above my head. My eyes search his, but there's nothing but anger in them.

His lips crash down on mine hard, punishing. I whimper under him, lust I can't fight exploding between us like a grenade. I twist and turn, trying to get away from the onslaught, but I can't help but surrender to it, relaxing underneath him, winding my legs around him. I feel him tense just before he rips himself away, staggering across the room. He turns, and his anger has been replaced by something far worse. Humor.

He laughs at me, panting hard on the couch, still aching for him to touch me anywhere. *Everywhere*.

'You're so easy. Such a dumb, little supe slut,' he chuckles. 'You really don't have a shred of self-respect. We laughed about you before, but you're even worse now. It's pathetic, Julia. *You're* pathetic.'

I sit up, trying to get my traitorous body under control and making sure my eyes stay dry. My chest hurts, and his cruel words have pushed all the worst buttons, reminding me of some of the more awful things Iron said to me in the Mountain while he was trying to break me.

'Nothing to say, sweetheart? That's not like you,' he sneers.

I don't trust my voice, so I just look at him impassively, and I watch his anger return because I'm not giving him the reaction he clearly wants. I feel some small satisfaction in that.

'You don't belong here,' he says. 'You're not *good* enough.'

I don't quite manage to stop my flinch this time, and he snorts, leaving the room.

I hear the door close and sniff a little. I stand up, letting out a harsh breath and promising myself that I won't let Daemon near me again. He's the worst of them all.

Chapter Twelve

KRASE

Krase

I'm watching Paris install yet another camera when I feel it. It's acute and painful, and it's coming from Jules. I let out what I think is an inaudible grunt, but Paris pauses and glances down from the ladder at me.

'Everything okay?'

'Fine,' I say with a frown because I'm sure as hell not going to talk to another incubus about my clan's female.

He doesn't go back to work, his eyes still watching me.

'We paying you by the fucking hour, or something?' I growl, impatient to get to Jules and find out what's wrong, except I have orders to stay here and keep an eye on Paris until he's done for the day.

He smirks. 'You seem different.'

I grunt. I know what he's talking about.

'So does Sie,' I say.

The last time I saw that big, quiet bastard, we shared an

unwelcome camaraderie in that we were both losing our minds. He wasn't so far gone as me, though.

'Are you almost done?'

'Yeah,' he says. 'You guys going out to feed soon?'

News to me.

'Probably,' I say instead of letting him know that I'm out of the loop. 'How do you know?'

Paris finishes screwing in a bolt. 'I heard Maddox talking to Iron about how to hide your identities.'

'You probably shouldn't be eavesdropping on my clan's business.'

'Sorry, just making conversation.'

'Well, don't. Are you done?'

'Yeah,' he says, coming down. 'For today. I got a few more to put up tomorrow.'

I nod and leave him in the hall because my job is done. I go directly to Jules' room, but she's not there.

Her upset is muted now, but it's still there, eating at her happiness, and I scowl. Jayce, Axel, and I made sure she was in a great mood when she left us this afternoon. When I find out who's made her feel like this, I'm going to beat the shit out of him.

It's dark outside, so I'm guessing she's in the house. But it won't be the library because Maddox and Alex are still in there talking.

I see Korban walking up the hall with Jane, and I tense a little. I haven't seen Jane since she was last here and I have an apology to make for my actions last time.

Kor snarls as I get closer, but ignore him, confident I could take him if I need to, though Jane is pregnant, so she probably shouldn't be made to worry that I'm going to kill one of her mates. I feel my other half's begrudging assent that we won't attack Korban for the female's sake.

'I wanted to say that I'm sorry,' I say to Jane.

She stops in the hall as I approach. She doesn't look scared of me despite the fact that I pretty much attacked her the last time she was here, but Korban snarls at me to get back.

I put my hands up and step away as he demands.

'The way I acted while you were a guest here was unpardonable,' I say. 'I wasn't myself, and although that's no excuse, please be assured that I will only ever give you the greatest respect in future, Ms. Mercy. On behalf of myself and my brother, Jayce, please accept our deepest apologies.'

'Thanks,' she says and starts off down the hell again.

I look after her, a little puzzled by her lack of reaction, but I turn and start walking towards my destination in the opposite direction when Korban glares at me.

I find Jules in the Parlor, sitting on the couch. I close the door behind me, and I turn the key in the lock.

She looks up at me as I approach but doesn't move. Her body is stiff when I sit next to her and pull her into my lap.

'You were content earlier,' I murmur in her ear. 'What's wrong, deamhan àlainn? Who made you feel this way?'

'Why can we feel each other? I've never heard of that happening with on-call girls.' she says instead of answering me, and I frown at this little tactic I've noticed she uses when she doesn't want to talk.

I choose my words carefully. As far as I'm aware, even she doesn't know the truth, and I don't want to scare her. She's flighty enough as it is. I haven't yet told the others, either. In fact, as soon as I could smell her, I used magick to subdue her scent again so none of them will be able to tell until the time is right. Sadly, I don't trust everyone in the clan at the moment.

'It's a side-effect of our intimacy,' I say, and it's not a lie; it's just not the whole truth. 'Are you going to answer my question?'

'It doesn't matter,' she says, putting her head on my chest and sighing.

'It does matter,' I persist, putting my hand over her heart. 'I can feel how upset you are now. Someone's been pouring poison into your ears.'

'We don't like it,' my darker side growls in the voice she knows isn't mine.

'Why do you care?' she asks, and I grin over her head.

She's fishing, but I don't mind. I'd give her every assurance I could to make her understand what she means to me. Us.

'I care because you're mine,' I growl. 'Because I love everything about you.'

'Shut up,' she scoffs. 'You can't.'

'I can,' I insist. 'Your hair, your smile, every inch of your mind and body are all the things I've ever wanted.'

'I'm far from perfect, Krase,' she whispers.

'Don't I know it, my deceptive little thief,' I say.

'You're putting me on a pedestal, and there's only one way to go from there.'

She sounds close to tears.

I tighten my arms around her.

'We all have our flaws,' I say. 'But I love everything about you, and I have since I met you. I love *you*, Julia.'

'It feels true,' she says very quietly with her head still against my heart that beats only for her.

'I'm not trying to trick you, mo chridhe.' I say. 'Now, who was it? One of the Iron I's? Korban?'

She shakes her head.

'One of us then. Not Axel or Jayce, not me. Maddox is cutting, but he knows how to skirt the line between decency and injurious banter.'

A run-in with Julian would have left her feeling furious and energized, not sad and despairing. My eyes narrow.

'Daemon,' my darker side snarls.

She tenses, and I know I'm right.

'Please don't do anything,' she pleads. 'He's right about—'

'Nothing,' I snarl. 'He's right about nothing. He's angry

because every single thing that's befallen him over the past two years was his own doing. He blames you because he's a fool. Ignore him until he comes to his senses.'

I lift her off me and put her on her feet, glancing at my phone when it vibrates and seeing a fortuitous message from Iron that might take Jules' mind off Daemon for the moment.

'You know, the horses were brought back to the estate this morning. Iron's about to go for a ride,' I tell her. 'Shall I tell him to saddle Pitch for you? He's the one you learned on, isn't he?'

She hesitates, nodding a little. 'But I haven't ridden since I was last here.'

'Ach, it's no different than riding a bike. Go out and get some fresh air, gràidh. Have some fun.'

She gives me a small smile. 'It *is* fun.'

I nod and message Iron back. He replies immediately.

'He'll meet you at the stable,' I tell her.

'What are you going to do?' she asks, sounding a little more herself.

'I'm just going to go for a walk,' I say innocently, and she rolls her eyes.

I unlock the Parlor door. 'You remember the way?'

She nods, and I let her go, closing it behind her and giving her a minute's head start. My eyes narrow as I open the door again and go into the hall. I sniff the air, locating Daemon almost immediately. He's outside.

I go through the kitchens and out the side door, crossing the grass instead of sticking to the paths to the tall wall that leads to a small, enclosed section of the garden not far from the forest.

'I thought you'd be happier,' I hear a voice saying. 'I got you back into the clan. What more do you want?'

That's not Daemon; that's his brother, Alex.

I slow my steps, not above a little spying. When I know they're just on the other side of the wall and that I'm upwind, I pause to listen.

'What's due me,' Daemon growls.

'There's nothing left of our father's enterprises,' Alex says, sounding long-suffering. 'After he and the others were killed and we freed the slaves, the rest was scattered to the winds.'

'I don't believe you.'

Alex's laugh is brittle. 'I don't care what you believe, Daemon. I have a mate to worry about now, a baby on the way. If there was money, I would give it to you if only so we don't have to go through this again. I wanted nothing from our sire. Nothing! Everything he had, everything about him, was tainted. He stole Jane. He and the others did vile—'

'I know,' Daemon growls. 'I know!'

'Because you waited to tell me what you knew so you could get the most out of it. I may have been given the title of Vicious, but you're more like Leonel than I ever was. I may have got you back in the clan, but I'll never forgive you for your part in what happened to her, Daemon. Never.'

I hear footsteps going the opposite way and peer through the ivy-covered archway that leads into the enclosed garden. Daemon sits alone on a stone bench, drinking from a whiskey bottle. He looks half drunk, no mean feat for a demon.

I come out of the shadows, and when he sees me, he takes another long drink.

'What the hell do you want?'

'Brotherly reunion not going well?' I snarl.

'About as well as can be expected in my family. We aren't like you and Jayce,' he mutters somewhat bitterly.

I almost want to tell him there's still time, but he's not in the mood to hear it, and I'm not in the mood to say it.

'You need to stay away from Jules.' I say. 'I won't have you hurting her.'

He laughs darkly. 'The supe slut get to you too? She's hard to resist when she's throwing herself at us all every other hour, huh? Guess it's worse for you, though.' He gives me a hard look.

'You *were* starving. Can't really blame you for falling for her, letting your dick take charge. Take it from me, though, big guy. See her for what she is. A liar and a thief and a fucking honey trap. She doesn't belong here.'

'Is that what you told her?' I growl low, picturing him spewing these despicable insults at my beautiful, vulnerable mate.

'That and more,' he replies without remorse. 'And I'll keep making sure she knows her place until she stays in it!'

'And what is her place?' I snarl.

He takes another long drink. 'I'd see her a slave in the lowest, filthiest human brothel I could find,' he says with a smirk.

My glamor is down, and I'm on him before he can say another word.

'You don't know anything about her,' I bellow. 'She doesn't deserve your ire.'

He struggles under me but can't dislodge me.

'No, *Crazy* Krase!' he bucks, trying to free himself to no avail. 'She doesn't *deserve* to be here. Maddox should have snapped her neck when he found her on the lawn and thrown her body down the well! Instead, you're playing house with a dumb, human bitch who thinks she's so much more!'

'She is more!' I roar, hitting him hard enough in the face to crack his jaw.

His face falls to the side, and the fight goes out of him suddenly. He's not unconscious; he's just not going to fight back. He'll let me pummel the shit out of him. My lips curl at the realization. I'm not going to be his tool for self-flagellation and loathing. If he wants to be punished, he can do it himself!

I lean close to his ear. 'She's more than you or I will ever be,' I murmur. 'You have no idea, but I hope I'm there when you find out.'

With a final push into his chest, I get off him and stalk

angrily back into the night. Maybe it's time they all knew the truth about Julia Brand.

I know Daemon and Maddox's anger would crumble in the wake of the facts, but there's more to this, to her.

Until I know what, I need to keep my silence.

The problem is, Maddox will cast her out within the month, and our mate won't be safe out there. We're running out of time.

JULES

I leave the house and make my way slowly to the stable, wondering if this is a mistake. Iron took me out a few times *before*. He basically taught me everything I didn't already know from movies about riding.

And I loved it.

The idea of getting back on a horse fills me with anticipation, but I wonder if Iron will really want me there. He's mostly avoided me since Krase's game in the forest.

I go into the stable, pausing inside the door to let my eyes adjust to the gloom.

I move through the building, looking in each stall until I find Pitch. His black head pokes over the stall door when he sees me, his ears twitching. Even though I've ridden him a few times, his size still shocks me. He's huge.

My lips curve to a big smile.

'Hey, boy,' I murmur, touching his silky nose. 'You probably don't remember me, but—'

His face is suddenly nuzzling against my hand, and he steps forward, butting it against my chest. Tears well in my eyes.

'You do remember me, don't you?' I whisper.

'Are you ready?'

I jump at the sound of Iron's voice, wiping my eyes quickly before I turn around.

He looks me over and rolls his eyes at my dress. 'There are some clothes that might fit you in the stall at the end,' he mutters. 'Lead him out when you're ready. He's all saddled up for you.'

'Thanks,' I say a little uncomfortably as I go into the last stall and find a shirt and some pants flung on a chair. They're the ones Iron got for me last time, I realize, finding my boots there too. Why did he keep them?

With a frown, I don them quickly and grab one of the many jackets hanging from hooks on the wall.

I go to Pitch, open the door of his stall, and take his reins.

'Ready for some fun, boy?' I ask.

He comes easily, and when we get to the stable yard, I take him over to one of the mounting blocks. I step up onto the large stone cube, using it to get easily onto Pitch's tall back, but, for a second, I'm afraid. What if it isn't like riding a bike at all?

'Are you okay?' Iron asks, bringing his white and brown stallion up next to mine.

'Yeah,' I say. 'It's just … what if I can't remember how?'

He regards me stonily, and I can't help but think that maybe coming out here was a mistake.

'Look, if you'd rather ride alone, I can—'

'No,' Iron interrupts. 'You'll be fine, Jules, I promise. I'm right here if you have a problem.'

I give him a wan smile.

'We'll take it slow first, okay? Just a walk down the lane and go from there.'

I grip the reins the way he taught me, and he gives me a nod when he notices. I try not to feel giddy at his silent praise, but I don't quite manage it.

We leave the yard side-by-side and turn down the gravel lane. I reach forward and scratch behind Pitch's ears.

'When I found the stables empty, I thought Maddox had had the horses sold,' I murmur.

Iron shakes his head. 'When the authorities took us in, Maddox was given half an hour to tie up loose ends. He had them all taken to a nearby farm to be looked after until we could return.'

I glance at him. 'I'm glad they're still here.'

Iron says nothing, and we keep to our slow pace.

The breeze picks up for a moment, and I shiver a little even though I'm wrapped up in a thick jacket. The air has a definite, wintery bite to it now. Though I suppose we're well into Autumn now.

I gaze out at the mountains.

'I love it here,' I say, not really meaning for him to answer and ignoring his soft snort.

'How did you do it?' he suddenly asks, twisting around and snatching my reins to halt Pitch.

'Do what?' I ask, taken aback by his sudden anger.

'Get Axel and Jayce to protect you in the Mountain? Make them and Krase fall for you?'

His questions take me by surprise, but before I can formulate any kind of response, he's talking again.

'I mean, fuck, Jules!' He runs a hand through his short, dark hair. 'Krase's mind was *gone*. We said goodbye to him! But now he's just *fine*?'

'I don't know what you want me to say,' I tell him. 'I don't know. I promise you I don't. If I am doing something, it's not on purpose.'

'Bullshit,' he hisses.

He leans forward, staring into my eyes as if he's trying to catch me in a lie. 'You're definitely a human, and that one little conjure you have on you wouldn't explain it,' he says half to himself. 'But I can't tell what it does ... not unless I explore it.'

His words about my conjure make me freeze. It's been working since whatever Krase did to fix it in the dungeon. But what if Iron tampers with it? Removes it? What if he *sees*? His fingers reach out to touch me, and I rear back, feeling like I might throw up.

'Please don't,' I whisper.

His eyes flick up to mine, and he scoffs, his hand going back to his reins.

'You're a great actress,' he mutters, giving them a snap. 'Come on.'

His horse walks off, and I follow on mine, going a little faster to catch up and trying to cover my upset. He's right, I am a great actress. But I know this isn't over. He's not going to let it go. He's going to find out eventually, and the thought fills me with dread.

We're silent for a while until he looks over at me again.

'You know, before the Mountain, I had little fae magick,' he says.

'I figured,' I murmur, making sure my voice sounds relaxed and *not* upset now.

He looks at me sharply, and I find myself trying to explain.

'I just mean ... when I was here before, I never felt it, and I heard the others saying that it was new for you.'

He sighs, looking away. 'I wanted it. All my fucking life, I wanted it. After my dad died, my mom sent me to her family in Ireland to learn, to try to unlock my power when it didn't manifest naturally like other fae children. My GiGi spent hours with me, teaching me to use magick I didn't have. It took three years for her to give up and tell the Council there was no hope for me.'

Iron stops the horse at a fork in the road. 'Do you know what the fae do with kids who don't show any power these days?'

I shake my head.

'They kick them out, Jules. Disown them. My mom wasn't even allowed to talk to me after that.' He snorts. 'Guess I was lucky I wasn't born a hundred years ago, or they'd have killed me.'

'I'm sorry,' I say, resisting the urge to touch him because I know he doesn't want that. 'Maybe they'd take you back now that you have some ...' I trail off at his vehement look.

'They didn't want me when I was 'useless'. Why would I want them now?' he snarls.

We turn down the dirt track to the left.

'Because they're your family,' I say, 'and because they were scared to go against the Council.'

He scoffs. 'Follow the rules or be punished severely.'

I pale at his words, words that are burned into my mind, words I heard a million times and wish I could forget.

'Want to race to the north bluff?' I ask so I don't keel over and vomit.

Not waiting for his answer, I use my heels to kick Pitch into a gallop, taking off down the dirt road before leaving it and racing over the meadow.

I can't help the grin that spreads over my face. Krase was right. I do remember how to do this. And I've missed it. I feel free!

I see Iron out of the corner of my eye and urge my horse to go faster, my smile wide.

'I'm going to win!' I yell into the wind.

I think I hear a response, but whatever Iron says is lost as the distance between us is doubled, and I press on, my destination almost in sight.

Pitch thunders across the wide wooden bridge that goes over the brook, his hooves echoing on the slats. I hear Iron just behind us and let out a whoop as we leap over a short hedge and enter the next field. We sprint across it, but I don't push Pitch anymore, my win all but assured when I glance back to see Iron only just clearing the same hedge.

I pull the reins and the black stallion skids to a halt by the tall oak tree we were aiming for. I look over my shoulder to find Iron almost upon us, and I cringe as he doesn't slow his horse until the last second. When he finally jerks to a stop next to me, the same smile is on his face.

'I told you you'd be fine,' he says.

'You were right, you were right,' I concede.

Pitch whinnies, batting the hard earth with his hoof, and I stroke his flank, 'I should have known you'd want more of a run than this,' I croon to him as I gaze out over the misty valley and snowy mountains.

I glance over at Iron, who's staring out at the scenery in front of us.

'Thank you for letting me come out with you,' I say.

He gives a curt nod, his smile fading.

'Well, I guess we should get back,' I mutter.

He turns his horse without a word, not saying anything until we arrive back at the stables a few minutes later. We dismount from our horses and take them into the paddock to unsaddle them. When they're safely back in their stalls, he finally turns to me.

'GiGi and the others aren't my family anymore,' he says. 'My clan are my family, Julia.'

There's a warning glint in his eye that makes me take a step back, but then he turns away, walking quickly back toward the house.

Left alone in the stable, I change back into my dress, leaving the riding clothes where I found them.

I go back to the house, entering through the kitchens and finding Tabitha at the stove. She gives me a smile.

'I think Jayce was looking for you,' she murmurs.

'Thanks,' I say. 'I'll go find him.'

She closes her eyes.

'He's in his room,' she says very quietly, and I wonder how much she knows about what's going on in this house.

Probably a lot. Probably everything. I let out a breath, hoping I can trust her as I give her another thanks and leave the kitchens.

I slip into the passages via the Parlor, and I knock quietly on Jayce's secret door, and it opens a second later. He's back in his paint-splattered jeans and no shirt on.

He looks surprised to see me, but he pulls me into his room and straight into his arms.

'Are you all right?' he asks.

I nod. 'Tabitha said you were looking for me, but if you're busy, I can come back—'

'No, I'm never too busy for you,' he murmurs. 'What happened earlier?'

I shrug, and he lets out a sound of displeasure. 'I won't ask you about it then. No doubt my brother will sort it, but you mustn't let anyone make you feel like that, lass.'

He caresses my cheek with the back of his knuckles, and I find myself sniffling.

'What do you all see in me?'

Krase's words and the ride on Pitch have gone a long way to making me feel better after Daemon, but the problem is that the bad stuff is always easier to believe. I'm afraid that everything Daemon said was true.

Jayce doesn't answer right away. Instead, he sits on the bed and draws me close between his legs, taking hold of my hands.

'Close your eyes and focus on me,' he says.

I do it, feeling him, where he is, and listening to his slow breath.

Something warm floods into my chest, making me shiver a little. It's like a flower opening in the sun, and inside is this feeling of happiness and contentment, how I feel when I'm with these demons.

'That's what I see in you,' he breathes. 'It's how you make me feel, Bana-Phrionnsa. You and no other.'

His hands squeeze mine, and I grip them hard in return. There aren't words for this, so I don't even try; I just lean down and kiss his lips gently.

I feel his smile, and I let out a tiny laugh as I open my eyes. He takes out his phone.

'What are you doing?' I ask.

'Just letting the Axel and Jayce know you're here.'

'I have something for you,' he says suddenly, standing up.

He goes over to his studio door and opens it.

'It's not finished,' he warns, 'but close your eyes. No peeking.'

I raise a brow at him but do as he says with a humoring smile I can't quite keep off my face. I hear him cross the room and then feel him behind me, covering my eyes with his hands.

'I already have my eyes closed,' I protest with a chuckle, but he just hushes me.

He walks me forward across his room. The smell of linseed oil and turpentine assails my nose.

'This is where you paint.' I whisper.

'Yes,' he replies. 'No one's allowed in here. No one but you.'

He lets me go. 'Open your eyes, Jules.'

I do, and my eyes fall on the canvas in front of me. My breathing stutters and my eyes swim. 'You—' My voice breaks. 'You *painted* her? For me?'

I try to wipe my tears away and take in the painting before me of Siggy in her web. He captured her so well, that look in her eyes that I didn't think anyone else could see but me, her bristly pedipalps that were a little brown along the edges when the rest of her was so pitch black. It's like I'm looking at a photo of her.

'I didn't think you'd have a picture,' he says quietly.

I turn to him and throw my arms around him with a sob. He looks surprised.

'I thought my last vision of her would be her dead on the floor of Dante's room,' I bawl, wetting his bare chest with my tears. 'But you *painted* her,' I say again, not believing that anyone would do that for me.

He's wrecked me.

I hold him tighter, wanting him to understand how much this means to me.

'Jules.' His voice sounds strained. 'I can't breathe, lass.'

'Sorry.' I let him go and pull back a little.

'Thank you,' I say with all the feeling I can muster. 'No one's ever done anything like this for me before.'

He takes my face in his hands. 'I would do anything for you.'

Chapter Thirteen

JAYCE

Her face is a picture on its own. Even if I couldn't feel her, I'd be able to see the gratitude in her eyes.

I hug her close and frown. I knew that Siggy was dead, but I stupidly hadn't realized the depth of her grief. She hid it from me somehow, probably without even realizing it.

She looks at the painting again and begins to cry anew. I hold her, my heart breaking. But only time will heal this pain. I can't help her with it except to hold her when she cries.

But I can do that.

I pick her up and carry her to the recliner in front of my computer, sitting in it with her and keeping her close.

After a long time, she quiets, and I realize she's asleep. I ease her dress off and put her in my bed naked, tucking her in and going back into my workroom. I look at the painting I did of Siggy. I was afraid I hadn't captured her accurately as I was only working from memory, but gauging from Jules' reaction, I needn't have worried.

I grab another of my easels and set it up with a canvas by my bed quietly. Jules has thrown off the covers, giving me a pleasing eyeful of her delectable curves and a very enjoyable model to paint.

I sketch her first, wanting this to be perfect because it's going on my ceiling when it's done. Then, I get my brushes and paints, and I begin.

I paint all night, and Jules is the perfect model, hardly moving at all during her slumber. She sleeps less fitfully than she did in the Mountain, I notice. Fewer nightmares, though I suppose that's hardly surprising. Still, maybe it also shows that she's not completely discontent here with us.

When I'm finished, I lay down in my bed and sleep the way I've been yearning to do since I was in the White Bunker with Jules, right next to her. I'm calm for the first time in weeks.

When I wake, Jules is still asleep, and as I lie in the bed next to her, an idea comes to me. I grin as I watch her, wondering how she'll react to my plan as she wakes. Careful not to disturb her, I tie her wrists to the corners of my bed and begin.

First, I use a very soft brush on her nipples, making them pucker and bead. I swipe down to her navel and abdomen, stroking across her body in zigzags to her mound. She shifts in the bed, murmuring a little, but doesn't wake.

Here, I change my brush to a coarser one with a thick, barreled handle, grinning as I stroke her sensitive lips with it, and she wriggles in her sleep.

I flip the brush around and wet the handle with my tongue, wanting it to slide in as gently as possible and not wake her up. I ease it into her slowly and back out again, fucking her with my thickest paintbrush gently. She whimpers, her legs falling open for me in slumber, and I grin wickedly as I plunge the handle deeper into her. Her hips roll.

I lean down, not stopping my rhythm, as I lick her clit with the flat of my tongue in circles. She moans, pulling on the restraints, but when I check, she's still unconscious. I keep it up, increasing my tempo, letting the glamor down from just my tongue. It becomes larger and coarser, flicking against her vulnerable flesh.

I groan, not far off my own release, and, this time, when I look up, knowing she's close, she's staring back at me. Her cheeks are flushed, and she's pulling hard on the ropes that are keeping her where I want her.

'Do you want me to stop?' I ask with a smile, plunging the brush in hard.

She cries out and shakes her head, and my demon tongue returns to her.

A few seconds later, her legs begin to shake, and she screams my name into the pillow next to her head.

I throw the brush on the floor and straddle her, taking in her prone limbs and loving that she's stuck in my bed until I release her.

I line up my cock and wink at her as I take my glamor down to see if my demon form pleases her as much as I heard Krase's did.

She takes in my large, slate-grey body, the twisted red horns, and I show her what I'm about to fuck her with. Long and ridged with a knot at the base.

As soon as her eyes widen in surprise and a little fear, I push into her very wet pussy gently, stopping before the knot because her channel isn't ready. But, with each thrust, my cock thickens to stretch her to take me fully.

She's panting, her mouth open, her eyes locked into where we're joined. She's nervous, but she doesn't say a word.

She trusts me.

The understanding has my dick broadening faster, and the noises she's making while I rut her are like music to my ears.

'Watch me fucking you,' I tell her, leaning back a little so she can see everything. 'Look how I'm stretching that pretty pink pussy. I'm going to stuff my entire cock inside you, and you'll take my knot like a good girl.'

I feel what my words do to her, hear her moan as I praise her.

'Do you like being mine to play with? To fuck at my leisure?'

She nods, her eyes finding mine.

'I don't deserve you,' I growl, surging forwards and capturing her lips with mine at the same time as the knot at the base of my shaft pushes into her.

She cries out in pleasure, biting her lip to keep herself quiet.

'No,' I snarl, 'I want to hear you squeal for me, lass. Cry out my name; thank me for the pleasure I'm giving you.'

She whimpers at my words. 'Jayce, please!'

'That's it,' I grind out with a groan. 'Just like that, my perfect, good girl.'

She screams my name as she finds her release, her muscles spasming as she gushes around the thick shaft that's still lodged inside her. My own body tenses, and I finally allow myself to come, throwing back my head and roaring loudly as I spill my seed as deeply into her as I can.

I collapse on top of her, and she kisses me, her body turning languid and sated.

She wiggles under me, and I grab her hips.

'No, don't try to dislodge it,' I murmur. 'You'll hurt yourself, lass. It'll go down in a minute if you're still.'

She relaxes under me, regarding me from under her long lashes. 'How does a demon have a shifter cock?' she asks.

I shrug. 'Maybe I can make it any shape I want.'

Her eyes widen.

'Or,' I say, 'perhaps Krase and I just have a little shifter in our family line, and I got the recessive wolf dick.'

'Recessive wolf dick?' She barks a laugh.

'Aye, like blue eyes in a family of brown.'

She giggles. 'Well, how long before your rare dick will let me up? I need to pee.'

I grin at her, untying her limbs deftly before reaching down to ease my deflating staff out of her, finding that it's small enough now.

She rolls to the side of the bed and gets up, her legs visibly wobbling as she goes into my bathroom.

'Have I broken you?'

She looks over her shoulder at me. 'Jury's still out.'

JULES

When I come back into the room, Jayce is on his phone, thumbs flying over the screen.

'Is something wrong?' I ask.

'No, Bana-Phrionnsa. Nothing's wrong. Just ... Maddox is looking for you.'

My heart begins to pound hard in my chest. 'Where does he think I am?'

Iron has said he believes he saw you going into the maze. That should give you a few minutes.

I nod and start looking for my clothes.

'Jules?'

I look up. 'You need to wash my scent off you, remember?'

I freeze.

'O-oh right,' I stutter, dropping the dress and going back into the bathroom.

I turn on the water and get under the stream before it's even hot, soaping myself vigorously and using the showerhead to douche myself the way Krase did, though it's far less pleasurable in the hurry I'm in. I'm out of the shower in less than five minutes and rush back into the bedroom.

Jayce approaches me, and I step back.

'It's all right,' he says calmly. 'You don't need to run. He knows the maze likes you and will try to hide you from him. He won't bother going in to find you.'

I nod jerkily.

'He won't smell me on you,' Jayce says, and his words calm my nerves.

'I'm sorry. I don't know why I'm getting so worked up,' I say. 'It's ridiculous.'

He shakes his head. 'It's all right. Everything is fine. Focus on me, feel me.'

I do what he says and find him sporting a Zen-like calm that's at odds with what's at stake. That's the problem, I realize. The money was important. It *is* important, but within a few days, everything I was afraid of happening has come to pass. There's so much more for me to lose now. I care about these demons, and being here again feels like I've come home even though some of the clan don't want me here.

It was so difficult for me to leave this house before. After the ball, it's going to be practically impossible to make myself walk out that door. I thought I'd be able to do my time and not let myself be affected, but I've completely overestimated myself ... and underestimated everything else.

I breathe deeply. I need to chill the fuck out because this anxiety is what's going to give me away to Maddox. Luckily, Jayce's calmness flows into me, and I'm freaking out a lot less within a minute.

'Thank you,' I say. 'How did you know that would help? Can all of you do that?'

Jayce gives me a full-on, gorgeous smile that literally makes me weak in the knees.

Oh, how far I have fallen.

He shakes his head. 'When you have a brother like mine, you find ways to project calm.'

I grin at him. 'Sounds about right.'

I get dressed quickly, frowning as I look at my wet hair in the mirror. 'Do you have a blow-dryer?'

'Sorry, no. But it's raining out, so it'll work with the story that you've been walking around in the maze for a while.'

'Okay.' I kiss his lips, careful to touch him as little as possible. 'Thank you for being you and for making me feel so much better,' I say with feeling. 'And thank you for the painting of Siggy.'

I clench my jaw to keep the tears away. 'No one's ever ...' My voice breaks.

'And that's as much a tragedy as you losing her,' he says softly.

I turn away, not knowing what to say to something like that.

'Take the passage down and then the long one that looks older all the way to the end. It'll bring you up in the center of the maze.'

I nod and, still not trusting myself to speak, I leave, taking the passages that I'm beginning to learn well. I reach the end of the tunnels in a few minutes and walk up the steps. It looks like a dead end, but there's a stone in the wall that looks smoother than the others. I press it and hear a click. The wall slides open, and I poke my head through, finding myself where Jayce said I would.

As soon as I'm out of the tunnel, the door slides closed, and the bench that sits on top of it straightens. You'd never know it was there unless you knew about it.

I start walking along the path. Knowing the maze, it'll let me out pretty easily. It likes me. The first time around, the clan warned me away from it, but I was drawn to it in the weirdest way.

Apparently, in Supeland, a row of hedges can be sentient, and this intelligent maze fucking *hates* almost everyone who enters it. It changes to make people get lost and traps them in squares of high, thorny bushes. Some of its victims never re-appear. Axel even told me about a rumor that the statues on the plinths that litter the paths came alive and killed a bunch of party guests in the 1700s. Why you'd want something that dangerous in your backyard, I have no idea.

Fucking supes.

But, for me, the maze ... I listen hard and hear the far-off strums of a harp ... plays music and leaves me presents like scarves and shoes. I like to think they're possessions others have simply misplaced in here rather than objects that have been stolen from corpses the maze has allegedly murdered.

As I walk through, every path I choose is the right one, and the music gets louder.

'It's beautiful,' I whisper to the hedge next to me and get this odd idea in the back of my mind that it's happy that I'm happy.

I exit easily via the main path and say goodbye. It's only polite. Plus, I think it's best to stay on the right side of Murder Maze.

I start walking back to the house, shivering in the drizzle. As I turn a blind corner, I run right into Maddox's chest.

'There you are.'

I mumble an apology, immediately wondering if I cleaned myself enough that he won't smell Jayce on me. I lick my lips where I kissed him goodbye, and I watch Maddox's eyes focus on my mouth.

Shit! He knows!

I keep my game face on, and I wait him out. My nerve has gotten me out of trouble more than once. Hope it doesn't fail me now.

'Were you looking for me?' I say breathlessly.

'Yes, for ages,' he grumbles.

'Sorry,' I say. 'I was taking a walk in the maze. It was playing music for me and everything, so ...'

He eyes the hedge next to us and lets out a grunt. 'It's dangerous,' he mutters.

I smile sweetly. 'Only because it doesn't like you.' I raise my brows at him. 'Me, it loves.'

'Fuck knows why,' he mutters. 'Come to the library. I have some folders to give you. I assume you still want to plan the ball?'

'Yes, of course.'

'Well, you haven't got all that long to sort it, so best get to it.' He leads the way, walking quickly, and I have to half-jog to keep up.

'Are the Iron I's still here?' I ask.

He stops abruptly, and I bang into him. 'Why do you ask?'

'Just curious,' I say, wondering what the problem is.

His eyes narrow at me. 'I've informed them of your proclivities,' he states.

'And what are those?' I ask, my tone as arctic as I suddenly feel.

He looks a little sheepish. 'Let's just say they won't be letting their guards down around you, and I doubt they'll allow their mate anywhere near you again.'

I blink at him.

Game face. Game face.

But it's very hard to keep the mask of indifference on this time.

'That's for the best,' I say. 'Wouldn't want me giving in to my baser, *deceptive* instincts.' I lean closer. 'And definitely wouldn't want me influencing their human plaything,' I whisper conspiratorially, and, I'll admit, a little pettily.

'Jane is their *mate,* not an on-call girl,' Maddox says, looking like I just insulted *his* mate.

The way he says her name is reverent.

Something in my chest clenches, and I let out a small cough to cover my involuntary gasp of pain. He wanted Jane to be theirs, I realize. But she chose the Iron I's over him and his clan.

'I stand corrected,' I choke out, ignoring the pangs of jealousy that have no place in this conversation or, in fact, anywhere near Julian Maddox.

'I'm glad we got that cleared up,' I say, walking ahead of him towards the library. Luckily, it's started to rain, so the stupid tears that leak from my eyes aren't noticed when he catches up and walks beside me.

I don't look at him, trying to think of things that don't make me want to bawl my eyes out. I'm sure I didn't used to cry all the time. These demons, the nice ones at least, have turned me soft.

Not conducive to survival, that little voice inside my head unhelpfully supplies. My internal voice of self-preservation has been so quiet lately I'd almost forgotten it was there.

The rain starts coming down in sheets, and I feel something get draped over my shoulders. Maddox has given me his jacket, and, for a split second, I could almost believe he gives two shits about me.

But that's not true. What actually just happened is that Maddox has given the evil, deceptive human con artist his jacket because chivalry runs high in him, and I'm still a female in need. His hatred of me is immaterial and totally irrelevant.

His hand on the small of my back urges me into a run. He even helps me up the slippery stone steps to the French doors of the library. He flings them open, and we get inside. I stand in the middle of the room, shivering despite his coat because, as usual, I'm wearing a fucking evening gown.

I shrug off his *fake olive branch* and hand it to him. His eyes are fixed on my sodden dress as he takes the jacket, and I watch his Adam's apple bob.

I follow his gaze to my chest and see that the wet chiffon is practically see-through.

Great.

I cross my arms over my breasts, looking away from him uncomfortably.

Bet he wishes it was Jane's honest boobs he could see right now, not my lying ones!

Stop it.

He clears his throat. 'Here,' he says, handing me a folder. 'All the usual discrete and supe friendly suppliers, so there shouldn't be any problems. You can use the landline in here to call them. They can invoice me directly.'

'Thanks,' I say, still not looking at him as I grab the folder with one hand and attempt to cover my chest with my other arm.

He's quiet for a moment before he speaks again. When he does, I realize that he's moved to his desk and sat down behind it. He's lord of the manor now. He's taken away our equal footing. Somehow, that makes me feel even more embarrassed to be standing here like this.

'I know it's against your beguiling nature, Julia, but I'd urge you to dress more appropriately ... if only for the cooler weather,' he says.

My cheeks heat. He thinks I'm wearing Haute Couture gowns like loungewear every damn day because I'm trying to seduce his clan?

'That will be all,' he says, no longer gifting me with his attention.

I frown at the floor, suddenly very angry at his insinuations. I don't deserve them.

'I don't have anything else!' I snap, my eyes rising and

locking onto him, blazing when he doesn't immediately look up from his fucking desk.

I swear if he ignores me or dismisses me right now, I'm going to ...

'I beg your pardon?' he asks, sitting back in his chair.

His eyes find me. He looks bored.

'I don't have anything else. I'm wearing the clothes from the closet in the room *you* gave me. If they aren't to your liking, then I invite you to find me some additional options that are more in keeping with your desired aesthetic!'

I turn on my heel, ignoring him when he calls my name.

Fuck Julian Maddox. He can kiss my pert, human ass!

Chapter Fourteen

MADDOX

I have to stop myself from going after her, apologizing for my awful behavior.

'This is for the best,' I mutter to myself, gripping the armrests tightly.

She's getting too comfortable here. *We're* getting too comfortable *having her here*. Lines need to be drawn. Boundaries maintained. That's why I let her have the task of planning the masque. It will give her something to do so she stays out of our way over the next few weeks. It also pushes her back into the category of 'employee' because things were easier when I could keep her at arm's length, and it's getting harder to do that. I'm hoping this will help.

I pour myself a measure of brandy and knock it back in one. The clock says it's barely 11:30. I've now started imbibing before noon, and I blame Julia Brand.

Letting out a groan, I stand up, willing away the uncomfortable hardness between my legs even as I can't get the vision that elicited my current state out of my mind. Jules standing in front of me in her wet clothes, her dusky areola clearly visible under the thin, sodden material, her nipples hard from the cold. How I wanted to rip that dress off her, throw her down on the rug before the hearth, and warm her up even as I ravaged her.

I sit back down a little shakily. I thought we could wait until the Iron I's have left, but I'll need to feed sooner. If I don't, I won't be able to stop myself from succumbing to our houseguest. And, if I do that, then not only will I be an abhorrent host, but a hypocrite as well after how I dealt with Axel and Jayce for giving in to those same impulses in the Mountain.

I take out my phone and message my favorite club manager, one I trust implicitly. Typically, we stay quite removed from most of our businesses. We're silent owners, absent majority stakeholders. But there are one or two establishments we've been known to frequent where we're referred to as 'VIP guests' only. We'll need a conjure or two to change our scents and appearances, but it won't be too difficult so long as we keep our wits about us.

I get a ping and let out a sigh. Tomorrow night is on. I let the others know on the group chat and then get to work, dealing with yet more of the issues that accrued during our incarceration. Less than a month until the ball, and all of this will be settled once and for all.

I bring up the cameras that Paris has already installed, finding Jules easily. She's in the Parlor, staring out the window. I know she likes it best in the library, but I can't have her in here with me even if she is only reading in the nook I had built after she left.

The devil only knows what valuable nuggets of information she'd soak up while my guard was focused on business associates.

There's a knock on my door. It's Iron.

'I've taken a look at tomorrow's guestlist, and eight o'clock would be better. Fae VIPs are due around ten,' he says.

I nod. 'Fine. Let the others know about the change.'

My phone rings, but he doesn't leave.

'Was there something else?'

'Yeah.' He comes in and shuts the door. 'What are we doing with Jules?'

I blink at him. 'What do you mean?'

'When we go to the club. We're all going, right? You're not thinking of leaving her here.'

I hesitate. I hadn't really thought.

'With Alex and his crew?' he continues when I don't speak. 'After what happened with Jane, it's not a huge jump to assume they might be wanting some friendly payback. I mean, we were ready to kill Korban and take her if Alex and the others were dead.'

Friendly payback in our circles can be anything from a prank to a slit throat, so I think seriously about what Iron is saying. 'On Jules? I doubt they'd see her as a target. I've already made it clear to them what she is and why she's here.'

'You did?' Iron shifts. 'Why?'

I frown. He looks angry but quickly schools his features.

'It's just that they already know too much about our clan business,' he elaborates. 'Anyway, even if you don't think they're a threat to her, do you really want to leave her unguarded? You know how slippery she is. Without supervision ...'

'You're right,' I say. 'Make sure she knows she's coming and what she needs to wear to look inconspicuous with us.'

He turns to leave.

'And, Iron?'

He looks back at me.

'You're in charge of her. Make sure the little mischief-maker stays out of trouble.'

Iron chuckles. 'I don't think anyone could stop that girl from getting into all manner of scrapes, but I'll do my best.'

I snort as he leaves, turning my attention back to the screens. Jules is still in the same place. She looks ... sad. As I watch, the door to the Parlor opens, and Jane comes in. My eyes narrow even as my body tenses as I wonder how they're going to react to each other for some reason. But Jules brightens, and they begin talking. There's no audio on the feed, so I don't know what they're saying, but they appear to be friendly.

It's odd. When Jane was here only a few weeks ago, I was sure she was meant for us. I knew what she was. I knew it almost as soon as I met her. When she chose the Iron I's, I was more than a little disappointed, but short of starting an all-out clan war, there wasn't much I could do besides using some leverage over her to make her give Krase more time. She did, to be fair, and I owe her for that because if she hadn't let him feed from her, there's no way he'd have survived long enough to get better. Now, as I watch her, I can't help but be glad we didn't succeed in making her ours. It's clear that she's not right for us.

I sit back in my chair, staring out the windows as I ponder.

I've asked Krase a few times how he was able to free himself from the darkness that was devouring him, but his answers have been vague, referencing obscure fae magick and meditation. I suppose we could call it a miracle and leave it at that, but if we believed in all that crap, we'd be angels, not demons.

I glance back at the screen and see Jules and Jane smiling at each other. Jules is telling Jane about something she's excited about. I know because her face gets animated, and her hands gesture a lot while she's telling a story. I let out a huff as it becomes abundantly clear that Jules seems entirely unperturbed that I instructed her to stay away from the Iron I's mate, and she agreed not half an hour ago.

My phone rings again. 'What?' I growl, finally turning away from the screen and already regretting the secret camera I had installed in Jules' room because I know I'm going to be glued to it whenever she's in there.

I tell myself it's because she can't be trusted, but I'm beginning to wonder if she's burrowing under my defenses the way she has with Axel and Jayce.

My eyes narrow. At least I'll be able to use the extra security to make extra sure she's not reneging on our deal. Part of me wants her to. I'd love nothing more than to turn her out onto the streets without a penny to her name. One final lesson to remember us by.

JULES

I wait in the library, feeling a little nervous.

Iron took me out riding again today. He was warmer somehow. He chatted to me about horses and his time in the military. He didn't mention my conjure once. When he let me know that the clan was going out to feed tonight, I wasn't surprised. I figured some of them would be getting a little hungry by now. I didn't anticipate that they'd be dragging me along, too, though.

When I asked why, Iron just shrugged and said they wanted to keep me close. Now, I'm sitting in one of the big chairs by the fireplace in the short, bodycon dress that Iron gave me to wear and high Louboutin stilettoes with their pretty soles that match the color of my clothes.

I hear the door, but it's not Maddox who comes in; it's Jane. She walks around, looking at the shelves and choosing a couple of books. I stay quiet, not wanting to get her into trouble if she's been told to stay away from me like Maddox said she would.

Her clan leader found us in the Parlor yesterday and whispered something to her that made her practically jump out of her seat, give me a salute goodbye, and drag him out the door.

He gave me a disgusted look as he left, so I guess Maddox wasn't bluffing when he told me he made sure they know what I am.

I sink into the seat further, but she sees me anyway.

'Oh, hey!' She sounds genuinely happy to see me.

'Hey,' I mutter. 'I can leave if you need me to.'

She frowns. 'Why?'

'Um, well, I mean, if you're not allowed to be around me ...'

'Not allowed?'

'Never mind.'

Jane comes over and places the books she chose on the table before sinking into the chair opposite me.

'Theo told me a little more about the Mountain. Sounds like a nasty place.'

I nod. 'It's a hellhole, but it is a supe prison. It's not supposed to be a vacation.'

'I didn't even know it existed until the guys were sent there. I didn't grow up around supes. But you said before that you've been in the supe world a long time?'

'Yeah,' I say without bitterness. 'I grew up in Supeland pretty much the only way a human can grow up around supes. Fast.'

'Yeah, their world is a different one, that's for sure.'

I relax, liking that she doesn't ask me about the specifics. Some people are so nosy, but Jane isn't at all.

She shifts in her chair with a groan.

'Still hating pregnancy?' I ask.

She grimaces. 'With a passion! Everyone always says what a magical time it is and how you'll glow and blah blah blah.' She waves a hand. 'One day, you'll get what I mean.'

Something about Jane's artlessness makes me smile. 'Actually, I won't.'

'No?' She looks unconvinced.

'I was in an accident when I was a kid. Got a piece of shrapnel lodged in my gut. Scar tissue.'

'Shit. I'm sorry.' She grimaces. 'I didn't realize.'

'It's ok.'

'No,' she mutters. 'It's not. I suck at reading people, and I put my foot in my mouth all the time. I'm so sorry.'

I give her a smile and shrug. 'It's really fine. I've known it wasn't going to be possible for me all my life, so it's not a big deal. I'm happy for you. Are you excited for the birth?'

She quirks a brow. 'I'm excited to have a baby,' she corrects. 'For the actual birth part, I've already told Theo I want all the drugs and whatever else he can do!'

'Will he listen to you?'

'He fucking better!' she laughs.

'Do you like being their mate?' I ask abruptly and then hope she doesn't think I'm trying to be rude.

'Yeah,' she says without hesitation. 'They're a little rough around the edges sometimes, but they love me, and I love them.'

'But ... you're human.' That is the only thing I can think to say.

She doesn't say anything for a minute, and I get the impression she's not sure what I'm saying.

'I mean ... actually, I don't know what I mean.'

'We started off a little rocky, but we've been through a lot together. I trust them,' she says. 'They're mine, and I'm theirs, and the baby is ours.'

She grins at me. 'Oh, you thought I was a human surrogate, didn't you?'

I nod hesitantly. 'I'm sorry, I—'

'No, it's ok, I get it. Things are changing, but most humans are still contracted to supes. I started out that way.' She shakes her head as she chuckles. 'Look, I gotta go. My guys are waiting for me, but don't worry, I don't need a woman's shelter or anything like that.'

She gives me a wink, and I swear I see her eyes change, but it happens so fast I'm not sure *what* I saw. She leaves quickly, closing the door behind her, and I sit back in the chair, wondering about Jane's relationship with the Iron I's. I mean, it's none of my business, and she's not unhappy. It's clear she doesn't need rescuing from the big, bad monsters.

I hear the door again, and this time it's Maddox. He's wearing a black tux, and though I tell my eyes to stop undressing him, they ignore me completely. I remember how he looked when he came out of the lake, the broadness of his shoulders, the rippling muscles. The tattoo. He looked powerful and predatorial then, but somehow, in the suit, he looks even more so.

I don't make a sound, not letting him know I'm there so I can observe him freely for a little while. He takes a link key out of his jacket and looks at it for a moment before he slips it back into his pocket. Then, he checks his phone and goes to the windows to look out at the dark, wet terrace.

When he turns back, he spies me and can't cover his surprise for a second.

'What are you doing hiding over there?'

I shrug, sort of not wanting to get up to show him what I'm wearing after his comments earlier, but he comes closer, and his eyes flick over me, lingering on the heels.

'Iron said this was normal to wear to where we're going,' I whisper, getting to my feet awkwardly to get it over with.

My eyes stay on his patent leather shoes, and I hear him grunt a 'you'll do'.

'Good,' I murmur, looking at the door as I hear it open again.

All five of the others stalk in, all wearing the same kinds of expensive and tailored dark suits. All five pairs of eyes stray to me, taking me in and locking on.

I clear my throat, trying to pretend my body isn't coming alive under their lustful stares. 'I think we need to get to where we're going,' I murmur, trying to make light of it, but even Daemon and Iron are practically salivating.

Maddox takes my arm, and I start, waiting for that inescapable heat that unfurls whenever he touches me, but nothing happens, and I realize he's wearing gloves.

'You're to stay with Iron at all times,' he orders quietly, 'and if you put one foot wrong, the things he did to you in the Mountain will feel like a walk in the park compared to how I've told him he's allowed to punish you. We can't afford any of your nonsense tonight.'

I snort at his words. 'Noted.'

But I notice the faces of Jayce, Krase, and Axel in my periphery, and I curse this thing between us because all three of them felt my spike of fear, how afraid I am of Iron turning his power on me. I can mask it like a pro on the outside, but it doesn't matter because I can't hide it from them.

I need to start trying harder to keep my emotions under wraps, muting the connections.

Axel takes a small step towards me, but Krase stops him with a surreptitious tug of his sleeve just as I'm thrust towards my keeper for the night.

Iron takes hold of my upper arm, and I shrug him off, giving him a dirty look that makes him smirk.

Maddox takes the link key out of his breast pocket and fits it on the door. I take a deep breath as I prepare to travel by portal. It always makes my stomach do flip-flops. Iron takes my arm again, and I glance at him.

'You're going where we go,' he says as if I'm going to somehow hijack Maddox's portal and come out at a different destination.

I watch them all disappear through, and an unwelcome thought crosses my mind as I reach the precipice. What if whatever's keeping me hidden here on the grounds doesn't extend to Maddox's properties elsewhere?

I pull back, but it's too late. Iron hauls me to him, wrapping an arm around me, and we're in the breach.

The trip is over within five seconds, thankfully, and we emerge in a back-room somewhere. I glance around. It's an untidy filing room. I hear music thumping not too far away.

'Where are we?' I ask Iron.

Maddox pockets the link key and opens the door we just came through, but on the other side of it is now a crowded bar.

I see Jayce and Krase glance at each other, looking half concerned and half wicked, and my eyes narrow as we walk out into the main club. It's busy despite the relatively early hour, and there are supes of all kinds milling around.

My mouth falls open as my gaze finds a stage at the front where a woman is strapped to an X. She has a corset on and heels, and she's being flogged by a large guy whom I get shifter vibes from. My eyes cut to the guys.

'A sex club?'

Maddox chuckles and looks at me like I'm a moron. 'Where else did you think we'd go to feed?' He glances at the others. 'Snacking only. Keep to the rules we agreed on.'

Snacking only. That means no sex. Something that was knotted up in me relaxes, and I try to ignore the fact that not only do I care if Jayce, Krase, and Axel fuck someone else, but Maddox, Iron and Daemon as well.

I'm so fucked.

A supe that appears to be the club's hostess, judging by her long, black dress and general lack of a waitress uniform, approaches us a little hesitantly.

'Can I get you a drink, sir?' she asks.

'Only if it's a martini,' Maddox answers, and she nods.

I frown at the odd exchange as we're led into a room that says, 'VIP Only'. There's a stage and a pole, a long couch, and a low table with a bottle of Champagne in an ice bucket and seven glasses waiting on it.

'Meredith will be in to see you shortly,' the hostess says with a polite smile and a deferring bow of her head.

'So far so good,' Daemon mutters.

'It'll be fine,' Krase says, sitting down and pouring a glass of Champagne. 'No one can see what we really look like or even smell like outside our group. The conjure is a good one. I've used it before.'

I sit down beside him, smiling at him as he hands me the glass, and I take a sip of my second favorite drink. I wonder if he can tell that I like it from my internal reaction as it fizzes over my tongue.

'Wait,' I say, taking in their conversation, 'so we don't look like us?'

'You do, but we're still meant to be in the Mountain, darling,' Maddox mutters. 'Do you really think we'd take such a risk before our pardons are finalized?'

I blink, sort of wondering what everyone else can see from the outside. Are they still hot incubi, or do they look and smell like bridge trolls? I stifle a small chuckle. Maddox pretends not to care, but he'd never go for the stinky bridge troll look.

'I guess not.'

The door opens, and another woman enters. She's dressed in a business suit, and she greets Maddox and the others with an incline of her head.

'Julian?' she says in English with a thick, French accent, coming forward when he nods and kissing both his cheeks. 'It's been too long. Although I know why, of course.'

She joins Krase and me on the couch. 'It's odd to be speaking to a friend you don't recognize.' She tilts her head as she looks up at Maddox. 'No need for the conjure here. If anyone sees you, they can't contact anyone from in here, and I've already ensured no one will remember you once they leave the club.'

Maddox regards her thoughtfully, and she shrugs.

'Of course, if you do not trust me ...'

'Trust isn't the issue, as I'm sure you know,' Maddox chuckles, but he nods at Krase, who takes something out of his pocket and fiddles with it.

Meredith blinks and then smiles at Maddox. 'It's good to see you properly.'

'And you. How's business?'

She rolls her eyes at him. 'You know this, mon ami.' She waggles a playful finger at him. 'I know you read my reports with a ... how you say ... fine tooth comb.'

Maddox nods. 'I mean the things we don't put in writing.'

Meredith's smile becomes sad, and she pats the seat next to her. 'Come. Sit.'

Maddox and the others do as she says, and her eyes flick to me curiously. She gives me a small smile and then turns her attention back to Maddox.

'The disappearances, they continue. Mostly Lower Fae. There's talk of a Gestapo, a private army taking them, and some other supes. But no one sees anything, or if they do, they are too afraid. Maybe they don't remember.'

'Has the resistance been in contact?'

'Ah! Fiona tells us nothing,' Meredith mutters bitterly. 'She is too powerful to care for our affairs, I think.'

'You're wrong,' Maddox replies. 'If Fiona has distanced herself, it's for a reason. The club is probably in the Ten's crosshairs somehow. She won't put her people in danger. You know that.'

'Perhaps,' Meredith concedes. 'Some of them do come from time to time. In fact, tonight, there will be two, but never in the main bar. They frequent the upstairs rooms and watch the shows from there.'

'How long do we have?'

'Two hours, maybe three. But I tell you when their people start arriving so you can leave.'

Maddox nods. 'What happened to the girl who disappeared before we were arrested?'

Meredith looks away. 'She is dead. She was found in the alley behind the club, in the rubbish. They must have had her followed. They knew she was spying for someone. But she never knew who, so at least she could tell them nothing. From what I heard about the state of her body ... they asked.'

Maddox stands, glancing at me. He gestures to the others. 'Go. Feed. Iron, take Jules to the bar.'

I stand up, and we leave slowly, Iron keeping a firm grip on me as we go back into the club's main room. The stage is empty for the moment, but there's a new 'set' for the next *show*. Iron and Daemon flank me. The others slink away, but I see them watching from the wall by the private rooms.

'Are they slaves?' I ask.

'Who?' Daemon surprises me by answering my question.

'The people on the stage,' I answer.

He chuckles. 'Volunteers only. You thinking of signing up, baby?'

His question makes me turn to him. 'Would you like it see me up there strapped down and getting a good whipping?' I ask.

I watch his mouth open and close like a fish, and his eyes go to the stage. I get the distinct impression he's imagining it, and I look away, my attempt to make him uncomfortable having backfired spectacularly.

He gives a low, somewhat belated chuckle. 'Only if I could be the one flogging the shit out of you,' he says sweetly before melting into the crowd.

I swallow hard. I need to stop goading him. It's only a matter of time before he loses it and chokes the life out of me.

Iron gets the barman's attention and asks me what I want. I order a pornstar martini, my actual favorite drink, and look away to take in the atmosphere. It's even busier now, and I realize that most of the newcomers seem to be male. It's some kind of party. I shudder as I notice the large group next to me, realizing they're all vamps and, by the looks of it, a very well-to-do coven.

I don't mess with vamps, not ever. All they have is time, and they're a special kind of nuts if you cross them. They never stop until revenge is theirs, no matter how long it takes. I already have enough regular enemies at my back to keep my attention. I don't need any like that. No, thank you!

But when I look over to ask Iron something, he's gone. My breathing picks up as I cast my eyes around a little frantically, trying to find him, stupidly worrying that I've been left alone. I've been by myself for years, and while I may not have frequented supe sex clubs, I've been to plenty of other, arguably more dangerous places. I can't see him through the thickening crowd. I can't see any of the clan.

I'm lowkey freaking out, and there's nothing like a human's heart pumping fast to get the attention of the bloodsuckers.

'Would you like to come to a private room with me?'

I jump and turn around, realizing I'm being spoken to.

'No, thank you,' I say without looking at the speaker who's propositioning me. 'I'm actually here with someone.'

He chuckles, and I look up. He's handsome and lithe and screams, 'I was almost guillotined in the French Revolution, but, huzzah, I was saved at the last moment by the Scarlet Pimpernel'!

There's even a cravat around his neck. Old habits die hard, I guess.

'No one comes here to be monogamous, chéri.'

I straighten up, and I woman up because looking weak in here is going to get me sucked dry. I sort of feel bad for all the supes I lured into Siggy's lair for her to slurp down. In some circles, a little bloodletting by a three-century-year-old vamp would just be me getting what's coming to me after I helped my spider buddy do all that 'murdering' in the Mountain.

I attempt to get my shit together in front of the vamp and chuckle as I lean back, making a show of surveying him.

'What's your name?' I ask.

'Pierre.'

I'm surprised he doesn't use all the titles he likely has. Most of them are pompous enough to, I hear.

'Victoria,' I say, holding out my hand palm down because I know he'll want to kiss my hand and also because you don't just show a vamp your juicy, blue wrist veins.

He does what I expect, watching me closely, and I grin.

'It doesn't work on me,' I murmur.

'What doesn't?'

'Your vampy voodoo.'

He looks intrigued. 'No? Why not?'

I shrug. 'Just one of the lucky few who can't be mind-frazzled, I guess.'

He smiles at me, clearly enjoying our exchange. 'And what would it take, mon amour, to get you in one of those rooms with me?'

My pornstar martini appears along with the accompanying shot of Prosecco. I turn my attention to it to avoid the question because there is no fucking way I'm going anywhere alone with this guy.

'You know, some people are adamant you have to drink the shot, but I like to pour it in,' I say, changing the subject as I add it to my glass. 'I'm a heathen, I guess.'

'I fucking hope so,' Pierre groans.

I take a sip of my drink, and my eyes roll upwards at the taste. The barman here sure knows what he's doing.

I startle as I feel a pale, cool hand caress my skin where my neck meets my shoulder, and I freeze, staring at Pierre. He's still for a moment as well. Then he yanks his hand back.

'You aren't what you seem,' he drawls, looking suddenly a lot more predatorial and way more intrigued than he was before.

Not what a human girl wants when she's in the presence of one vamp with boundary issues, much less thirty.

'No?' I take another sip of my drink, trying to keep my heart from ratcheting up and giving away my fear to the entire bar.

'Non, chéri, you are not. I think perhaps you need to go back to your master.'

My stomach bottoms out at his words. How does he know?

I force a chuckle and take a large gulp of my drink while inside; I feel like I might just throw up my martini all over this guy's fancy silk cravat.

'I don't have a master.' My voice comes out sounding almost normal, and I smile at him.

'Oh, I think you do.'

I'm suddenly pulled backward into a hard chest and look up to see, out of all the members of the clan, the one most unlikely to save me.

'Daemon,' Pierre says, smiling darkly, and I see one or two of the other vamps look over when Pierre says my savior's name. 'It's been so long. We feared the worst when you disappeared. Wait until McCathrie learns that you've returned. He'll be thrilled.'

'I had some business to take care of,' Daemon says smoothly, his eyes focused solely on the vamp in front of me. 'But please do tell McCathrie I'll be by to see him very soon.'

'I will,' the vamp sneers.

He takes a final look at me that makes me suddenly very afraid he'll say something about what he thinks he knows in front of Daemon, but he just winks at me.

'Until next time, chéri,' he purrs in such a way that I know he'll do everything he can to ensure there *is* a next time.

I smile, hoping it looks natural.

'Until then,' I say quietly.

Chapter Fifteen

IRON

I'm almost to the bar, cursing Maddox for calling me away from Jules when he'd told me to stay by her side. She was only left unguarded for five minutes, but her face has paled, and I see a member of McCathrie's coven has already moved in.

Fucking bloodsucker.

I get ready to snap his neck to send a non-fatal message that won't start a war when I see Daemon swoop in. He touches Jules like she's ours, giving her our protection by the gesture, and I relax a little. I wouldn't trust him alone with her, but she's not in danger in public with him.

My eyes narrow as I watch him speaking to one of them. He knows them well. It must have been while he was out on his own after Maddox kicked him out of the clan. I knew he'd have gotten involved with some of the seedier organized crime syndicates. It's the only way he'd have survived out there. But I had no idea he'd stooped to working for the vamps.

I wonder if Maddox knows. I'll bet he doesn't. He would

never have let Daemon back in if he did. The bloodsuckers don't just let you out once you're in their pockets.

He starts walking away with Jules, and I intercept them, grabbing Jules and pulling her a little too hard towards me. She stumbles into me, and I catch her, murmuring an apology and noticing she still looks jarred by whatever the vamp was saying to her, though she's hiding it well. She looks up at me with wide eyes, and I get lost in them for a moment.

Until I hear Daemon's low growl, I focus on my clan brother, stifling my own snarl.

Has he forgotten she isn't actually ours?

'How deep in are you?' I sneer.

He takes a step back. 'I don't know what you're talking about.'

'Sure you don't.' I smirk at him. 'Maddox wants to talk to you,' I lie.

'What about?'

I shrug. 'Probably about McCathrie if he just saw you talking to his guys.'

'I wasn't talking to them,' he mutters. 'I was making sure the dumb human didn't get herself lured into one of the private rooms to get fucked and sucked.'

Jules opens her mouth, looking affronted, but I take her arm and turn her away, taking her to the other side of the bar where it's quieter. I can practically hear her teeth grinding.

'He's right, you know.' I say, ordering her another martini. 'The vamps are dangerous.'

'Please,' she mutters. 'Act like I'm a dumb human, like I have no clue what's going on. Underestimate me, Iron.' She snorts. 'It works for me every time in Supeland.'

My hand snaps out, and I take her chin in a firm grip, making her look at me.

'Thinking of making trouble for us again?' I ask, unable to keep the anger from my voice.

She bats my hand away and doesn't look scared even a little.

'Why don't you make me tell you if I am?' she hisses. 'Oh, no, wait, that doesn't work on me. You have to torture me for hours and then trick me to get me to tell you shit.' She glances around. 'But this isn't the right time or place. Too bad.'

'Isn't it?' I murmur too low for her to hear.

Her drink appears on the bar, and I hand it to her. She drinks it in one, staring at me angrily.

Another show starts on the stage, and the lust in the room increases. It's enough to sate me for a few days, but don't even look at what's going on up there. I want something else, something I've been denying myself when it's clear half the members of this fucking clan aren't doing the same. I want a piece of the pie.

'Come on,' I say.

'Where?'

'I'll show you,' I say cryptically, ensuring she's curious.

I move away from the bar, not bringing her with me but making sure she's following. There's a hallway with private rooms and an unmarked door with a keypad at the end. I put in the code and go into the dark room.

I'm already second-guessing myself, but I can't resist as I wait until she's inside, and I close the door behind her.

'Are you scared?' I drawl in her ear.

'No.'

But she is. I can hear it in her voice just a little.

I move away from her, reaching up and turning off the security camera before I turn on the dim light.

I hear her gasp at what she sees, but she doesn't run for the door.

'How about now?' I say.

Her eyes find mine. 'What is this?' she asks me.

'A little fun if you want it,' I say, not moving towards her, wanting to give her every chance to leave if that's what she decides to do.

She swallows hard but takes a step into the room. 'What is this place?'

'It's where we come to play. Privately. We're the only ones with the code.'

'To feed?'

'Yes. Among other things.'

She takes in the pieces of furniture in the room, each one specifically designed for dark deeds.

'When Krase caught you in the woods, I was so pissed that he locked me in that fold.'

'I know,' she murmurs as she walks around. 'You wanted to save me.'

'No, Jules,' I growl. 'I was pretending even to myself, but I wasn't going to save you.'

I grab her from behind, and she jumps but doesn't scream.

'All I could think about was that I was so close to breaking. I was made to watch Daemon do what he wanted in the Mountain, and then I was forced to watch Krase too,' I whisper. 'I wanted it to be my turn. I needed it to be my turn.'

I turn her around so she can see my face. 'Do you trust me?'

She shakes her head.

'Because of the Mountain.'

Jules gives me a tiny, hesitant nod, looking down at the floor.

She's more scared of me than I realized. She's just so good at hiding it around the supes that it's very difficult to spot. I wanted her to be afraid before. I liked it. But I'm cursing myself at how I handled her interrogation in the Mountain. I was so focused on following Maddox's orders, so angry that my brothers had succumbed to her. Whatever was going on in my head because of that place made me ruthless and cold as ice. It wasn't meant to be personal, but it was. I did things, said things to her that keep me up at night.

'I'm sorry about the Mountain,' I say, cringing a little. 'I can't excuse what I did, but I'll never use my power to hurt you ever again.'

She doesn't look at me. 'I don't want to talk about it.'

I tilt her head up to see her eyes. 'You have my vow, Jules. I won't break it.'

'Thank you,' she whispers.

'You believe me?' I ask, relief flooding through me.

She nods. 'A know how important vows like that are in Supeland.'

'But I can't forget what you did, the things you said, how you fucked with my head,' she whispers, looking away. 'No matter how hard I try.'

I don't speak for a minute, surprised that she's said it aloud. Jules isn't the type to show weakness, but that she is with me is telling.

'I have an idea,' I say, tilting her chin up to see her face again and gauge her reaction. 'What if I compelled you here and now, but everything I made you do led to pleasure?'

Pain. But I don't say that last word.

She tenses, and her eyes dart up to mine.

'What do you mean? What will you make me do?' she asks almost inaudibly.

'Feel very, very good.' I let go of her, and I step away even though anticipation is rolling through me that I might *finally* have the human who's taken over my every waking thought for days.

'I won't do anything you don't want,' I tell her. 'You can leave right now, Jules. The door isn't locked from this side.'

She swallows hard, and she nods without discussing any clear boundaries with me. I frown at her inexperience.

'How many men have you been with?' I ask.

'Three,' she whispers.

I can't hide my shock. 'I thought–'

I shut my mouth as her cheeks redden. I may not deserve her trust, but I'm not going to abuse it. I'm going to make sure she loves this.

'Turn around, spread your legs, and bend over.' I order, imbuing my words with power.

She jerks as she tries to fight the magick on impulse but does what she's told, just as I knew she would. Now, it's my turn to swallow hard as her short dress rides up, giving me an amazing view of the bottom of her ass cheeks and her plump pussy lips through her gauzy underwear.

'You will tell me to stop if you want me to stop,' I command.

I lightly touch her panties with the tip of my thumb, and I hear a tiny gasp. It comes away damp, and I chuckle.

'Wider,' I growl and watch as she struggles to follow my order in her high heels, her hands resting flat on the floor.

Her eyes follow me as I move around the room, gathering things I may need for our impromptu little tryst.

'Get down on your hands and knees,' I bark.

She does what I say.

'Crawl to me.'

I see a flash of anger in her eyes, followed by something else entirely, and I grin. She likes this even if she doesn't want to like it.

When she gets to me, she pauses and stands when I tell her to.

'Take off the dress. Slowly.'

She looks up at me, her eyes wide, and draws the hemline up and over her head.

'Stop,' I command while her head is still covered, and she can't see what I'm doing. I take in her tits framed so nicely by an expensive-looking, black balconette bra and the little matching panties she's wearing that makes me wonder where she got them from. *Or who.* The others have been giving her things, I realize. Has she been ignoring Maddox's deal with her?

I doubt I'd have noticed if she was. When I'm not taking her out riding, I'm shut in my room running the estate and some of the businesses while Maddox is engaged in playing catch-up and kissing Council ass to get us pardoned.

'Take off the bra.'

She unclasps it and lets it fall down her arms.

'I think you've been a naughty girl, Jules,' I say as I pull her gently over to the table in the middle of the room and push her forward gently onto it. 'I think some punishment is in order, don't you?'

She struggles a little as I strap her down and secure her legs wide enough that I have complete access to her ass and pussy. I leave her heels on.

'You can tell me if you want me to stop, and I'll let you go,' I remind her just in case.

She says nothing, and I grin.

I feel the globes of her ass, slapping them a little. She doesn't make a sound, and I frown, taking the crop I brought over and drawing it up her slit.

'Do you know what this is by the feel of it?' I ask.

'No.'

'Have you ever been spanked before?'

'Yes.'

'Did it hurt?'

'I have a high pain tolerance,' she says.

'Hmm, maybe you do, but you've never been hit with a riding crop on your bare little asshole, I'll wager.'

She strains against the leather and twists around. I'll bet she can just see me through the fabric over her head. I imagine her pleading eyes, though I can't see them.

'Tell me to stop if you want me to stop,' I say again.

She remains silent, and I fondle her pussy with a grin. 'I think you like this. I've noticed after a ride, you get this little look on your face when you dismount, and your ass is sore. You like a little pain, don't you?'

She tenses a little. 'I–I don't know.'

'There's no need to be embarrassed. A lot of people do.' I lean in closer. 'I'm one of them,' I whisper and hear her gasp. 'Do you want to stop?'

'No,' she breathes.

'Good girl.'

I step back. 'Talking to vamps,' I murmur, 'fucking other members of the clan even though you were warned not to.' I tut at her. 'Not the behavior that's expected from a good little human guest of the estate.'

Her body goes rigid, but I wait until she relaxes, and only then do I deliver the first stinging slap directly onto her asshole with the flat end of the crop.

She squeals and struggles, ripping off the dress that's still around her torso and trying to stand, but the thick straps hold.

'The straps are made for supes,' I tell her. 'You're not getting out of them unless you ask.'

I caress her back. 'Do you want me to stop?' I whisper.

'No,' she whimpers. 'I think ... I do like it.'

I smack her ass cheeks, but it doesn't elicit the same reaction from her at all, so I tap her delicate hole again. She cries out and then moans, twisting around with tears in her eyes this time, but she doesn't say a word.

Ten times, I swat her vulnerable flesh, and ten times, she cries out for me but doesn't tell me to stop.

When I'm finished, she's quivering and panting. She's gripping the sides hard with her hands, and her legs are ramrod straight in her heels. She looks fucking amazing.

'I think this fae would crawl naked through iron shavings if it meant I'd get to see you like this,' I murmur.

She pulls at the straps in impatience, and I laugh, stroking down her back to her ass and dipping between her wide legs.

'We're not finished yet,' I tell her, plunging two fingers deep into her sopping wet pussy. 'Hmm, you did enjoy your spanking.'

She gasps as I finger fuck her, whimpering as I take them out and ease them into her ass. I push them in and out a few times to see how she reacts. When she whimpers, and her hips buck a little, I unzip my pants. She hears and swivels her head to look at me, her cheeks still wet. She's breathing hard.

'Do you want me to fuck you?'

She nods, her eyes not leaving me.

I add a third finger to her ass, stretching her, and she moans, collapsing back down to the table as I ease my dick into her cunt.

'You feel just as amazing as I knew you would,' I whisper, starting slow because even in my human form, I'm pretty big.

She writhes under me, making little noises of pleasure that soon have me pounding her into the table with my cock and my fingers.

'You like that, princess?' I grind out.

'Yes!' she squeals.

I smile and do what I've been dreaming of since I watched Daemon's fingers working in her at Dante's table since Krase fucked her in the forest. Only this time, I'm not just a spectator.

I demon-up, my entire body growing, my fingers and my cock included.

She makes a sound between a pleasured moan and a pained squeal as my body changes. I stretch her and fill her more than she ever has been before. She bucks against my fingers, moaning my name. Her energy fills me, its potency making me feel a little dizzy.

'Your tight little pussy is choking my cock,' I groan, pumping into her faster, harder.

She screams loudly as she comes, her entire body quaking under me, her shoes falling off as her legs scramble to gain purchase. Her holes squeeze my dick and my fingers, and I find my own release, pushing into her deep and seeding her. The image of her round and pregnant makes me groan in pleasure.

'I'm going to breed you,' I say darkly, not really thinking about my words.

But she goes rigid under me, and then I *feel* her. She's shocked and confused and suddenly sad.

I put my glamor back on and pull out of her, stepping back in surprise. I didn't realize I'd be able to read her emotions. This has never happened to me after feeding before, and I'm not sure what to make of it.

I release her from the straps immediately, and she rises and teeters on her feet, not looking at me.

I frown, putting aside the fact that I *can* feel her in favor of what I *am* feeling from her. I had her consent and made sure she could stop at any time. What happened? This wasn't like what I did to her in the Mountain, I remind myself. She wanted everything I did. I made sure of it.

Feeling the urge to fix whatever it is I've done, I pick her up and sit her on the table facing me, being careful with her no doubt sore body.

'What's wrong?' I ask, not beating about the bush.

She shakes her head, eyes avoiding mine.

'Did I hurt you?'

Her brow furrows.

I sigh. 'I mean, did I hurt you in a way you didn't want?'

She shakes her head. 'I liked what you did. Even the things you made me do. I didn't think I would, but ... it was different than in the Mountain. You were different then. Cold. All business.'

She touches her chest and looks up at me. 'You feel different than I thought.'

I take a small step back warily. She can feel me as well. The thought of her knowing me so intimately has my eyes narrowing to slits while she's not watching me. How did she do this? Is this how she took down the others? Did I just play right into her hands?

'You're surprised,' she says like we're talking about the weather.

Fuck. This.

I lock every emotion down fast, numbing myself as much as I can, and she frowns, looking up at me in askance. She can tell the difference.

Can't read me anymore, little snake.

I smirk as I glance at my watch and then look at my phone. No one's messaged, and luckily, we still have a few minutes to clean up because I don't think I could explain what just happened to Maddox. I wouldn't want him to know how I succumbed to her anyway.

I shuck my clothes quickly.

'Come on,' I say, picking her up and taking her into the bathroom.

I turn on the water and wait for it to heat up, putting her under the spray when it's warm. She grabs the soap, but I take it from her gently.

'All part of the service,' I chuckle, but I'm wondering if she knew this would happen, that we'd have this bridge between us. She has to have, right? She's been with three of the others. Can they feel her, too? Can she feel them? What is her game? What if she tells Maddox what we just did?

I wasn't part of the deal with Maddox, so if she does tell him, she doesn't lose anything. *I* could, though. Maddox values trust. Respect. Loyalty. I'm his second, and I've noticed Daemon trying to worm his way in. I'm not giving him the ammunition to take my place.

My scent needs to be absolutely gone from her. No evidence. Her word against mine because I'll be the one who's believed, not the thieving, human conwoman.

But she lets me wash her, allows me to move her this way and that to make one-hundred and ten percent sure there's not a hint of me left on her when I'm done.

When I get below the waist, I hesitate before washing her intimately with my soapy fingers, but I have to be the one to do it in case she tries to leave traces of me for Maddox to scent on purpose.

She stifles a whimper when I'm too rough, but I feel her arousal spike too. I hate the way it makes me want to fuck her again here and now. I thought having her would stop me from wanting her, get her out of my system. But it's done the opposite. What is this? Why do I want this human?

My phone rings, and I curse, shutting off the water.

'Maddox?' I say over the receiver, and her eyes widen.

She grabs a towel and begins to dry herself vigorously as I answer, but I don't have enough reception to hear more than a broken crackle of Maddox's voice. I watch her movements almost lazily but am gratified that she doesn't seem to want Maddox to know what we just did any more than I do.

'I'm coming,' I say loudly, cursing again over the static before hanging up.

I dry myself off and grab my clothes off the floor. I need to leave before her so no one sees where we've been together. Luckily, the bathroom is down this hallway, too.

'It's okay,' I say as I take in her almost frenzied movements. 'We still have a while before the fae are due. Finish up in here, and I'll meet you by the bar in a few minutes.'

She nods, and I leave without looking back, grabbing my jacket and tearing open the door.

I walk through the bar, scanning it for the others, and I see Daemon loitering by one of the anterooms.

I start making my way through the crowd toward him, but I'm beckoned by Jayce to the room we were first shown into when we got here.

When I get inside, the door closes, and he and Krase bar my way.

'Where is she?' Krase growls.

'Safe,' I say.

'What did you do?' Jayce hisses low.

'Nothing!'

'The hell you didn't,' Axel says from the couch next to me. He stands up and pushes me in the chest. 'We all felt it. What the fuck did you do?'

'Nothing!' I say again as I stagger back. 'She needed the bathroom.'

My eyes narrow as I properly take in their words. They *can* feel her, too, and the way they're acting ... whatever started in the Mountain with Axel and Jayce has continued despite the deal Jules made with Maddox. And Krase is fucking her as well.

'Shit. I was right. *All* of you? With her? Maddox is going to throw a fucking fit when he finds out.'

I shake my head and ask myself again how she was able to do this. 'Fuck.'

'How's Maddox going to find out?' Jayce says with a snarl. 'He won't so long as you keep your mouth shut.'

Krase grins, pushing me into the door behind me.

I let him.

'You won't escape his wrath either. You didn't tell him about the woods. You're just as culpable, Iron, and don't you forget it. Maddox and Daemon don't find out. Not until the time is right.'

I shake my head. 'What? What the hell are you talking about? You think he'll make her sign?'

I look at both brothers. Do they actually think Maddox will lock her into a contract?

My dick stiffens at the thought of her bound to us. Do I *want* that?

My hand comes up to my chest, and I realize it aches. I can

still sense her right now, but it's a shadow of how intense it was before I locked it down. I'm not sure what it is I'm feeling from her at the moment.

'He'll never go for it, and, in case you've forgotten, this isn't a goddamned democracy. What Maddox says, goes.'

Axel snorts at my words and turns away. 'She's unsettled,' he says to the others who nod. 'Something that happened in the club tonight shook her to her fucking core.' He casts me a withering look that I ignore. 'I'd say it was you, but it happened while she was at the bar.'

'The vamps were there,' I say. 'One was talking to her before Daemon got to her.'

Krase nods. 'Aye, and she didn't like what he was saying one bit.'

The door opens, and Maddox enters the room.

Speak of the devil ...

All of us shut up, but Maddox doesn't seem to notice we were in the middle of something.

'I've been trying to call you!' he snaps.

I take my phone out. 'Reception isn't good. I couldn't hear you.'

He looks agitated. 'Where is Jules? You were told to keep her with you.'

'She needed the bathroom,' I shrug.

'You left her alone?'

I give Maddox an incredulous look. He was the one who wanted me back in the room with him and Meredith, making me leave her alone at the bar earlier.

'What's the big deal?' I ask. 'This is our club. Besides, Daemon claimed her in front of vamps. No one will mess with her.'

'The fae are early!' Maddox hisses. 'They've already begun to arrive. We'll need to leave. Now.'

JULES

The shitshow of the evening hits me as soon as Iron leaves the dim room. I lean heavily against the table I just got railed on.

I fucked Iron, or, or accurately, he fucked me. In sex club. In a *sex room in a sex club*.

He spanked my asshole, and it hurt, and, for some insane reason, unlike most of the pain I've experienced before, I loved it.

I put my hand over my heart and frown. He didn't like that I knew what he was feeling. Right now, I can sense the others, but he muted himself almost instantly. I'm not getting much at all.

Four down, two to go, I think bitterly.

I throw on my clothes quickly. What am I thinking? I ask myself this every day, but I'm no closer to figuring it out. My life is circling a drain, and I'm going down very soon. Maddox WILL find out, and regardless of what these demons keep doing to me, only then will I be well and truly fucked. Why am I so drawn to these incubi? I could go out on a limb and say that being around so many males in the Mountain made me go supedick crazy, but I haven't been drawn to the Iron I's at all. In fact, I feel a little repulsed when I'm around them.

It's completely the opposite with Maddox's clan, though. Even though I know Maddox and Daemon would laugh at me, and be cruel, a part of me still wants to go find them and beg them both to fuck me every which way from Sunday. Maybe even up on that stage.

I mean, what kind of a girl wants guys who hate her to do that to her? I thought I had some self-respect, but maybe it was all for show. Maybe I never did have any at all; I was just going through the motions. Maybe it was taken from me when I was still just a kid.

In the bathroom, I make sure I'm not disheveled before I leave the room, shutting the door firmly behind me. I walk out of the hallway and towards the bar, scanning the room but not seeing the guys anywhere.

My eyes pass over a Lower Fae by the other side of the bar, and I do a double-take. His back is to me, but I'm sure I recognize him. He turns to talk to someone, and I gasp, throwing myself back into the hallway and against the wall, my heart hammering in my chest. I haven't seen that fucker in years, but I'd know him anywhere. More importantly, though, *he knows me.*

I need to get out of here without him seeing me.

There's a stairwell.

I noticed it when Iron brought me down the hallway earlier. I'm shaking so badly I can hardly walk as I turn and try to make it to the last door on the left as quickly as possible, hoping against hope that it's unlocked and there's no alarm on it.

I reach it and push the bar. It swings open, and there's no buzzing or ringing that I can hear. I slip past the threshold and close it gently behind me, taking off my shoes and carrying them as I run silently down three flights of stairs.

When the steps run out, I push through another door at the bottom and find myself in an alleyway. There's garbage and broken glass. It's dark, the only light coming from a neon sign on the side of the building that bathes everything in green and blue light. I have no idea where I am, not even if I'm still in the human world.

I slip my shoes back on and walk down the steps, skirting around the refuse and trying to ignore the smell of rot.

There's a sound by the dumpsters down at the end of the alley, and I slip into the shadows near the building out of the sign's dim light, glad it's dark out, until I hear an animalistic growl just behind me.

I freeze and cringe as I turn, finding a pair of glowing red eyes behind me.

What the hell is this thing?

I take in the creature before me. It's like a huge dog, but not a wolf or a shifter. It's like a giant, shaggy Doberman.

'Hello, puppy,' I try.

It snarls at me, and I take a step back, but it doesn't move. I'm scared, but I'm not wet-my-pants terrified after some of the weird shit I saw and heard in the Mountain.

'I had a friend scarier than you,' I tell it, deciding that, like the supes upstairs, showing fear equals death. 'Now, hush. I'm not here to take your food or fight. I'm just going to hide out in the shadows with you for a little while.'

It makes doggy-talking noises at me and sits down. Something moves behind it, and I realize it's got two tails that are now wagging.

'Good boy,' I say.

The tails wag harder, thudding against the ground.

I grin and put my hand out.

He sniffs it and tilts his head adorably.

'I know,' I coo, 'I don't have a scent at the moment, but I probably don't smell all that exciting anyway, even if you could scent me.'

I hear more growls in the shadows and see five more sets of eyes appear in the darkness at the first dog's back.

Shit.

But he swings his head back towards them and snarls. The eyes disappear.

Thanks, bud,' I murmur at my new friend.

I peer around the corner as I hear the door open, getting ready to run if it's the fae, but it's Krase who comes out into the street.

I relax immediately, wondering how he found me so fast.

'She's out here,' he says, staring at his phone, and I let out a small sound of annoyance.

'He's got me tagged like a dog,' I mutter.

I'm sort of glad but also annoyed that I'm glad that he knows where I am all the time.

I side-eye the hound. 'No offense.'

I see the others come out of the door behind Krase, who's still looking at the phone, but I know he must be able to feel me now. He's just playing to Maddox and Daemon, who are looking around the alley. Iron, Jayce, Axel, and Krase are basically looking right at me. They know exactly where I am, irrespective of the tracker Krase has on me.

'Time for me go. Bye, Fluffy,' I say, and I step out into the light.

'Looking for me?'

I see relief in Krase's and the others' eyes, but it's Maddox who comes to me. It's not to hug me, though.

'Where the hell were you?' he thunders.

'Looking for you,' I spit just as angrily. 'Then I saw some fae in the bar, and I took the nearest exit like any other human who has an ounce of self-preservation!'

He lets out a noise of frustration and mutters something about the vexing female.

'It's dangerous out here these days,' he says, pulling his fingers roughly through his disheveled blonde hair. 'There are packs of hellhounds roaming these streets! Do you have any idea what they'd do to a defenseless human like you?'

'Sit for me and wag their tails? Get a name like Fluffy?' I smirk at the angry demon in front of me and give him a wink. 'Careful, Maddox, you almost sound like you care.'

I swear I hear one of the others snigger, but when I look at them, they're all so stoic that I can't tell which one it was.

'Come on,' Maddox growls, grabbing my arm and hauling

me back to the side exit I took. He throws the link key to Daemon, who attaches it to the door and opens it.

The portal is quick, and we arrive at the library in record time, Maddox still gripping my arm like he's afraid I'll up and disappear.

'You can let go,' I murmur, and the fingers go slack.

I don't look back at him as I follow the others out of the library. I make for the stairs because I'm dead tired after my evening of supe fun.

'Jules?'

I turn to find Axel.

'We're going to watch a movie. Want to join us?'

Jayce is behind him, giving me an encouraging nod, and I give them a smile because this is the first time they've asked me to hang out since I got here, but I shake my head.

'Consider me Cinderella,' I chuckle, gesturing to the grandfather clock by the wall near the stairs that's showing it's about five minutes from midnight.

'Are you okay?' Jayce asks.

He steps closer and lowers his voice. 'Something happened in the club. We felt your fear multiple times, Bana-Phrionnsa.'

'I'm fine,' I say, turning and ascending the stairs as I push all my emotions down.

I definitely need to find a way to mute my feelings, I think as I go into my room and close the door. Otherwise, it's only a matter of time before they learn about my past. The thought of them knowing everything makes me sick to my stomach. I touch my chest and can't feel the brand. The conjure hiding it is still working fine.

I peel off my dress and get into my bed, glad I made it back in one piece and realizing how at home I feel in this house.

Fuckety fuckety fuck my dumbass self.

I fall asleep almost instantly but wake in the night to find Krase in the bed next to me, his arms around me while I sleep.

He doesn't say anything, just holds me, and I fall back into a deep sleep.

--

I wake to a grey and wet morning, feeling unsettled but trying not to because I don't want the incubi to feel it too and start asking me questions I can't answer about last night.

I frown at the empty bed next to me, sure that Krase had been here. But he's gone now.

I get up and pad to the bathroom, following my usual morning routine. I stare at myself in the mirror. I look the same, maybe a little healthier. Regular food and sleep will do that, I guess.

I go into my closet. When I turn on the light, I find a note on the dresser.

These should suffice. ~ M

In the drawers are tank tops and yoga pants, jeans and stretch pants. That was fast. When did Maddox find the time to do this? When did they even get delivered?

Supes.

I let out a breath and pull on a grey tank with some pants. They're soft and stretchy. He even remembered socks.

When I'm dressed in 'normal' comfy clothes, I feel weirdly better. Don't get me wrong, I love a top-tier Armani as much as the next girl, but sometimes you just want to veg on the couch instead of feeling as if you have to sit like you're balancing a book on your head.

I grab the folder that Maddox gave me, deciding to get to work on this party I'm supposed to be planning. But there's no phone in my room, so I go downstairs to make the calls to the suppliers. I already made a list of what I need to book, so it's just a question of doing it.

I see Jane in the hall and give her a wave.

'Hey,' she says. 'We're leaving today. Sorry, I thought we'd have more time to hang out, but,' she shrugs, 'incubi.'

I nod. 'Incubi.'

'Hey, look, uh ...' she lowers her voice. 'I don't know if you know, but Korban and I had to stay here for a while when Alex and the other Iron I's got put in the Mountain.'

'Oh? No, didn't know that.'

'Well, I just ... I don't know what you have with these guys, but it was kind of weird. They were pretty close to killing Korban.'

'I thought they were friends.' I say.

'Yeah, it's like some kind of demon territorial thing. Maddox wanted a mate. I fit the bill, but I was contracted to the Iron I's ...'

'Did you *want* to be with Maddox?' I ask, not sure if I want to hear the answer.

Jane looks disgusted. 'No way. No offense, but ew. Besides, he came to his senses, and it all worked out.'

I frown. 'So then, why are you telling me?'

'Because you shouldn't trust him,' she whispers. 'He's slippery as fuck. Nothing he says is the whole truth. Same with Daemon.'

'Noted,' I say. 'Incubi.'

She snorts. 'Fucking incubi.'

Chapter Sixteen

DAEMON

'I'll see you.' Alex says, looking for a second like he might hug me, causing me to take a step back.

Instead, his arm goes around his mate, who has hardly looked at me even once the whole time she's been here.

'Yeah,' I say, my eyes flicking from her to him.

I watch as my brother leaves through the portal, taking Jane and the rest of his clan back to the newly built mansion they have in the forests just outside of Metro.

Jane waves goodbye to Jules, and I wonder how close they could possibly have gotten while she was here, but Jules waves back with a genuine-looking smile on her face.

The portal closes, and our guests are finally gone. I feel like I can breathe again.

I side-eye Jules. *Almost.*

Maddox sits back down at his desk, looking through some paperwork.

Jules, who's suddenly dressing in loungewear instead of

evening gowns, approaches him. My eyes narrow. What's her angle now?

'Thanks for the clothes,' she says to him.

Maddox looks up, his expression bored, but I watch his fist clench as he takes Jules in directly.

'I didn't choose them,' he drawls with a roll of his eyes.

She chuckles, and he raises a brow.

'I was just imagining you actually looking for clothes in a normal department store.'

He snorts. 'I wouldn't do that for anyone, let alone you.'

I think I'm going to see anger in her expression, but I should have known better. She ignores his barbs.

'Well, thanks anyway,' she says more brightly than she has any business being when he's treating her like shit to her face.

Dumb supe slut.

'Get out,' I snarl at her, and she flinches just a tiny bit at my growling words.

Upsetting her is more than a little gratifying, and I find I want to keep messing with her.

I push a pen off the desk. It lands in front of her, and I watch her stoop to pick it up, giving me a great view of her tits in that tank top. Maddox's eyes roll over her ass while he pretends to work.

She puts the pen back on the desk, ignoring my smirk as she walks out.

'Iron said he's received some news about Robertson,' I say once the door shuts and we're left alone.

I sit in front of the desk, watching Maddox stare at the door Jules just left through, his expression unreadable.

He blinks. 'Yes. As of a fortnight ago, he was still alive, but he's in the wind. I'm having our contacts search for him. I've put a bounty on his head.'

I nod. 'And the fights? They starting up again soon?'

'Yes, we need the revenue stream until we're properly up and running again. The pardons will come through next week, but we need to wait until All-Hallows for the official announcements. After that, we'll be nigh on untouchable. I spoke with Alex, and we decided on a fight next month. Sort it, will you?'

I nod, glad I'm being given tasks again. Maybe Maddox is finally forgiving me for Jules, really letting me back into clan business.

'I saw you speaking with Pierre La Croix at the club,' he says.

I just about hold in my grimace. 'Look, there were times out there when—'

He looks up. 'I understand, and I don't need the details. But whatever business you have with McCathrie, finish it. No split loyalties.'

I nod, glad he's giving me a chance. I was afraid he'd just kick me to the curb once he knew I had unfinished business with the vamps.

What I can't tell him, though, is how much money I owe them and how fucked I am if I can't pay it back soon. I thought I'd be able to get something out of Alex, but he's adamant that our father's clan left nothing when they died. I need to get another plan together and fast since Pierre knows I'm back now. I saw him writing on a napkin from the bar after we spoke.

Smart, old-school fucker wrote himself a note so he'd remember he'd seen me even after the club magick wiped his memory when he left.

I stifle a sigh. Wish I'd never had to get in bed with the vamps, but here I am.

'Will that be all?' I ask, and Maddox nods. 'Keep me updated.'

I leave the library, feeling like hitting the pads for a while. I go up to my room to change. My phone rings, and I sigh as I see who it is.

I answer in a clipped tone with just my last name. 'Mackenzie.'

'Daemon,' comes the soft, vampiric drawl that makes me grit my teeth. 'Meet me at the club.'

'Now?'

'Now, my dear friend.'

The line goes dead. *Fuck.* I've been summoned. I thought I'd have more time.

Abandoning my gym plans, I go back through the house, grabbing a link key from the top of the grandfather clock, where we always keep a spare, and skirting around the cameras.

I use it on the nearest closet, and it deposits me in the club we were in last night. It's early and quiet, so I find Pierre quickly. He's sitting in the middle of the venue, not even bothering to hide our meeting.

'I wondered if I'd have to send someone to get you,' he says, taking a sip of his very red drink.

'Not at all,' I murmur smoothly, sitting down at the table across from him.

'Let's get to the point, Daemon. You owe us a lot of money, and time is running out for you. When will you be settling your debt to McCathrie?'

'I just got out of the Mountain,' I say apologetically.

'Yes, I gathered, and I'm wondering how you escaped. I'll bet it's a good story. I'd very much like to hear it one of these days.'

'Perhaps. Anyway, I was in jail. I'll get the money to McCathrie as soon as I have it, but ...'

'This isn't a charity, Daemon. You have until the end of the month. Payment in full.'

I sit back in my chair and hear it creak. 'That isn't going to be possible. Kill me if you must, but you definitely won't get your money then.'

Pierre takes another sip of his drink. 'I did enjoy speaking to your human, Victoria, last night.'

I shift in my seat again, not liking even her fake name on the vampire's lips. I don't say anything.

'What if I told you that giving her to us would solve all your problems?'

I stand up abruptly. 'I'm not a skin trader!' I hiss, wanting nothing more than to beat the shit out of this asshole and tear out his heart for even suggesting I sell Jules to the vamps.

'Not for *that*,' Pierre mutters. 'Though I'm sure I'd enjoy a taste.'

'For what then?' I growl, taking my seat once more. 'What possible use would a human have to you if not for feeding from?'

Pierre smiles darkly. 'You really don't know who you've got there, do you?'

He laughs, and my eyes narrow. 'Does this have anything to do with … Tamadrielle?'

The vampire sputters at the name and hushes me at once, looking all around us as if someone could be lurking. 'Quiet, you fool! The walls have ears! Never utter that name. Never let anyone hear it from your lips.'

He heaves a melodramatic, unneeded breath.

'But, yes,' he says low and eyeing me meaningfully, 'the human is worth a lot to some.'

I regard the vampire coldly, not giving anything away. The deal is as clear as he's going to make it. I give Jules to them, and they absolve me of the debt I owe them.

'Who is ….'

'Ask your human.' He laughs. 'She knows that name.'

'I don't believe you,' I sneer.

'She'll have his mark on her. A brand on her body.'

'I've seen her body,' I half lie. 'There's no brand.'

Pierre chuckles low. 'She's got a conjure on her. Remove it and see for yourself if I'm telling the truth.'

I stand. 'I'll be in touch.'

'Make it soon, Daemon,' he warns.

I nod and leave immediately, a plan forming. If Pierre is right about Jules, then I won't be selling her to McCathrie; I'll be going straight to the source for top dollar. I look at my messages and copy the number Paris got for me through the Iron' I's private detective. Their guy's good if he's found Tamadrielle's number already when no one's even allowed to say the High Fae fucker's name. I save it to my phone.

First, I need to find out if Pierre is right about Jules.

JULES

The wind in my face takes my cares away, and I urge my giant horse faster, laughing when he leaps over a fallen log, and I feel the pitch and roll in my stomach that makes me giddy.

I hold him tightly between my knees and let go of the reins, closing my eyes and spreading my arms wide. I feel like I'm flying.

I hear Iron's shout from behind me and open my eyes, taking up the reins again and casting a look behind as I ease Pitch to a canter, and Iron comes up next to me.

'Are you trying to kill yourself?' he demands.

'Sorry,' I say guiltily.

I hear him swear under his breath, and I hide a grin.

'I thought you were too far back in my dust to see that,' I tease, laughing at his answering growl.

A speck of cold rain lands on my cheek. 'Want to race back?'

He shakes his head. 'You're in too reckless a mood,' he mutters. 'You're going to break your fool neck.'

He's very angry, I realize. He's furious.

With me.

'I'm sorry,' I say, turning to face him properly, not even

having to pretend I'm contrite. 'Really, Iron. I promise I won't do that again.'

'Fine,' he says, pulling out his phone. 'I need to speak to Maddox, so I'm going back to the house directly. You take Pitch to the stable, and I'll take care of him later.'

'Okay,' I say, but he's already galloping away.

Suddenly feeling morose, I head back to the stable and put Pitch inside. I give him some hay to munch on until Iron comes, and then I go to the last stall to take off my riding clothes.

I'm in the middle of changing when a hand closes on my forearm. I'm whirled around and slammed into the wall before I can even see my assailant.

I scream as my head hits the wooden slats, and when I look to see who has me, my eyes find Daemon. The smirk on his face makes me quake.

'You can't hurt me,' I cry, 'Maddox promised—'

'You were the one who didn't keep to the deal,' he snarls. 'Fucking supe slut!'

I'm sick of him calling me that!

Angrily, I push him hard in the chest, succeeding in making him take a couple of steps back, and I know my strength surprises him because he swears and doubles down in his effort to grab me.

I try to dart around him, but he succeeds in taking me by the throat like he always seems to, but he doesn't squeeze; his gloved fingers just keep me where he wants me.

'This clan is my family,' he growls, backing me up to the wall again. 'And when someone like you messes with my family, we have a problem.'

He looks away from me for a second as if he's having to make himself do whatever he's going to do.

'You don't have to do this,' I whisper.

He turns back, and his eyes flash. To my horror, I feel the conjure on me start to shift.

NO!

'You can't—'

'Actually, I can,' he snarls. 'It's amazing what I've picked up from Jayce and Krase over the years.'

I'm shaking my head a little, panicking as I try to pull away from his hard grip.

Daemon's other gloved hand is suddenly over my mouth, and my panic rachets up, my eyes pleading for him not to do it.

'Stop struggling. I'm not going to hurt you, baby,' Daemon drawls.

But I do struggle, and somehow, I twist out of his grasp.

His eyes narrow when I'm able to keep him from grabbing hold of me, but then he smiles darkly and shows me his hand. He rips off the glove and advances towards me.

I move backward to stay away, knowing how I'll feel if he touches me.

'Using your own tricks against you has a certain poetry to it, right?'

I shake my head, begging, but he ignores me.

He takes me by the throat again, and desire immediately slams into me, making my body give up the fight. My limbs turn heavy, and he subdues me easily, keeping me in place while I put every ounce of my energy into not moaning, not wrapping my legs around him. I'm panting. My hooded eyes don't leave his.

My skin tingles, and I let out a sob.

'NO!'

I renew my struggle in Daemon's grip, somehow getting past the haze of need, scratching at him, kicking. But he doesn't move an inch. I grip his hand that's at my neck hard.

Daemon chuckles at my futile attempts, his fingers caressing my neck and making me stifle another moan.

'What are you hiding?' he growls low.

I'm shaking my head as much as I'm able with his fingers around my neck, my lip quivering.

'Please, don't,' I whisper.

But his eyes harden. 'You brought this on yourself, baby.'

This can't be happening.

But it is.

I feel the conjure that keeps my scars hidden fail, and my heart lurches, the fight going out of me completely.

Daemon finally lets go of me, and I almost sob in relief when the need for him all but disappears.

'Let's see what Julia Brand is hiding,' he sneers with a grin as he steps back.

I don't want to watch his face, but I can't seem to tear my eyes away.

He freezes, his shocked eyes that are on my body darting back up to mine for a second and then down again.

I was in the middle of changing, I remember dully. All I'm wearing is lingerie. He can see almost all of me.

A hiccupping laugh bubbles out of me.

'Don't you like what you see?' I choke out. 'If you wanted a look at me, all you had to do was ask.'

'Baby ...' Daemon breathes faintly. His eyes are tortured when they finally make their way back up to my face.

I ignore him.

'Want to view it all?' I ask. 'Take a look. See the cuts, the brands, the symbols they cut into me.'

I twirl slowly for him, numb.

'Who did this to you?' he snarls, grabbing me and turning me back to face him.

His bare hand elicits a deep, mortifying moan from me, my back arching at his touch. He jumps back.

'Jules,' he whispers.

Chapter Seventeen

IRON

I'm frozen in shock. She finally notices me in the doorway and lets out a tortured wail that breaks me out of my motionless state.

'That the hell is this?' I snarl, wrenching Daemon away from her. 'What did you do?'

'I didn't—I didn't know,' he whispers.

He looks back at Jules. 'I'm sorry, baby. I didn't know.'

The connection I have with Jules tells me exactly how injured she is as if I couldn't already see it in her face. She's just standing in front of us, shivering, tears leaking from her eyes. I don't want to look, but I can't help it.

'This was what you were hiding with the conjure?' I ask, feeling like a piece of shit.

I glance at Daemon. *But not as big a piece of shit as he is.*

'What did you do?' I snarl. 'How did you even know how to—'

'It doesn't matter,' he says, turning away. 'Fix it. Help her. I don't know how.'

'You sonofabitch,' I hiss, and he recoils.

I approach Jules slowly. She doesn't even seem to see me. I can't help but take a closer look at the scars; my stomach is churning.

There's a brand in the shape of an elaborate 'T' on her chest just above her left breast. Burn and knife scars litter her arms, her stomach, and her torso.

'Who did this to you?' I ask, trying to keep the anger from my voice so I don't scare her.

She doesn't show any signs that she's heard me.

'Jules.'

Nothing.

But she moves, angles her body away from us, wraps her arms around herself, and leans against the wall. I can't help my sharp intake of breath when I see her back, and I hear a similar sound from Daemon.

I thought the front was bad, but the back is worse. More knife cuts, more burns, signs of multiple whippings.

I swallow hard.

'Jules?'

She lets out a harsh breath, the soft sobs ebbing. I feel her anger just before she surges off the wall.

She pushes me so hard that I stagger back a couple of steps.

'It's okay,' I say quietly. 'It's okay.'

She wipes the tears from her cheeks and levels us both with such a look of malice that it makes me wince a little.

She looks directly at Daemon, and her lip quivers. Then her eyes find me. Her sudden laugh is brittle and broken.

'No, sweetheart,' I mutter, horror rising as she makes a show of turning for me like she's modeling an outfit.

All I can do is stand still, like a macabre voyeur in a play I'm not in control of.

'Read them all,' she invites in a whisper. 'You can, right, Iron? What do they say? I've always wondered.'

'Who hurt you, baby?' Daemon asks again.

'What, this?' she asks, gesturing to her body as she picks up one of the jackets and some pants off the chair.

'I would welcome this torture a thousand times over if it meant I never had to see you ever again,' she says to Daemon stiffly.

With that, she walks out of the stall.

Neither of us try to stop her. We don't move at all.

'It's fae,' I mutter.

'What?' Daemon asks from behind me.

'The scars. I thought they were just burns, but it's fae. Old fae.'

'Why would a fae brand power symbols into a human with no magick?' he asks.

'I don't know. Fuck!'

I round on him. 'What the fuck was that?'

'She had a conjure on her. She was hiding something. I thought—'

'You have no idea what you've done, you selfish asshole,' I mutter. 'Maddox was right to kick you out. You're not one of us. Not anymore, Daemon.'

He freezes, opening his mouth to speak, but nothing comes out for a minute.

'Fuck this,' he mutters, striding from the stall and elbowing past me on the way out.

'Shit!' I run my hands through my hair, pulling at it.

I let myself feel her properly for the first time since the club when this bond flared to life. The pain that burns its way through me and forces the air from my lungs tells me I need to find her now.

I leave the stable and turn down the path towards the house, using our connection to feel for her since she still doesn't have a scent, thanks to Krase.

I stop in my tracks, and my gaze turns towards the wood. She hasn't gone back to the house.

I walk quickly, at times breaking into a run as I follow a trail I can't see or smell. But I know I'm going the right way. I just know.

It doesn't escape my notice that how I view Jules has changed. Whether it's being able to sense her true feelings, or the time we've been spending together ... or the fact that she almost gave me a heart attack when she was messing around on Pitch earlier. She's not what I thought, and I realized today that I care about her a lot.

I break out of the tree line and look frantically around the pond, finding her sitting on a rock that juts out over the deeper water. She has the jacket on, but her bare legs are dangling down over the edge. I sigh in relief. I knew she hadn't done anything yet because I could sense her still, but I can almost feel her thoughts of self-destruction. I glance at the murky surface, and my heart leaps into my chest.

I approach her cautiously. I don't say anything; just make sure she can hear me approaching. I sit next to her, not touching her as I watch her in my periphery.

She's not crying; she's not doing anything but staring at the water.

'I'm sorry,' I say quietly.

She turns to look at me, her eyes dull.

'It's not your fault.'

She looks back down at the water.

'I know you can feel ... where my head is,' she mutters softly. 'I've thought about doing it a thousand times. Just let it end. Float away.'

I don't say anything as her suffering flares in me, bringing tears to my eyes.

'Do you know what stops me?'

'Revenge?' I ask.

She barks out a small laugh and then looks surprised.

She opens the jacket and looks down. 'I haven't looked at the real me in a very long time,' she whispers. 'I thought it would have gotten easier.'

She thrusts it back together, hiding her body from herself and from me, her chin wobbling.

I want to tell her it isn't bad, but that would be a blatant lie. It's awful, but it's not because of how it looks; it's because her marks tell the story of *years* of suffering. Pretending to her that it's less than it is undermines what happened to her, what someone did to her.

Someone I'm going to kill, I vow silently.

I close my eyes and concentrate, putting the conjure back the way it was before Daemon fucked with it, and she straightens with a small gasp.

'I thought he'd destroyed it,' she whispers, her voice breaking.

'No, I just displaced the magick ... like breaking a circuit,' I say. 'It's back as it was now. No one can see, Jules, and I promise no one will mess with it again.'

She nods, her jaw tight as she forces back tears.

I raise my fingers to her cheek and turn her to face me gently. 'Who did it, Jules?'

'Doesn't matter. It was a long time ago.'

I don't ask the other questions that are eating me up inside.

JULES

Iron sits with me in silence until the sun is low in the sky.

I'm angry and upset *and tired*, but the reality is that I

expected Daemon to do something shitty. Like Maddox, he thinks the worst of me, and he must know how close I'm getting to the others. What he did hurts worse than the torture ever did right now, but this is Supeland, and I'm a product of it whether I want to be or not.

Even after everything that just happened, I'm alive, and that's a win. I'm even a tiny bit relieved. Both Iron and Daemon saw every burn and cut that I've kept hidden for so long, but neither turned away in revulsion. I didn't realize I was so afraid of what the clan would think if they ever saw me like that, but I was. I was terrified.

But they didn't look disgusted ... not by the scars themselves, at least, just the fact that I have them at all. And Iron didn't *feel* repulsed.

In fact, what I've been experiencing from him since the stable is his guilt and remorse, his anger at the ones who did this, as well as at Daemon for his part in it.

Despite what happened, there's no scar-shaming here, at least. After the past few awful minutes, I don't know why that matters so much to me, but it does.

'Thank you for fixing the conjure.' I say. 'You didn't have to do that.'

He rubs his chest. 'Yes, I did, Jules.'

'Is it because of the link between us?'

I look at him and see him shake his head a little.

I sigh.

'I'm sorry that we're connected, but I've been thinking about it, and I'm pretty sure it wasn't me,' I murmur.

He glances over at me. 'What do you mean?'

I roll my eyes. 'I know you all think I'm doing it, that I have some nefarious plan, or that I'm luring you guys in somehow, but I'm just a human. What power could I have over you? *You're* the incubi.' I huff. 'Blame yourselves if you can't control your magick.'

I shudder as I think about what Daemon did. How he subdued me in the barn; he knew what his touch would do to both of us. I could see it in his eyes when he took off the glove. But he was able to stay in control of himself while I was turned into a puddle of sexual need.

Not fair!

'No,' I say with certainty. 'It can't be me.'

He lets out a breath, eyeing me. 'You're not what I thought.'

I give him a small smile and wrap my jacket around me tighter, eyeing the pants on the rock next to me that I should really put on because I'm starting to get really cold.

I start to get up, but he turns towards me, putting a hand on mine to stop me. I tense up because I can feel what he wants to talk about.

'We need to ... I need to ask you about the symbols, Jules.'

I hide my flinch and look down at the water again.

'What about them?' I whisper.

'They're not ... You said you didn't know what they were.'

'I don't. They–' I swallow hard and try again. 'They never said what they were doing or why.'

'So you were just tortured for no reason?'

I take a steadying breath. 'Yeah.'

He looks apologetic. 'How long did it go on for?'

I shake off his hand and stand up abruptly. I grab my pants and take a few steps away from him to put them on, trying to think about what to say because I've never spoken about it to anyone.

'For a long time,' I say over my shoulder. 'I know there was a reason, but they never told me what it was.'

I wrap my arms around myself.

'And why would they?' I say bitterly. 'You saw the brand on my chest, Iron. You must know what it means.'

'That you were a slave.'

I nod, still not looking at him. 'They branded symbols into

my flesh. Sometimes, I was beaten or given the lash. Sometimes, they'd take a knife and draw it through the scars of the symbols that they put on my skin like they were canceling them out, and then they'd brand me with others.'

I turn back and finally look at him when I don't feel anything from him, trying to glean something from his face, but he gives me nothing.

'Who?' He *sounds* angry, but I have no idea why.

What does he care? Incubus pride thing, maybe.

'I told you. It doesn't matter who,' I say as I turn away. 'Revenge isn't an option.'

I take a few more steps to the tree line before I look back at him again, done with this conversation.

'Don't tell anyone about it.'

I mean it as a demand, but it comes out like a plea.

Mildly disgusted with myself, I leave him in the forest, and I'm glad he doesn't follow me as I take the path back to the house.

When I get inside, I see Tabitha lurking. She beckons me, but before I can go to her, the library door opens, and Maddox steps out.

'I thought that was you. Can I have a word?' He asks me.

Afraid it's something I've missed for the party tomorrow, I nod and come into the library with him. I sit down in front of the desk, and I put my game face on because I'm dealing with Maddox.

'Is something wrong?' I ask.

He regards me with a detached expression. This doesn't bode well.

He doesn't speak for a minute. He's probably just trying to make me uncomfortable, so I just stare at him because I've had enough of being intimidated today.

I suppress a shiver as my mind is drawn back to the barn, and I push it away.

Finally, Maddox stands.

'Drink?' he asks.

I nod because, after the past hour or so, I sure as hell could use one. I accept a brandy and take a sip, leaning back in the chair and closing my eyes.

'You seem tired,' he remarks.

I crack one eye open and glance at him. 'So what if I am?' I countered. 'Do you really care whether or not I'm sleeping well?'

He looks amused but doesn't answer.

I give him a look.

'Spit it out, Julian,' I say. 'I'd like an early night before the party tomorrow. *Is* something wrong, or are you just bored?'

'Nothing's wrong,' he says.

He sits back behind his desk, but then he seems to think the better of it and moves around it to lean against it in front of me instead. It's as if he's trying to put me more at ease, make our interaction less bound by his social constraints, but all it's doing is making me nervous.

'I have a proposition,' he finally says.

Great. Another proposition ... because the last one went so well.

'What is it?' I ask, glad he's finally getting to it.

'I don't think that you should leave after the masque.'

He delivers the bombshell calmly, but I'm only just about able to keep my mouth from falling open.

'You don't want me to leave?' I ask faintly, and I frown at him. 'I don't understand. The only reason that you wanted me here was because—'

'Yes, well.' He clears his throat. 'I've received some information that changes the situation somewhat.'

His eyes turn predatory, and I lean back a little, feeling like a deer in the headlights. I don't usually see this side of Maddox.

My eyebrows rise in surprise as I realize what he's getting at.

'You want me to contract with the clan,' I murmur.

'Yes,' he says. 'If we're to remain on the right side of the law after tomorrow evening, your presence here will need to be legitimized. You will be paid handsomely, Julia.'

I shake my head. 'I don't understand. Why me? You don't even like me.'

'That's not entirely true,' he mutters.

Bullshit.

'You don't trust me then.'

'Fair,' he mutters.

'What on earth could you want me to stay here for?'

'For Krase,' he whispers, his eyes boring into me. 'I don't know how, but there's something about you that has enabled him to somehow come back from a place no one should have been able to bring him back from.'

I cross my arms over my chest as I feel my ripped jacket sliding apart slightly.

'Why do you think I had anything to do with it?' I ask.

'I don't have another explanation at the moment, and I'd rather not take the chance of losing him again.'

He glances down at my arms.

'Are you cold?' he asks, changing the subject.

'Yes,' I lie because I don't want him to know that I have nothing on under this ... or be forced to come up with an explanation as to where my clothes went.

He looks slightly perturbed but says nothing more as he turns and opens his safe in my presence. I don't let my look of surprise show as I watch him key in the long code. He doesn't even try to hide it.

Does he trust me? He can't.

'All I ask is that you think about it,' he says, handing me an envelope. 'The contract.'

I take it from him carefully and sit back, letting out the breath I've been holding. 'What about our other deal?'

'This would circumvent our other bargain, and you wouldn't get paid until your contract was up,' he replies. 'But if you're staying here with full room and board as well as anything else you need, what do you require the money for now anyway?'

He has a point. If I stayed here, if I did take him up on his offer, I wouldn't need the money until I left.

'And would all of you feed from me? Axel and Jayce—'

'Yes.' He levels me with a hard stare. 'You would be the entire clan's.'

'What about Axel and Jayce?' I say in confusion. 'You wanted me to stay away from them. You thought I had some terrible power over them. What's changed?'

'Once you're contracted, it won't matter. You'll be under the magickal law of the clan. Whatever it is you've been doing, whether it be on purpose or inadvertently, will be nullified. The problem won't be a problem anymore.'

I regard him for a moment, wondering what else their clan magick will do.

'How long would the contract be for?' I ask finally.

'Three years is standard for these types of things.'

I sit back in my chair to consider. It would certainly give me time to come up with an actual plan. I might even get enough money by the end to sort out something a little more permanent instead of leaping from conjure to conjure, hoping for the best. But it would also mean letting all the clan feed from me, have sex with me.

'I'm not sure that you're selling it to me all that well, Maddox,' I remark.

I take a slow sip of my drink.

He leans in closer, his eyes fixed on me. 'Well, how about this then? A million for three years, Julia.'

I choke on my brandy, and he crosses his arms, the ghost of a smile on his face.

'A million *dollars*?' I sputter as it burns down my throat.

'Pounds, darling.'

My mouth almost drops open. I could buy a home *and* have

enough to have border conjures put around it with that. I'd be free and wouldn't have to run anymore. I could even settle out here in Europe somewhere.

I get to my feet. 'I'll think about it,' I say vaguely.

'Is everything ready for the party tomorrow?' he asks, changing tack.

I nod, feeling a little dazed. 'I've triple-confirmed everything is ready, so long as the guests know where to come and when.'

He grins. 'Good. That will be all.'

I give a faint nod and wrap my ruined jacket more tightly around me as I make my way to the door.

I go back up to my room, slipping off the jacket and throwing it across the room in a sudden burst of anger as soon as the door is closed.

He knows he's got me. The money is too much to pass up.

But I'd be the clan's for three years. Could I do that?

I don't know.

I didn't want to leave yet, and this is the price to stay. And what pressing things do I really have going on out there right now anyway? My entire life is here. How pathetic is that?

But despite Maddox and Daemon, Jayce, Krase, Axel, and maybe even Iron have made me feel things that I've never felt before, things I never thought I'd have.

I look at myself in the mirror.

'I could stay here with them,' I whisper, staring at my bare upper body, the scars now completely invisible.

I run my hands down my skin. Can't even feel them now. I stare at myself for a long time before I go to bed and close my eyes, deciding in my half-dreaming state that I will contract with the clan.

Chapter Eighteen

MADDOX

I sit at my desk, staring at the chair where Jules was just sitting. I try to stop myself. I try not to give in to the temptation, but I open the window on the video feeds, and I click on the one for her bedroom.

I see her walk in, closing the door behind her, and I frown as she takes off the jacket that I could see in here was ripped to buggery. There's nothing underneath.

I stare. 'It's not because I'm interested,' I say to myself.

Who ripped her clothes? At the moment, I know where everyone is except for Iron and Daemon. In fact, I could have sworn I saw Iron taking Jules riding earlier. Did Iron do this?

I watch as she throws the jacket across the room and stands in front of the mirror. She touches herself in an innocuous manner, but it's enough to make my cock start to grow under my desk. I wasn't lying when I told her I didn't dislike her. I don't understand it. But this human has done something to us. It shouldn't be possible, but I think I have to face the fact that our little human guest is more than she appears. What, I can't say. Though Krase seems to have his suspicions, he hasn't bothered to tell me what they are.

My gaze falls on my collection of books on succubi. I've thought about this a couple of times and discounted it, but what if ...

Impossible.

There would be markers, and I knew Jane was one immediately. Jules isn't the same.

I stare at our soon-to-be-on-call-girl a little while longer, watching as she gets into bed and falls asleep.

I hear the passage door to the library open. I don't bother glancing up because I know it's Daemon. My eyes narrow slightly as I take in his swagger. He's happy about something.

'Where have you been?' I ask.

He shrugs. 'Around.'

He comes to stand in front of my desk.

'Jules came in earlier,' I say. 'She looked a little worse for wear.'

I watch him, but I see nothing as he shrugs again.

'You know Jules,' he says. 'She's always getting into mischief.'

'I've asked her to contract with the club,' I say, watching his reaction, and I'm sure I see surprise, followed by something a little bit more sinister. 'You don't agree?'

'We can get on-call girls from anywhere,' he snorts. 'Why that one?'

'Simple. She's already here,' I half lie. 'We don't have to worry about forms and time. Vetting.' I chuckle. 'We already know Jules' faults.'

Daemon's lip curls with dark amusement.

'When?'

'After the masque,' I tell him.

'I won't be feeding from her.'

I give a small laugh. 'She's not for you.'

'Who, then?' he sneers.

'Ah.' I see him roll his eyes. 'Crazy Krase.'

'Not so crazy now,' I murmur, sitting back and steepling my fingers.

'No, I suppose not. You think she has something to do with that?'

I tilt my head, 'Truthfully, I don't know what to think, but I would rather not have Krase fall back into that pit of darkness. Odds are he wouldn't escape a second time.'

Daemon nods. 'I think it's a good idea,' he says, surprising me.

'I'm glad I have your approval,' I mutter, and he seems to miss my sarcasm as he turns to leave, walking nonchalantly across the room like he hasn't got a care in the world.

I stare after him, knowing there's something wrong, wondering if he actually has taken care of his little vampire problem yet.

My phone rings, and I answer it on autopilot while I deal with business. At least our coffers are filling faster than anticipated, and it looks like I won't have to pay Jules. At least not for another three years. By then, a million shouldn't even put a dent in our accounts. I can thank Krase for the extra time, I suppose.

At first, he was adamant that it wasn't Jules who had done it, but then he came to me late last night and told me he needed her here. Against my better instincts, I acquiesced. I still don't trust her, but if Krase thinks she helps, then I'm willing to try. At least if she's contracted, I'll have a little bit more control over the human who resides in our house. At the moment, as a guest, she has far too much leeway and freedom. As a contracted on-call girl, she'll lose many of her human rights for the term she signs up for.

I wonder if she'll say yes or simply take the cash and run. I thought money was her only motivator, but she didn't immediately say yes to my proposal. Considering she's been living here for weeks, I still know far too little about our little human, and that's going to need to change ... in the interests of clan security, of course.

The person on the other end of the phone says goodbye after prattling on for at least ten minutes about who knows what, and I gratefully put the phone down. I get up, closing the window on the screen that's watching Jules sleep.

I glance at the clock. It's not late, but I find I'm finished for the day.

My eyes fall on a box on the table by the hearth. I forgot to give it to Jules. I pick it up and take it upstairs with me, going silently into Jules' room and depositing it on the bureau where she won't miss it.

Before I leave, I stand over her, watching her face in sleep.

No, I don't trust her, and I don't want to trust her. I wasn't even intending on feeding from her even if she does sign, but I can already feel my resolve thinning when it comes to her.

'How are you able to do it?' I whisper. 'How are you able to burrow underneath my defenses?'

I turn away and leave her bedroom, going to my own and practically throwing myself into my bed.

The Champagne is flowing. The masked guests have almost all arrived. There's a string quartet in the ballroom playing soft music for everyone to enjoy. There are flowers everywhere.

I have to admit, as I walk around playing the good host, greeting all of the rich and powerful supes who have come to celebrate our pardons officially coming through, that Jules has done a good job of organizing tonight.

The part of me that has been worrying since we returned starts to relax. Soon, we'll be able to put all of this behind us, get back to our lives, be free of lawlessness – Well, perhaps, *outward* lawlessness is a better way of putting it.

Daemon stands next to me in a black tux with a matching demon mask over his entire face. We're all matching tonight except for Jules. She hasn't come down yet. I've only seen her from afar all day because she was dealing with caterers and other suppliers coming to the house, and I find myself impatient to hear her answer to my proposal.

'Everything seems to be going well,' I murmur to Daemon.

He nods. 'Yes, I have to admit it. Jules did do a fine …'

He trails off, and I look at where his gaze is going. My eyes widen when I see her in the red ball gown, a glittering feathered mask over her face, her hair in elegant up-do.

I can feel myself stiffening, and I have to look away, gritting my teeth. Now is not the time.

'It appears she's graced us with her presence,' Daemon mutters, and there's an edge to his voice that I don't like.

'Make sure you know where the council members are at all times,' I order.

'I remember the brief,' he mutters, his eyes locked on Jules.

He takes a flute of Champagne from a member of the catering team who's walking around with a tray and begins to wander around the room, pretending to mingle.

I make my way to Jules, who's standing by the door, looking a little bit intimidated. When she sees me, she gives me a small smile.

'You've outdone yourself,' I say.

I take her hand and put it to my lips. 'I knew you'd look lovely in red.'

'This is from you. I take it?' she asks.

I nod.

'Thank you. It's lovely.'

Her eyes don't stay on mine for too long. Instead, they bounce around the room.

'Looking for someone?' I ask.

She shakes her head. 'No, I don't know any of your guests,' she says.

I stifle a grin as I pretend not to hear the 'thankfully' she whispers at the end, and grab her a glass of Champagne from a tray. As I hand it to her, she takes it with murmured thanks, and her fingers brush against mine. She starts and visibly shivers. I almost do as well.

This happened before, and I thought it was her doing, but she looks uneasy. In fact, she's made so sure that we haven't touched since then that I wonder if it shocked her as much as it shocked me. I stand close, and I run a finger down her arm. It's like a flame igniting in my body and in my loins. My eyes roll back in my head behind my mask.

'Come with me,' I say.

'But I just got here,' she murmurs breathlessly.

She still follows me as I take her into the library, though.

I close the door and lock it. Then, I press a button on the wall by my safe. All the windows leading to the garden frost over, giving us some privacy.

'I'd have your answer,' I growl, feeling on edge and a little bit out of control.

'You could have asked me that out here,' she says quietly.

'Your answer, darling,' I grind out.

She gestures to my desk. 'I signed it.'

I almost breathe out a sigh of relief. It must be because Krase's sanity is safe now. I lock up everything I was feeling, confident that she's ours now.

'Turn around,' I command her softly.

She gives me a puzzled look but does as I say, and I put a

necklace on her, clasping it at her throat. It's chunky and golden with ruby-colored stones in it that match her dress.

She looks at herself in the gilt mirror over the mantle, and her eyes meet mine in the reflection.

'Thank you,' she murmurs.

'It's not worth anything,' I mutter. 'It's for appearances' sake.'

I chuckle, knowing I'm being a cad but needing her to know her place here from the very beginning. 'As if I'd trust you with anything valuable.'

I see some of the spark in her eyes dim, but then she adjusts the necklace slightly and turns around to look me in the eye.

'You're finally learning, Julian. Good for you!'

With that, she goes to the door, unlocks it, and slips from the room.

It takes everything in me not to call her back and apologize.

This is how it needs to be with her. We'll keep her for Krase's sake, but she needs to stay at arm's length. She's an employee. Nothing more.

JULES

I whip a drink off a tray going past me and sip it slowly. I'm not getting drunk tonight, regardless of how I'm feeling, because I'm not an idiot, but I'd love to right now. I finger the necklace Maddox gave me and wonder what that was all about. I knew it was fake as soon as he put it on me. Doesn't have the weight of real gold. That didn't hurt, but his words to me definitely had the desired effect.

I find myself needing another drink and make an effort to pace myself.

At the end of the day, this might be a civilized event, but every one of these assholes is a supe, a rich, entitled one, and nothing good ever comes from a human losing their faculties around a bunch of supes.

I take a look around, finding couples dancing on the dance floor of the ballroom.

I see Jayce and Axel and give them a small wave, wondering if they know Maddox asked me to contract to the clan yet. Krase comes to me and gives me a small bow.

'May I have this dance?' he asks.

I nod, and he takes my hand, twirling me effortlessly into an old-fashioned waltz that I only know how to do from old movies. He whirls me around and around on the dance floor until I'm breathless and actually really enjoying myself. We don't say anything to each other, but I can feel how happy he is. He knows I'm not leaving after the party. In truth, despite Maddox's games, I'm happy I'm not leaving as well.

As soon as he stops, Jayce cuts in and swirls me around some more. By the time Axel appears, I'm laughing and a tad dizzy. We dance for a little while, and then I beg to stop for a bit to catch my breath and have a cool drink.

He goes off to get me something, and I'm standing by myself, just taking in the ambiance with a silly smile on my face.

Then I catch sight of someone, and my heart lurches in my chest.

'It can't be.'

I make my way through the crowd to where I saw who I think I saw, telling myself the whole way that it's not possible and pushing away the links I have with the clan. I don't want them to know how I'm feeling.

But then I see her ... and it is *her*. She looks a little different, older now.

VENGEANCE AND VIPERS

I watch her for a minute. She's talking to a couple of older shifters who look like they might be Council members. She's on the arm of a large shifter alpha.

She excuses herself a minute later, and I see my chance, moving to intercept her when she's out of her date's line of sight. I put my hand on her arm, and she turns.

'Mom?' I ask.

She looks shocked, her eyes widening, but covers it quickly.

'I'm sorry,' she says. 'I think you have me confused with someone else.'

I shake my head, and I grip her a little tighter. 'No, I know it's you.'

'Let go of me!' she hisses, and I do, taking a step back.

My eyes fill with tears. 'I thought you were dead. They said you were dead. They said you and Dad were killed in an accident.'

She swears under her breath, a smile still plastered to her face.

'Don't you know anything?' she whispers angrily, glancing around. 'Not here.' She looks around again. 'Somewhere private if you really want to do this.'

I nod, ushering her out of the ballroom and down the hall to the Parlor. I open the door, hoping it's empty. I poke my head inside and practically push her in when I see no one there. I shut the door behind us.

I hug her tightly despite her animosity. I can't help it.

'It is you,' I whisper. 'I don't understand. Where were you? Why did they tell me you died?'

She returns the hug for a moment but then pulls away.

'Don't you get it?' She chuckles a little, looking like she can't believe she's having to spell it out for me. 'I did what I had to do.'

'But you left me. You left me with the fae, Mom,' I whimper, tears clouding my vision. 'I'm not your mother.' She says it with a roll of her eyes.

I take a step back. 'What?'

I shake my head, not comprehending. 'Of course you are.'

'No. I was never your bio mom. We were ordered to pretend. John, your 'dad' and me.' She shakes her head. 'We weren't even a couple. They gave us a baby, and they told us to raise you and keep you safe until they came for you.'

I sit down heavily on the couch, feeling sick.

'Raise me for what?'

She shrugs. 'You'd know better than me. We just did what we were told. They owned us all. They said if we did the job, they'd free us when it was done. One day, they came, and we'd kept our end, so they kept theirs.'

Tears come to my eyes, and she sighs like I'm an inconvenience to her.

'Look, I'm sorry if they never told you, but I did my job, and I held up my end. I'm free now. I have a husband, kids of my own. They don't know about my past, and I want to keep it that way.'

But why—

She paces away from me. 'If I'd said no, I'd have been punished severely, and they would have just picked someone else. You know how it works.'

I nod. *Yeah, I know how it works.*

'What are you doing here?' I ask.

She flashes me a ring. 'I told you. I have a family now,' she says.

I take a deep breath. My mom's gone from dead to fake in the space of two minutes.

I stare at her.

She looks bored.

'Who am I?' I ask. 'Can you tell me? Who were my real parents?'

She shakes her head. 'I never knew anything about your biological parents or where you came from. I can't help you. I'm going to go back to the party now. You stay away from me and my husband, do you hear me?'

I nod numbly.

She steps forward. 'And, just in case you're too stupid to realize, you can't tell anyone about this,' she says, her voice sharp. 'No one can know that you met me. In return, I won't tell anyone that you're here either, but you keep your mouth shut, Julia.' She looks me up and down. 'Because we both know he didn't let you go, did he?'

I shake my head.

'Don't you dare try to make me feel bad!' she hisses. 'If it hadn't been me, it would have been someone else.'

She turns away and goes to the door. 'He always gets what he wants. They all do.'

The woman who I thought was my mother leaves the room without looking at me again, and I'm left alone, reeling.

That was my mom. I loved her. Was it really all pretend for her all that time? I stay where I am, afraid I'll faint or something if I get up.

Who am I? Who were my parents? Are they dead? Why was I taken from them? Why did they do all those things to me?

'I don't understand any of this,' I whisper to myself.

I can't go back to the party now. I just can't. The door to the Parlor opens, and a tipsy couple stumble in, giggling. I leave the room quickly as they enter, wanting to be alone. But there are people everywhere, and I don't want to see any of the clan right now, either.

I make for the kitchen, slipping inside and belatedly remembering that the catering staff are using it as their base of operations.

I make my way quickly across the room to the back, feeling stifled and lightheaded.

I need some air!

I run out of the house with a gasp, my head spinning. I close the heavy door behind me, leaning on it as I try not to cry.

'Are you okay, sweetheart? What's wrong?'

I look up to find Tabitha propped up against the brickwork, smoking a cigarette.

'Those are really bad for you,' I gasp, and then I burst into tears.

I find myself wrapped in her arms.

'It's okay,' she coos. 'It'll going to be fine. You let it out, honey.'

'I-I just saw someone,' I sob, 'Someone I thought was dead.'

'Oh, sweetheart,' she murmurs. 'That must have been a shock.'

She doesn't ask me anything specific, and I'm grateful. I squeeze her hand.

'Thanks,' I whisper.

'Come with me,' she says firmly. 'You must be freezing out here without a jacket on.'

I nod, realizing that it is actually really cold out here tonight.

Tabitha leads me back inside and left into what used to be the scullery. I see she's set up a couple of chairs and a small TV. She looks at me a little bit sheepishly.

'I didn't think anyone would mind if I took this as my break room.'

'I don't mind,' I whisper.

She sits me down on a chair and looks down at me, opening and closing her mouth as if she wants to tell me something.

'I'll get you some tea,' she mutters abruptly, bustling off and leaving me to the dull droning of the TV set.

She comes back a few minutes later, carrying a small porcelain cup with flowers painted on it.

'Here we go,' she says, handing it to me.

'Thanks.'

She sits down across from me.

'I need to tell you something,' she says.

'You're not my real mom, are you?' I half-joke.

She frowns. 'No, dear, I'm not your mother.'

She opens and closes her mouth again, letting out a sigh.

'What is it?' I ask, starting to worry.

'It's just ...' She gets up and looks out the door, making sure there's no one close by. She closes it and turns back to me. 'You know how I can tell where everyone is?' she asks.

I nod. 'Yes. You told me it's your magick.'

'Well,' she wrings her hands. 'I can also count bodies.'

My brow furrows.

What the hell is she talking about?

'For example,' she goes on, 'out in the main kitchen, there are seven.'

'Okay,' I say slowly, wondering if there was a little something extra in that cigarette she was just smoking outside.

'And, in this room right now, there are three.'

Yep, definitely wasn't a normal cigarette.

I frown at her. 'Me and you. That's two.' I say.

She comes closer. 'No, dear.'

She puts her hand gently on my lower abdomen.

'There are three.'

I rear back in the chair, almost toppling it over.

'That's impossible!' I say. 'No, that that's not true. I–I can't have– They told me ...'

'Whoever they were,' Tabitha says quietly, 'they were wrong, and I never am. It's early, very early, but you're pregnant, Jules.'

I gape at her for about a minute.

'Why did you tell me?' I ask her finally.

Tabitha looks worriedly at the door. 'I just thought you should know before you made any big decisions.'

My eyes widen—*the contract.*

Julian literally told me he'd never trust me with anything

valuable. Iron's words come back to me from the Mountain. They'd take it from me as soon as it was born.

'Thank you,' I say, taking her hand. 'Please don't tell anyone.'

She squeezes mine back, and I leave the kitchen, slowly going back through the party to the library. I slip inside and go to the desk. The contract I signed is gone.

It's too late.

Feeling numb, I go back through the party, taking pains not to be seen by any of the clan; I drift up the stairs and into my bedroom. I stare at myself in the mirror as I take off my mask, my eyes going down to my abdomen. There's not even a bump, but I believe Tabitha. I didn't think it was possible, but somehow, I'm pregnant.

What am I going to do?

KEEP READING FOR CHAPTER ONE OF VIPERS AND VENDETTAS!

Snag Your Copy!- VipersandVendettasVV3
If you enjoyed this book, please consider leaving a text review. Even one line is so helpful to your friendly neighborhood author! xx
Do you need to talk to SOMEONE about this book? Join Kyra's Secret Spoilers Group on Facebook or my Denizens Discord!
Also, sign up to my mailing list to recieve a steamy novella in the Dark Brothers and Aforethought universe!
Finally, keep reading for a taster of **Demons and Debts, Book 1 in Desire Aforethought. (Set in the same world with several cameos!)**

If you enjoyed this book, please consider leaving a text review. Even one line is so helpful to your friendly neighborhood author! xx

Do you need to talk to SOMEONE about this book? EVERYONE is on Discord!

Also, sign up to my mailing list to receive a steamy novella in the Dark Brothers and Aforethought universe!

xx Kyra

CHAPTER 19
Chapter One Vipers and Vendettas

Jules

The clang of my chains wakes me in the dark. I sit up slowly against the wall. I can't feel my fingers, but that's not unusual. I'm so used to the cold down here that I don't even shiver anymore.

There is a dim blue light flickering faintly on the stone where the passage in front of my cell curves, and I struggle to stand. If I'm not ready to meet him, he'll make it worse for me later.

Using the wall, I inch myself to my feet and lean heavily against it as I beat back the dizziness that threatens to send me back to the hard floor. I inadvertently graze one of the fresh, puckered burns, and I clench my teeth as I let out a muffled and inhuman sound of pain.

The flicker gets brighter, and I hear his footsteps, Toramun, the jailor who comes for me each time, who always stands in the corner relishing my pain while Grinel and Volrien carve me up and burn their symbols into my flesh. His job comes later. He'll administer the beating that always follows while the other two look on. Sometimes, Tamadrielle comes to watch as well, but he always leaves angry.

I'm not as stupid as they think. I know they're doing this for more than brutality's sake. They're trying to make something happen, but whatever they're waiting for never does, and I'm glad. I'm not sure how my life here could be worse, but I know the fae well enough now that I'm sure their cruelties have no limits.

Toramun comes into view; his face lit up in blue from beneath his chin, where his conjured ball of light hovers at his chest. It makes him look more grotesque than usual. All of the High Fae I've ever seen come to Tamadrielle's house have been beautiful. But this one's face is scarred. When he takes off his uniform to bare his torso when he gets too hot beating me, I see marks all over him. His body is twisted and broken.

I gaze down at myself. I suppose I have as many scars as he does now, though.

He opens my cell door with a word of power that doesn't work for me. I know the drill, so I don't tarry. I shuffle forward and hold out my manacled hand. He unlocks it without a word, and I stand in front of him, looking past him at the wall as he looks his fill of my body that's clad only in an old, grubby bra and a pair of ratty underwear.

He lets out a groan as his calloused hands gently move the cups of my bra down so he can see my tits. Whenever he handles me down here in the dark, it's always carefully, almost reverently.

I hate it.

I hate that he's the only one in my life that touches me softly. I hate that after a particularly painful session, I sometimes almost look forward to this little ritual of his.

'Very nice,' he coos, rubbing his fingers over my cold, hard nipples.

He angles my face so that I can't help but look at him.

'Once he's done with you, he's promised I can have you,' he

says, drawing a hand down my cheek and throat to my beating heart.

I keep still, and my face stays completely blank. I don't speak to him. I never do, not to any of them. The only sounds they ever hear from me are the screams they elicit, and that's all they'll ever have. It was a vow I made to myself, and I won't break it.

'Don't worry. I'm not going to leave you down here once you're mine. You're going to be upstairs in the barracks with me. Won't that be nice?' He groans again. 'You'll be in my bed with me every night. Won't that be better than the floor?'

His hands move down my body, and I try not to show any revulsion as he cups me over my underwear. He leaves his hand there as he watches me. I stand impassively, keeping my breathing even and slow even when he nudges my foot with his boot to open me to him further.

A chime sounds through the hall, and he lets out a sound of disappointment as he stops groping me. He grabs my arm in the first punishing grip of the day and walks me back through the tunnel.

It's a thousand paces to get to the winding stone stairs. I think I've counted them about as many times.

There are twenty-two steps up to the main dungeon where the rest of the prisoners are. Almost all are supes, and they're all waiting at the fronts of their cells to ogle the human girl as she's brought through.

I ignore the lecherous stares and the muttered threats about which of my holes they're going to destroy first. I already know Tamadrielle has ordered that I remain a virgin for now because two of the kitchen slaves attacked me one evening, and the fae lord gave them to the supes in the dungeon for the night. Afterward, he had them dragged still half-alive back to the kitchens, and their throats were slit in front of everyone. Then, their bodies were hung up on the wall over the fires to slowly burn to nothing as a reminder to the rest. I guess he put a conjure on them so they didn't smell, but you couldn't miss them. None of the human slaves have touched me in desire since then, only anger or apathy. That's allowed.

Some might view Tamadrielle's edict as a mercy of some kind, and I suppose it is, but no doubt Grinel and Volrien have advised him that keeping my hymen intact is necessary for their 'science'. It's not meant to be kindness. If they thought my being raped every night by a minotaur would help them achieve their ends, no doubt I'd be nursing a sore cunt every morning.

I'm pushed up more stairs, Toramun's hand lingering on my ass and squeezing. He's getting bolder. He'd never have risked that even a few weeks ago. Something is changing, and that never bodes well for me.

It's clear that whatever their reasons for torturing me, it's not going the way they wanted. Maybe Tamadrielle is finally losing patience with the pair of fae he pays to hurt me.

We arrive in the main house and go up the back stairs the human slaves use to get around without bothering the fae. The 'lab' door is right in front of us.

As usual, my body locks up, and my steps falter at the sight of it. I try to be brave. I don't want them to see how scared I am, but I can't seem to help it. This is where all the worst things happen.

My breathing stutters.

Toramun doesn't miss a beat; he just picks me up and throws me over his shoulder. He's used to this, after all.

My mind and vision are swimming as we enter the white room. Tamadrielle's 'doctors', as he calls them, are already waiting. I'm put on my feet in the middle of the space and told to stand still. I'm poked and prodded. A burning salve is pushed into the wounds they made a few days ago that are starting to go septic.

I realize belatedly that Tamadrielle is here. He's never here this early.

What is going on?

He stands by one wall, looking me over as he would any other *inadequate* possession. He lets out a slow breath through his nose. He's annoyed.

He waves Toramun out of the room without looking at him, leaving me with him and his other two fae employees.

'This goes on too long. You promised me my desired outcome months ago,' he says smoothly, his tone belying the anger in his eyes.

Grinel and Volrien look at each other quickly, their haughty movements over me faltering as they begin to, rightly, fear for their lives.

Grinel turns towards his master; head lowered in subservience. 'My lord, we've not even exhausted half of the variations we can try. My most sincere apologies for your time being taken so. We know, of course, how busy you are, sir. If you would permit us, we could have her taken to our personal laboratories in the city and let you know when we have made the progress you desire.'

'No,' Tamadrielle says, his eyes fixed solely on me. 'I told you. She stays here. Increase your sessions by ten percent.'

'My lord, that is not advisable.'

The fae lord's flashing eyes finally turn to Grinel. 'You presume too much.'

Grinel's eyes lower to the floor, and he practically quakes under Tamadrielle's anger.

'Forgive me, my lord. I only mean that she will continue to weaken if we keep increasing. She must be given time to heal. Then, there is the question of space.'

'Space?' Tamadrielle snarls, gesturing around the room. 'What more space can you need for your activities?'

Activities.

An unusual sort of anger stutters through me but can't gain purchase, like sparks flying from a flint onto damp kindling.

My suffering is *activities*.

'Forgive me, lord. I meant on *the subject*. We're running out of canvas.'

Tamadrielle lets out a hum, walking around me as I stand in silence, not looking at any of them. 'So I see.'

Without warning, his hands snatch the cloth of my bra and underwear, wrenching them off my body. The worn fabrics rip easily, and my eyes fly to his for a second as I gasp.

'There. Some additional, unblemished *canvas* for your tools.' He sees me looking at him and snorts at me. 'So, you are still in there. I thought your mind broken long ago, child.'

He grasps my chin and makes me look into his eyes. Anger grows inside at this new humiliation as he stares at me, and I can't hide it.

He rears back, a look of shock on his face for a second, though he doesn't let go of me.

'There!' he says with barely contained excitement. 'I saw it! Just for a moment. But it was there!'

'My lord? What did you see?'

I notice the fae scientists hovering in my periphery, looking worried but very hopeful.

He doesn't answer them. 'Continue with the present course. I have business that will take me away for a week or more. When I return, I expect to see more results than your paltry offerings thus far.'

'Yes, my lord.'

'Of course, my lord.'

Tamadrielle goes to the door, casting one final look at me before he leaves.

Toramun re-enters once his lord is gone, and his eyes light up in anticipation when he sees all my clothes are missing. I hide my emotions, going back to staring straight ahead. I ignore the guard as he chains my arms and legs tightly so I can't move more than half an inch in any direction.

Grinel comes forward first, looking over the symbols they put on me last time. He puts a marker tic on a couple and an X on all the others. I know the drill, and my heart starts pounding as the silver knife is brought out. I grunt as all the new brands except the first two are sliced cleanly and deeply through.

Then, it's Volrien's turn. He's already heated each brand over a brazier set on the table. Each one is on its own metal rod. Eight today. The most I've had at once is six. I swallow hard, but I'll be vomiting by the third. I always do. That's why they don't feed me for twelve hours prior to these sessions. They don't like it when I puke on their shoes.

'The same as we discussed?'

Grinel nods. 'I think that's best, don't you?' He glances at Toramun. 'Be ready to begin embedding the magick the very moment the last mark is made.'

Toramun nods, grabbing the first instrument he'll use to make me scream for him. A short whip – his favorite for the first marks he puts on me to cause me the hurt they say is needed for their magick to take.

Volrien steps forward, and I look past him at the wall, steeling myself for the pain, breathing hard through my nose and clenching my teeth. He puts the first one on my ribs under my breast. I squeal as it touches me, the hiss and the stench of my own flesh burning, making me turn to the side and dry heave. The next two are put on my shoulder at the same time, and my body shudders in the restraints. The next four, he puts in a square on my hip, and my leg jerks a little as I try to escape the biting of the metal. He gets to the eighth.

The last one.

I'm sobbing quietly. The others he did quickly, but he makes me wait for this one.

I feel his fingertip brush my breast, and my tearful eyes fly open just in time to see him press the final one into the vulnerable skin above the nipple. My loud scream is followed by other squeals and whimpers as the heat of the burns dissipates, and all that's left is agony radiating out from them. This is the pain of the magick burning through me.

As soon as he's clear, I feel the first lick of Toramun's whip on my back hard enough to split the skin.

I feel woozy, my eyes closing as I droop in the chains.

I hear one of them order something I can't quite make out, and I hear a snap. I jerk awake as I smell the ammonia under my nose.

'Idiot! Beat her unconscious too soon, and we'll have to do these same symbols over again,' Volrien is hissing at Toramun.

After that, my scarred jailor takes it easy, only making my blood splatter on every fourth or fifth strike. The other two fae watch for a while, making sure whatever they've done to me is working properly. I don't feel any different. But I never do.

Toramun throws the whip to the side as soon as the fae are gone, choosing a switch instead. He begins to cane me hard, starting on the backs of my thighs and moving up to my ass, where he stays for a while.

By the time he stops hitting me, the shadows in the room from the light outside have changed dramatically. He's shirtless and dripping with sweat. My cries have mostly ceased now, and he only draws a pained whimper out of me when he hits me extra hard. I know he's tired now, and I'm not surprised when he stops, and the other two fae re-enter. They check my marks, and I'm given the smelling salts again. I'm released from the chains, and I sink to the floor.

I wonder if this beating has been worse than the ones before it. Usually, I can stand afterward, but I can't get up today.

I'm dying, I realize. What they're doing to me is killing me, and my body can't take much more. I was going to bide my time, wait, and make my cache a little bigger, listen, and learn a little more, but it's going to have to be soon.

Very soon.

Toramun nudges me with his boot, but I ignore him. With an angry snarl, he drags me to my feet by wrapping his meaty fist in my hair and pulling me up. He grips me like that until my legs finally hold me. A ragged shift dress is flung at me, and I put it on, shuddering as it touches the many new lacerations and burns decorating me. I'd rather have nothing on. Clothes hurt, and they mean I'll be working in the house this afternoon.

The thought fills me with excitement and with dread.

It's going to be today.

Toramun takes me by the arm and pulls me out of the room. When I stumble, he casually snaps my forearm and grins at my weak scream.

'The price for not giving me enough of those pretty cries in there,' he whispers. 'We'll remedy that once you're in my bed, girl.'

Cradling my broken arm, I follow him meekly down to the kitchens, ignoring the humans who stop and stare. None of the slaves here are treated particularly well, but none of them are treated like I am.

They decided between them long ago that I must have done something awful to incur their lord's wrath, so they handle me with the appropriate level of revulsion.

I'm taken into the scullery, and Toramun orders one of the lower fae overseers to fix my arm so that I can work.

She puts a healing conjure on it without a word, giving me a vicious pinch on my leg for her trouble when it's done.

One of the cooks tells me to wash dishes, so I stagger over to the sinks and start clearing the mountain of washing up that's likely been accumulating since last night.

Luckily, I'm left alone to work.

As the minutes go by and the pain ebbs, my mind begins to clear a little. Tamadrielle is away for at least a week, I think he said. It'll be a few days before my next session, but odds are I won't survive another. My body gets weaker with every single one.

It needs to be today or never. I won't get a better chance than this.

I already know how I'll do it. I've been planning it for a long time. They think because I don't talk, that there's something wrong with me. I've heard the guards calling me witless. They tell each other that Toramun has struck me too many times in the head. They argue with each other sometimes because many of them believe that all humans are addled in their heads, so I'm no different from the rest of them, regardless of how many times Toramun has smashed my forehead into a wall to show his power over me in front of his fellows.

They always underestimate me, and I'm counting on it. I just need to keep my vacant eyes open and my ears listening.

I feel one of Tamadrielle's personal soldiers coming up behind me. I always know when they're nearby. I'm a punching bag for many of their ires, but this guard is particularly sadistic. He doesn't usually come down to the kitchens, though.

That's another thing that's different today. Yes, something is going on, and I have a feeling it has to do with me. Whatever it is that Tamadrielle's been wanting to see in me, he saw it briefly today.

Was it just my fury he wanted? Was all of this to see how angry I would get? It's impossible to say with the High Fae. So many of the things they do and say make no sense to me.

The guard comes at me with a wire garrote, looping it around my neck. He'll stop short of killing me, but I pretend to struggle because I know that's what he wants, and it'll be over sooner that way.

So, I play my part. I flail and choke and go down on one knee until he lets up, and I make a show of gasping for breath even though I could have gone another twenty seconds more.

'You're to light the fires,' he orders, kicking me until I get up off the floor.

I rise and nod as I stare at the ground. My eyes flick up, and I see him looking at me with disgust. I make my way over to the full coal scuttle by the door and heft it up onto my hip, trying to ignore the pains that shoot through my body at the action.

'You get more and more pathetic every day,' he laughs.

I keep my eyes off him as I shuffle to the door and leave the kitchens, more than a little elated. It doesn't matter what order I start the fires in, and half the rooms don't have guards on them when Tamadrielle isn't here.

I begin enacting the plan that it's taken me so long to develop. I've spent years watching and listening and waiting. I can't mess this up. They'll make sure I never get a second chance.

I make my way slowly to the upstairs rooms as I always do, performing my role the exact same way and at the same speed as usual. Nothing can seem amiss.

I light a fire in the lord's apartments first, noting that his travel suitcase is gone from his closet. He's already left. Why have I been told to light the fires? I roll my eyes.

Fae.

I go to the next room. It's his cruel fae wife's, but she's never here, thankfully. I make sure there's no one lurking as I kneel beside the bed and pull out the bag that I keep stuffed under the frame. I've been taking things for months, amassing a pile of trinkets and fae magickal items. I knew a High Fae as wealthy as Tamadrielle would simply have them replaced rather than waste his time waiting for them to be found.

I've never been suspected of making things go missing. A human would never dare, and thanks to all the conversations I've listened to, I have an idea of how much they're worth. I think I have enough for my plan to work.

I lift my dress, and I tie the bag around my bare waist, wincing when the string digs into the broken skin from Toramun's whip. I stand up, having to use the bed frame for support for a second. I let the dress down and glance at myself in the mirror. The bag can't be seen.

I heft the coal scuttle and set the next few fires in the grates, wondering, as I often do, why the fae don't just use magick for everything instead of having an army of slaves and servants.

Another adorable fae idiosyncrasy, I guess.

When I'm finished upstairs, I head down, forcing myself not to rush now that the end is in sight. I ignore the guards completely as I slowly make my way into the library. It's empty, just as I knew it would be. It smells musty and old. I don't like this room much because Tamadrielle is always in here.

I set the fire in the hearth in case the guards are listening for my usual routine. Then, I cross the room to Tamadrielle's desk silently, and jimmy open the top drawer with the ostentatious, jeweled letter opener he keeps in the gilt holder with his pens. I open the drawer carefully. He has a spare link key in here. I know he does.

When I don't immediately see it, my heart begins to pound. What if he's taken it with him? My whole plan hinges on this. If I don't have a link key, I can't get off the property. My fingers brush something under a pile of papers, and I dig under them, finding the little gold box. I sigh in relief.

I grab the papers from the drawer and go back to the hearth. The fire is burning away happily. I light the papers in my hand on fire and take them to the long curtains, dropping them on the floor. They catch alight quickly and begin to burn. I catch sight of a pair of leather shoes, and I snatch them up on a whim because I'll have to escape barefoot otherwise.

I put the link key on the door to the closet, my hands shaking. I've only ever seen this done. I've never actually used one myself.

I think about the market I came through as a kid, just after mom and dad were killed and the fae lord's men brought me to him. I was scared and alone, but I remember that place and every sight and sound and smell like it was yesterday. It was the first time I'd realized magick was real.

I glance back and smile darkly. The room is very much on fire and filling with smoke. I open the door and gasp at the shimmering portal in front of me.

It worked!

I grab the link key off it, and I step through, my stomach lurching as I'm propelled through a dark tunnel by some unseen force.

I stagger from a door out into a bustling street. No one even looks twice at me. I glance around like I have a reason to be here even though I'm human and dressed in rags. I see a tent with a bored woman in front of it. She's a sprite or a pixie, I think.

I make my way over to her.

'Can you tell me where the bank is, please? I'm meant to be meeting my lord there,' I say smoothly.

I started practicing speaking and talking with confidence in my cell at night months ago when I realized you can make people see and hear what you want them to. The fae do it all the time.

She looks me over, but if she thinks it's weird that I'm dressed in a sack with some oversized men's shoes on my feet, she doesn't say. She points down the road. 'No more than five minutes that way.'

I thank her and walk quickly down the old-fashioned cobbled street with my head held high. When I find the bank, I go past it a ways and to an adjacent alley, hoping that the fae soldier I overheard speaking to Toramun in hushed whispers last week before he locked me in my cell was telling him the truth about the red door here.

I find it. So far, so good. I knock lightly, and a peephole opens.

'Password?' rasps a voice from the other side.

I keep my expression blank, but I didn't hear the soldier say anything about a password. I'm sure of it. I was hanging onto every word while I was pretending to be nonsensical. I'd even let a little drool out while he was talking for good measure.

'There is no password,' I say with a smile, letting myself appear self-assured.

That was how the Low Fae in Tamadrielle's household got the humans to do what they wanted even though they usually had about as much magick as the human they were ordering around. The fae ooze confidence with those they consider lower than them, and it's one of the reasons they get what they want all the time.

Sure enough, the door opens and I walk into a dimly lit hallway. The walls, ceiling, and floor are all black. The short, stocky man on the door is a goblin with stringy grey hair and large eyes.

'Go to the left and all the way to the end if you have something to sell besides yourself, human.'

I say nothing; I just turn and walk slowly down the corridor. I take the left fork. I go through a conjure that feels like a cold curtain, and the hall opens out into a small room. A man sits at a desk, writing numbers in a large book. He looks human. He's got short brown hair and a square jaw. He's dressed in a brown suit, sort of like what I'd imagine a professor would look like. There are even leather elbow pads on the jacket he's wearing.

I cough, and he looks up, doing a double take.

He leans back, watching me with interest. 'Don't usually get humans in here,' he remarks. 'At least not ones so young as you.'

'I'm older than I look,' I say.

'Doubtful,' he chuckles but motions to the chair in front of his desk. 'Sit then, my beauty. Tell Jack what you've come to sell.'

I don't mess around. I yank the dress up at the side, being careful to show as little of my goods as possible, and start untying my pouch of loot.

'Whoa, I don't deal in flesh, my dear. You want the other hallway,' he says, putting a hand up and looking away.

'I'm not selling myself,' I say, emptying the bag onto his desk. 'I'm selling these.'

He stares for a moment, and I know I've surprised him. 'Where did you get all this, girl?'

'Do you really care, or are you just trying to give me a hard time?'

He glances up and smiles. 'No, I don't really care. But do you know what these are?'

I snort. 'I should. I took every single piece from the lion's mouth myself.'

He leans back, eyeing me and flicking one of the pieces back into the pile nonchalantly. 'Well, most of it is relatively invaluable. I mean, I could take some of it off your hands, I suppose.'

I roll my eyes, instinctively knowing he's going to start lowballing next. I've heard the cooks talking to suppliers in the office before, trying to get the best quality for the lowest prices.

I start shoving everything back in the bag. 'I don't have time for this,' I say, hoping he won't call my bluff because I don't know of anywhere else I can take this stuff.

'There's no need to be hast—' he starts.

When I don't stop packing up, he puts a hand over mine.

'Stop what you're doing,' he growls, and the words echo oddly through the room, through my skull.

He relaxes and takes his hand off me like my staying is now a foregone conclusion.

I stare at him for a second, and my eyes narrow.

'You're a vamp,' I mutter. 'Fuck.'

I heave a sigh and start packing up again, wondering where I'm going to be able to get rid of my haul at a fair price, if not here.

He looks surprised, shocked even, as he watches my movements resume.

'My powers of compulsion don't work on you,' he murmurs.

I shrug. 'Guess not.'

'I think we got off on the wrong foot,' he states.

I glance up at him. 'I know the stuff I have is valuable. Some of it is rare, too.'

'I think we can do business,' he says, and I scoff.

'Not if you're going to set me up to get cheated.'

He puts a hand up. 'Let me see the merchandise again. Please.'

I let out a slow breath and dump out the bag again. I pick through it myself this time, forming two piles.

'I want a bag of silver for this,' I say, pointing to the pile with the least amount of value, the trinkets with magick that aren't all that rare, just good quality.

The second pile has some very interesting and quite unusual objects in it. I know for a fact that one has been in Tamadrielle's possession for centuries because I heard him bragging to one of his friends about it once. He missed that one. He had servants searching for it for ages.

'For these, I need a conjure to keep me hidden from magick forever.'

The vamp chuckles. 'The first pile, fine. We have a deal, firecracker. The second though, I'm afraid not. A forever conjure? You're looking at several million dollars for something like that. There's not enough here for that.'

I don't show him my disappointment. 'How long, then?'

He shrugs. 'A year, maybe.'

I sit down heavily in the seat. 'I need more than a year,' I whisper.

He nods, steepling his fingers as he regards me. 'I like you,' he says.

'Great,' I mutter.

'You've got potential,' he continues, 'and a useful little gift if vamp compulsion doesn't work on you.'

I sit back and watch him, hiding my shaking hands and

keeping my anxiety in check by counting the books on the shelves behind him. 'Potential for what?' I hear myself asking.

He claps his hands, making me jump. 'I'll tell you what, how about I give you the silver, a years' conjure, and then you come work for me?'

'I don't even know you,' I say.

'Sweet girl,' he looks me up and down with a critical eye. 'I think we both know you don't know anyone outside the estate you just escaped from. But I could use a go-getter with your skills.'

I stare at him, my heart pounding. If it's that obvious to him where I just came from, others will quickly realize, too. 'You want to give me a job? Doing what?'

'What it looks like you've already been doing, girl.'

'Okay,' I say, not letting myself second guess.

I have nowhere else to go anyway.

He grins, glad I've agreed so quickly. 'What's your name, kid?'

'Victoria.' I give him the name easily. I've been practicing that in my cell at night, too.

'Cute name,' he says. 'How could you tell I was a vamp, Vicki? I take my fake tanning regime very seriously.'

I shrug. 'Don't know. But I can always tell a supe.'

He gives a small chuckle. 'Another useful talent in Supeland.'

He gets up from the chair. 'Here.'

He throws a jingling pouch across the desk and then turns around to grab a box from the shelf behind him.

He turns back in time to see my dress hiked up again as I stow the bag of money, and this time, he whistles low.

'Those fae cunts really fucked with you, huh?' he says quietly, taking in my scars.

I pull my dress down quickly, wilting a little under his scrutiny. I've never had anyone staring at them or commenting on them before. Everyone where I'm from was used to seeing them, so no one bothered to say anything about them.

I'll need to keep my entire body covered, I realize, or having a conjure to keep me hidden from magick isn't going to do a damn bit of good. Tamadrielle's people will find me as soon as someone sees the marks and blabs.

Jack opens the box and takes out a golden medallion. I move to take it, but he waves me back.

'No, sweet Vicki, the object is just a case for the conjure.'

He closes his eyes and says some fae words while he holds the round disk in his hand. When he's done, he chucks the medallion in the trashcan by the desk.

'How will I know it works?' I ask him.

He smirks. 'The fae fuckers won't show up at my door looking for you,' he says. 'Trust me. I don't want them turning their heads my way, either. It's in both our interests for you to be hidden from their tracking spells.'

I frown at him, not trusting him for a second.

He sighs. 'You'll start to feel it if you concentrate. Like a buzzing in your body. When the tone changes, the conjure is getting to the end of its life, and you need a new one.'

'And if it stops completely?' I ask.

'Start running.'

I nod. 'Thank you. Where can I go to get some clothes and clean up? Are there places to rent close by?'

Jack snaps his fingers, and a door opens. 'My apartment is upstairs. You can stay in my guestroom until you're on your feet, okay?'

'I can't say with you,' I say, my eyes wide. 'You're a stranger.'

'Stranger danger? What are you, twelve?' He laughs. 'But it's cool. You're right. We don't know each other yet. I'm a vamp. You're a human. I understand. There's a hotel down the street or some lodging houses across the way.'

'Thank you.'

He shrugs. 'They'll ask questions, though.'

I regard him as I weigh my options. There aren't really any right now. He knows I'm going to say yes to the room. I can't have people asking questions I can't answer. And is this really any more dangerous than how I've spent the past few years with the fae? Sure, there are a few things he could do to me that haven't already been done, but at least I'd be getting something out of it. It's not ideal, but I can be pragmatic if it means I never have to see Tamadrielle and his sadistic minions ever again.

'Why are you doing this?' I ask.

'I told you. This is business, and we can be very useful to each other. It's purely selfish, so don't get any ideas that I'm some benevolent benefactor, Vicki-bear.'

'I'm not letting you drink from me,' I say, just to see how he reacts so I know what to expect. 'Nothing else either.'

'Relax, Victoria, you're not my type.'

I nod and glance down at my burns, not able to help myself from wondering if that's why I'm not his type, even though I'm glad he's not interested.

'No, it's not the scars,' he says quietly, correctly guessing my thoughts.

My cheeks heat. I don't like being so easy to read.

'Fuck,' he mutters wearily, going back into the box and drawing out another gold disk, this one the size of a coin. 'When did I get so soft?'

He points at me with one finger. 'One freebie, and that's it,' he says.

He chucks the coin into my hand, closes his eyes, and says more fae words.

My body tingles, and I cringe. When I open my eyes and look down, there are no scars on my legs. My grateful eyes fly to his, questioning.

'It's not a forever conjure, and the scars are still there,' he says, looking a little embarrassed. 'And it won't cover up anything that isn't fully healed, so stick to long pants and turtlenecks for a few weeks. So long as the spell remains intact, no one will see the marks nor feel them, and it'll last your whole life, okay?'

I nod, my lip quivering, trying to hold back tears of gratitude. My whole life? He might as well have given me a forever conjure. No one will see what they did to me.

He waves me away. 'Go upstairs. Shower. Go to bed. The guest room is at the end of the hall. We'll talk about what you'll be doing for Jack Enterprises tomorrow.'

I nod, not trusting my voice. I start going to the stairs, each step like a weight lifting off my shoulders. I think I've landed on my feet for the first time. They can't find me. They'll never be able to hurt me again.

By the time I get to the top, I have a smile on my face that hurts a little because I haven't been this happy since before the fae lord 'took me in'.

I'm going to be okay. I'm going to make sure of it. No matter what.

I wake up with the memory of that first day of freedom fresh in my head. I haven't thought about that time in years.

I sit up slowly, my head pounding. I'm tired. I feel like I didn't sleep at all last night. I get up and turn on the shower. I stare at the wall while I wait for the water to heat up.

I'm pregnant.

My mom and dad aren't dead, but they aren't really my mom and dad.

I signed a contract to be the clan's on-call girl.

I put my head in my hands. Before the party, all I wanted was to stay here however I could manage it.

Now, I'd give everything to leave.

I never thought this would be a problem. When I read the contract Maddox gave me, I skimmed the contraception part because I never dreamed I'd need it.

I look down at my stomach. It shows nothing. How can I love something so much when I haven't even seen it, when, for all intents and purposes, it's just a collection of dividing cells right now that aren't even visible to the naked eye?

But I do.

My heart beats faster as I think about the predicament I've got myself into.

'I won't let them take you,' I whisper.

I get into the shower and think of how I'm going to do this. I have time before I begin to show, but not three years' worth. As soon as I leave, they'll come after me now that I'm considered theirs, and I have no doubt they'll find me if I can't get a conjure on me the moment I get out of here.

Escape is my only option. Tears come to my eyes when I think about what else I'm going to have to do. Krase, Jayce, and Axel won't believe I could have done this. I need to make them think this was a long con, that I only got close to steal from them again.

They're going to hate me, but it's for the best. Otherwise, I know they won't stop looking for me once I'm gone. Like last time, they'll try to find me and fail. They'll move on if they think the worst of me. I won't be worth it to them if they don't care about me anymore.

Even the thought breaks my heart. I love Axel, Jayce, and Krase. I care about Iron, and even Maddox is worming his way in slowly somehow, even though he's a snooty prick.

I won't miss Daemon, but I sort of understand where his head is. He blames me for what he went through without the clan and with the vamps. I think it was bad for him. I wish I could fix my part in what happened, indirect though it was.

But the baby is more important than anything else.

I push my emotions away. I already know how I'm going to do this.

I get dressed in pants and a tank, putting on some sneakers and a sweatshirt like I'm going for a walk.

I know where the cameras are, so I leave my room and go downstairs. I pass the grandfather clock and frown. I know they keep a link key in the groove at the top for emergencies, and I was going to use that, but I can't reach it without getting caught by the camera.

I grit my teeth, trying to think of another way as I smoothly make my way to the library. I pretend to take my time choosing a book and then go over to the last of the French doors where the camera can't see me anymore. On the way past Maddox's desk, I grab the cordless phone.

I stare out the French door as I huddle by it out of the camera's view and call the number I memorized long ago.

Someone picks up. 'Jack?' I whisper.

I hear a snort. 'Been a long time, Vicki-bear.'

'I have a good haul. You want in … for old-time's sake?'

'You know I do, but no more freebies. You try to screw me this time, and I just know you'll get picked up by the fae. I have that feeling.'

Same old Jack, but he's all bluster, and he hates the fae. He'd never turn me in, not to them.

'I understand. I'll be there soon, and … I'll need a conjure.'

'Of course you will,' he sighs. 'Same old Vicki. Is that it?'

'One more thing. Do you know the name Daemon Mackenzie?'

There's silence on the other end. 'Yes,' he finally says. 'Brother to Alex Mackenzie, leader of the Iron Incubi Motorcycle Club. Heard he got in deep with the vamps. They made him sign himself over to them. Guess he figured it would be enforcer-type stuff, but they chained him up in one of their brothels. They did the usual: starved him, sold him, kept him drugged, and used him to bliss out the clients for a ton of cash. He was in there for about eighteen months. Last I heard, he'd bartered for release, but he can't pay his debt with them. They're putting a bounty on him to be brought back sometime this week.'

I choke out a thank you, and I put down the phone. I move back across the room, putting the phone back in the cradle as I pass.

My hands are shaking. Holy shit. I hadn't realized how bad it had been for him. No wonder he hates me. Because of me, the vamps locked him into sex slavery and whored him out. Despite how he's treated me, guilt gnaws at my gut. I can't just let them take him back to that. I'm not that much of an asshole, despite what he thinks of me.

I pick up my book and leave the room, going through the house to the kitchens and out the side door. I meander through the garden slowly before I go into the maze.

I feel it perk up at my presence and smile a little. 'I think you're going to be the only one who misses me when I go,' I say quietly.

'I have a favor to ask you,' I say, settling on a bench. 'Sometimes you give me presents, and I ...' I look at the hedge beside me, feeling a little dumb for talking to a bunch of leaves. 'I wondered if I could make a request.' I edge closer. 'I need a link key,' I whisper. 'Would you be able to get me one?'

Nothing happens, and I let out a breath. It was a long shot, anyway. I'm just going to have to grab the loot and make it to the clock to get the link key before they can figure out what I'm doing. The other keys are in the library, too, but they're in a separate safe, and I haven't seen anyone unlock that one. I can't get into both safes and get out of there before I'm caught because as soon as either one is opened, even with the code, Maddox's phone will get pinged. There just won't be enough time.

I sigh heavily. I'd rather have everything together by the time I open the safe to grab the diamonds, but I'll make it work somehow.

I stand up to go, but as I do, something falls from my lap into the grass by my feet.

I bend down, heart hammering. No way.

My fingers close around it, and I pick it up the box slowly. It's heavier than others I've held, and when I can see it properly, it looks different as well. Older. It's gold and covered in delicate filigree, whereas all the ones I've seen have been plain. But it's definitely a link key.

I chuckle. 'You must have had this awhile,' I mutter.

Not knowing what else to do, I stroke the leaves next to me. 'Thank you,' I say. 'I hope I can make it here again one day.'

But I already know that isn't going to be possible. I'm about to burn this bridge again, and this time, I'm making sure there is going to be no rebuilding after I do.

Now that half my plan is in place, my stomach drops as I think about the rest. My body feels heavy as I leave the maze and make my way back to the house.

I sit in the parlor and take a deep breath. With everything in me, I push the connections I have to the others away as completely as possible. I make it so that I can't feel anything from them, and they won't be able to feel anything from me. Barely holding back tears, I sit back to pretend to read and wait for them to come to me so I can start making them hate me.

It's only five minutes before the door opens. It's all four of them, concern etched on their faces.

I force the pang of guilt back.

'Do you need to feed?' I ask, keeping my expression bland.

Krase and Jayce step forward with matching frowns. The others glance at each other uneasily.

'Are you all right, gràidh?' Krase asks.

'I wish you wouldn't call me names that I can't understand,' I mutter with a roll of my eyes. 'And, yes, I'm fine. Why wouldn't I be? I signed the contract to become the clan's last night. Three years of safety and security.' I smile like the cat who got the cream.

'What's wrong with you?' Iron asks, his eyes narrowing.

'Nothing at all. Why?'

'You don't seem yourself,' Axel says, his gaze moving over me.

'I just think we should keep things professional from now on. I got what I wanted, and so will you. You can feed from me whenever you want. Fuck me whenever, however you like. I'll even pretend to be lulled if that's what gets you off.'

I stand up. 'Do any of you need to feed?' I ask again.

None of them answer.

'Look,' I say with a roll of my eyes. 'I'm really sorry, but my contract states that I only have to feed you. I'm not obligated to spend time with any of you, so if you're not hungry ...'

I leave the room, a puzzled smile on my face.

Krase comes after me first. I knew he would.

'Julia.'

His use of my name almost makes me wince, but I manage to keep it in.

'Yes?' I ask, turning with a polite smile as if I have no idea why he might be upset.

'What is this?'

I laugh. 'I don't know what you're—,' I put my hand over my mouth with a small, affected gasp. 'You think the past few weeks was real.' My mouth falls open as if I can't believe it. 'Wow. I must be a better actress than I thought,' I mutter to myself. 'Look, I'm sorry if you got the wrong idea, but you know me, Krase. I'm a survivor. It's dangerous for a human out there. I knew Maddox was going to cut me loose after the party, so I made sure you guys wanted to keep me here.' I take a step back. 'At least now we all get what we want, right?'

He doesn't say anything, but I see the darkness leaching into his eyes. The other guy is pissed even if Krase is pretending he isn't. But I know he won't turn on me that fast. These are just the seeds. The real betrayal comes later. This little scene will just make it easier for them to swallow the main event.

I turn on my heel and go upstairs, closing myself in my room and pretending to read until it's dark.

Someone knocks on my door once, but they leave when I don't answer.

At two a.m., I grab a jacket and go downstairs. I already know where the creaks in the floorboards are, so I avoid them easily and get into the library without a problem.

Show time.

I let out a breath and pretend this isn't real.

I look up into the camera in the corner and give it a little wave. 'I'm guessing this thing has audio. I hope so because there are a few things I wanted to say before I left. There was a little confusion earlier. Maddox, Daemon, you were right not to trust me. I'm only here for one thing. Another payday.' I scrunch up my face and fake cringe. 'I know! I'm sorry, but I'm a little behind on my rent, and you guys just make it so easy. Maddox, thanks for the opportunity to feed the clan for the next three years, but no thanks.' I chuckle. 'What I should really be thanking you for is opening this safe in front of me.' I tut as I twizzle the dial. 'Silly, silly.' I put in the first number and turn around for the camera again. 'Iron, this is for you— a little friendly advice. Don't get in touch with your family. They got rid of you for a reason, sweetie, and I doubt it actually had anything to do with your lack of magick.' I put the next number in.

'It's funny,' I say. 'If Axel had just killed the arania when he had the chance, none of this would have happened, so this is basically his fault. But, Maddox, don't kick him out, or the vamps will probably turn him into an incubus whore like they did with Daemon.' I turn and look directly at the camera. 'Did you know they chained him up in a basement for months? I'll bet you did. But you still didn't help him. In fact, you sort of abandoned him. Huh. I always thought you were a better leader than that.'

I shrug and turn back around, grasping for something to say to Jayce that will make him hate me, too. It comes to me quickly, and I close my eyes, forcing back tears. 'Jayce,' I say, my voice almost breaking, 'you should probably take that painting back.' I swallow hard, and I make my words as nonchalant as I can manage. 'I know it was meant to be some grand gesture, but the thing is, I was only using the arania to stay alive, and I don't really want to think about the Mountain anymore.'

Bile rises at my untrue words about Siggy, and I choke out the rest quickly.

'Krase, I know you're lonely, and you wanted me to stay here with you happily ever after, but do you really expect me, or anyone, to believe I saved you somehow? We all know you're going to sink back into that pit of darkness, and Maddox is going to have to put a bullet in you. I can't help you. I'm a human. That's it.'

I roll my eyes at the camera and let out a laugh. 'I literally can't believe you all fell for my "poor little Jules" routine.' I shake my head. 'Anyway …'

I put the final number into the safe and open the door.

'Well, I'm out of here. Sorry, you got burned by me again.' I give the camera a wink. 'It's not personal, guys. Don't bother trying to find me, either. You won't. But, hey, maybe I'll come back one day, and we can do all this over again. Maybe you won't get the wool pulled over your eyes. Third time's a charm, after all.'

I empty the safe, grabbing the jewels in their little velvet bags and boxes and thrusting them all into a small backpack. There's one box I leave, but I put it all the way at the back, so it looks like I missed it. It's a ring that belonged to Maddox's mother. I know his dad pawned the rest of his mom's valuables when he was a kid, and I can't bring myself to take that, too.

I close the safe with a click when it's cleared out, and, just for a second, my emotions get the better of me. I close my eyes, stifling a sob, but I touch my stomach and get it together. The baby is what matters, and I'll do everything I have to do to protect him or her. I wipe my eyes and step back, turning to give the camera a finger wave.

'It's been fun as always, guys.'

I put the link key on the main door and think about the fae market. I open the door and grab the link key as I go through.

More tears blind me, but I make it to the other side, and I close the door behind me, leaning against it for a second before I cast myself off into the street.

It's lively and full of supes, and I walk quickly, not making eye contact with anyone. I get to the bank and cross the street, going down the alley to the familiar red door.

I knock once, and the shutter opens.

'Password?'

'Hey, Bruce,' I say with a drawl. 'How you been?'

The goblin on the other side does a double-take before he lets out a soft chuckle.

'Been a while, sweetheart,' he says as he opens the door. He gestures down the black corridor. 'You remember the way?'

'Yeah, I remember,' I say quietly. 'Thanks.'

I walk down the corridor, the diamonds heavy in my bag.

I go through the conjure curtain and find Jack at his desk. He glances up when he sees me.

'Looking good, Vicki.'

'You too, Jack. How's the vamp life?'

'Forever, baby.' He grins. 'What you got for me?'

I open my bag and take the diamond necklaces out of their pouches and boxes. Laying them out for him to see.

'You really are something, you know that?' he breathes, taking out a magnifying glass and peering at them. 'Lovely.'

When he's satisfied, he sits back in his chair. 'I can give you a conjure to hide you for three years and half a bag of silver for this stuff.'

I wince. 'What if I had two bags of gold? How much time could I have on a conjure then?'

'Five months, probably.'

I wince.

Five months isn't enough time,' I say.

'Best I can do, Vicki-bear.'

I let out a breath. 'Come on. We both know you have conjures that'll work for years in there. I'll pay you back, I'll—'

'That's enough, Victoria,' he says sharply in his vamp voice, and I frown.

'Doesn't work on me, remember?'

'I remember,' he growls. 'I remember you doing a job for me and skipping town with the cash, Victoria. How much goodwill do you think you have left to use with me?'

I throw my hands up. 'Fine! If you want to drag up shit that happened forever ago! I'm sorry, okay? I didn't want to do it if that helps, but my conjure was failing, and I didn't have the money for a new one.'

He sighs. 'Same old story, Vicki. It doesn't fly anymore. We all got problems, and you stopped being mine when you stole from me.'

I sink into the chair in front of his desk. 'I brought you diamonds, though,' I say hopefully. 'That counts for something, right?' I smile. 'Come on, Jack. Please?'

He rolls his eyes, and I give him a grin. 'You're going to single-handedly ruin me, you know that, don't you, Vicki-bear?' He puts his head in his hands and groans as he stands up. 'More fool me for having a soft spot for the best little human con artist this side of the Breach.'

He gives me a bag, but I shake my head. 'I need some in human money. Dollars. The rest in gold.'

He raises his brows but delves into a drawer and brings out a wad of bills. 'Here's a grand. That's all I have in human right now.'

He grabs the box of conjures off the shelf behind the desk and rummages through it. 'Okay, you're in luck. I can give you six months.'

I nod. 'It'll have to do until I can figure something out.'

He holds up the disk and says the words, and I sigh with relief.

'Thanks, Jack,' I say, putting my warm hand over his cold one and squeezing it a little. 'I am sorry for what I did. You didn't deserve that. You were good to me.'

Tears come to my eyes, and I blink them away.

He looks down at my hand and then back at me, his face grim. 'How much trouble are you in, Vicki-bear?'

I chuckle. 'You know me. The usual amount.' I stand. 'I'm going to portal to a human place on the other side of the Veil and do some pretending,' I say. 'But I'll do some jobs for you if you want. If you feel like you can trust …'

'Aw, fuck,' he mutters. 'I have something coming up. I'll let you know.'

'It um …' I glance up at him. 'It can't be anything dangerous, okay?'

His brow furrows, and he laughs. 'You always used to ask me for the opposite.'

'Yeah,' I mutter, 'but things are different now.'

He gives me the two bags of gold, and I heft them up.

'Can you have them delivered to someone?'

'Who?'

'A vamp named Sheamus McCathrie?'

He purses his lips. 'Did I teach you nothing?'

'Relax, Jack. I don't owe the vamps. It's for a ... friend.' I choke on the word, but regardless of what I said on camera, I do want to help Daemon. I need to.

He sighs. 'I can have it delivered. Who's it from?'

'Daemon Mackenzie.'

'Helluva friend to give up this kind of cash for,' he remarks, his eyes boring into me. 'He the father?'

I'm not surprised Jack knows. He can probably sense it vampire style, or something.

'Not your business, Jack.'

CHAPTER 20
Need More Demons?

DESIRE AFORETHOUGHT SERIES-

Caught in the clutches of five formidable Incubi bikers, neurodivergent Jane Mercy navigates a treacherous world of dangerous secrets, unyielding passion, and looming threats.

Will she emerge unscathed, or will the sizzling world of demons shatter her, piece by piece?

Succumb to an intoxicating realm where incubi masters awaken dark desires and debts are paid in the throes of passion. (on Kindle Unlimited)
https://geni.us/DesireAforethought

DEMONS AND DEBTS (AUDIO BOOK NOW AVAILABLE!)

When debts call for desperate measures, will a deal with demons be the path to salvation or damnation?
https://geni.us/DemonsandDebtsAudio
https://geni.us/DemonsandDebts

🚴 **Hot Monsters/Supernatural Biker Gang**
🧠 **Neurodivergent Strong Heroine**
🔍 **On the Run Mystery**
💚 **Paranormal Romance**
👯 **Reverse Harem**
😼 **Enemies to Lovers**
🔒 **Dark Past/Secrets**

DEBTS AND DARKNESS

In the darkest corners of desire, will she find freedom or lose herself forever?
https://geni.us/DebtsandDarkness

🔥 **Emotion Manipulation by Incubi**
🌕 **Hidden Secrets & Deceptions**
😈 **Hate-Love Dynamics**
💃 **Dancing to their Tune**
🌑 **Self Preservation vs Demons**
👯 **Reverse Harem**

VENGEANCE AND VIPERS

🩶 **Enemies to Lovers**

DARKNESS AND DEBAUCHERY

Caught in a web of lies, betrayal, and heartache, can she conquer the darkness and reclaim her life?
https://geni.us/DarknessandDebauchery

🕊️ **Gilded Cage**
🔍 **Unknown Enemies**
⏳ **Race Against Time**
🧩 **Deciphering the True Self**
🌈 **Pursuit of Happiness & Freedom**
🧩 **Reverse Harem**
😈 **Enemies to Lovers**

CHAPTER 21
Demons and Debts
DESIRE AFORETHOUGHT: BOOK 1
(SERIES COMPLETE)

CHAPTER 1

JANE

When life hands you lemons, make lemonade!

Someone told me that once and it always stuck with me, not because it made me feel better on dark days, but because it's such a dumb thing to say. It's like a meme on your feed with a mountain background or a cute kitten and message on it saying something like 'Don't worry! You got this!' or 'Make someone smile every day, but never forget that your someone too.' (Yeah, with that 'your'.)

I don't think the people who made up these little proverbial sayings and uplifting generic messages had a group of stalkers dogging their steps either. I mean, seriously, for one thing, what kind of fucked up lemonade can you make from a scenario where people you've never seen threaten to hurt anyone you come to care about, people who never let you make a home anywhere? How do you make the best of *that* shit?

I already have my hand on the door when I freeze. I can hear a tune from an old juke box. The song it's playing is dated; not the kind of music that would be on a playlist in a crowded wine bar. There's a pool table inside. I can hear the balls knocking against each other, low chuckles, the clink of glasses, and errant, female laughter.

I shouldn't have come here. I told Sharlene the same thing, but she said these guys are the meanest and have the most muscle in town … for a price.

I hear someone snigger behind me and voices murmuring. I glance over my shoulder to see two human guys in their leathers, standing with their bikes and sporting the patches of some MC I've never heard of. I'm not surprised they're there. This is a biker bar after all. They're watching me, talking about me. Cold, calculating eyes take in my jeans and old sneakers, the oversized thrift store jacket that I bought to keep me dry, but is nowhere near waterproof enough for the amount of rain we've been getting lately.

Not giving them the chance to say anything to me directly, I yank open the door. I don't need any trouble. I got more than I can handle as it is and that's the only reason I'm here.

My senses are hit with the force of a sledgehammer, my usual defenses crumbling like a dried-up sandcastle on the beach. I automatically keep the cringe inside. I wish I could put my earbuds in just to help with some of the louder noise, but that would look too weird now. The cacophony of sound that had been muffled before makes my steps falter. The neon signs over the bar glare at me, and the smell of smoke and stale air assails me. I almost take a step back, call this whole thing off.

But I can't. What's waiting for me if I don't do this is worse than a little discomfort.

So I push it down, wondering why it's so hazy when lighting up indoors has been illegal forever.

I survey the room, not even trying to pretend I belong here as the second-hand smoke chokes me a little. There are quite a few people sitting around. I can see some others playing pool at the back. As I make my way over to the bar, I garner a few curious looks, but no one approaches me.

I stop and stand in front of the one and only bartender. He's about a foot taller than me with dirty blond hair just long enough, *just styled enough* to look like he simply rolled out of bed, giving the impression that he can't be bothered to go get a haircut because he just doesn't care. But I'm not fooled. Guys, just like girls, have to put in the effort to be *this* hot. It's not a natural occurrence no matter what he wants people to think. This guy is all mirage. There's nothing real about him.

Hot Guy ignores me for long enough that my waiting for him to look up becomes awkward even though he's not serving anyone. I'm standing right in front of him and he's intentionally not letting his gaze fall on me.

So rude.

This is a college town and I've gotten used to dealing with pretty boys like him in the diner over the past few months, but as the irritation mounts, I forget my usually crippling social anxiety. I push away the sensations screaming at me to go somewhere dark and quiet and just zone out for a few hours.

'Excuse me,' I say lightly, pretending I haven't even noticed his BS.

He finally looks at me and I'm caught. I'm ensnared by eyes that are the color of molten caramel with little flecks of gold that catch the lights even low as they are. My breathing stutters and I swallow hard. I've never felt anything like this.

His knowing smirk is enough to shake me out of my embarrassing reaction and I frown at him. What was that? What is *he?*

The realization hits me, and I take a step back, my nostrils flaring on a gasp I try to keep under wraps.

Incubus.

I should have known he was one of them even though I've never actually met one of his kind before. In general, the supes move in very different circles from humans, but I know they hang out in this bar. That's why I'm here.

'You break down or something?' he asks in a lazy drawl as if I'm taking up his valuable time.

But something in his eyes makes me think that, like the rest of his appearance, this is a show he's putting on. There's something about me that's intrigued him, and I don't like it. The last thing I need is his full attention.

'I'm looking for the Iron Incubi.'

He barks out a loud laugh and I can't hide my wince. What if their gatekeeper won't even let me talk to them? What's my plan if I can't get their help?

Leave, a helpful voice inside my head supplies. *Get on the first bus out of town before bad things start to happen here too.*

But I can't do that. I need this all to stop. I'm so tired. I just want to live my life. I don't want to go to a new town, live on the streets for the first few months, get some shitty job that doesn't ask questions so I can beg my way into some hellhole apartment on the worst street. And then do it all again in a few months just like I always have to do when they track me down. They always find me. The thought of it makes me want to curl up and cry.

But I don't. I'm here so this can finally be over.

Hot Guy doesn't say anything, his gaze roaming over me, and I get the feeling I've somehow baffled him and he's trying hard to figure me out.

Who knows, maybe he's the kind of guy it's *really easy* to confuse. Even a hot incubus can't have looks *and* brains, right?

He gestures with his chin to the darker area where the booths are.

'They're in the back by the pool table,' he says.

I incline my head in thanks, grateful he's not throwing me straight out on my ass.

I walk through the smoke that's heavier back here, trying not to cough. I can make out murmured talking and the feminine giggles I heard from outside.

Grinding to a sudden halt, I have third thoughts at the juncture where the floor changes from old wooden boards to an industrial carpet; the kind with brown toned patterns to hide the dirt. It doesn't work here. I sort of don't want to touch *anything.*

If I go past this line, there's no turning back. Forcing myself to raise my eyes, I'm taken aback by the men in front of me even though I should have expected this level of good-looking.

There are more hot AF men back here. Two of them stand at the wall like sentries, one's by the pool table in the middle of a game and the other two are sitting in a lone booth with the woman whose laugh I could hear before, I realize belatedly.

'What the fuck is this?' one of them asks, putting a little snort at the end.

My eyes follow the voice to the two men leaning against the wall. The one on the left was the one who spoke, I'm sure. He's got brown hair, a shaggy haircut, and the beginnings of a beard along a jaw so chiseled I could swoon like a debutante. This one *actually* doesn't care what he looks like I'm pretty sure, but he's as gorgeous as Hot Guy at the bar and he's got a broad set of shoulders that I can't seem to ...

I tear my eyes away.

Don't get drawn in. You know what they are. You never even notice guys like this. Pulling you in and lowering your defenses is literally what incubi do.

As I look over all the men here, I realize that four of them are even better looking than I originally thought. They could literally all be freaking underwear models if the toned arms I can see are anything to go by. The fifth one my eyes hardly land on. I don't think he's one of them.

I scrutinize the small woman in the booth that I just barely noticed. She's pressed up against one of them and I look away immediately. He's massive and he's feeding from her ... just a little and she's probably not unwilling, but her eyes are glazed over. If she was in control of herself when she came in here, she isn't now. At least they aren't fucking her at the table, I guess. Though from the sounds she's making, I doubt it'll be much longer before they are.

That'll be you if you don't get your shit together.

I silence the thought that comes after that image – that they'd never want someone like me – for multiple reasons. Firstly, I'm trying to be kinder to myself, mostly to get Sharlene off my back because she keeps saying I need higher self-esteem. Secondly, the truth is that if they're hungry, what I look like doesn't matter. They might not want to feed off a homeless drifter, but they will feed if they need to.

Kind thoughts!

The one who spoke is looking past me and I turn my head to see Hot Guy shrugging behind the bar.

'What do you want?' asks one of the guys at the pool table to my right. He sounds bored and annoyed at my interruption.

My eyes find his dark and foreboding ones. He's got a short, black beard that matches his hair and ... *I want to run my fingers through it?*

No, Jane!

'We already have enough humans to play with.'

He glances at the booth where the woman is now letting out a series of strangled moans and a couple of the guys nearby chuckle.

'Try your luck in a couple months, sweetheart.'

I cant my head at him as I try to work out what he ... *Oh! ... ME?* My eyes widen. 'Oh! No.'

'No?' he asks, the menace in that one word making me glance at the nearest exit, which happens to be past him. 'Too good for us, human?'

'I mean that's not why I'm here,' I mumble, mortified that he'd assume I thought I was better than anyone. Is that really the vibe I give off?

'Gonna have to speak up, little girl,' the other one by the wall says and I glare at him.

I'm not a loud person and my voice never seems to carry all that far.

'That's not why I'm here,' I say more loudly, putting the effort in to be heard.

The one with the dark beard walks forward slowly until he's right in front of me looking down his nose at me as I'm forced to tilt my head up. Shit, he's tall. He could probably break me in half. Sharlene was right. These are the kind of men I need at my back. I'm not leaving here until they work for me.

***

Vic

As I stare the girl in front of me down, I can't help the frown that creases my forehead. She's not the usual type we get in here; the townie girls looking for the quick high they've heard we can provide while we feed. If the girls who try their luck here could be bothered to do their research, they'd know we aren't allowed to just take humans in off the street to snack on anymore. There's an extensive process now. Interviews. Contracts.

This one's older than I first thought when I noticed the sneakers and the faded jeans. I'd have put her at around eighteen when she came in, but she's probably in her twenties. Her brown hair is scraped back into a ponytail and her matching eyes don't stay on mine, constantly moving. I stifle a snort. Yeah, she knows what we are and she's afraid she'll get ensnared by one of us.

I glance over at Sie in the booth, just making sure our wildcard isn't still starving enough to lunge at this one, but it looks like Carrie, the blond contracted to us who he's playing with at the table, has taken the edge off. He's watching the one in front of me, but he's got his needs under wraps for now. He smirks at the little brunette, doing something to make Carrie scream her release without even looking at her. I sigh, Carrie's sexual energy sating me a bit just from my proximity to the action. When I look back down at the human girl before me, her wide eyes are locked on Sie's, and I can tell my lieutenant is imagining fucking her.

Interesting. He hardly looks at humans at all these days. I practically have to make him feed.

'What do you want from us if it's not a good, hard fuck?' I ask and grin at the shock she's trying to hide.

She pulls herself together quickly though and gives me a level stare. It almost appears as if she's looking directly into my eyes, but she's actually looking at the wall past me to the side of my head. She thinks the eyes are the only way I could capture her. I bet she's never had direct contact with an incubus before. Her knowledge is second-hand at best.

Silly little human.

'I want to hire you,' she says.

I wasn't expecting that, but I don't let my surprise show.

'What kind of dumbass problems a girl like you got?' Korban sneers from his place by the wall.

She doesn't answer him, hardly even notices him. Instead, she looks at me – well, almost. She's still avoiding my eyes.

'Stalkers,' she says, and I hear a couple of the other guys chuckling low.

I don't laugh with them. The others here might not understand what a stalker can do to a woman, supe or otherwise, even if he never touches her, but I know how life-destroying it can get.

Not that I give a shit about this woman per se.

'A stalker, huh?' I look her up and down and I see her shiver a little. 'What do you have to pay with?'

I'm surprised that the first idea that pops into my head is that she has no money and she'll have to pay us with her body, and I push away the thoughts of her on her knees before us. We aren't allowed to do that shit anymore, I remind myself.

'*Stalkers*,' she corrects me. 'As in more than one.'

That gives me pause. The others too.

'How many?' asks Theo.

He's sitting in the booth waiting for his turn after Sie's had his fill of Carrie.

The girl in front of me glances over at him, and I notice she takes pains not to look at Sie though *he's* still watching *her*. I wonder if he's going to be a problem.

'I don't really know, but there's a group of them.'

Probably some of the frat assholes from the local college.

'Payment?' I ask again.

She hesitates.

Korban pushes himself away from the wall and takes his shot, grinning from beside the pool table. 'You didn't come to the Iron Incubi without something to trade, did you, princess?'

'No,' she says quietly, and her shaking hand begins to unzip her oversized jacket.

Fuck.

I'm standing here with bated breath, hoping for a glimpse of what's underneath like a teenage boy. I swallow hard and turn away, pretending to ignore her while I play my turn. Yellow to corner pocket.

I miss, but everyone's eyes are on her anyway.

'Your body's the payment?' Korban asks as he slides closer, and I shoot him a warning look.

Feed from her before she's signed an agreement, and the supe authorities WILL find out. Unlike some, those are the rules we have to live by, and, in return, the cops mostly leave us alone. Besides, we have three girls living at the house already. We don't need another.

But she looks baffled for a second at his words, not afraid. And then she lets out an incredulous laugh.

'No.'

She pulls out an amulet and all of us look just a tiny bit disappointed. How does this girl have us all practically salivating over her? It's not usual, not even when we're hungry and that realization is enough to make me want to flip the kill switch on whatever this is. She looks, smells, feels like a normal human, but something isn't right.

She draws the necklace over her head and holds it up.

'We don't deal in jewel—' I begin, getting ready to shut her down and get Paris to boot her out the door.

And then I get a good look at the blue, iridescent stone set in a cage of silver hanging from an iron chain.

Even Dreyson, one of the human prospects, takes a step forward. 'Is that a—?'

An orc stone.

'So what happened?' I interrupt. 'You go to the wrong place at the wrong time in the wrong outfit or something?'

I sound bored, but I'm looking at this girl with new eyes.

Does this little human have any idea how much that bauble in her hand is worth in our world?

I'm guessing not and I hide the gleam in my eye. We're about to get the payday of the year and all I need to do is send one of the prospects to take out the trash.

'Something like that,' she says. 'Doesn't matter where I go. They find me. They do ...' Her eyes get a faraway look in them. 'Bad things.'

Her head gives a little shake. 'I work over at Gail's. My friend Sharlene said you might be able to help me. Can you?'

I hold out my hand and she lets the dull, cerulean gem fall into my palm. I feel the hum of power as it touches my skin and I know I'm right. How the fuck did she get an orc stone?

'We don't usually do this sort of thing,' I begin and see Theo rolling his eyes in the booth, 'but we'll take care of your little problem for you.'

Her hand clenches the thick chain hard as I curl my fingers around the pendant. Her eyes are suddenly boring into mine.

'You'll keep me safe, get rid of the group who wants to hurt me to the best of your ability. In return, you can have this necklace, and only this necklace, as payment. The terms are final.' She says the words clearly. 'Who will bear witness?'

I give her a slow smile and watch a blush climb up her throat to her face. She's not unaffected by me even though I'm not using my power, and she's not stupid for a human either. She'll make this official through all the right magickal channels.

Unfortunately for her, those ancient laws were written by the fae. They're sly as fuck and, holy shit, are there some fun loopholes. As I look at her, it strikes me as weird that she seems to know some basic rules about our world, but not others. I frown. Is she a cop? They've tried to infiltrate us before with human prospects, but not in ages. But I'm not going to stop the deal. That orc stone is worth calling in some old favors if we get any trouble from Johnny Law.

'I'll witness,' Paris says from behind her. He's left the bar unattended, and I give him a look, but there's no one here to serve anyway.

She jumps a little as he clasps her wrist and mine in his hands and he looks at her oddly for a second before he closes his eyes and says the binding words that make the deal unbreakable ... for her anyway.

'It's done,' I say. 'Dreyson, go with her and see to her little problem.'

I'll let the others know my suspicions about our new client on the DL later. Until then, Dreyson won't do or say anything in front of an outsider anyway.

The human prospect pushes himself off the wall and glances at Carrie. Sie's still feeding from her lust, and he looks a little disappointed since he sometimes gets to have a little fun with our contracted girls once we've had our fills.

'You prove yourself with this and that's it. You're one of the Iron I's,' I tell him.

Dreyson's face lights up at the promise. 'I won't let you down, Vic!'

'Keep it professional though, huh?'

He nods, looking a little surprised that I'd spell it out, but he's a ladies' man and this one is off-limits.

I pull on the chain that's still wrapped around the girl's fingers. She looks up at me and then at her hand as if she can't quite bear to let it go. Maybe she does know what it is, she's just so desperate that she'll give it up anyway.

'What's your name?' I ask.

'Jane,' she whispers, letting out a small breath and dropping the necklace.

With a mental high five to myself, I pocket it immediately and go back to my game without another word. As far as I'm concerned, we're done and when I look back after taking my next shot, she and Dreyson are gone.

KEEP READING ON KINDLE OR LISTEN ON AUDIBLE

https://geni.us/DemonsandDebtsAudio
https://geni.us/DemonsandDebts
<3

🎄 **Remember Giselle, my little helper from the Aforethought Trilogies?**

Well... now this little fae is about to (*ermm*) sparkle in her own story filled with twisted tinsel and forced proximity in ***"Wrath and Wreaths,"*** exclusively in **Volume Two of the Snowed In Why-Choose Anthology Set** –

<u>NOW AVAILABLE</u> on Kindle Unlimited! 🎄

> *Ready for your snow-melting tease?*
> *Think tinsel's just for decoration?* 😏
> 🔥 ***WAIT UNTIL YOU SEE HOW GISELE USES IT*** 🔥

KEEP READING!

CHAPTER 22
Wrath and Wreaths Sneakpeek

<3

Adam

I hear a soft moan, and I shut my mouth. My eyes cut to her, widening as I see her hips undulate, and she whimpers a 'please'.

Drake gives me a smug look as her unfocused eyes flutter open lazily. She's still pretty out of it.

'She's our prisoner,' I whisper. 'You can't ... You heard what she admitted to Jack. Don't you think she's been mistreated enough?'

He rolls his eyes at me. 'She clearly knows her own mind. If she weren't strong, the dragon wouldn't want to mate her.'

'So, what do you propose?'

'Let her make her choice. You. Me. Both.'

I can't hide my surprise. 'You'd share her?'

He shrugs. 'If that's what my mate wants.' His eyes move over *me, assessing. 'You're annoying, but you aren't weak. You can help protect her from her father and the other fae.*

'What if she wants neither of us? Will you abide by her wishes?'

'Of course.' Drake gives me a slow smile. 'But she won't deny me. You, maybe, but she feels me just as I feel her. Why do you think she's so hungry for me after one kiss? Her very being understands that I can sate her.'

I scowl, hoping that what I'm feeling isn't jealousy. I hardly know this girl, but I don't think I've ever been so interested in a female before, and definitely not a fae female. This has the hand of fate written all over it, and mages don't fuck with fate.

'The injuries I healed will still ache for a bit,' I say, sitting back in the chair. 'Don't start anything with her that's too strenuous, even if she seems amenable.'

Drake nods and sits on the bed beside her. 'Gisele,' he murmurs, cupping her face. 'Wake up, gorgeous.'

Her eyes open again, and she blinks at him in adorable confusion.

'Gorgeous?' she asks, her eyes flicking to me in artless bewilderment that quickly turns cynical when she sees I'm watching. 'Look, Dragon Santa. I know I'm tied to a bed and all, but don't take that as confirmation that I'm an easy lay, okay, chief?'

Drake roars a laugh at her words, putting his hands up and getting off the bed. 'I just brought you some soup, sweetheart.'

She quirks a brow at him. 'Well, I'd love to eat it, Dragon Santa, but ...' she waggles her wrists in her bindings, 'I'm a little tinselled up.'

I snap my fingers, and the tinsel goes slack, leaving her wrists. She glances at me as she sits up with a grin, clearly thinking that's the end of her internment, but I snap them again, and they wind around her waist instead so that she can't move off the bed. She scowls at me from her now-seated position.

'At least the dragon brought me soup,' she mutters. 'You suck, Wizard Santa.'

But then she frowns, moving her torso this way and that. She pulls up her tank top and looks at her stomach. Her eyes fly to mine. The world-weary jadedness is gone, and she looks baffled again. 'You healed me. All of me.'

I nod.

Her lower lip trembles, and I watch as she bites it hard. She looks completely slain by my actions, and I hate how clear it is that so few have ever treated her kindly.

'Why would you bother to ...'

'My dad was a lot like yours,' I mutter.

She gives me a small, knowing nod. 'I take it back,' she says quietly, blinking rapidly. 'You don't suck. What's your name, Wizard Santa?'

'Adam,' I say.

'I like Wizard Santa better.'

Her eyes move over the suit appreciatively, and I grin. 'You have Santa kink, don't you, baby girl?'

Her eyes widen, and I stalk closer to the bed, relishing her widening eyes and her small intake of breath.

'Bet you have a daddy kink, too,' I murmur.

She licks her lips. 'Well, I do have the daddy issues to fit the mold,' she says a little breathlessly.

I glance at Drake and raise a brow. He returns the look.

'Drake is going to feed you, now, sweetheart, and I want you to eat every bite.' I take hold of her chin when she looks a little uncertainly at the dragon shifter. 'Eyes on me,' I order and watch a blush creep up her cheeks as she looks at me. 'Is that clear, Gisele?'

'Yes,' she breathes.

'Yes, what, princess?'

'Yes ...' She licks her lips. 'Daddy?'

Holy shit! I don't think I've ever been so turned on in my life.

'Good girl,' I murmur, watching her throat work and hiding

a smile and a tent in my pants as I go back to my chair and sit down.

Gisele

Oh, my fucking god! Did I just call one of my captors, Daddy?!

In a bit of a daze, I let the other one feed me like Wizard Santa, I mean Daddy Santa, I mean Adam! told me to. I keep glancing at him and then at the other one, half mortified, and half turned on.

Ready for more?

Unwrap three volumes of snow-blanketed steam *(that's a thing, right?)*. From heart-pounding dark romance to spine-tingling paranormal encounters, these stories have everything your delightfully dark heart desires.

😍*And the best part? It's all for a good cause; proceeds are helping The Cancer Research Institute and The World Central Kitchen.*
Snowed In Charity Anthology Set

Newsletter and Discord

SIGN UP TO MY NEWSLETTER AND DISCORD AND STAY IN THE KNOW!

Members also receive exclusive content, free books, access to giveaways and contests as well as the latest information on new books and projects that I'm working on!

It's completely free to sign up, you will never be spammed by me, and it's very easy to unsubscribe:

www.kyraalessy.com

https://geni.us/KyraAlessyDiscord

Acknowledgments

For my kids, who will hopefully never read this book. I hope this series saves our house from the increased mortgage rates because I'd hate to have to go get another job.

For my grandkids, who I hope do read this and recognise how fucking epic their granny was when she was young and fun.

For me as an old woman. (If I've survived his kooky, fucked up planet). OMFG, stop being so fucking OLD and go tear some shit up!

xx 2023 Kyra

About the Author

Kyra was almost 20 when she read her first romance. From Norsemen to Regency and Romcom to Dubcon, tales of love and adventure filled a void in her she didn't know existed. She lives in the UK with her family, but misses NJ where she grew up.

Kyra LOVES interacting with her readers so please join us in the Portal to the Dark Realm, her private Facebook group, because she is literally ALWAYS online unless she's asleep – much to her husband's annoyance!

Take a look at her website for info on how to stay updated on release dates, exclusive content and other general awesomeness from the worlds and characters she's created – where the road to happily ever after might be rough, but it's worth the journey!

Also by Kyra Alessy

WRATH AND WREATHS: A SNOWED IN CHARITY ANTHOLOGY

Unwrap three volumes of snow-blanketed steam *(that's a thing, right?)*. From heart-pounding dark romance to spine-tingling paranormal encounters, these stories have everything your delightfully dark heart desires.

😈 *And the best part? It's all for a good cause; proceeds are helping The Cancer Research Institute and The World Central Kitchen.*

Entire Set > Snowed In Charity Anthology Set

I'm Here> Snowed In Volume Two

DESIRE AFORETHOUGHT COMPLETED TRILOGY

Caught in the clutches of five formidable Incubi bikers, neurodivergent Jane Mercy navigates a treacherous world of dangerous secrets, unyielding passion, and looming threats

DEMONS AND DEBTS

When debts call for desperate measures, will a deal with demons be the path to salvation or damnation?

https://geni.us/DemonsandDebtsAudio

https://geni.us/DemonsandDebts

DEBTS AND DARKNESS

In the darkest corners of desire, will she find freedom or lose herself forever?

https://geni.us/DebtsandDarkness

DARKNESS AND DEBAUCHERY

Caught in a web of lies, betrayal, and heartache, can she conquer the darkness and reclaim her life?

https://geni.us/DarknessandDebauchery

VENGEANCE AFORETHOUGHT TRILOGY

When hearts are the real treasures to be stolen, can a con-woman outwit the demons of her past?

VILLAINS AND VENGEANCE

She stole from them, lied to them, and now they're her prison mates.

In a world without exits, trust becomes the rarest and most deadly commodity.

https://geni.us/VillainsandVengeance

VENGEANCE AND VIPERS

https://geni.us/VengeanceandVipers

I was supposed to be their downfall. They were meant to be my revenge. But the chains that bound me have now tangled us all.

VIPERS AND VENDETTAS

https://geni.us/VipersandVendettas

Six seductive demons, bound by venom-laced passion, teeter on the brink of salvation and ruin.

a former slave waging a final stand for a life far beyond her darkest dreams.

DARK BROTHERS COMPLETED SERIES

In a world of darkness, the intertwining fates of fierce women and brooding mercenaries challenge the very essence of love and war.

SOLD TO SERVE

In a game of power and survival, will she be the pawn or the queen?

https://geni.us/SoldToServe

BOUGHT TO BREAK

Liberation comes in many forms... sometimes in the arms of the enemies.

https://geni.us/Bought2Break

KEPT TO KILL

When your salvation lies in the hands of beasts, will you conquer or crumble?

https://geni.us/Kept2Kill

CAUGHT TO CONJURE

Unleashing the power within, a witch's redemption, or the world's doom?

www.kyraalessy.com/caught2conjure

TRAPPED TO TAME

In the arena of love and war, who will reign - the damsel or the dark fae?

https://geni.us/Trapped2Tame

SEIZED TO SACRIFICE

With forgotten sins and unseen foes, will memory be her weapon or her downfall?

https://geni.us/seized2sacrifice

For more details on these and the other forthcoming series, please visit my website / join my mailing list!

https://www.kyraalessy.com/bookstore/

Printed in Great Britain
by Amazon